RELIVING
FATE

BOOKS BY NATASHA PRESTON

RELIVING FATE

NATASHA PRESTON

ISBN-13: 978-1547224029

Zoë, Rocco is yours.

ONE

BELLA

Twelve years on, Celia's death still hangs around the house like a bad smell. Her room has remained untouched to this day. Twelve years, and not a thing has changed in there. No one but me goes inside, and I'm sure as hell not moving her shit.

Her worn clothes still litter the floor, and a gross empty glass is on the bedside table, collecting a thick layer of dust. I occasionally clean her room because it's clear that Mum and Dad won't, but for the most part, I leave it alone.

Nervously biting my lip, I tiptoe inside. I'm home alone, but I'm not sure how Mum or Dad would react if they caught me in here. They must know. Olivia, my twin, would tell our parents in a heartbeat if she found me here.

Fucking snitch.

Celia's room is always cool. She died during a particularly hot spring, so her radiator was turned off. When I'm in here during the winter months, I still don't dare turn it on. Isn't there…something about not messing with the dead's possessions? Like Karma? Well, I don't know, but I'm so not up for being haunted by my own sister—not in the Casper sense anyway. I'm haunted by what happened to her every second of every day.

We all are. It follows us around, like having a dark, stormy cloud constantly above you.

There have been a lot of seconds in those twelve years. I'm shit at math, so I have no clue how many, but it's loads.

Most of my early memories of her have faded—I was six when she was killed—but I remember the last few months before she died as clear as the day she was murdered. She had been going out more, argued with our parents all the time, and stopped caring about school.

In that time, she wasn't the same girl. I didn't understand why my big sister no longer wanted to play Barbies with me anymore. Of course, I get it now. What sixteen-year-old wants to play dolls? It was more than that though. Celia was cold and withdrawn and had changed beyond recognition.

What happened to you?

I look over my shoulder, up the long hallway before I turn back and pad deeper into her room. When we moved to this house, Celia was twelve, and Olivia and I were two. It was decided that Celia's room would be the last one, so Livvy and I would be closer to Mum and Dad.

It was as if my parents knew Celia wouldn't be here now. Her room is tucked away at the end of the dark corridor where it can be forgotten.

Only nothing about her or the way she died will ever be forgotten.

The sickening girlie walls have faded to a much duller pink now. While she was going through her change, she decided to paint her room a pale blue. But she didn't have time. Two years ago, I mentioned painting it for her, and Mum freaked out, like I'd suggested we exhume her fucking body.

So, it's staying pink.

I cross the floor and sit on her bed. Her perfume is long gone, but I can still smell her in here. I like it. It makes me feel close to her. I lie down on her bed—I've not done that before; I've only sat here—and my head hits a hard object in the pillow.

What is that?

I sit up, my butt sinking into her soft mattress, and twist around. Cautiously, in case it's something I really don't want to see, I reach into the end of the pillowcase.

Please don't have a dildo in there.

It's a book.

Thank God.

Thank you for not having a sex toy stuffed in there, Celia.

Taking it out, I see it's not just a book.

"You kept a diary," I whisper.

How could no one have known about it?

I'm not sure if I should look—it's private after all—but I know I have to. There might be things in here I need to know. Probably things I really don't, too.

I'm not sure when I became so obsessed with finding him—*her killer*—but all I know is that I'm not going to university this September, my relationship with my parents has plummeted, Livvy is more like a stranger than a twin, and I don't really care about any of it right now.

This has to be done.

Sod privacy.

As I flip the diary open, I'm filled with a sense of familiarity. Celia's writing is exactly how I remember her speaking. She was like me. Or I'm like her.

> *Today, I snuck out with Steph and Nancy, and we met up with Hugo, Davis, and Jack again. Nancy thinks I should move on and forget Hugo, but I can tell he likes me, too. He's just scared because he's older, and I'm still stupid 16! I can't wait for my birthday. 11 days and counting!*

> *As soon as I'm 17, everything WILL be fine. I'll be able to get a car, have more freedom. Dad will freak though. Technically, Hugo is an adult, but I'm not apparently! I don't care. I'm falling in love, and there's nothing anyone can do to keep me away from him.*

I stop breathing and it causes my lungs to burn. She never mentioned a Hugo; neither did any of her friends after she died.

So, who the bloody hell is he? Steph and Nancy know who he is. But, if Hugo had anything to do with her death, wouldn't they have told the police about him? Unless they believe the bullshit story of how she died.

Surely, they would have mentioned him anyway though? They were her friends.

Celia's death was ruled as a burglary gone wrong because there wasn't a suspect, motive, or anything to suggest otherwise. And there had been three break-ins the month previous, so the police thought our house was targeted during the carnival, and Celia must have spooked the burglar.

It all worked perfectly for the bastard who took my sister's life. But there's something wrong with the story.

I know *there is.*

After Celia's death, the break-ins stopped, but I still can't help thinking there is more to what happened that night.

Stuffing the diary under my top to hide it from the empty house, I go back to my room. Facebook is a good place to start. Maybe Steph and Nancy are friends with him. I can stalk online like a pro. Seriously, I would be an asset to MI5.

Flipping the lid of my laptop open, I sit on my bed and cross my legs. Maybe this is the start of answers—*real* answers. Someone needs to be locked up for what they did to my sister. I have no idea if Celia knew her killer personally, but if it was a thief, he could've run instead of murdering her.

I click on Steph's profile first and scour her Friends list. Anyone I don't know or anyone who looks shady, I click on and search their Friends list, too.

"Isabella?" Mum calls, making me jump out of my skin.

Shit, she's home early!

I leap off my bed and shove Celia's diary under the loose floorboard in my walk-in wardrobe.

A much better hiding place than a pillowcase, FYI, Celia.

"Coming!" I shout. My heart is going a million miles an hour. She could have caught me.

I get downstairs faster than Usain Bolt and follow my parents' voices into the kitchen. They're putting groceries away, both looking at Celia's birthday cake that's taunting them from the counter as they work.

She would have been twenty-eight, but she will forever be stuck on sixteen.

"Nan and Grandad's for dinner tonight, remember? You're not staying there though, Bella," Mum says, raising her perfectly plucked eyebrows.

My mum is flawless. She won't even leave her bedroom without makeup on. She has chocolate-brown eyes and long, dark hair. Dad's hair is a shade darker than Mum's, and his eyes are hazel.

Celia, Olivia, and I all look alike, all carbon copies of our mum—only I inherited Dad's hazel. It was the only way people could tell me and Livvy apart when we were little.

"I'm staying," I reply. "And I already okayed it with Nan."

She sighs, her nostrils flaring the way it does when I piss her off. "*Isabella*, I am telling you, you're not staying the night there. I'm the parent. I make the rules, and I don't care if you're *eighteen* or not." She tries to mimic my voice, but she fails miserably.

I roll my eyes. She worries when we're not home, but I feel safer out of this house than in it.

"I stay the night all the time. I'd rather be there tonight."

"Bella, enough," Dad says, stepping in.

Mum doesn't do discipline well, and Dad always steps in eventually. Still, we all know that I'll be staying at my grandparents' tonight. I understand their concern. Celia spent most of her time at Nana and Grandad's in the last year of her life, and they're scared the same thing will happen to me.

"I want to stay at theirs tonight."

I *need* to.

"You know what tomorrow is, Isabella," Dad says sternly.

His words slam into my chest.

I force tears in my eyes. "You think I could ever forget?" I've tried. It's impossible. "Dad, please. I *can't* wake up here on her birthday."

Mum's hard expression softens, and I know they won't push it anymore. Tears work every time. Truth is, I can't cry anymore. Celia's been gone for twelve years, and I've missed her every second of them, but crying doesn't provide answers.

Answers are all I want now.

"Oh, Bella," Mum says, tilting her head.

She's crying. *Shit.* My stomach swims with guilt, but needs must and all that.

"Please. I'll come home in the morning, I promise."

She rounds the worktop and pulls me into her arms. The hug is awkward. I wrap my arms loosely around her. "Of course. We're sorry, love. We didn't realise how hard this has been on you."

"That's okay," I say, breaking the hug and wiping a fake tear from under my eye. "What time are we leaving? I need to pack a bag." *And grab Celia's diary.*

"At four. Olivia should be home soon," she replies.

"Right. She'll be home at just before four, unable to peel herself away from Mr Personality."

"Isabella," Dad warns.

My parents adore Livvy's boyfriend, Harry, because he's responsible and mature and sensible.

Boring, boring, boring.

Harry and I share a mutual dislike of each other. He thinks I'm childish and that I have a hold over Livvy, and I think he's a sad, jealous prick.

Raising my hands, I say, "Fine, sorry. Anyway, I'm going to get my things ready."

"Do you have a card for Celia yet?" Mum asks as I walk away.

Freezing on the spot, I take a deep, ragged breath. "I have one, yeah."

I want to do the birthday and Christmas thing for her—she's still every bit a part of our family—but it's never easy.

"I'll leave it on the mantelpiece with the others," I say as I rush out of the room and rub the ache in my chest.

I miss you, Celia.

Back upstairs and in my room, I pull out my travel bag and throw some clothes in it. If no one else were home, I'd read more of Celia's diary, but Mum isn't huge on boundaries, and knocking is apparently optional. So, I stuff it between my clothes and ignore the itching in my hands to grab it and read the whole thing now. My self-control is waning.

I could just sneak a quick look.

Biting my lips, I calculate the probability of being caught with it. I could say it's mine.

Pah, like that's believable.

As I reach for the bag, a noise from the hallway interrupts me. I pull my hand back as Livvy pops her head around my door.

"Hey," she says. Her smile is bigger than mine.

She loves people, and she loves life. I…do not.

Personality of the Year is with her, and he gives me a tight smile. Harry would rather spit in my face than be civil, but Livvy is all about the twin-bond thing, so he's never rude to me in front of her.

"Hey," I reply. "How was…whatever you were doing?"

"We just spent some time with Harry's family; they took us to play tennis."

Whacking a ball with a bat. Fun.

"Great," I say, trying so, so hard to keep the sarcasm out of my voice.

I love my sister, and I never want to make her unhappy, but—*fuck me*—she lives a dull life. Still, at least she has one.

"Ready for tomorrow?"

She sucks in a breath, and Harry puts his hand on the small of her back. "As I'll ever be."

"Same." I nod, picking up my bag and Celia's card. There are so many things I want to write in the card, but no one else can know, so I keep it simple and impersonal.

Offering me an affectionate smile, Livvy tilts her head, and I'm suddenly scared she'll want to hug me too. We haven't hugged in…I don't know how long. Even though I love my family, I feel a complete detachment to them most of the time.

It's because of Celia.

Maybe, if things had turned out differently, they'd have had her and not me.

I'm being stupid, of course. They would never want us to change places, but guilt pretty much strips all rational thought.

"Mum said you're staying at Nan's?" she asks.

"Yeah."

Her dark eyes turn black. "Really, Bella?"

"I'll be home early. What's the problem?"

Harry's eye twitches. Oh, he'd love to voice his opinion right now. I'll be there for Mum and Dad tomorrow, but I can't wake up to Mum's crying. I just can't. They don't understand, and it's my fault.

"Fine," she snaps. She pulls Harry across the hall to her room.

We might share the same genes and shit, but we're *nothing* alike.

Lucky her.

TWO

BELLA

Nan ushers us into the house, and the smell of freshly baked bread has my stomach rumbling.

"Food?" I say, giving Nana my puppy-dog eyes.

She likes to feed us—well, anyone really.

"Ten minutes," she replies. "Grandad's making pasta."

"Score," Livvy says, linking arms with Mum and Nana before walking into the kitchen.

Mum doesn't look for me to take her other arm.

I'm not touchy-feely.

Dad and I follow behind, and we meet Grandad in the kitchen. He's stirring pasta sauce on the hob and bobbing his head to some seriously old-sounding music. Turning around, he greets us with a smile. I go over to him because he's not the hugging type either. He's safe.

"How are you, kiddo?" he says.

Still *kiddo* even though I'm eighteen.

"I'm good, Grandad. How's old age?"

"You're only as old as you feel," he replies as I mouth the words along with him.

"And how old do you feel today?"

"Thirty."

I snort and rest my elbow on the worktop beside the cooker. "Yep, still old."

"It'll creep up on you before you know it."

It should have been creeping up on Celia.

"Please. I have ages yet. Can I have a taste?" I ask, pointing to the sauce.

"Have I ever said no?"

He gets a fresh wooden spoon from the pot of a thousand utensils and hands it to me. The sauce is good, and I have another taste before he removes the spoon from my hand.

"Let's save some for everyone else."

"Why? We all know I'm your favourite."

He laughs and kisses my forehead. I do get along with him best. I love them all equally, but I'm closer to Grandad—probably because we both have a general dislike of people and lean more on the sarcastic side.

"How are you feeling about tomorrow?" he asks.

"Just peachy."

"I know how that feels."

Celia spent a lot of time with our grandparents in the year leading up to her death, so it hit them really hard, too. Now, I'm filling that void, and I think they love having a teen around the house again. Can't think why.

"You'll stay a while tomorrow, right?"

He smiles, and his dark eyes lose their shine. "Of course I will. Nana and I will take you home in the morning, leave you all to visit Celia in peace, and then join you."

"After breakfast at the café?"

"Absolutely. I want a full-works omelet, and I'm not eating the regurgitated-looking monstrosity your nan makes."

I laugh and take a look over my shoulder at the same time he does. Nana is deep in conversation with my parents and Livvy, so they didn't overhear. There is only one dish that woman can't make, and it's one of Grandad's favourites.

"That sounds good to me." The first part anyway. Celebrating Celia's birthday is never enjoyable.

Nan and Grandad serve dinner, and shortly afterward, Mum, Dad, and Livvy leave to go home. I feel like I can breathe as soon as they're out of the house. Everything they want for me and expect of me is suffocating. They don't know how much I want to be what they believe I can be, and they have no idea what's standing in my way of it.

Nan and Grandad watch *Britain's Got Talent*, which is ironic because ninety-nine percent of the show proves we do not, and I force myself to sit through it. I'm antsy, and I wish they'd just go to bed already.

Half an hour has passed when they finally start yawning. Although they fall asleep quickly, I need to wait a good twenty minutes before I sneak out. It's almost ten p.m., and I'm tired. The last thing I want to do is go traipsing around town, but if I want answers, I can't sit on my arse.

At 10:13 p.m., Nana starts to yawn, and five minutes later, her hand covers Grandad's wrist. I know from experience that she's telling him it's bedtime. They go together every night, neither one of them willing to leave the other behind. It's kind of sweet really.

"We're heading up, Bella," Grandad says even though there is no *up* in the bungalow.

"Yeah, me, too." I fake a yawn, which leads to a real one, and stand up. "Night," I say.

"Good night," they reply at the same time.

This little routine has been rehearsed many, many times before.

I head to the family bathroom with my bag and pretend to get ready for bed. They have an en suite, so I know I won't see them again until morning. I don't change because I'll be leaving soon, but I need to go through the motions. I brush my teeth and take off the small amount of mascara I'm wearing. Makeup doesn't interest me, mainly because I've watched Celia and now Livvy spend absolutely ages in front of the mirror, perfecting their looks. I'd rather have a lie-in. Besides, when I attempt to do my face up, I just look like an extra from *The Walking Dead*.

Closing my bedroom door, I make sure to slam it enough that Nana and Grandad hear but not too much that they think something is wrong.

Now, I wait, and I despise waiting.

Time is a bitch when you're waiting for something. Usually, I can lose a few hours with Facebook and days with Netflix, but I need to concentrate, so I can hear when it's time to make my escape.

Twenty minutes later, I hear Grandad's snore.

Yes! He's asleep, so it's time to go.

Nana is asleep already, as she's usually gone the second her head hits the pillow. I open the window and hoist my leg over. I kind of feel like a ninja boss as I leap over, close the window, and dart across the front garden.

Or I just look like I'm off my face on acid.

It's June, so sunset is later in the evening, but it's dark enough that I probably won't be seen or at least identified.

For the last couple of months that I've been wandering around town when sleeping at Nana and Grandad's, I've been going to the main high street. Today, against all my instincts, I turn in the other direction. It's the shitty part of town where you lock your doors as you drive through and don't make eye contact with anyone.

This had better lead somewhere, Celia.

I pull my leather jacket around my body and fold my arms. It's not at all cold out, so I don't zip it up, but I'm nervous, and I don't want to be stabbed.

Right, because leather is basically armour.

Houses slowly slip from manicured lawns to old kitchen appliances on overgrown lawns. A river runs through the whole town, so I head toward it in the hopes that I won't attract too much attention. At some point, I'll have to talk to someone, but now, I just want to know where people hang out and what they get up to.

Turning right, I head toward the river where the greenery gets thicker, and you can't tell who would sooner stab you in the eye than who would help you carry your shopping bags.

This is a bad idea.

If Celia did hang out around here, then she was stupid.

Why would she choose *this?* I mean, the bad-boy thing is hot and all, and it looks like there are a lot of them around, but I'm not sure I'm willing to die for it.

Hugo must look like a Greek god. Or Nick Bateman.

The warm breeze sends chills down my spine, and I look over my shoulder. No one is around, and I hear no other footsteps on the floor, but I still feel like I'm being followed.

God, this place gives me the creeps.

Standing taller, I continue as confidently as I can while my legs feel like jelly, and my heart is jackhammering in my chest. I don't know where the hell I'm going, but it doesn't matter, especially not if I find Hugo. My safety stopped meaning that much to me a long time ago. The only thing that matters is finding the man who killed my sister.

I owe her.

When I was younger, there wasn't a lot I could do but live with the guilt. Now, I can try to find him and hope the guilt will lessen when I do. Obviously, I know I have to be careful. Celia was terrified of someone, and I'm not dumb enough not to be scared, too. Heck, I am scared. Like really, really scared.

Keep going.

I eventually stumble upon a small river beach. The same river is behind a white railing in the nice part of town. Apparently, safety and drowning risks aren't important here. Down on the mud is a group of people hanging out, drinking and sitting around a bonfire. It's odd, as there are teenagers and adults, some who look well into their forties.

What kind of party is this?

"Who the fuck are you?" a deep voice snaps.

I spin around and have to do a double take. My frozen heart skips a beat. He's *gorgeous*. Tall, muscular, short and dark hair, and caramel eyes framed by a ring of chocolate.

Asking if I can lick him seems entirely inappropriate.

He doesn't look pleased to see me though.

I prepare for a fight. It doesn't matter how gorgeous you are; if you're an arsehole to me, I'm going to fucking own you.

Or you're going to die because he looks like he can handle himself.

"Are you a police officer?" I ask.

His nose scrunches slightly as he frowns. He looks confused, and it's cute.

"I'll take that as a no, so forgive me if I'm being rude, but jog on."

The shock of my words is evident on his expression even though he tries not to react. Too late; it's clear that he's not used to people standing up to him, so that puts me at an advantage.

"You need to watch your mouth, little girl," he threatens.

"Or?" Perhaps I'm a bit too gobby, but I don't like his attitude any more than he likes mine, and I won't be intimidated.

He takes a step closer, and his caramel eyes turn darker. If he wants to play the big, bad guy, he really needs to ugly himself up. "Or I'll make you. Am I clear?"

"Yes, I have no problem understanding, but that doesn't mean I'm going to listen. Now, unless there's anything else, I'd like to get on—"

"What're you doing here?"

Sighing sharply, I narrow my eyes. I don't like questions. "I recently moved nearby, so I wanted to explore the area."

"At this time of night?"

He doesn't believe my story about moving here.

"It's eleven," I deadpan. "If I'm keeping you up—"

"Isn't it past your bedtime, sweetheart?"

Patronising fuck.

"Want to come tuck me in?" I shoot back.

His eyes smoulder, and I realise that maybe that wasn't the best thing to say. I mean, I would absolutely go there, but he's pissing me off too much right now.

"Name," he demands.

He's bossy.

"Bella Hastings."

"Good. That wasn't so hard, was it?"

I ignore that. "What's yours?" I ask.

He smirks, and I know I'm not getting it. He can't be Hugo; he's too young. He looks to be in his early twenties, and Hugo, assuming he was older than Celia, will now be in his thirties. This is getting me nowhere.

"Well, this has been a delight. It was nice to meet you," I say sarcastically.

I turn to walk away, but I don't get far because his hand circles my wrist, and it steals my breath. I'm not sure if I'm more scared that he'll hurt me or annoyed that the contact makes my hormones freak out.

"What're you really doing, Bella?"

I snatch my arm back and stand my ground. "I'm checking out the area. What don't you understand about that?"

"Watch your back," he says. Then, he disappears into the darkness of the night.

I watch until he turns up again, closer to the fire. There's about twenty feet that's unlit between where I am and where the fire is, and knowing anyone else could pop up makes me jittery. I have things to do, so I don't dwell on it, and instead, I walk into the dark area, so I can spy on the insanely good-looking, weird guy.

If this is where Celia escaped to all those years ago, then I question her sanity. It's strange. I wouldn't want to hang around with old people.

What do they all have in common anyway?

I'm jumping to conclusions. *They could be family, but if they were, why wouldn't they be at home and not at the saddest-looking river beach I've ever seen?* The bleakness doesn't exactly scream *party*.

There's something about them, about them being out of the way, that makes me think there's more going on and that Celia's been here—probably anyway.

It's not like I'm fucking Sherlock Holmes, so, really, I need to look at everyone, everywhere. Someone *has* to know Hugo and *has* to remember Celia. The fact that no one has ever come forward shows just how deep in the shit she got herself.

People don't talk when they're afraid.

That doesn't exactly make me feel confident about finding him…or living to tell the tale. Whatever happens, happens. Celia deserves to have him pay. Maybe then my family can start living again.

THREE

ROCCO

I watch her *not* leaving from the shadows on the furthest side of the fire with the crowd on the other side. She shouldn't be able to see me too well from here, but I have a pretty good view of her.

Who the fuck does she think she is?

If she were checking out the area, she would've left by now. There's nothing here worth seeing. Never has been, and never will be.

That leaves one option; she's looking for something. Shit goes missing around here all the time. The key is not to have anything you care about, and then you won't give a flying fuck when it's gone.

Come on. Leave.

I don't know why I give a damn. The nosy bitch has it coming if she thinks she can wander around here, alone in the dark, and have nothing happen. I'm surprised she's not been mugged yet.

What the hell is she doing?

She's not leaving. I clench my fists.

Stupid girl.

Though I know I'm not responsible for her, I still find myself walking toward her again, keeping to the edge of the brambles where she's trying to watch everyone inconspicuously. I take long strides, eager to get to her before someone else does. She's doing a pretty good job of hiding. No one else—that I know of—has noticed her.

As I approach, I hear her heavy breathing. The girl has confidence and courage, but right now, she's petrified.

So you should be, little girl.

"You're not gone yet," I say after watching her for another second, making her jump.

She spins around. Her posture relaxes as she recognises it's me—not that she should since I'm a complete stranger to her.

I've scared her, but the only indication is the slight flinch in her compelling hazel eyes that she quickly recovers from.

"Well, your observational skills are second to none," she says dryly.

Her smart mouth is nothing new...but she is. Usually, good girls from the right side of the tracks run fucking fast after stumbling upon this shithole.

"What're you doing here, Isabella?"

"How did you know my name's Isabella?"

Really?

"It's not much of a stretch from Bella."

"Whatever," she snaps, narrowing her eyes.

There's no denying the girl is beautiful, sexy, and full of attitude.

"I told you what I'm doing. New to the area and all, I'm just looking around. Am I not saying it right?"

"Nothing here you need to see."

"Do you own this land?"

I glare. "You should leave."

"No."

Fuck me, she's stubborn.

She folds her arms, and it pushes her leather-clad breasts out. "Why're you so precious about a stupid river beach? You don't even have proper sand."

I want to laugh, but I catch myself. *Who the hell is she?* "I'm not worried you'll fall in love with it and bring the tourists with you, Bella."

"Hmm," she murmurs, stepping forward and tilting her head. "What are you worried about then? Why is my presence making you go a tad crazy?"

I don't know.

"You think I'm crazy?"

"Well, I'm certainly not putting money on your sanity."

"Bella, leave."

"Weird Dude, no."

"Have it your way, but don't say I didn't warn you."

"Warn me about what? The tide going to come in soon?"

Oh, for fuck's sake!

She's so infuriating that I want to smash her head against the rocks and shag her over the bonnet of my car at the same time.

"Warn me about what, Weird Dude?"

"Rocco!" I snap.

Fuck, I gave her my name.

"Huh? Who's Rocco, and why do I need to watch out for him?"

Is she serious?

"I'm Rocco. Stop calling me Weird Dude. Please."

"See? Isn't it nice when we get along, Rocco? So," she says, stepping around me so that I have to turn my body to watch her, "what exactly are you warning me about?"

"Where the hell have you really wandered in from?" I ask.

She makes me feel drunk.

"I told you the truth, Rocco. Perhaps you could extend that courtesy to me. You're warning me about something. Why?"

"Because this isn't the place for girls like you."

"You don't know the first thing about me."

"No? You're not some bored teen, looking for excitement?"

"Excitement?" she seethes.

And I know I've guessed wrong.

"You're fucking clueless, so back off. I don't need anyone looking out for me, so go back to your party or whatever the hell this is, and leave me alone."

She spins on her heel and marches off. At least she's gone.

Or not.

She gets about six feet away and then stops. Turning around, her eyes are firing bullets at me.

"Forget something?" I ask.

"Yes, actually," she replies, stomping back. "You're a prick. I really fucking hate it when people assume things about me. I'm not some perfect, privileged princess, like you seem to think. Stop judging people who you know sod all about!"

Man, I've really worked her up. It's hot. Her pretty hazel eyes are alight. This is clearly something that pushes her buttons, and I want to do it over and over again.

"Please accept my humble apology," I say with a bow.

She glares again. "You've got to be the most annoying person on the planet."

"I was going to say that about you," I reply.

Why does she rub me the wrong way?

She's just a stupid little girl who, despite what she says/shouts, doesn't have a clue about the real world.

Still, I'd love it if she started rubbing me the *right* way.

Lightly shaking her head, she closes her eyes. "I'm over this. See you around, Rocco."

"Good luck with whatever you're searching for, Isabella."

She gulps, and for the first time, I see a glimmer of weakness and pain. I don't want to let her walk away. I'd be lying if I said she didn't intrigue me. Her attitude is hot, and I can tell it'd be fun to be around her, but it's a bad, bad idea. I'm the fucking one who's bored, and I really don't need some girl I have no business being attracted to keeping me occupied.

"Good luck getting out of here," she replies before walking away.

It's like she sees right through the bullshit. No one is dumb enough to think you'd stay in a place like this by choice.

I didn't know I was so transparent when it came to how much I wanted out. But there have to be bad places for there to be good places. It's luck, which one you're born into.

Isabella's good. Rocco's bad.

Mixing those two would be chaos and would never end well.

I watch her until she's out of sight, and I turn around, hearing someone approach. My hearing's good; it has to be. There's always someone waiting to rush you and steal the nothing you've got.

"Who was that?" Ellis asks.

I've known Ellis since I was two, and I trust him more than anyone else. He has light-blond hair cut short, a square jaw, and dark green eyes. I don't think he would go out of his way to help me out, but we have each other's backs because that's what you're supposed to do. To survive in this place, we have to be more than one person, but it's all about honour. It doesn't look good if you don't watch out for your own.

"I dunno. Some girl got lost."

"She's smokin', man. You're not tapping that?"

"I'm good." I'm not. Her sassy attitude has got me all hot and hard, but I'm not about to act upon the urge to go pick her up. Plus, I'm certain she'd tell me to piss off.

"Damn. You calling dibs, or can I take a crack at it if I see her around?"

"If anyone's getting in there, it'll be me."

"Fine. You always see the fittest ones first."

"That's because you're always more concerned with getting drunk," I say, nodding to the JD in his hand.

"I can do two things at the same time, brother."

"Lucky women."

"They are fucking lucky. I'm hung like a donkey."

"I need a drink," I say, heading to the beer cooler.

Faith, one of the older members of the group and the mother hen, always keeps us boys stocked with beer. It's her thing. That, and looking out for the young teens wandering the streets.

"You're not following Belle?"

I stop and turn around. Ellis lifts his eyebrows and points over his shoulder with his thumb. He knows her name. He knows it wrong, but he still knows it.

"Do you know her?"

"Shit," he says, laughing. "Her name's really Belle?"

"No, it's Bella. You guessed that?"

What's going on?

"Nah, bitch looked like the chick from *Beauty and the Beast* when she was all tarted up."

I'm concerned with the fact that he's watched *Beauty and the Beast*. And I'm not sure how *tarted up* Belle gets, but Bella was wearing jeans, a Metallica T-shirt, and a leather jacket.

I shake my head. "Whatever, man. I'm sure I'll see her around again."

After all, she's not one to take on board anyone's warning.

Frustrating woman.

I grab a Coors and pop the lid with my teeth. Bella's gotten to me, and I'm pissed about it.

Who the fuck does she think she is?

People don't just stroll up here, and if they do, they don't hang around and give one of us lip. A few lads who tried in the past got their arses handed to them. It might be a shithole around here, but it's ours, and no one's taking it.

Craig stops beside me and takes a swig of his beer. He clicks his tongue and angles his beer toward Dillon.

"He wants in?" I ask, guessing what he's talking about.

"Wants to prove the size of his cock. Not sure it'll be worth your time."

I shrug. "Got nothing else to do."

Craig drops his stubble-coated chin in a nod. "I'll set it up."

Then, he's gone.

Craig's not wrong; fighting Dillon isn't worth it. Hell, it's not even worth getting out of bed for, but it's been a slow month, and I'm getting restless. I have a build up of energy that needs releasing, and I don't think any of the girls around here will be able to help. I need some good old-fashioned violence.

Or I need to get under Bella's skin, the way she has mine. Bickering with her tonight provided more entertainment than Vanessa, Eve, and Hayley putting on one of their shows. Those girls are dirty and know how to work a crowd, but arguing with the entitled princess was more fun.

Shit, balls are about to shrivel up and die.

Maybe I need sex.

I drop my empty on the floor and make a play for Vanessa. Hayley has her tongue down Craig's throat, and Eve is nowhere around. I'm not letting some little rich girl fuck me up.

Vanessa's posture loosens as I approach, and she gives me her best sexy face.

"Hello, handsome," she husks.

I'm not in the mood for pleasantries. I lift my eyebrow and unzip my jeans. She's on her knees without another word, but all I can picture is Isabella's smart mouth.

FOUR

BELLA

I don't even know who he is, and I don't particularly want to, but he's royally pissed me off.

Actually, I lied. I *do* want to know him. He lives here, and he doesn't seem interested in killing me. Really, I need to befriend someone; it could only potentially help me find Celia's killer.

It's definitely not normal for young people to want to hang around old people. At least, it's not for me. Rocco makes me think there's more to it though; he wanted me out of there. And that kinda makes me want to go back. Often.

I walk back up to the road and along the path. From up here, I can still see the bonfire and Rocco's friends' silhouettes. Even though it's too dark to distinguish him from everyone else, I think I can see him.

He knew too much. People usually believe whatever crap excuse I give them but not him. And I don't like his questions.

I turn away from him and scour the other side of the road. There's a bar and a hell of a lot of boarded up buildings.

Come on, Hugo.

"You didn't get too far," Rocco says from the darkness.

My heart leaps into my mouth for, like, the millionth time tonight. I need to be here, but I sure as hell don't like it.

"What the fuck are you doing, lurking around like a psycho?" I hiss.

"I dunno. Same fucking thing you were doing while lurking behind the bushes."

"I very much doubt that." I walk past him and try to ignore his heavy footsteps on the concrete behind me.

Why is he following me? He has some serious problems. Or I'm about to be kidnapped.

The second the thought enters my head, my heart starts to race. I clench my fists.

Shit, I knew he was a bit strange, but I never thought he was kidnap strange.

I know absolutely no self-defence, and that's one of my biggest regrets right now. What I'm doing is dangerous; I know that.

So, why the hell did it never cross my tiny mind to learn how to protect myself?

I'm so bloody out of my depth here.

How the hell did my big sister do this? Ha, she had two friends with her. Safety in numbers and all that. Or it should have been anyway.

"Okay, why are you following me?" I snap, merging most of the words together. It'd be a miracle if he understood all that.

He stops dead, startled. His big caramel eyes widen. It's almost like he's never dealt with a woman before. It's…kinda cute.

"Jesus. What was that again?"

"Why. Are. You. Following. Me?"

I try to sound as pissed off as I feel and stand my ground. He can't know he's scared me. It's over if I show weakness. I have absolutely no time to be weak.

"I told you, you shouldn't be around here."

"So…what? You're escorting me home? No offence, but you don't strike me as a gentleman."

"Oh, I'm the furthest thing from a gentleman, sweetheart, but if anything happens to you here, we'll all get pulled in for questioning."

Charming.

"I'm touched, Rocco, really, but something tells me the people who would do anything to me are drinking with you on your fake beach. I can take it from here, thanks." I start walking again.

"Hey, Bella," he says.

"What?"

"Take care of yourself."

I'm momentarily stunned at the sincerity in his voice, especially since, five seconds ago, he was only worried that my brutal murder would bring questions to his doorstep.

"You, too, Rocco."

This time, when I walk away, he doesn't follow, but I feel him watching until I'm across the road and headed back to the good part of town. Besides, he's very good at popping up unannounced, so I don't know if I've seen the last of him.

The lights are still out in the bungalow when I get back to my grandparents'. Both are early risers but heavy sleepers, so I know I have a good few hours before they wake yet. My bedroom window is pushed shut—how I left it—so I pull it open and climb through.

My grandparents' house is the most homely place on earth, all soft colours and warm smells. I much prefer it here, but it would break my mum's heart if I moved. She's already stressing over Livvy moving to university in September.

I've applied, but I'm not going. It just seems pointless when the only thing I want to do is find the man who killed my big sister. I promised myself and my parents that I'd deflect only until next year. Guess I'll have to figure out what I want to do with the rest of my life.

No pressure or anything.

Grandad's soft snore fills the back end of the house where the bedrooms are. I change my clothes and get into bed. Tonight is as close to *something* as I've gotten so far. Celia was sneaking off from Nana and Grandad's to go somewhere, and what I found tonight is all about after-dark activities.

Hugo has to be there.

27

Dread washes over me like an ice-cold shower.

What if Hugo wasn't just a friend of hers? What if he's the killer?

If her diary entries are to be believed, Celia wasn't scared of him, but perhaps she didn't write in there if he'd changed. Flicking on the bedside lamp, I shove my cover off and reach into my overnight bag.

I couldn't have thought of this during the day?

Stifling a yawn, I pore through the pages after she met Hugo. All they say is sad, soppy stuff that infatuated teenagers write. Celia was one of those girls who makes me gag, writing things like, *I already know I love him*, and, *We're going to be together soon*. She even has her name and his encased in a huge heart on the back page of one of the last entries.

Really, Celia?

So far, it's all been pretty one-sided. Everything she wrote is about how much she likes him, how amazing he is, and what she wants their future to be like. No mention about his feelings or any attraction toward her.

Awkward.

The way she wrote about him and how enthusiastic she was, there's no way she would have skipped over them kissing or him telling her he liked her. There could have been an argument between them. Maybe he felt like she was stalking him or something like that. But that doesn't really add up. What she wrote in here doesn't suggest that he was ever violent or that she was scared.

I flick back through the last entries, trying to pick up on anything I could've missed, but the more I read, the less convinced I am that Hugo hurt her. But I obviously don't know.

Whatever happened between them—or didn't happen—I have to find him.

It's slowly creeping up to two in the morning, so I put the diary away and slip into bed. I'll need all the strength I can get for going home later.

Nan wakes me up in the morning, and her eyes are glossy.

Happy birthday, Celia.

"Morning," I mutter, feeling my heart deflate. There's nothing I want to do less than go home and deal with today.

"Good morning. How are you?"

"I'm...okay. I miss her."

"We all do. We stick together, remember?" she says.

I nod once and sit up. "Right. Is Grandad up yet?"

"He's getting dressed. We need to leave soon."

"Okay, I'll quickly throw on some clothes. I'm starving."

"That's exactly what your grandad said." She smiles and gives me a hug that's full of pain and protectiveness.

When Celia died, my whole family pulled together, and we've been that way ever since. Kind of. My relationship with my parents is strained most of the time.

"Have you spoken to Mum?"

"Yes, a minute ago."

My throat is dry. "And?"

"They're all doing okay. Livvy was upset first thing, but she's looking through old pictures now."

A part of me wants to go home right now, and another part wants to run away. I feel like a fraud. "Okay."

"Hey," Nana says, patting my hand. "Bella, no guilt now. We understand why you need some time on days like these."

I found her. I saw my big sister like that, and there isn't a day that goes by when I don't think about what happened, but on anniversaries and birthdays, her death is *all* that goes through my mind.

"Thanks," I say, giving her the only reply that'll end the conversation. "I'll get dressed then."

Nana stands up to let me out of bed, and I don't look back as I grab my bag and escape to the bathroom.

I close and lock the door behind me, and then I take a deep breath.

I can do this.

My hair is a mess, and I look like I've not slept in weeks. Livvy will be polished and looking like she's ready for the catwalk. I look ready to be shipped off to a psychiatric unit.

Dragging a brush through my hair, I attempt to salvage something about my appearance. My dark hair is far too long, almost down to my hips, but it's about the only girlie thing about me, so I absolutely refuse to cut it short.

I pull on my shorts and a Fall Out Boy T-shirt, tie my hair in a messy ponytail, and go back out. Nana is sitting in the living room, but Grandad is still getting ready, probably trying to choose the most appropriate shirt for the day. He does like his shirts on special and difficult occasions. Not sure what difference it makes.

"Who is...Fall Out Boy?" Nana asks, reading the name off my top.

"My future husband's band."

Nana's lip quirks in a smile. "I remember those days. I was going to marry Elvis Presley."

"Had to settle for Grandad, did ya?"

He chooses that moment to walk into the living room and scoffs. "Settle? She landed herself the catch of the day."

"Just the day?" I tease.

God, I wish I could live here until I moved out on my own.

"Watch it, you." Grandad laughs. "Are we all ready, or do you two need a little more time to antagonise me?"

"What do you think, Bella?" Nana says.

Before I can reply, Grandad holds up his hand. "All right, whoever's not in the car in the next thirty seconds pays for their own breakfast."

We don't need to be told twice. Nana and I make the quickest dash for the car.

"Can I drive?" I ask, leaning against the driver's door as Grandad locks the house.

He turns and laughs. "Not a chance. In the back, Bella," he replies as he presses the unlock button.

Rude.

I passed my test four months after my seventeenth birthday, so I've been driving a while now. My parents thought Livvy would pass first because she's focused and driven, and she pretty much excels at everything, but I bossed it for once.

It takes only a few minutes to get to the café, and as soon as I walk into the door, I see Rocco straightaway. He looks even better in daylight, and my heart goes crazy.

Great.

FIVE

ROCCO

Ellis shovels half of a sausage into his mouth in one go and chews. We're in the local café for breakfast because neither of us can be fucked to cook.

"You always feel like you're being watched in here, man?" he asks.

I can see chewed sausage and beans churning away in there.

"Yeah, because we're always being watched in here. They're probably waiting for us to skip out on the bill or swipe something on the way past."

The café is wedged between the good part of town and where we live, so it gets the people with money and the people waiting to steal the money. The owners are decent and come from a working-class background, and by all accounts, the money the place makes doesn't allow for a flashy lifestyle. But what they have, they want to keep. I don't believe in shitting where you eat, so they'll never have any hassle from my end. We don't come here very often though. I prefer to eat without an audience.

"Wankers," Ellis mutters, forking the other half of the sausage into his mouth.

I push my food around the plate. After three coffees and a bacon sandwich, I'm not feeling the omelet.

"Craig asked me to sort the bets," he says. "I thought you weren't interested in fighting Dillon?"

"I'm not really, but I've not been offered anything in a while."

"You could just use a punching bag if you needed to get off. Or a woman."

It sounds an awful lot like he is telling me to raise my hand to a woman, but I know what he means. To Ellis, sex is no different than fighting. You release all of that pent-up tension and frustration, so why not do it the way that gets you an orgasm? His long-term fuck buddy would agree. Though, deep down, I think Izzy is more to him than just a shag.

It's not like that for me. I need both. Ever since I walked in on some guy beating my mum, I've been up for a fight. As soon as I was old enough, the first one I picked was with him.

"Thanks. I'll think about it," I murmur.

There's only so much a fight or a woman can do anyway. The feeling of my skin burning and screaming can only be smothered for so long, no matter what I do.

"No, you won't."

"Then, why did I say it?" I snap.

Ellis flashes me a shit-eating grin. "You're such a fucking pussy, man."

"Piss off."

He's the only guy I can stand, and right now, he's really ruining it.

"You heading to the gym more this week?" he asks.

The gym is a gym in the sense that you pay to use the fitness equipment, but it looks more like a dirty old shed.

"Maybe. Dillon isn't a threat though."

"Mate, The Hulk isn't a threat when you get going."

Thinking of every man who abused my mum, I'm untouchable, thanks to my ability to paste their faces on my opponents. It probably isn't healthy or whatever, but it means I can handle myself while bringing in a decent amount of money.

"You about to help me train?"

He nods and stuffs another heaping spoonful into his mouth. I knew he would because there's fuck all else for him to do until next week when debts need paying.

I drain a strong mug of coffee and flick my finger up for a refill when Bella and what looks like her parents or grandparents walk in.

Jesus, she's even more beautiful in the light.

I know I should look away, but my eyes are drawn to her like a magnet.

Her long, dark hair is tied up, and she's wearing black jean shorts and a grey top. Her legs are begging to be wrapped around my shoulders. Written across her boobs is *Fall Out Boy.* I have no idea what the fuck that means.

She's animated and smiling, which is new to me. Last night, she was full of attitude, and it was a lot of fun. Probably the most fun I've had, and that says a lot about how dull and empty my life is.

"Who's the chick?" His green eyes narrow as he recognises her. "Wait, she's the one from last night, isn't she?" Ellis asks, checking out what's caught my attention.

"Yeah, that's her. I'm not sure exactly who she is yet."

Every time I think I've got her all worked out, she surprises me. Like, right now, there's none of the gobby bullshit. She's a normal girl, out to breakfast with her family.

"She's smokin', man. You really should fuck her," he says.

"Probably will eventually," I reply halfheartedly, still watching Bella.

She turns, and I see her freeze as she spots me. Her eyes widen, and she stumbles a step.

Her mum or maybe her nan points to the table next to ours, but she shakes her head. It makes me smile. She tries to suggest another table, but there's some sort of disagreement. The one next to me is the only window table left, so I guess that's the preferred seat—though not for Bella.

Her expression is priceless as she trails behind her family to the table.

"This table's rubbish, Nana," she whispers.

Her grandparents then.

"There's nothing wrong with it. Sit down, and act eighteen."

Fucking hell, eighteen?

She acts about twelve. Unless that is just an act. It's hard to tell with her.

"Good morning, Bella." I smile.

She jabs her tongue into the side of her mouth and scowls. "Hello, Rocco."

Bella's nan looks between us and then picks up her menu. She's not looking at it; rather, she's using it to pretend like she's not listening in.

"How've you been?"

Bella's lips thin, and she gives me a don't-drop-me-in-it look. Ah, no one knows she was out. She's a fucking adult, so why would it matter?

"Fine," she replies instantly. "You?"

"I'm good. It was nice to see you the other day."

Her nan looks up. "When was this?"

Bella looks like she's going to reach across and strangle me. "The shop last week, Nana, when you asked me to get bread and biscuits."

Her lie came so naturally, without a second thought. I'm used to that, so I don't know why it doesn't seem to fit well with Bella.

"Okay, love. What are you having?" her nan asks, accepting Bella's lie at face value.

"Fried egg on toast, I think."

"Do you ever have anything different, Isabella?"

"No, I don't."

"Are you ready to go home after breakfast?"

Her eyes darken, and she bites her bottom lip. It's sexy even though she's doing it because she's unsure.

"I will be when I'm fed."

Ellis cocks his eyebrow and boots my foot under the table. "What?" I snap.

"You're staring." He leans in. "You like her."

I nod and take a gulp of my coffee. "What're we doing after the gym? I'm bored as fuck."

He shrugs. "Nothing planned. Don't think we're needed."

Great, another mind-numbing day then.

"I need to do something, man," I say. I'm restless, and I hate sitting around.

Bella's nan leaves her table and walks over to her husband at the counter. She is at the table alone now and staring holes into the menu even though she's decided on what to eat already.

"Are you sneaking out tonight, Bella?" I ask once her nan's out of earshot.

Her head doesn't move, but her eyes shoot daggers at mine. "I didn't *sneak* out," she lies.

"Good, because you're a little old to be doing that."

"You don't know the first fucking thing about me. I thought we'd established that."

Ellis laughs and kicks his feet up on the chair beside me.

"That doesn't mean you're not too old to sneak out of—"

She holds her hand up and snaps, "How about you concentrate on your coffee, and I'll wait for my breakfast? There is no need for us to engage in conversation. Ever again."

"You brought the bitch out today, huh?"

She looks away and clenches her jaw.

"Don't get me wrong, *Isabella*; I like it."

"You're a dickhead."

"You love it."

Her grandparents return to the table, so her focus shifts to them, and she's all smiles. I know I should just leave her alone, but I haven't had a girl in my life who is feisty and confusing in…forever.

She's beautiful, strong-willed, frustrating, and perfect to play with. I usually only get enjoyment out of things that are less than legal. Nothing about Bella is dangerous, and she's a female who isn't easy. I'm drawn to her even though I have a feeling she'll be more trouble than she's worth.

"We doing one? I'm bored," Ellis asks.

"Yeah," I reply, pushing my mug away.

I need to put some distance between me and Bella. Things would be easier if she'd just let me fuck her, but since that doesn't seem likely, I need to get away.

SIX

BELLA

Olivia's and my car is in the drive, so I get to be the late one again. It's worse today, being Celia's birthday.

Mum, Dad, Olivia, and Harry are sitting in the living room when I walk inside. Nana and Grandad went into town when they dropped me off, and they'll be back here in a little while. They let us visit Celia alone and go later.

They're looking at photos of Celia. Since Harry and Livvy got together three years ago, Harry has been here every year for Celia's birthday.

"Bella," Mum says with a smile.

She's been crying, but I can tell she's happy, too. Celia's not here, but we still love her and celebrate her life. My sister gave our family a lot in her short sixteen years, and we aren't going to forget that just because she isn't here.

I can't smile. I have a hole in my heart and dread churning in my stomach.

"Hey," I reply as I sit down in the armchair.

I've never felt more single, sitting in the lonely chair, while Mum and Dad share one sofa and Olivia and Harry share the other. But I don't have the capacity to open up and let another person into my life. My parents, both sets of grandparents, and twin sister are enough. Boyfriends take up too much time that I just don't have.

I never quite know how to act on Celia's birthday. We try to move on and take her with us, but there's been no closure. We don't know who killed her and why. I feel like we're just going through the motions, and we're half-stuck in the past.

"How are you doing?" I ask.

Mum smiles and grips Dad's hand.

"We're okay, love. What about you?" he asks cautiously.

They treat me like glass on her birthday and the anniversary of her death.

"I'm okay."

"Are you?" Olivia asks.

"I found her, Livvy, but I'm okay." My stomach feels like it's full of lead as I remember that day.

Breathe.

Celia was always full of life, so seeing her cold and lifeless was torture. It still is. Images like that don't fade. I'll always see my big sister's dead body. It's just something I have to live with.

Fuck today.

"Are you?" Mum asks, repeating Livvy.

I feel like saying *no* to get them off my back, but if I do, there will be all sorts of comfort that I just can't deal with at the minute. Years ago, we promised that we'd make today a celebration, and the others can cry as much as they want, but I owe Celia this much.

"Yes. When are we visiting her?"

"We were just waiting for you," Dad says, standing up. "I'll grab my wallet, and we'll get out of here."

First stop is the local florist where Gloria will have the biggest, brightest bunch of flowers waiting for us. She does it every year and never charges. Celia did two weeks' work experience in that florist when she was fifteen, and then she took a part-time job there a few nights a week and Sunday mornings. Gloria loved her, too, and this is something she can do to feel useful, helpful. Celia would have appreciated it.

We walk down the street, into the heart of our sleepy little town. It's one of those cute places where everyone knows everyone, but Celia's murder cast a shadow over this once perfect town.

People stop for a second to say hello and to tell us they're thinking of us. Everyone remembers every anniversary.

Mum pushes open the door to the florist, and the scent of summer hits me.

I remember coming here on the few occasions when Celia picked Olivia and me up from school because Mum was working her shift at the doctor surgery. We'd sit out back, and Gloria would grab us a snack and put the TV on. Occasionally, if we were quiet, we were allowed to help out with one of the arrangements or restock the buckets with flowers or top up the water.

Gloria's face this morning is her sympathy face. She tilts her head to the side and softly greets us, "How are you?" Her striking blue eyes fill with tears.

Mum nods her head. "We're okay. This day will never be easy."

"No, of course not. Her flowers are ready though, the most colourful ones in the delivery."

"Thank you, Gloria," Dad replies.

"Anything I can do. I'll just go and get them."

Livvy laughs, and I follow her gaze to the old, rickety wooden footstall—one that Celia fell over when she backed up without looking. Livvy and I laughed until we couldn't breathe, and once Celia got over the initial shock, she did, too.

"Remember the look on her face?" I say.

Livvy looks back and grins. "I'll never forget that."

"Bless her, she fell down like a sack of shit."

Dad glances over his shoulder and gives me a look full of warning. *Language, Isabella.*

Oops.

I mouth, *Sorry*, and he turns back.

Gloria comes back with a gorgeous bouquet made from peonies, lily of the valley, roses, lilies, and gerberas—all bright and beautiful. Celia would have loved them. She was full of energy.

"Oh, Gloria, they're perfect," Mum says.

Every year, they are. Gloria's skills are insane.

"I'm so pleased you like them," she replies.

Dad gets his wallet out and Gloria holds her hand up, shaking her head, same as every year.

"Thank you," he says sincerely. He wraps his arm around Mum as she takes the bouquet from Gloria.

"You're welcome. I thought the world of her, too."

I leave, and Livvy follows. Things were about to get sentimental, and I already feel like I'm being suffocated. I take a deep breath the second I'm outside.

"You okay?" Livvy asks.

"Will be."

Today needs to end. It's barely fucking begun, and I'm already done.

"You never open up as much as the rest of us," she says.

That's because I can't.

"People are different, Liv."

"Yeah, I know that. Maybe it would help you to talk to us though. It helps me, and I know we're not the same, but I honestly think you need some help."

"Wow."

"No"—she sighs—"that's not what I meant. I'm not saying you need a shrink, but I think it's pretty obvious that you need a better way of coping. I don't just mean with Celia but other things, too."

"So, you are saying I need to see a shrink."

I don't like where this is going at all, and I can't even blame Livvy. If things were the other way around, I would want her to get help, too.

"If that would help you, then, yeah, see a therapist."

"I'm fine, Livvy."

"Yeah? Where are you going to uni? What's your plan if you don't go? Will you live with Mum and Dad? Do you want to get your own place? Have you thought about having someone in your life, a friend or boyfriend? Do you even want that?"

My head is spinning.

"Okay, I've not decided about uni this year. If I don't go, I'll get a job," I lie. "I'll live at home until I can afford to move out. I don't need anyone. Pretty sure I'm too high-maintenance for a boyfriend." When I say *high-maintenance*, I mean, messed up. I'm not capable of putting anyone or anything before my quest to find Celia's killer.

I've never had a proper boyfriend, but I think they require a certain amount of time and attention. I don't have that to give. It's why my last and only two pitiful attempts to be with someone ended very soon after they began.

She folds her arms. "Come on, you're going to find someone. You just need to let yourself be happy."

How can I do that when our sister was murdered?

Celia will never do the things we have the opportunity to do. Livvy deserves it, but I don't.

I don't care if I never have anything as long as my sister gets justice.

You could tell them.

I scrap the idea before I put too much thought into it. They can't know. Selfishly, I can't lose them either. I might not be close to my parents or sister, but I don't know what I'd do if they cut me out of their lives because they found out the truth.

We arrive at Celia's grave five minutes later, and Mum grips ahold of Dad. The massive guilt slams into my chest harder than a fucking freight train.

I'm so sorry, Celia.

"Hello, darling," Mum says, sitting down at the grave.

Dad sits, too, and puts his arm around her. Livvy takes her place beside Mum, so they're both supporting her. I don't know where to go or what to do. It's always the same. I must seem heartless.

"Happy birthday," Livvy whispers.

I swallow a lump the size of the Grand Canyon and look up to the sky. *Don't cry, don't cry, don't cry.*

This day is so overwhelming that I feel like the world is about to swallow me whole.

It will be over soon. I just need to be strong for a little bit longer.

I watch over their shoulders as the three of them talk to Celia. The times I tried, I ended up choking on guilt when I opened my mouth.

"We miss you every day, but we know you're still with us," Dad says.

I wish I could believe that she was still here, too. Maybe then I wouldn't feel so awful every second of every day.

We need to hurry this up. It's fucking horrible.

"Isabella, would you like to say something?" Mum asks.

No, I don't want to say something!

I never want to.

"I'm okay, thanks," I mutter in response, trying not to feel like the worst person ever.

The things I want to say to Celia aren't anything I can say in front of my parents and sister. I made a promise.

"I think it will help," Mum says in a low voice while staring at the ground.

Dad puts his hand over Mum's. "Love, we all grieve in different ways."

It's his way of saying, *Leave her alone*, and I appreciate it.

Talking to my dead sister's headstone won't help me move on from her death like it does for them. I'm glad they're able to find peace, but I can't.

At least I can't yet.

SEVEN

BELLA

I can maybe get away for two hours, but any longer than that, and Mum will be blowing up my phone. After spending time at Celia's grave and sitting in silence back home, I need to be elsewhere.

The air in the house is getting thinner.

While Mum and Dad cuddle on the sofa and talk about their firstborn and Livvy goes to meet Harry again, I head out to my shared car and leave home behind. There's only one place I want to be right now.

Rocco hasn't told me where he lives because we've had, like, two short conversations, so I drive around, taking random turns and heading back in the direction of the river.

I take a left, and, yep, I'm totally lost.

Finding him is going to be like finding a needle in a haystack. But I need to because he's my only connection to this place. I can't let him slip away and be left with nothing to help me find Celia's killer.

Swinging the car around at the dead end, I head back the way I just was. It doesn't help that there are rows and rows of similar-looking houses, many boarded up. I could really do with a big flag of Rocco's face flying high over his house.

This is dumb. I'm dumb. I'm not going to find his place.

And I think I'm kind of a stalker.

After fifteen minutes or driving in what appears to be circles, I park near a supermarket and get out. That, I recognise, and it's not far from the river, so I walk toward it to see if there's any sign of the man I can't get out of my head.

If I don't find him, this will have been a waste of time. But it beats walking the streets near home for a couple of hours. I don't have any friends to escape to, and it only bothers me on this day each year. It's a day when I *really* need somebody.

And I have no clue why I'm looking for Rocco to be that person. But I am.

"Bella?"

I turn to see the person behind the voice. The guy Rocco was with in the café jogs toward me.

Please say he's off to meet up with Rocco.

Giving him a smile, I take a sweep of the area behind him, and he's definitely alone. "Hi…"

"Ellis," he says, giving me his name. "You looking for Rocco?"

Yes.

"I was just in town."

He smirks, seeing straight through my stupid lie. "He'll be at the café. We're supposed to meet there in five."

Yay. Okay, I rock at finding him. Well, eventually anyway.

"Oh…"

"Come with me," he says, shaking his head, amused.

Great, I'm that transparent.

"Thanks, Ellis." I fall in line with him because I have no idea where I'm going.

We pass empty commercial buildings, and I think one actually looks like it burned down. Ellis walks fast, but it's not fast enough.

"How are you?"

With a frown, he says, "I didn't think you'd be much of a small-talk girl."

"Just trying to be polite."

"Ask me what you really want to know."

Fine.

"Is that your natural hair colour?"

Laughing, he gives me a what-the-fuck look. "Well, I did ask. Yes, it is. Why?"

"It's just *way* too blond."

"Um...I don't know what to say to that."

I shrug. "You don't need to say anything."

He shakes his head and looks forward. We turn a corner, and then he glances at me again.

"There's something about you that Rocco likes."

I look up through my lashes, trying to act innocent even though I'm a little taken aback.

"Please," he scoffs. "That's what you really want to ask me. Look, Rocco doesn't think about girls, and he doesn't seek out female company...unless he's looking for a quick shag."

Er...nice?

"Well, has he said anything about me then? Because, the couple of times we've been together, we've mostly just bickered."

"You've clearly not known him long. He doesn't talk about his feelings."

No, I've known him for about three minutes!

We walk in silence for a few seconds, and I wait for him to elaborate.

Then, how do you know? How. Do. You. Know?

I press my lips together to stop the words from bursting out. He can't feed me tiny bits of information like that and then go silent.

Seriously, he needs to start talking.

"I can tell what you're thinking, Bella," he says with a laugh. "We might not have deep and meaningful talks into the night, but I know him. Without even thinking, he's brought you into conversations. That's never happened, and he's known you for only a day. That's big for him."

That's big for anyone.

But I like where this is going.

I want to quiz Ellis further, but we arrive at the café. It's not the one my grandparents take me to, and I've not been here before. It looks severely run-down, more of an old shack than a restaurant.

Note to self: Don't eat here.

We walk through the door, paint peeling off it, and I'm hit with the smell of grease.

My hair is going to be gross when I leave.

The walls are an off-white, but I'm pretty sure it's just because it's old and covered in God knows what rather than a choice of colour.

Ellis sees my distaste and laughs. "You'll need to shower, but their all-day full English breakfast is good."

I open my mouth to tell him there's no way I'm eating when I spot Rocco. He's sitting in the corner, facing us, but he's not looked up from his phone yet.

My first instinct is to freak out over who he's potentially texting, but that would be batshit crazy of me. Plus, Ellis just told me that Rocco likes me. Probably. Mentioning someone a few times might not count.

It's not until we're right at the table when Rocco looks up. He sees me first, and the surprise is evident. His dark eyebrows rise, and he sits back in his seat. Folding his arms, he smirks.

Jesus, he is beautiful. Aren't you just supposed to get butterflies around someone you're attracted to?

I have fucking *Game of Thrones*-style dragons going on in my stomach. My attraction to him is coupled with intrigue and a whole lot of nervousness. He's exactly what I need to help me find Celia's killer.

"Look who I found," Ellis says.

He takes a seat so that I'm forced with facing Rocco. Not that I'm complaining.

"What're you doing here, Bella?" His voice is rough and sexy as hell and does things to my insides that makes me want to drag him into the nearest restroom.

"I was bored," I reply.

Telling him the truth isn't going to happen. Rocco and his friends can't know why I'm here. I came to get away from the crippling sadness at home, not to talk about it. And, if I tell them my sister is dead, they'll have questions.

I bloody hate *questions.*

"Wow, nice to know you have to get really bored before you pay us a visit," Ellis says sarcastically.

I lean my elbows on the table and tilt my head in his direction. "Ah, but I didn't come to see you."

"Ouch." He clutches his heart and then nudges my arm.

When I look back at Rocco, his expression is hard.

Yeah, I was so not flirting with Ellis.

Quite like that he's jealous though.

At least I think that was jealousy.

When the server comes, Rocco and Ellis order the all-day full English, and I opt for chips. It seems so much safer, and I'm hungry.

"Are you being a princess about the food here?" Rocco asks once we're alone again.

I fold my arms. "I bet there is no real meat in the meat here. And they don't even mop the floor, which everyone can see, so what makes you think they're cleaning the kitchen?"

Rocco eyes me like he's not sure I'm even human. "Why the fuck would I think about that shit at all?" he says the words with conviction.

But I don't miss how his eyes snap to the floor.

Yeah, dude, it's fucking filthy. Enjoy your plate of dirty, processed arseholes and hooves.

We fall into an easy conversation until our food arrives. I pick up a chip and inspect it to make sure there's no mould. Result: It looks okay.

"I swear, best food in the world right here," Ellis mumbles, shoving a massive forkful into his mouth.

I turn my nose up. "Gross."

"Stop being a little princess," Rocco teases.

"I'm not, but that does not look good. Your food is sitting on a layer of grease. You know that's probably taking a month off your life each time you eat it."

He shrugs, never taking his eyes off me. "It's worth it."

"Doubt it."

"I'm not making it past fifty anyway," Ellis says.

"Fucking hell, man, not this again."

"What?" I ask, looking between them.

Rocco shakes his head, discouraged. "Ellis seems to think that, after fifty, your dick and sex drive start to decline."

"I'm just sayin', I don't see a point if you can't have sex. What else in life is there?"

"So, what happens when you get to fifty?" I ask.

"I'm going to have one fuck-off huge weekend, do every drug imaginable, and shag as many women as I can before I OD."

I raise my eyebrow at his stupidity. "Wow, life goals."

"Death goals," he corrects. "Tell me a better way to go."

He's talking about taking his own life on my murdered sister's birthday, and I can't get angry at the waste. For the first time since she died, I feel hope. Being with Rocco and Ellis is the only time I've felt a sliver of the carefree teenager I should be. They're fun, and I haven't realised, until now, how much I needed that.

I could easily become lost with Rocco. Part of me wants that. If I can just forget, then I can have a normal life.

You owe Celia. You owe her.

I don't deserve a normal life, not until I put this right first.

"Old, in your sleep, and surrounded by people you love." It doesn't sound like an end I'll get, but that doesn't mean I don't want it.

"Nah, I'm with Ellis here," Rocco says the words, but his eyes say something completely contradictory.

He wants my version of a perfect end. I want to call him out on it, but that would be kind of a dick move in front of Ellis. Also, it would make me sound like a needy psycho, and I'm not down for that.

"Can we talk about something else now, please?" Just because I feel okay to talk about this subject today doesn't mean I particularly want to discuss it.

"Done, Bells," Ellis says.

Sure, call me whatever you want.

"Tell me honestly, which one of us is better looking?" Ellis gestures between himself and Rocco.

Ellis isn't bad-looking, but there's no comparison in my eyes.

The tall, dark, and handsome man staring at me will win every time.

"Rocco," I say, smirking at Ellis.

"Ah! You're killing me, Bella."

I glance back at Rocco, and he's smug as fuck. The way he looks at me, sort of like I'm dinner and the only woman on earth at the same time, is like nothing I've experienced before. I've had guys want to be with me, but they were just after sex.

"See, bro? You just don't do it for her," Rocco teases.

Yep, this is definitely appropriate conversation for my third encounter with this stranger.

A stranger I weirdly feel like I've known for a long time. It's probably because I'm not used to feeling comfortable around anyone.

"If it helps, I'd pick you over the rest of the men in here," I say to Ellis.

It won't help.

"Oh, thank you very fucking much. You'd do me over all the *old* men. Thanks. My pride has been restored."

I laugh. "You asked, so you brought this on yourself."

"I didn't think anyone would be blind enough to choose that prick over me," he says, playfully narrowing his eyes at Rocco. "Anyway, kids, I'm gonna do one. Play nicely together."

He chucks some cash down on the table and exchanges a look with Rocco, and I have no idea what it means. Rocco does though, as he glares back.

"What was that about?" I ask innocently, knowing full bloody well that he's not going to tell me.

Frustrating idiot.

"What?"

Yep, not going to tell me.

"What're you doing for the rest of the day?" he asks, folding his arms.

God, I would love to chill with him, but I can't be here too long. Soon, I'll have to go home and pretend like being there isn't excruciating. My family always talks about Celia today and on the anniversary of her death. To me, it's too much. It brings everything back, and I'm that terrified little girl again.

"I have a family thing," I reply, turning my nose up.

"You seem thrilled."

"I'd rather be anywhere else."

"You don't get along with them?"

"Not so much. It's okay though. I get along well with my grandparents." *They don't care that I'm not a carbon copy of Livvy.* "Do you feel sick yet? I feel like you should after eating that."

"Try it before you write it off."

"I'll pass. Hey do you have WhatsApp?"

He frowns, looking at me like I'm speaking a different language. "A what's app what?"

I laugh at his confusion. Oh my God, his frown is adorable.

"It's a messaging app on your phone, like text but you don't have to pay."

"I don't pay to text either. I don't really do it."

"You don't text?"

"Ellis, maybe a couple of times a month, but—"

I hold my hand out. "Wow. Okay, give me your phone."

He pulls a face like he definitely doesn't want to hand over his phone to a virtual stranger who keeps randomly turning up. "Why?"

"Because I'm putting WhatsApp on it. You can message me."

"I can text you if you put your number in."

"Hilarious. I don't want my parents to see your number on the bill. They'll ask questions."

He puts his phone in my outstretched hand. "Can't you just tell them I'm your pimp?"

I roll my eyes and ignore his comment. It would be funny for, like, a second, but then there would be shouting, and they'd have to meet him. I'd likely be grounded—or they would *try* to ground me anyway.

After getting Rocco to enter the pin in his iPhone 4— yeah, really—the app downloads. I add my details, and we're all set.

"There," I say, handing it back. "Now, you don't have to miss me so much."

"Oh, thank God," he mutters sarcastically.

He can joke all he wants, but I know he's happy to see me, too. Whatever this is between us, after only a day, I like it. It's nice to have a friend.

Can he be called a friend already?

"Shall we get out of here then? I really should get home."

Nodding, he reaches for his wallet.

"How much do I owe?" I ask.

He gives me a flat look. "Just get your bag, Bella."

"I don't expect you to pay for me. This isn't the 1950s."

"Isabella!" he snaps.

"Wow. Okay, Mr Grumpy."

He raises an eyebrow instead of saying anything.

"Thank you, Rocco."

"There. That wasn't so bad, was it? Don't you think it's so much nicer when you're not being bratty?"

"No, I don't. And, if you're honest with yourself, you don't think that either. You like to be challenged."

He grunts. "Well, you sure are a challenge."

"You're welcome. Where are you going now? My car is near the supermarket."

"I'll walk you back. And what car do you have?"

"A Fiat 500."

His nose turns up. "Don't call that tin can a car."

I get up and grab my bag. My phone is on silent, and I can feel it vibrating with a call, probably from Mum. "You're so funny. You know, I don't think I've ever met anyone as hilarious as you. You should do stand-up at the Apollo. And I share the car with my sister; it was her choice."

He grabs my elbow, rolling his eyes, and leads me toward the exit. "I think you should be quiet now, Bella."

"Nuh-uh. You don't want me to."

"Right now, I do."

We walk out of the café, and four men are involved in a fight across the street. Fists and feet are flying everywhere as each one tries to inflict the most pain on the other.

Rocco doesn't even blink.

Each one of them looks like they're in their thirties.

"What the hell is that?"

I've seen pathetic fights at school, but they were broken up by teachers pretty fast. This is something completely different. Blood is everywhere. They're rolling around in a pool of their mixed blood, and it makes me feel sick. This is vicious and brutal.

Brutal…just like my sister's death. Is it one of them, Celia?

I'm cold. Icy cold.

Rocco puts his arm around me, and I think I'm more stunned at that than the fight. His fingers lightly dig into the flesh of my hip as he holds me close.

"That's just another day in paradise," he mutters as he quickly ushers me back toward my car.

I look over my shoulder, memorising the faces of the four men. I think I recognise a few of them from the river, but I could be wrong because I only saw them for a matter of minutes.

I'm coming back here as soon as I can.

I won't give up, Celia, I promise. I'll make this right.

EIGHT

BELLA

Sunday brings a breath of fresh air. It's no longer Celia's birthday. The house returns to its post-Celia normality. Mum and Dad are in the kitchen, where they spend most of their time, drinking coffee and talking. Livvy is rushing around, getting ready to go to Harry's for the day.

All I plan to do is binge-watch *Gossip Girl* and eat. Since sixth form is out for revision before our final exams, I'll have plenty of time to stay with Nana and Grandad.

"Morning," I say to my parents as I hone in on the pot of coffee. Caffeine dominates my bloodstream, and I need my fix.

"Morning, sweetheart," Mum says.

"We're going to the car boot today. Want to come?" Dad asks.

Do I want to spend all morning walking around outside, looking at tables of other people's old shit?

No, I don't.

"Do you know me at all, Dad?"

He laughs. "It was a long shot."

"Thanks, but I'm Netflixing today."

"Perhaps you should study," Mum suggests.

"It's Sunday. Sunday is for Netflix."

"I'm sure that's not what Sundays are traditionally for," Mum says, her lip twitching in a smile.

"Depends on whose idea of tradition you're talking about."

Livvy waltzes into the kitchen on cloud nine. She probably just had another ten-minute fight with Harry over who should hang up first.

Vom.

It's eight thirty a.m., and she's perfectly groomed and ready for the catwalk. I look like I was just mugged.

"Coffee?" I ask.

Livvy nods. "Thanks. So, today, Harry and I are…"

And that's when I switch off.

Mum and Dad listen to Livvy reel off her list of super-sickly-sweet plans for her and the dickhead boyfriend while I make drinks.

I add milk to our coffees, more to hers since she prefers it far too weak, and put them down on the table. Livvy gets the chopped fruit from the fridge to make a fruit salad for breakfast, and I grab the box of raspberry Pop-Tarts. We fail so hard at being twins.

"Thanks," Livvy says, nodding to her coffee as she joins our parents.

When my Pop-Tarts are done and molten-lava hot, I follow.

"Bella, I was thinking about getting my nails done one day this week and wondered if you'd want to come, too?" Livvy asks.

She's positive I'll say no, or she wouldn't have asked quite so formally.

Honestly, I'd rather pull my nails off than go have them done by some orange-tanned lady who won't stop talking to me, but I've not spent much time with my mum and sister recently, so I find myself nodding. I should try, right? "Sounds good."

Actually, it sounds like hell, but I'll get over it.

"Great," she replies, sitting up straighter, clearly pleased that I proved her wrong.

I love my sister to death; she's the other half of me. But, sometimes, I resent her for being the one who gets to be normal. I'd give anything to not have seen Celia like that. Livvy is the girl whose big sister was murdered. I'm the girl who found her murdered big sister.

"Just nails though, right? They're not coming near my face with any of that mud shit."

"Bella," Dad warns at my word choice.

"Just nails," Livvy says. "I promise."

"I'm hoping to stay with Nana and Grandad Tuesday to Thursday, so any other day is good with me," I say, looking to Mum and Dad for their approval since I technically haven't brought it up with them yet.

Now that I'm eighteen, it's not that they can really stop me from staying anywhere, but they've had enough to deal with, and I don't exactly make things easy on them.

They share a look, and Livvy stays quiet to see how this goes.

"All right, that's fine with us," Mum says.

Huh? I expected a fight.

"Thanks."

"As long as you keep up with your exam revision there," she adds.

I hold my hands up, totally okay with that condition. "Will do."

Mum smiles and turns to my sister. "Livvy, do you need a lift to Harry's?"

"Er," she says, looking over at me.

Since we share a car, we have to bloody book it in advance.

"I'm not leaving the house today, so do what you like," I reply.

"Then, I'm fine," she says to our parents.

Mum ushers Dad out of the house in a hurry in case the neighbours sell out of all their old rubbish in the next hour. *Un-fucking-likely.*

"So, you're really staying in today?" Livvy asks.

My sister seems to think that I should be out with friends like normal eighteen-year-olds. My group got bored of me a long time ago. My mind is still very much in the past, so I make a terrible friend.

"Yep."

"Why don't you come to the cinema with me and Harry?"

I laugh before I can stop myself. "Sorry, but being a third wheel to you guys is the absolute last thing I want to do."

"You wouldn't be a third wheel; you're my sister."

"That's right, and sisters shouldn't go on each other's dates. I'm fine, Liv. I like my own company." I might not like it in twenty years when I'm living with thirty cats, but for now, I'm cool.

She sighs and purses her lips. I hate that she pities me. There's nothing wrong with not being a people person. Most people are wankers anyway.

"When you get home, why don't we watch something?" I suggest.

We won't. We rarely do anything like that anymore, but the thought makes her feel better.

"Sure," she replies. She pops a chunk of melon in her mouth. "I might come to Nana and Grandad's with you one night."

No. Absolutely not.

If she's there, I can't sneak out. We share the spare room at theirs, and I don't fancy my chances with her sleeping in the same room. But I can't really tell her that.

"Yeah? I thought you'd want to spend as much time with Harry since there's no school, and we don't have to be home as early." *That's right; use her boyfriend as an excuse.*

"I do, but I feel like we don't spend much time together anymore. I miss that."

"We're doing nails." I'm torn between actually wanting to spend more time with her and wanting to cause an argument, so she won't want to be anywhere near me.

"I know, but—"

"Livvy, you don't have to feel bad. We're adults now, so we're going to do different things. It's perfectly normal, and it doesn't mean we're any less twin than before."

It's all true even if I am just saying it so that she'll stay the fuck here.

"I guess. As long as you're not mad at me for being with Harry so much. I feel like you don't like him sometimes."

Oh, I don't like him all of the time but not because she's always with him.

"We might not be besties, but I definitely don't dislike him because you're together so much. Stop stressing, and just be happy, okay?"

I need her to be happy, or what's the point of me keeping quiet for the last twelve years?

"Have fun with Harry today," I say as I make a quick exit to my room.

I can't think about Livvy's worries at the minute. When this is all over and done with, I'll work on my relationship with my sister.

Carefully taking the steps with my coffee, I'm relieved to be in my room. I close the door and put my iPod on. Livvy knows not to disturb me when music is blasting from my room. But I don't need time to sulk by myself. I need time to read Celia's diary.

Yeah, I win the sister award.

> *Me and Nancy spent the evening with Hugo and Jack tonight. Jack was all over Nancy like a rash, but Hugo barely touched me! What the fuck is wrong with me? UGH! Nancy says he's just being a gentleman, and it's clear he likes me because he spent the whole night flirting. I don't know. Sometimes, I feel like he*

wants more, and other times, I think I'm a delusional twat.

I love Celia to bits, but she was definitely a delusional twat. The guy obviously didn't return her feelings, but she couldn't take the many, many hints. I fucking hate him. If she hadn't been so obsessed with him, maybe she'd still be here.

Fighting with every urge to lob the diary at the bloody wall, I turn the page with shaking hands. The paper is dented where she angrily pressed the pen down too hard. Even if Hugo had nothing to do with Celia's death, I still want to strangle him. She was hurting, and none of us knew.

Cass thinks I should just go for it and jump him. He doesn't seem shy, but that doesn't mean he's not. If he wants me to make the first move, I don't mind doing that, but after the way he threw that skank off him the first time I saw him, I'm scared to go for it in case he shoves me away too.

I drop the diary. I don't remember this page.

My heart is pounding.

Some skank made a play for Hugo, and he threw her off him?

Is that what happened to Celia?

Did she go for it and make a fool of them both? Was Hugo tired of girls coming on to him?

I slap my hand to my mouth as bile hits the back of my throat. My sister could have been murdered by someone she was infatuated with.

Shit. Have I found Celia's killer after all?

First, I have to actually find Hugo.

I shove the diary back in its hiding spot under a floorboard in my walk-in wardrobe. Then, I get ready and leave the house before my absence is noticed. No Netflix for me now, I guess.

Since Livvy has the car today, I head to the bus stop. Buses run regularly between my town and Nana and Grandad's, so I won't have a long wait.

A few of Livvy's friends are at the park as I power walk past them. I really don't want anyone to stop me. I don't want small talk. I want to find Hugo. They're sitting on the back of the bench—because that's obviously cooler—and drinking Coke.

Rock-'n'-fucking-roll.

They're loud, obnoxious, and overdoing the play-fighting to the point of embarrassment.

Livvy would say, *We're just having a laugh*, but here's a news flash: You're not fucking funny.

It's not hard to see why I don't have friends.

"Bella?"

Damn it.

I think that was Kayleigh. Her voice is soft and kind, but it's false. I don't have the energy to engage in any type of conversation or have a bitch-off with her, so I keep walking.

Stupid tart.

Seven minutes of power walking and some burning thighs later, I reach the bus stop. It's empty, apart from one old lady who's sitting on the bench, clutching her wicker handbag like she's waiting for me to try and wrestle it off her. I know I don't look my best today in old skinny jeans and a Muse T-shirt, but bloody hell.

Keeping as much distance as I can in a tiny bus shelter, I check the timetable. There's a bus due in ten minutes.

Score.

Turning, I sit down on the metal bench at the opposite end to Purple Rinse and stare ahead with a small natural-resting smile, trying not to look like a teen mugger. It's exhausting.

Livvy had better enjoy our bloody car today.

"I feel like I'm always waiting for a bus," she says after a minute of glorious silence.

Oh, she's decided I'm safe then.

I force a laugh and turn my head away. We so don't need to engage.

Out of the corner of my eye, I see her take a book out of her bag.

Thank God. I suck at small talk.

Although this woman isn't a twat, I'm relieved when we get on the bus and sit on different sides. She doesn't try to speak to me again, but as I get off two stops later, she does smile, which I return.

Nana and Grandad's house is a two-minute walk from here, so I'm at theirs shortly after getting off the bus. I let myself in and head to the kitchen.

They're both sitting at the table, and they do the same double take as they see me.

"Bella, we weren't expecting you, love," Nana says.

"Yeah, it was kind of a spur-of-the-moment thing. Are you busy?"

"We're never too busy for you."

I feel like I'm home.

It's such a relief to be back with my grandparents. They fall asleep at nine p.m. like good little old people, and I leave very shortly after.

I take the same route to the river as before. Only, this time, I have a small hammer in my bag. Small but not a kid's hammer. The area is dodgy, and a weapon makes me feel safer. I'd probably be shot or stabbed before I could get it out of my bag, but whatever makes you feel better, right?

Soon, I'll be back with Rocco—not that he knows—and I know he wouldn't let anything happen to me. Well, I hope he wouldn't.

I turn the corner, and there he is, leaning against a broken bus shelter. Momentarily stunned, I freeze on the spot, as it feels like the hammer has been used on my heart.

The attraction I feel toward him is bloody insane and hits me like a goddamn train every time I see him. No one should look that good. His torn denim jeans hang low, and a black

T-shirt hints at the hard muscles underneath. Short black hair is styled to perfection, and his dark caramel eyes scan the area.

There's no getting away with it; I'm going to have to speak to him. Hugo is out there somewhere, and I need to find him. I march over to Rocco and halfway realise I don't really know what I'm doing or what I'll say. My stride wavers, and I consider turning and running in the opposite direction, but I'm committed now.

He looks over, and his face hardens. A face that's sporting a nasty black eye.

"What happened?" I ask.

"Got hit."

Well, duh.

"What are you doing here?"

"I…" *Totally can't stop thinking about you, as irrational as that is at this stage. And, you know, I'm looking for a killer.*

His eyebrow kicks up, and I can see the sarcasm on his face.

"Checking out the area?"

"Very funny. I'm going for a walk…if that's okay with you."

"I'm not your dad, Isabella."

Thank God.

"Does Daddy even know where you are?"

I narrow my eyes, my patience with him starting to run thin. *What's his problem?*

"He does not."

"I wonder how he'd react."

"He'd be fucking livid. But he's not going to find out."

He laughs. I really like the sound of his laugh.

"You do know you're legally an adult, so you can go wherever you like, don't you?"

"Yes."

But, if I do, my parents will worry themselves sick, thinking something will happen to me, too. I owe them more than that. Plus, they pay for everything and don't expect me to get a job while I'm in full-time education.

Damn, that'll be changing soon.

"But you're a good girl. Of course."

"Tell that to my parents," I mutter. In my family, I am definitely not the good one. "Show me around. The places I haven't seen."

"Why?"

"You live here, so you know where everything is. I kind of don't, so if you wouldn't mind…"

"If I do mind?"

I shrug. "Then, be pissed off while you're showing me around."

That gets a proper laugh out of him, and the sound makes my heart leap. Not good.

"*Please*, Rocco," I add.

"Okay, fine. But you should know, the guys are pretty…full-on with fresh meat. You're still fresh to them."

And to you?

"I'm literally two seconds from kicking your shin." *Fresh fucking meat.* "Show me around, and tell your lechy friends, if they come within five metres of me, I will rip their balls off."

Rocco smirks and starts walking. I follow.

"You should probably see someone about your anger."

I should see someone about a lot of things.

He leads me down the road that I avoided last time. I want to pull him right and go toward the river, but I asked for this.

"Where're we going?"

"I'm showing you around, like you asked."

"Sure, but where are we going specifically?"

"To meet up with Ellis."

"Where is he?"

"At his house."

I sigh and clench my fists. "Where is his house?"

"Not far."

Helpful…

We pass a row of houses, and I swear, every second one has boarded up windows and graffiti. It's not a good look, especially the giant yellow knob on number 101's door. Being here is worse in the dark, too. Everything looks ten times bleaker. I wonder where Rocco lives. He's not mentioned any family—not that I'm surprised. He barely barks a one-worded response and never starts a conversation unless it's to piss me off.

"Would you rather have legs the size of carrots or arms the length of lampposts?"

He stops dead in his tracks and turns to me, staring dumbly.

"Ah, at least I know you're human. Honestly, can you please give proper replies to the questions I ask? It's called respect."

"Jesus, girl, you need to be tested."

Not the first time that's been mentioned.

"You won't talk about where we're going."

"I told you!" he seethes. He looks completely lost, like someone just handed him a newborn he has no idea how to look after. "Ellis lives at 53-A Rose Court. There! Now, why don't you lead the fucking way?"

I fold my arms over my chest. "I don't know where that is, do I?"

"And that's my point. What the fuck difference does it make if you know where we're going if you don't know where we are?" He throws his hands up in the air and breathes hard through his nose.

Neither of us is going to win here, so I concede. I don't have a lot of time, and I refuse to waste it arguing with him on the side of the road. "All right, fine. Can we just keep going, please? I'd like to get there today."

"Has anyone ever told you that you're impossible?"

"Oh, yeah," I reply. "No one seems to tell me anything else."

"Maybe you should try harder to, you know, stop."

"No. I might be impossible, unpredictable, immature, and a complete mess, but I refuse to change for anyone."

His lip quirks. "Good girl. You might be borderline crazy, but at least you're true to it."

Cheeky sod.

"Take me to Ellis's house!"

I just asked a practical stranger to take me to meet another practical stranger. Perhaps he is right, and I am crazy. Still, I need to do it. Oh God, what if Hugo and Rocco are related? His mum might like the ending-in-the-same-letter thing that my parents seem to be huge fans of.

Okay, you're getting way ahead of yourself.

"Do you have any siblings?" I ask as we walk toward his friend's.

"None that I know of."

What?

"That you know of?"

"My dad got about, but he took off before my first birthday and never really spoke to me again, so I guess I'll never know."

Nice.

"*Oh-kay.* Hey, are you ever worried that you'll marry a girl, and she'll turn out to be your half-sister? Shit like that happens all the time, you know."

He glances at me out of the corner of his eye, and it's that what-do-I-do-with-a-newborn look again.

I shrug. "Sorry. It's just…it happens."

"You should stop watching daytime TV."

"I probably should."

Rocco stops and nods at a house in the middle of a long terrace.

"This is it then?" I ask.

"Yeah," he replies as he walks up the short path.

No knocking; he walks through the door, so I follow. The house is small and dated with old paint decorating the walls and threadbare carpet, but it's kept clean. I've only met Ellis once, so I don't really know him, but I did expect his place to be more modern.

"Ellis," Rocco hollers through the house.

There can only be, like, two rooms in here, so there's really no need for so much noise.

"Outside!" a rough voice shouts back.

We walk down the hall, past a closed door, and through a small kitchen. Ellis is outside, sucking on a cigarette like it's a lolly. His eyes dart to me, and he nods.

"Hey, Ellis," I say.

"Bella wants a tour guide," Rocco says.

What the fuck? Is he about to palm me off on his mate?

I'm about to explode when he adds, "Want to come, too?"

Ellis looks at me again and then shrugs. "Sure. You fucked her yet?"

"No, he has not," I snap. I grit my teeth. "I'm not looking for a lay. I just want someone to show me around before it gets even darker."

There is definitely something wrong with the people around here. Maybe they're here because they're all insane and lacking manners rather than lacking money.

Rocco laughs and tilts his head in my direction. "She's far too high-maintenance. Wouldn't be worth it."

I have never been more insulted in my life, and because of the nature of the insult, I'm also annoyed at myself. "You utter bastard!"

He smirks, his eyes catching mine and preventing me from looking away. "Hey, if you want to prove me wrong…"

So, I might have walked into that one.

"Shall we go?" I say tightly.

Rocco is all smiles.

I walk between them along the cracked path toward somewhere. Apparently, we're going to the local pub, which I am not at all happy about.

"Are we going in?" I ask as a decrepit building comes into view.

The White Rabbit looks like a dive. The window near the door is boarded up with some sort of metal-looking contraption. Nothing about it makes me want to go inside. It's opposite the river.

"No, we're showing you around," Rocco replies.

Ellis is frowning, and I have a feeling he assumed we'd be getting a drink. For whatever reason, Rocco doesn't want me to go in, and I'm so grateful for whatever that reason is.

"What? So, we're just going to walk around?" Ellis asks, sounding really put out.

"If you don't want to come…" Rocco responds.

Ellis grumbles out an, "It's fine," and we walk straight past.

Did Celia go in there?

She mentioned a pub in one of her diary entries but not which one.

"Are there any other pubs around?" I ask.

"Not for miles. The rest of 'em were trashed before I was born. This is the only one I've ever known," Ellis replies.

So, Celia did go in there.

Fucking idiot.

And, suddenly, I want to go in, too.

"Sounds like you go in there a lot," I say.

Ellis snorts. "Both me and Rocco were brought up in that pub. When alcohol is about all you got to brighten the shit pit that is your life, you take it. My parents and his mum spent most days there, and so do we. And so do most other kids as it goes."

Yeah, wow. My mum went mental on my dad when he took me and Livvy to a pub when we were nine. It was one of those family-friendly ones with the outdoor play area, too. Rocco's life really isn't anything like mine.

I want to shove them both down and quiz them on Celia. If they hung out at the pub all the time, they must have seen her on occasion. Sure, they were probably only about ten, but they might remember. I'm blatantly different to everyone else here, so Celia would've been, too.

They also must know Hugo. Or at least know of him. I feel like I'm finally getting closer to finding the man who might have killed Celia, and it gives me an incredible high. I owe her this, and after it's done, I owe it to us both to do something with my life.

Although that something might well be the World Record for Watching Netflix.

NINE

ROCCO

Ellis left us after ten minutes for some woman who'd texted him—probably Izzy—and he'll be shagging her right now.

I've shown a couple of places to Bella, but thankfully, she hasn't push for more. She seems more interested in bickering and flirting with me. I'm not complaining.

As we walk back toward my car, Bella chews on her lip, which I find sexier than I probably should.

Don't get hard. It'll be embarrassing.

"What?" I grunt.

"I don't know. It feels like the end of the night, but I don't want it to be yet."

Shrugging, I pull her to a stop. "So, don't go yet."

What the fuck are you saying? Get rid of her.

She blinks up at me, and I know that look. As tough as she is, she wants someone. I can't be that someone. I don't know how to do more than sex. I wouldn't know where to start with a relationship, and I categorically know I would fuck it up on day one.

"Where do you want to go? No offence, but I don't much feel like walking the streets anymore tonight," she says.

I wonder if she means just tonight or if she doesn't want to walk the streets ever again.

Has she found whatever she was looking for?

"Er, my place?"

Tilting her head, she pouts. "And what are you expecting?"

"Blow job." I keep a straight face for added effect.

Her eyebrows shoot up. "Excuse me?"

Nope, can't hold it in.

Laughing, I nudge her shoulder, and she bats me away. The physical contact is electric, and that's completely unexpected.

"You're the biggest dick I know!"

"Thanks. Wanna see how much you can get in your mouth?"

She whacks my arm.

Fuck, I'll keep this up if she keeps touching me.

"You know what? I'm going home, and you go take a cold shower!"

"Wait, wait," I say, gripping her wrist as she starts to leave.

I don't want you to leave. I should want you to leave.

"Are you done being a pervert?"

I pretend to think, but then she tries to leave again.

"Okay, I'm done."

"Good. Take me back to yours then," she says.

"Oh, Bella, you keep setting them up."

"Keep it up. What do I care? You obviously enjoy rejection."

"Please, you're clearly obsessed with me."

She tugs her wrist from my grip, but I hold on harder.

"I'm not obsessed with you. Maybe I'm just bored."

I grin. "Uh-huh."

"If you're going to be a twat, I'm really going home."

"I'll stop now." *Because I really want you to come home with me. Get it the fuck together.*

Though I know this is a terrible idea, I can't cut her loose.

Maybe I'm the one who's obsessed. There is something about her that's addictive. She's stunning, and she has a body to die for. I want her more than I've ever wanted anyone before, and she just needs to sleep with me, so I can get her out of my system. The one thing I have going for me here is that I'm not close to anyone. That can't change. I can't have a weakness.

Against my better judgment, I take Bella back to my flat, and she looks around. My place is small, a tiny kitchen just big enough for a cooker, fridge, cupboard space, and two-seater table. My living room barely fits a three-seater sofa and TV, and my bedroom is only big enough for a double bed.

But it's clean and home, somewhere I can get away from everyone. I watch her look around, biting her lip. Taking a breath, I look away. I'm fucking desperate to kiss her. Usually, I would just go for it, but everything with Bella is different. We're both walking in the dark here.

"Your place is nice," she says, giving me a genuine smile that touches her eyes.

"There are shoeboxes bigger than my flat."

She grins at my exaggeration.

Don't kiss her.

"It's still nice. We have a lot of space at home, and it always seems so empty."

I clear my throat and force my gaze from her mouth to her eyes. "How many people live at home?"

Her eyes flick to me for a second before she looks away. "Four of us. Can I use your bathroom, please?"

"Yeah, sure. Just through there," I say, pointing to the door off the kitchen.

She can't get away fast enough and practically sprints to the bathroom.

All right, what the hell just happened?

One minute, she's fine and cocky, and the next, she's acting weird and rushing off.

Unless that's just her?

I've not even known her for a week yet.

Shit, not even seven days.

Why does it feel like so much longer?

Bella comes back out after a minute, and her eyes look red. Her smile doesn't cover the sadness, but she probably thinks I wouldn't notice, so I don't bring it up. It is bothering the shit out of me though. I want to know what's going through her head. I want to know why she's really here.

The more I see her, the more her secrecy bothers me.

"You good?" I ask.

"Yeah. I'm starving though. Can we order pizza?"

It's almost eleven p.m., but okay.

"Good pizza or shit pizza?"

"Oh, I wonder," she says sarcastically.

I roll my eyes. "The good place doesn't deliver."

She drops down on my sofa, getting herself comfortable. I should hate that.

"Ugh, shit pizza then."

"Really? You'd rather eat greasy pizza than get up off that fine arse of yours?"

Glaring off into the distance, she kicks off her shoes and tucks her feet under her legs. "I'm not moving, so unless you want to go, greasy pizza, it is."

"Yeah, okay. I can't be bothered either."

Ridiculously, I want to stay in with her. It bugs me that I can't read her. I'm not arrogant enough to think I know everything that goes on with everyone around here, but I'm not usually this crap at guessing a person. I can normally tell if a person's intentions are honourable or if they are a backstabbing wanker. Bella, on the other hand…nothing.

I don't exactly trust her, but I also don't *not* trust her. Certain things, I think I've cracked, and then she'll say or do something else, and I'm back to square one. I don't like that, especially with someone new.

How much trouble can one eighteen-year-old girl be though?

Bella reels off her ridiculous list of toppings, and I place our order. She's really going to regret suggesting this when she's hugging the toilet tomorrow, throwing up grease.

"So, I'm guessing you live alone? This is definitely a bachelor pad."

I've been living alone since I was fifteen, and there's no way I could share a place with anyone again.

"It's all mine," I reply, slumping down beside her.

"What do you do?" she asks.

"Sometimes, I work at a repair garage with Ellis."

"And the rest of the time?"

Of course she's pressing it.

"Organised fights are where I get most of my money from. The pay is decent, and I don't lose."

Her mouth falls open. "Rocco! That's dangerous."

"Did you miss the part where I said I don't lose?"

"No, but still, you could be hurt."

"Doesn't happen." Not seriously anyway. "So, I'm guessing you want to live alone?" I ask to change the subject.

She frowns before letting it go. "Oh my God, moving out and living alone would be a dream."

"Why? Are things really bad with your parents?"

She turns her nose up. "It's complicated, but let's just say, I'm not the favourite daughter. What about you? Where are your parents?"

"Like I said, my dad left when I was young. He's now dead, and my mum's dead."

Her mouth drops open. "Rocco, I'm sorry. What happened?"

Shrugging, I silently wish I'd brought beer in from the fridge. "She OD'd on crack."

I have never seen a person's eyes bulge so much as Bella's.

"I don't really know what to say to that."

"You don't need to say anything. She was a shitty mum and a shitty person all around. I'm better off without her."

I might sound harsh, but she was never there, not even when I was a kid. She didn't care if I was fed or if I was happy. All she cared about was fucking the next guy to get money for her drugs.

"Well, I'm sorry. You didn't deserve that."

"No one does, but we're not all born to rich parents in big houses."

Frowning, she fiddles with her sleeve. "We're not rich."

Wealthy then. She definitely has money. I can tell by her perfect hair, even when it's messy, and the quality of the things she wears. Plus, she's got a car to share with her sister.

"Whatever. It's cool. Anyway, I got over it a long time ago. Actually, I don't ever remember crying over her."

"She was still your mum."

"Only in the sense that she brought me into the world."

Bella looks down. I've never spoken about this, so I wasn't really sure how someone would react if I ever did. Bella looks out of her depth.

At least she understands a fraction of how she makes me feel.

"I'm sorry."

"Are you ready to talk about something less awkward?" I ask, smirking at her.

Her shoulders sag in relief but not too much because she has good posture. Like a dancer. "Definitely!"

Oh God, is she a dancer? That would just about seal the deal.

"What do you do in your spare time? Besides come and pester me?"

She narrows her eyes. "Not much really. Netflix and music. I used to dance, but I gave that up last year."

Bingo.

"Pole dancing?"

Her hazel eyes glow. "Fuck off. And, yes, I did do *fitness* pole dancing in one of my classes."

"Why did you give it up?"

Why? That is so hot. I would give my right arm to watch her pole dance. Shit, this isn't helping me hold back from kissing the crap out of her.

"Wasn't feeling it anymore."

Her eyes glaze over, like she just metaphorically left the room. There's more to it, a real reason that she's holding back, but she's completely shut down, and from experience, I know when to give up. Bella won't tell me, not yet anyway.

Damn, why do I keep thinking about her like she's going to be around forever?

In the inevitably short time we have together as friends, she might never tell me what happened to make her love of dance disappear.

"Yeah, I got bored of ballet, too," I joke, bringing her back.

She laughs and playfully smacks my arm. "Have I told you lately how funny you're not?"

"Yes. Are you going to take your top off or what?"

"Nice convo change...and, no." Her eyes linger on mine for a second too long, and she presses her lips together.

Yeah, I'm struggling, too.

She looks away and grabs the remote. "Let's find a film before I have to go home."

I can think of a few other things I'd rather be doing, but I go along with it. For the first time ever, I don't want to rush.

TEN

BELLA

I wake up at the crack of dawn by some fucking annoying singing.

"*Livvy*," I growl.

She's in the shower, singing like she's being murdered.

She fucking might be in a minute.

Outside, birds are chirping along with her.

Jesus, does no one want me to sleep in?

Grabbing my phone, I send a quick message to Rocco because he's the only person on the planet who I like right now. He's also the only person on the planet I've liked so much in such a short space of time. I can't stop thinking about him.

> I hate showers. I hate birds. I hate my sister.

I press Send and wait. His reply is almost instant, and just seeing his name on my screen makes my heart jump.

> Why are you talking to me at 6 a.m.?

Oh, is it early? I hate everything!

> Go back to sleep, Bella. You're even more impossible when you're tired.

I can't go back to sleep now.

> Well, I fucking can! Message me in four hours.

Unacceptable.

I hit another reply when he doesn't message back.

I want to talk now!

I stare at my phone, willing him to message back faster. My texts with Rocco have become one of my favourite parts of the day. We were comfortable around each other straightaway. I'm still not totally comfortable around my family, and I've known them for eighteen years. He's about the only person who I message.

Yep, I'm a massive loser, and besides my twin, Rocco is the only one to WhatsApp me.

Let's get the tiny violins out.

Another minute passes by. I am totally watching the time tick by at the top of the screen.

It hits me. *The bastard isn't going to reply.*

That little shit has probably put his phone on silent and gone back to sleep. Now, I'm mad. I want to sleep again, but I can't because Cher's reject is still screeching her stupid head off in the bathroom.

I throw my cover off and hunt for something to wear. Most of my clothes are piled up on my cuddle chair, so I root through them for a pair of skinny jeans and an oversize T-shirt. That'll do. It's too early to think about outfits. I don't even bother to apply any makeup because I'd probably just poke myself in the eye right now.

Stumbling out of my room, still half-asleep, I go in search of coffee before I leave the house. Livvy is still in the shower.

How bloody dirty is she?

When I get in the kitchen, Dad is sitting at the breakfast bar, drinking coffee and looking through uni brochures.

"Morning. Coffee's in the pot."

I grunt, "Thanks."

Laughing, he properly looks up from checking out another uni I'm not going to. "Ah, I forgot you're not the morning one."

"Can you hear her?" I ask, pouring a large mug of coffee.

"I think the whole town can."

"She's too happy."

"Can you be too happy, Isabella?"

I take a sip of black coffee. *Can I get this through an IV?*

"At six in the morning, you can. At the risk of starting an argument, what are you looking at?"

"Nottingham University looks lovely. You were right to apply there. They have a good music programme."

Why, oh why, did I apply to any unis?

Well, I did it to shut Mum and Dad up when they were going on and on about my fucking future. Now, they're badgering me to go through with it.

"Uh-huh."

"Have you made a decision yet?"

"Nope," I reply, sitting down next to him.

"Isabella, you don't have long left to decide."

Yep, and I plan on stringing this out until it's too late to accept my place. I don't want to go to uni yet.

"I'm not sure I want to accept if I get the grades, Dad. You and Mum need to let *me* decide what I want to do with *my* life."

His eyes cloud in disappointment, and it makes me feel like shit. I have to look away. If he knew the truth, he wouldn't care so much about what path I chose. He probably wouldn't even want me in the same house as him.

"I don't know how we're supposed to stand aside and watch you make a huge mistake."

"Please, you got pregnant with Celia when you and Mum were eighteen, and if you'd listened to your parents, then she wouldn't have been born. I promise you, I'll make a well-thought-out decision about what I feel is the best for me, and that's the best I can do. Okay?"

Dad grits his teeth. He has nothing to come back at me with because he knows I'm right. If he didn't follow his parents' demands, then he can't expect us to either.

"Anyway, I need to go. I'll see you later."

"Where are you going?" he asks.

I put my mug down and reply as I walk away, "Meeting a friend."

Dad doesn't really know who is or isn't my friend, so he doesn't question it. Livvy would know straightaway and be suspicious. Thank God she's now murdering Snow Patrol in the shower.

I take the keys to the 500 without clearing it with Livvy. She'll nag at me again, but I honestly don't give a shit. I care less than I did when she made a bloody schedule.

I laugh as I think of her schedule printed on glossy paper with colour blocks to indicate who got the car when. She didn't speak to me for a whole day after I laughed solidly for, like, five minutes. The girl is insane. We've never used her schedule.

She will chase me down if she catches me, so I get in the car, slam the door, and peel out of the drive. I wrench the gearstick into fourth and curse Livvy's choice of manual drive. All my fault, of course, because if I'd been at the family meeting—yeah, legit, a meeting—about it, then I could've had my say.

It doesn't take that long to get to Rocco's, but today, I'm extra impatient, so the drive is dragging. Finally, I pull up outside his place, cut the engine, and get out.

I might not be your biggest fan, 500, but please still be here when I leave.

Turning so that I can watch and make sure the car is locked, I spot a girl over on the opposite side of the road. She's maybe a little older than me and dressed in a mega-short denim skirt and a skimpy pink top that hovers above her belly button. Written across the boobs is the word *Superstar.* I don't think she's made it since her makeup is running down her face, and her hair is a ratty mess. She's a prostitute, and it looks like she's just on her way home.

Where is home?

She can't be older than twenty.

Surely, someone misses her?

My family might be a bit dysfunctional, and I might not fit, but I don't know what I would do without them.

I watch as she walks along the road before stopping and getting in the back of a blue car.

Okay, time to get inside.

Rocco is probably still asleep, so I'm really going to enjoy this. I jog to his door, hover above his doorbell, and then jam my finger in it.

After a few seconds of the constant ringing, I hear Rocco shout…something. It's hard to make out a word, but it sounds like a lot of swear words all strung together.

This is excellent.

After my rude awakening from Livvy this morning, I don't feel too crappy now. His words become much clearer, the closer to the door he gets.

"All right, for fuck's sake!" he bellows as he rips the door open.

I remove my finger from the bell and smile. "Good morning, sunshine."

"Isabella," he growls, narrowing his eyes. "What are you doing here?"

"Duh, I came to see you." *And your naked chest. Hello!*

My eyes fall on that six-pack and slide down to the top of the V. Heat spreads through my body like wildfire.

Oh, wow. Wow. Wow. Wow!

Coming here this morning is the single best idea I've ever had. Ever. I'm instantly on fucking fire.

He clears his throat because my eyes are still way lower than his face. "Why, Bella?"

It's hard, really hard, but I force my gaze upward and smile. "I visit. We do that now."

His glare turns deadly, and I try to keep a straight face.

"We don't do that early in the fucking morning!"

"Are you going to invite me in or not?"

"No."

I roll my eyes and walk past him. He makes no move to stop me, like I thought he would.

"Do you have plans today?"

"Well, I was going to sleep in…"

"Me, too, but my sister, Livvy, didn't."

"I don't see why your sister getting up has to affect me," he grumbles, following me into the living room.

I sit on the sofa, and Rocco drops beside me. He's close. His naked arm is pressed against mine, and it feels electric. I glance up at him through my lashes, and he smirks. He definitely feels what I'm feeling.

I've told him I'm not jumping into bed with him, but kissing is different. But I don't know how much self-control I'll have once his mouth is on mine.

"Tell me about your family," I say to distract myself.

He stills and tilts his head to the side as he frowns, like he was expecting anything else than what just came out of my mouth. "Why?"

"Because you know about mine." *Sort of.*

"So?"

"Really? You're not seven, Rocco, so don't be an evasive, childish dickhead. We're supposed to be able to talk about things. I want to know about your family. And, actually, how old are you?"

Sighing sharply, he leans his head back against the sofa. "I'm twenty-two. Grandparents are dead, same as my parents. No aunts, uncles, or siblings."

"Oh," I mutter.

Wow, I had to ask.

Everyone he had is gone.

"Rocco, I'm so sorry."

God, he's all alone.

He looks over. "Don't be sorry. There's nothing to miss, so don't give me that face."

I'm doing a face?

"Sorry," I mumble.

Oh God, was I giving him the same face people give me when they hear about Celia?

I find it hard not to feel for him because I know how much it hurts. I'm still not over my big sister's death.

"Isabella, stop being sorry."

"What happened to them?"

There has to be a reason he doesn't even have aunts, uncles, or grandparents.

He looks up at me out of the corner of his eye. "Why do you want to know all of this, Bella?"

"I want to know everything. Aren't you at all curious about me?"

He lifts his eyebrows. "Full disclosure? I can ask you anything?"

Fuck.

I swallow. "Sure." *Come on, it's not like he's going to ask if I have a dead sister.* "But, first, tell me about your dad."

"He was sort of murdered."

My eyes bulge, and at the same time, my stomach bottoms out.

"I…what happened?" *And how can you be sort of murdered?*

Rocco places a hand on my leg and squeezes. He thinks I'm worried or scared or something to that effect. He has no idea how close to home this is hitting.

"He was a fighter in his new town and—"

"What the fuck, Rocco? You fight!"

He jumps at my sudden outburst. "Chill out. I'm better than he was."

"Are you fucking serious? *That's* your argument?"

"No, that's my reason. Nothing is going to happen to me. I'm not going to make the same choices or mistakes as either of my parents, so take a breath."

I don't like this one bit. And he wouldn't like what I'm doing, following Celia here either.

Is what he's doing really that different from me?

Yes, fuck, it is different from what I'm doing.

He's going into something, knowing full well that he could get killed or seriously injured. I, on the other hand, don't have the same danger. This place and these people are just what I assume were involved in Celia's death. It's a pretty educated guess, considering there were no links to anything dodgy in all other aspects of her life, and I've only just discovered she would come here to meet a mystery guy. Still, Rocco's fighting is worse.

"What happened? How did he die?"

"It was a bad punch. He went straight down. It was instant."

"You were there?" *This is getting worse by the second.*

"I was. He left when I was a baby, but I'd occasionally see him when he reappeared here to fight, never visited me though."

I frown, and strangely, it makes Rocco laugh. His dad was an arsehole.

"How old were you?"

"Nine."

He was just a kid, too. I want to tell him all about Celia, so he knows he's not alone. We were both so young when we lost someone.

"Rocco…"

"Don't say sorry."

Pressing my mouth together, I nod. "I won't." Then, I ask, "Why did you watch his fights?"

"You think I wanted to know him?" he asks, raising his dark eyebrow.

"Yeah, it's only natural that you would."

"I guess. Things were shitty at home with my mum always high and fucking around. I liked watching him fight. He was savage, but he also lost control, and that's why he died. He left himself open, and the other guy took advantage."

"Do you fight because he did?"

"No, Bella, I don't want to follow in his footsteps. He was a street fighter, not a surgeon. I do it because I need money, and I know I'll get it."

"You know, regular jobs do that, too."

"No, thanks."

I roll my eyes. *That's just great.*

"And you were young when your mum died?"

He nods. "Yeah. Fifteen."

Jesus.

"Did you...did you see that, too?" My heart flutters as I wait for his reply.

"No, I was out. I found her when I got home."

My God, his life hasn't been easy.

"Who was there for you once she was gone?"

"No one, but she was never there for me when she was alive. I've always taken care of myself."

"I wish I'd known you sooner," I whisper.

He smirks, and his eyes light up. "You want to take care of me?"

Yes.

"What? You wouldn't let me?" I challenge.

"I'll let you take care of something," he replies, lifting his eyebrows at his innuendo.

"The meaningful talk is done now, I see."

Rubbing his forehead, he sighs in exasperation, but uncharacteristically, he doesn't snap. "Bella, please, I don't want to do this right now."

I scoot closer, practically sitting on him, and smile, trying to offer comfort. *What else can I do?* "Okay, no more talk about your parents." *For now.*

He doesn't reply because he's staring at me like he can see right into my soul. I bloody hope he can't.

ELEVEN

BELLA

Rocco watches TV with very little interest. It looks like his mind is ticking over and over.

Is he thinking about his parents?

He might have been very cold and matter-of-fact about it, but it must have hurt.

I can't believe that he lost both of his parents.

Why would anyone want to walk away or put drugs before him?

"Rocco?"

He turns his head. "Hmm?"

"Are you okay?"

"Yeah. Why wouldn't I be?"

Because you just talked about your past and your mum dying!

When my family talks about Celia, it sometimes takes every ounce of my self-control not to scream at them.

"You just looked spaced then, is all."

I want him to talk. I want him to tell me how it really made him feel when his mum died. And I'm the biggest hypocrite because I don't want to tell him about my sister.

"What do you usually do while watching TV?" he asks.

"Huh?"

"When you watch TV, you don't just sit there and stare at a screen, right?"

I purse my lips and glare. "No, I do not. I also regularly check my phone, flick through magazines, randomly burst into song, paint my nails—the list could go on and on."

"Thank fuck I'm not a girl."

"If you were a girl, you'd like it."

"If I were a girl, I'd never leave my room."

Gross.

"That's lovely, Rocco," I mutter sarcastically.

"What would you do if you were a guy for the day?"

"I'd get someone to kick me in the balls, so I can see why men turn into little bitches when that happens."

He looks me dead in the eye. "You can't even comprehend the pain."

"No, I'm sure nothing a woman could ever go through would be as bad as that."

"Don't give me that childbirth crap. Women do that more than once. I have no desire to ever get kicked in the balls again."

"Okay, I have no experience of childbirth, but I still think you're full of shit right now."

Laughing, he throws his arm over the back of the sofa. His hand brushes past my hair, and my breath catches.

"Probably."

"You think you'll have kids one day?" I ask.

He gasps, faking surprise. "Isabella, we barely know each other!"

I roll my eyes at his comment. Obviously, I wasn't asking to have his children.

Rocco chuckles at his own joke. When his smile fades, he asks, "Do you want kids?"

"No, I don't," I say.

"I do someday."

God, I wouldn't know what to do with a baby. Way too much responsibility, and I saw how broken Mum and Dad were when Celia died. You couldn't pay me enough to get me to risk that.

He smirks. "You might one day. I can see you with several kids."

I laugh and shake my head. "Absolutely not. There's no way I'm ruining this figure. I'll be a cat lady. Nah, actually, that's too cliché. I'll have something cool, like racoons."

Rocco's doing that staring thing again, like he's not quite sure what to do with me. "So, you want to be a crazy racoon lady?"

"Over cats? Sure. Or maybe I'll just travel the world. If you don't settle down, where do you think you'll be?"

"Six feet under probably."

"Death? Wow. And you think my goals are weird."

"Why are we even talking about this?"

"Because you spaced."

"I've never gotten off topic so hugely before you."

"You're welcome, mister." The doorbell rings, and I give his chest a shove. "Ooh, pizza! I have some cash."

Yep, pizza again.

I reach for my bag, but Rocco gets there first and launches it across the room. It hits the wall and lands on the carpet with a thud.

"Okay, what the actual fuck was that?" I shout in disbelief.

Chuckling, he stands up and pulls his wallet out of his pocket. "I've got this."

"And you couldn't have just said that?"

What's wrong with him?

"I could have, but that was funnier."

With my mouth hanging open, I watch him walk past me and out of the room. He just threw my handbag.

"If my phone is smashed, I'm going to break your dick!"

Retrieving my bag, I rifle through it until I find my beloved iPhone. I don't know where I'd be without it. My love for my phone would be a whole lot less pathetic if I had friends to contact. But Netflix app? Hello! Plus, I can stalk beautiful celebrity men on Twitter and Instagram.

Rocco comes back through with two pizza boxes. He raises an eyebrow.

"You are lucky my baby isn't broken," I say, holding up my phone.

"I didn't even throw it that hard. And, anyway, I would've replaced it."

"So not the point. Would you be okay with me throwing your stuff, huh?"

"Bella, use your mouth to chew instead of talk, yeah?"

Really?

I glare at the prick.

His mouth kicks into a smirk. "Better still—"

"Don't finish that sentence!"

Bloody dickhead was about to tell me to suck him. Not happening.

Rocco sits and opens both boxes. "It's getting cold, Bella."

"Ugh, fine, but I'm only still here because I'm hungry."

"That, and whatever you're running from."

It's not what I'm running from; it's what I'm running to.

And it's a really, really dumb idea. But, hey, it could all be worth it.

I grab a slice of pizza. When Rocco leans back, he kinda moves over, so his arm is now touching mine. There is a whole other space next to me, but we're still sitting cramped together.

Should I move?

He can't, but he definitely had more room before he scooted over a fraction.

Okay, I really don't need to overthink this.

Just eat your fucking pizza, you moron.

He grabs the remote and starts flicking through the channels on Freeview. No Sky or Netflix app on his TV.

What does he do when he's home?

Ugh, women probably.

If he thinks I'm going to be another notch on his bedpost, he's fucking tripping.

"Hey, what's your number?"

He abandons his quest for something less shitty than some car programme. The answer is *anything*.

"You want to know how many women I've slept with?"

I shrug. "Sure. Why not?"

"Why?"

"Er, why not?" I repeat.

He's silent for a second, and at first, I think he's just considering whether to tell me or not, but then I realise he's bloody counting.

For real, he doesn't just know that?

Stupid slut.

You don't care. You've known him for a few days, and caring about how many women he's bedded is pathetic. Don't. Be. Pathetic.

"It's around fifteen."

"Around?"

"I don't remember them all, Bella."

I figured that much.

"Wow. You don't even know how many women you've been *inside*."

He rolls his eyes. "What's your number?"

"Two. And they sucked."

Both guys were while I was desperately trying to act like I was fine and moving on from Celia's death. I jumped into relationships, and obviously, it didn't go well either time. Apparently, I'm not supposed to have a normal, happy life.

So, yeah, racoons, I guess.

"Only two?"

"Are you saying I look like a slut?"

He doesn't even flinch, so he's clearly not worried that he's offended me. "No."

"Then, what do you mean by that?"

"Well, you're sneaking out to hang around in shit neighbourhoods. Doesn't exactly scream virgin or long-term-relationship type."

"I don't even know what you think it *screams*."

"Just a few more men."

Right.

"Well, at least I know my number, Mr Slut." I take a huge, unladylike bite of pizza.

"Okay, now, I'm sure you've been with more than two."

"Huh?"

"You can fit that much in your mouth, so you must be—"

I punch his arm and swallow. "Don't even finish your sentence. You will never know how much I can fit in my mouth."

"Yeah, of course, I won't," he says sarcastically.

"Wow, you're very sure of yourself."

I'm not sleeping with him. Not even if he begs.

Probably.

He smirks and picks up another slice of pizza. "We're both impossibly good-looking; it's only a matter of time."

I can't come up with a decent comeback quick enough because my stupid hormones are going crazy over Rocco saying I'm impossibly good-looking.

Get ahold of yourself, Bella.

"Cat got your tongue?" he says.

"No," I reply, narrowing my eyes.

"Then, can I?"

"Oh, smooth, Rocco! Do you really think—"

He cuts me off…with his lips.

Hell yeah!

His hand wraps around the back of my neck, and he holds me still. It takes me a nanosecond to respond. I grip the muscles over his hips and hold him when I feel like I'm about to fall away. His lips are on mine, and—

Holy fuck!

They're soft, but the way he's kissing me is firm, and it's so freaking maddening.

Rocco moans as his mouth guides mine in the most perfect kiss. This is doing nothing to curb my obsession with him.

Rocco's tongue sweeps my top lip, and I almost fucking implode. My fingers dig into his skin, and it makes him kiss me deeper.

I really could get used to this.

"Bella," he groans against my lips. "If you're serious about that no-sex-yet thing, you need to stop me now."

Pulling away is something I know I will regret, but I can't let this go too far before I'm ready, so I sit up and look at him. His dark eyes look black and full of lust. He takes a breath and flops his forearm across his lap.

"That's not the last time we'll be doing that, Bella."

"Let me know once you've calmed down," I reply, smirking.

Inside, I'm happy-dancing and doing all that shit I mock teens for. I'm one of them now. Rocco is more than a pretty face with a body sculpted from heaven itself. He's hope.

TWELVE

ROCCO

Bella hasn't come over for the last eleven days. Eleven. I'm fucking keeping count. Even though she does my head in most of the time, I like being around her. And I like kissing her even more. That first time, she stayed until almost three in the morning. We put on a film but didn't see a second of it. I had to keep stopping kissing her because, like the first time, it was going to get out of hand.

Over the last week and a half, I've spent a lot of time texting her, but it's not the same. I'd rather spend time with her than Ellis. And I suppose it doesn't hurt that she's very easy on the eyes.

Bella sends me a message on WhatsApp. I know it's her because I only use it to talk with her. And, when I say I use it, I mean, she downloaded it and teased me for not already having the stupid app.

So, how much are you missing me?

There's no way I'm telling her that. I don't even want to admit it to myself. I can honestly say, I've never missed anyone before in my life.

> Wait…you're Bella, right?

I wish I could see her face. I want to see those eyes narrow and her mind tick over as she thinks of something witty to hit back with.

Her reply comes faster than I expected.

> No, it's one of the "around fifteen." Guess which one.

Very good, Bella.
I should've known she would bring that up.

> Er…#7?

> Of course you don't remember names, slut! Who was lucky number 1?

Sending back *your mum* is too obvious. Also, I'm working on getting in Bella's pants, so it's probably best not to bring her mother into anything, even as a joke.

> One of my high school teachers.

It wasn't, but I'm nowhere near done with this. She's too much fun.

> Hey, me, too!

She's lying. Right? She's definitely lying. Come on, of course she is.
I really hate the fucking idea of her being with someone like that. Or anyone. I want her for myself for however long we're going to hang out.
If I could just get her to agree to a friends-with-benefits arrangement…

> Were you in school regularly enough for that? Anyway, tell me what you're wearing.

I don't like that subject anymore.

> Nothing. Want to see? ;)

Well, that has to be the stupidest question in history. But it's a trap.

> You already know my answer, Bella, and we both know your comeback.

Ten seconds later, I get a topless picture and choke on my beer.

Fuck. Me.

I punch my chest, still coughing, and stare at Bella's perfect chest. I can't believe she sent that. It's definitely her, too. She's angled it, so her face isn't completely on show, but I'd know those lips anywhere.

> Shit, Bella. Come over. Now!

> Sorry, washing my hair.

> You're better than that comeback, Isabella. If you can't get away, give me your address, and I'll sneak in.

Oh God, please give me your address.

I know she lives in a nice town, but I have no idea where, and it would be impossible to find her.

> Sorry, I'm not ready to up my number just yet.

She said *yet*. I'll take that. Despite knowing that it would be a bad idea to get involved with her beyond the fragile friendship we have, I wouldn't think twice about taking her to bed. One day, she'll disappear and live the perfect little life she's supposed to, and I'll be a distant memory.

I'm fine with that. Someone like me isn't supposed to be with someone like her. But, while I have her, I want to enjoy it. Repeatedly. Bella knows we'll happen eventually. She just enjoys driving me crazy and giving me blue balls.

> I'm here whenever you want to get lucky for a third time.

> Thanks! I'm coming over…but not for that, so get your head out of the gutter.

Good.

I don't care if she's just coming to argue with me.

God, I shouldn't be this excited. Have I ever been excited before?

My mum was always too wasted to do anything at Christmas, and there's not really been much since.

Bella is my fucking Christmas!

I need to get control of this.

Bella knocks on my door thirty minutes later, and I'm right there. I hold my hand on the door handle, giving it a few seconds so that I don't seem so fucking pathetic.

"Hey," I say, opening up to let her in.

My eyes go straight to her chest. She's perfect even if her clothes are obstructing my view. It really doesn't matter; I won't ever forget what she looks like.

She clicks her fingers, drawing my attention to her face. "Eyes are up here, pervert."

I shut the door behind her and grip her hand, stopping her from rushing off. "Take your top off."

Laughing, she playfully punches me in the chest. "You've already seen more of me than you need."

"No, I really haven't."

"I'm hungry. Feed me. And no innuendos!"

I should really buy more than bread, cheese, and beer if she's going to hang around a lot.

Great, because buying food for her is really helping me keep some distance.

"Toast?" I offer.

She gives me a look. "Is that all you have? I can cook."

"You cook?"

Shrugging, she heads to my kitchen. "How hard can it be?"

"Look, this might not be the flashiest place, but I don't want it covered in smoke and—"

"Have some faith. I won't burn your place down…probably. Do you have home insurance?"

I raise my eyebrow. "Do you think I have home insurance?"

"Well, be prepared to lose your home then."

I'm always prepared to lose everything at any point.

"Turn that sweet arse around, Bella. We're going out."

"Aw, you're taking me on a date," she says sarcastically, tilting her head and trying to look cute and innocent.

I wouldn't have the first clue what to do on a date. Unless having sex and leaving so fast you'd beat an Olympian qualifies as a date.

Bella probably wouldn't think so.

"I bet all the dates you've been on were to posh restaurants."

She bites her lip, and it does nothing to help the blue balls.

Take your top off.

"That's not the point," she replies.

"Ah, I was right."

"Fine, show me what you do on a date."

I raise my eyebrows. "I would be more than happy to. I'll get the condom; you strip and drop to your knees."

Her mouth falls open. "Come on, that's not all you do on dates. That's not even a date!"

"You want me to show you what I do?"

"Where are you taking me to eat, Rocco?"

"Diner down the road."

She walks back toward the front door, but I stop her with my arm.

"Just so we're clear, you're not getting naked?" I ask.

"I'm not getting naked."

I lower my arm. "Damn."

Shoving past me, she shakes her head, but I see the smile she's trying to hide.

Why do I feel like she's going to drive me insane before letting me get close to that body? Fucking hell, she definitely is eighteen, isn't she?

"Isabella, tell me you're not underage."

She turns on her heel. "Huh? I'm eighteen, Rocco. Unless you have a different law in your part of town to the rest of the UK, I've been legal for two years now." Leaning in, she whispers, "I can even drink."

I nod. "Good." I've never been too concerned with the law, but I draw the line completely at underage girls.

"I don't even want to know why you asked that. Where's this diner?"

I grab my phone, keys, and wallet, and we head out.

Bella doesn't walk around with her eyes darting everywhere now. She no longer thinks someone is going to jump her wherever she goes. She's getting confident in being here.

We enter the diner, and I nod to a table. A few locals are in here, and they seem very interested in us.

Maybe I shouldn't be out with her much. I don't want anyone to know I've got a weakness…because that's what she is to me now. Before Bella, there was nothing anyone could hurt me with. I care about her, and it's really fucking nice to have someone I can be myself around.

She sits opposite me and grabs a menu. "What's good here?"

"The burger isn't shit. You're also safe with the coffee."

Her eyes flick up to me. "Those are my only choices?"

"No, but you asked what's good."

"Okay." She closes the menu. "Looks like it's a burger and coffee."

I smile. "Good choice."

Rolling her eyes, she slaps my hand. "Hey, why are people staring?"

Hitting was unnecessary.

"I don't date."

"Oh, this is a date?"

Out comes the girl who makes me want to strangle her.

I take a breath. "You know what I mean."

She laughs and nods. "Yeah, I do. You're fun to play with though."

Is this a date?

I don't exactly hate that idea, and I don't know what to think about the fact that I don't hate it.

"Hi. What can I get you guys?" Leigh asks.

Leigh is a year older than me. At school, she was adamant about going off to London to make it as a model. At fourteen, she took a job here to save for her bus ticket. I don't know what fucking bus she plans on taking, but nine years later, she's still here.

"Burger and coffee for us both, please," I say.

"Can I not order for myself?"

I take another breath. She'll regret ordering anything else from here.

"Go ahead."

"I'll have the burger and a coffee, please," Bella says to Leigh.

Bella looks smug, lifting her eyebrow and the corner of her mouth, and I want to bash my head on the table.

Leigh laughs and writes down our order. "It won't be long, guys."

"Do you do shit like that on purpose?"

She must. No one is that naturally aggravating, surely. And why the hell do I like it so much?

She bats her eyelashes. "I really don't know what you mean." Looking at the menu again, she purses her lips. "Hmm, are there any decent desserts here?"

"No."

"Ugh, that sucks. I want ice cream or cake. Or both."

Who the fuck is this girl?

Bella licks her bottom lip as she puts the menu down, and my blood sets alight in my veins. I want to grab her and fuck her over the table.

If we just get it over with and have an afternoon in bed, I might be able to forget about her.

Like that'd happen.

The revelation slams me in the fucking face. I wouldn't sleep with Bella if that meant she would be out of my life.

Jesus.

I take a jagged breath as the air gets knocked from my lungs. This has never happened before.

Since I first saw her, everything in my world has been animated. Meeting her was like being released from a prison. I'm not sure she's getting a good deal out of…whatever we are though.

I clear my throat. "We can get cake and ice cream after. There's a supermarket nearby, and they have a bakery."

"Very gentlemanly, Rocco. I didn't know you had it in you."

Yeah, neither did I.

She's changing me, and I want to embrace it, but I'm terrified.

THIRTEEN

BELLA

I left Rocco's just after three in the morning, wishing I could stay longer. When I'm with him, I don't have to try so hard just to get through the next minute. He was so sweet, taking me to get a massive tub of ice cream and cupcakes. Whatever I wanted, he was willing to make it happen.

Now, I'm driving back home, and the closer I get, the more I want to turn the car around. With Rocco, I can be myself. I can relax, and I don't have to act like I'm okay...as much as I do with everyone else anyway. There is no way I can tell him about Celia.

In a few short hours, my family will be up, and I'll have to pretend. I'll pretend that everything is all right and that I haven't failed them all so badly that they'd never want to see me again.

Over the years, I've gotten fairly good at making it seem like I'm fine after losing my big sister.

I pull the car into our drive and shut the engine off. They're all pretty heavy sleepers, so it's unlikely they would've heard anything.

Creeping up the path, I press lock on the key fob, and the car makes a quiet beep. The house is pitch-black when I get inside, and I don't dare turn a light on, so I use my phone to illuminate my way.

I could do this in the dark, but sometimes, Dad leaves his bloody shoes lying around, and if I fall, I'll probably scream. Can't see them sleeping through that, especially after Celia.

I take the first step to go up to my room, and the landing light turns on.

Shit.

"Bella?" Harry says, rubbing his eyes.

Tucking my phone behind my back, I smile. *Okay, why did you just hide your own phone, you dickhead?* The car keys are still in my hand.

"Hey, Harry. What's up?"

His eyes narrow, and he looks suspicious as hell. "What're you doing up?"

"What're you doing here?" I shoot back. *Can he not just bloody stay home for one night?*

"You're really going over old ground?" he asks in a snotty tone that makes me want to punch him. Rolling his eyes, he walks down the stairs.

Don't worry about letting me go up before you come down.

"Whatever." I step back down, look away, and wait.

"Why are you walking around in the dark?" His eyes dart to my clothes. My obviously not-pyjama clothes.

Great, there is no way he won't tell my parents what time I rolled in.

"I was at a friend's and didn't want to wake anyone."

"Unlikely. You don't have any friends."

See? He's a wanker of the highest calibre.

"My God, I can't wait for Livvy to get bored of your sad little married life with three kids and a traditional family home and cheat on you with your own brother."

"Leave Livvy out of this," he growls, narrowing his eyes to slits.

"Sure, if you leave Livvy…"

"Are you trying to blackmail me into leaving your sister?" He stops at the bottom of the stairs and cocks his eyebrow.

Folding my arms, I pretend to think for a second and then shake my head. "No, I really think I'd prefer to watch her cheat on you with your brother."

He leans into my personal space. I'm not intimidated.

"You really are a jealous, bitter bitch."

I yawn, bored of him now.

Harry and I will never get along, no matter how much Livvy wants it. I'd like to think that, if it ever came down to it, she would choose me. But I would never ask her—not because I'm scared she wouldn't, but because I love her, and I couldn't put her in that position.

So, I just hope that, one day, Harry will.

"Yeah, totally. I want you all for myself," I mutter, unable to be any more sarcastic.

"Sometimes, I wonder."

I laugh. A lot. Holding my stomach, I crouch over and tuck my head under my body. "Jesus, Harry! Okay, that was brilliant. Honestly, I know you can't possibly think that because, you know, I would rather get fingered by Freddy Krueger, but *that* was funny."

He grits his teeth and folds his arms harder. "Keep this up, Bella, because you're the one who's going to end up sad and alone."

"Fuck you, buddy," I say, pointing to him. "I'll have my racoons." Not giving him a chance to reply because I really don't care, I walk upstairs with a big smile and don't look back.

Once in my room, I change and brush my teeth in my en suite. My phone beeps, and I know it's Rocco. No one else would be messaging me at three thirty in the morning. Or any other time really unless it's Mum, Dad, or Livvy.

Are you home, or did you crash your roller skate of a car?

> You'll be happy to know, the car is fine, and I'm home. My sister's boyfriend is a mega prick though.

What did he do???

Three question marks. Rocco is angry, probably gritting his teeth and imagining the worst. I should let him punch Harry in the face. It would be like Christmas.

> Just talking shit. Nothing I can't handle.

I get into bed, put my phone on the charger, and send him another message before he's replied to my last one.

> Now going to sleep. If you wake me, I'll cut off your foreskin in your sleep.

At least you'd be touching it.

Rocco's reply makes me laugh. He's such an idiot. I don't reply because it will only lead to more conversation, and I'm too tired. But, tomorrow morning, I do plan on getting a naughty pic from him. My body warms at the thought.

Down, girl.

It takes me longer than usual to fall asleep because Rocco is on my mind. Rocco and dirty things. It's distracting and frustrating. When I do go to sleep though, I'm completely out of it.

In the morning, I'm woken up by my stupid sister again, but thankfully, when I look at the clock, I see that I don't have to suffocate her in her sleep. It's after ten a.m., and I'm feeling pretty awake already.

I get out of bed and grab my phone before heading downstairs. Livvy is just ahead of me on the stairs.

She looks over her shoulder. "Morning, Bells."

"Hey. Why're you happier than a clown on crack again this morning?"

"Don't you want me to be happy?"

I deadpan. "No, I want you to be miserable forever."

"Hey, if uni doesn't work out, you can go to comedy school," she says sarcastically.

"I don't think they teach funny, Liv."

Where's her lapdog?

Hopefully, he's left already, so I won't have to deal with him.

My phone vibrates in my hand, and it causes my heart to beat a little faster.

Don't get ahead of yourself.

I follow Livvy into the kitchen and check my message when she's distracted with making a pot of coffee.

Do I get the naked bottom half today?

I should have guessed.

> No. I've sent you my boobs, and you've sent me...SWEET FUCK ALL. So, pay up or face having just one picture to wank over for the rest of your life.

I chew my lip as I try not to grin too much at my phone, or I'll give it away, and I don't want Livvy to know about Rocco.

That'd be an interesting conversation. *Mum, Dad, I've been sneaking out of Nana and Grandad's to see a man I barely know, and I've sent him a nude picture. And, FYI, he's an illegal fighter.*

I'm sure it's every parent's dream for their kid.

> Isabella, I can get nudes from at least ten different women in about five minutes.

> Go on then!

I'm calling his bluff. And I really hope it goes in my favour because I don't like the thought of other women sending him pictures of their naked bodies at his request. Not at all.

It's probably not a good idea for me to send them either because that shit doesn't ever disappear from the internet, but despite not really knowing him for long, I trust him more than anyone else in my life.

Wow, I'm dumb.

How have three universities offered me a place?

Well, probably because they don't know me. Funny enough, I didn't put, *Is willing to sext*, on my applications. Though, if I had, I wouldn't be having the uni battles with my family on a daily basis.

Hindsight.

Rocco texts back.

> I don't want pictures from other women.

Well, hello, cloud fucking nine.

I like him a bit too much.

Grinning, I send back a flirty message and wait for his reply.

FOURTEEN

ROCCO

I drain the last of my beer and watch everyone at the river from the window in the pub. A night here used to be satisfactory, but now, I'd rather just hang out with Bella. Our texts are getting hotter, and it makes me want her even more, if that's fucking possible.

It's something I need to get over because she won't be around forever. Maybe I won't hate it when she's not around anymore. Yeah, right. I already don't like it when she goes home, let alone like the thought of never seeing her again. Jesus, I'm not sure if I've changed for the better.

"Where is she tonight?" Ellis asks, smirking, as he stops right in front of me.

The prick always looks so fucking smug when he's talking about Bella. He knows I care about her. I hope no one else does.

"How would I know?"

I hope he can't tell that I actually do know.

She's out to dinner with her family, and then she's going to her grandparents', so she can sneak out with less risk of getting caught.

"Oh, I don't know…because you spend all of your time with her now."

"No, I don't." It's a shit comeback, but I don't have the energy to argue with him. I don't want to talk about Bella here.

"Of course not." He gives me a side-glance and smirks again.

"I'm very close to punching you in the gut, prick."

"Hey, no need to get violent. You don't have to hide her from me, man."

I grit my teeth, not entirely sure where to take this. Ellis would never fuck me over—I'm almost certain of that—but I still don't completely trust anyone. If I have to push him away a little more to protect her, then I will.

Why is she more important than my oldest friend?

My God, my life is one confusing mess, even more so since Bella came into it.

"Yeah, I know I can trust you with her."

He clears his throat. "I like her, too."

You've got to be fucking kidding!

My head snaps in his direction, and he holds his stomach, laughing at my reaction.

Shaking his head, he takes a step back as he says, "Calm down. Not like that! I just mean, she's cool. I can see why you like her so much."

"I don't like her *so much*."

Yes, I do.

"We don't talk about our feelings, hopes, and dreams, Rocco, but if we're going to talk, at least don't lie. She's important to you. That's why you're so on edge when she's out in public here, and it's why you don't want to discuss her in front of all these people."

Fuck him.

My groin vibrates where my phone is stuffed in my pocket, saving me from having to think of something to come back at Ellis with. However, I don't need to continue arguing with him because his face is a permanent smirk as he watches me pull my phone out.

Gritting my teeth and ignoring the twitch in my hand that wants to punch my oldest and only friend, I open the text from Bella.

> Fine. You win, arsehole. I need to know that you didn't text any sluts.

Last night, I might have planted a little doubt over texting someone else after she accused me of being obsessed with her. I knew she would give in and ask eventually.

I've known her for only a matter of weeks, but she should know that I wouldn't do something like that. Nothing has mattered more than her before, and I'm not risking what we have—whatever that is—over cheap sex with some skirt.

> What do you think?

> I think you really are too obsessed with me to mess around.

"What's she saying?" Ellis asks.

Laughing, I put my phone down on the table to make her sweat a bit before I reply. "She's saying exactly what I thought she would."

If you peel away the layers of confidence, cockiness, and toughness, there's insecurity at her core. There's shit going on with her family that I don't expect her to share with me anytime soon, but when she does, I think I'll understand why she is the way she is. Not that I'll admit it to her, but I desperately want to know everything. I want to get an A in Isabella.

I've never gotten an A before. When I dragged myself out to attend school, the most I got were Ds.

"That her again?" Ellis asks, tilting his head toward my beeping phone.

"No doubt." I pick it up.

> You're being a bitch, Rocco!

I'm busy, Isabella.

Yeah, right! Tell Ellis I say hi…AND TELL ME NOTHING HAPPENED!

Nothing happened. You know that.

Good. I'm at yours. Where are you guys? I'll come and meet you.

No fucking way.

I stand up and down my drink. "I'm leavin'," I say to Ellis. There's no way I'm having Bella here tonight, We've already had a drug deal out back and a boring bar fight.

Stay in your car. I'll meet you there.

Shocker! See you soon.

She might think I'm overprotective. I don't give a shit. The girl isn't coming here.

"Have a good night," Ellis says, chuckling under his breath.

I plan to.

Once out of the pub, I jog toward my flat where Bella is waiting. Her ridiculous car is parked behind my jeep. She gets out as she sees me approach.

Fuck. Me.

Her hair is tied up. It's messy, like she put it up and then ran a marathon.

Motherfucking shit.

Her bare neck is on show and begging for my teeth to sink into her skin. My dick immediately responds. She'd better give it up soon. I'm going crazy with just my hand and her picture.

"Hi," I whisper around the lump in my throat as I stop an inch in front of her.

I'm far too close, completely invading her personal space, but I don't care, and she doesn't seem to either.

She bites her lip, and she's lucky that I have such amazing self-control.

"Hi, Rocco."

Come on, go down. This could get embarrassing. Why am I always hard around her?

She's the first person to get me up just by looking at me.

Shit. I'm not fifteen anymore, so what's going on?

"Where were you? I hope I wasn't interrupting."

I shake my head and say, "I wasn't doing anything," instead of what I'm really thinking. *I would drop anything to see you.*

Go and find the Jack Daniel's, Rocco. You need a drink.

"You were out though? At the river?"

"Yeah. The pub after that."

"Will you take me?"

"No." *Absolutely not. Fuck no. Not happening.*

She frowns and folds her arms, our moment now long gone. "Why not? I won't embarrass you."

"That's not what I'm worried about."

"Then, what are you worried about?"

Damn it.

"Nothing's worrying me. I was just there, and it's boring. I'd much rather have you entertain me inside."

"There's plenty of time for that."

Really?

"But I'd like to go out. You never take me out."

"Yes, I do."

"Not that much. Please. I'd like to hang out with your friends."

"Ellis has probably left to shag Izzy, and I don't really like the rest of them." *Stop pushing it.*

"Rocco," she whines like a bloody toddler.

Oh my God. Don't tell her to do one. You want her here.

"I'll take you there next time you're over."

"Why next time?"

"Why not?" I spit through gritted teeth.

She sighs sharply. "You're being ridiculous. I'm going to the river. Are you coming or not?"

My eyes twitch. "Doesn't look like I have a choice, does it?"

"Perfect." She smiles triumphantly and takes my arm. "So, what have you done today? No bruises, so you didn't have a fight."

Her voice is always slightly quieter when she talks about me fighting. I like that she hates it. I'm not used to having someone care about me, and it feels *really* nice.

"No, no fight. I helped Ellis at the garage for a bit. What about you?"

"I had to put up with my sister's ever-cheerful attitude all day. Then, my parents drove me insane at dinner with their uni talk. I swear, they're on repeat with that."

"They want you to go. You should go. It's all about partying anyway, right? You wouldn't have to get serious about a job for another two or three years. It's a win-win in my book."

"Yeah, there is that, but I think I would rather just work. The whole learning thing is so overrated."

"Preaching to the converted, Bella. What would you do if you got a job though?"

Her lips purse, and her eyebrows draw together as she thinks about my question. I'm not one for having plans, but Isabella is on a different level. I know I can take care of myself; she just assumes she can.

"I haven't gotten that far yet."

"Pole dancer?" I offer. "I know a few strip clubs."

"Why doesn't that surprise me? No, thanks. I don't really like people, so dancing for them would suck. Plus, there's the whole doing-it-almost-naked thing. It would just be a total drag."

"Wow, Bella. What's wrong with people?"

"Most of them are fucking idiots. You hate them, too."

"You're not wrong there."

We turn the corner, and the fire at the river comes into view. She's still holding my arm. I don't know if it's best for people to see her with me, so they know to back off or not. People don't generally screw with me because I don't hold back when I fight, but I've probably pissed some people off, and they might see her as a way to settle the score.

I hesitate. This feels wrong. Ellis was right when he said I cared about Bella, and this isn't exactly the place you bring someone you care about. The other side of the fire barely hides three guys dealing drugs. You don't even have to deal inconspicuously out in the open here.

"Let's just say hello and then go to the café. You must be hungry."

She's always hungry.

Bella shakes her head and gives my hand a tug. "I'm cool for now. Who're you going to introduce me to first? Do you spend time with anyone else outside of the beach?"

"Just take a quick look around, so we can leave," I snip. "You know I don't like people, so, no, I don't spend time with anyone but Ellis."

Christ, this is going to be painful.

FIFTEEN

BELLA

Rocco is tense as we approach the large—and probably illegal—fire on the dirt, halfway between the road and water. I'm pretty sure you can't just go around, lighting fires wherever you want, but there are things around here that get overlooked all the time.

"Who are they?" I ask, angling my forehead to a group of three girls.

They're probably a similar age to me; one looks like she could be a few years younger though.

He grunts, "No fucking idea."

All right.

"Don't you know everyone around here?"

"I don't take a register, Isabella. They're probably like you…but from a slightly less posh area than yours and a slightly less shit area like mine."

Well, he's about as cheerful as a rainy Monday.

"I thought you said once that not many people come here."

He glances at me out of the corner of his eye, and his face is hard, like he's absolutely had enough of my shit. "Not many like *you*."

I probably don't want to know what he means by that, so, *whoosh*, thought gone.

"Should we go and say hi then?"

His lip curls in disgust. "I don't know them."

"Yeah, I got that, but you don't usually know someone before you've met them!"

"You wanted to be introduced to the people I knew. Let's just get that over with, okay?"

Aren't I glad I came here tonight?

Rocco is being unnecessarily difficult. I want to know who they are because I've seen a few teenage girls wandering around.

Are they like a new generation of Celia?

I need to know where they came from and why they're here. And I need to find the elusive Hugo.

I want all that soon preferably. Every second I spend with Rocco, I can feel myself being sucked into something completely different, something that looks a lot like a life, and I can't allow myself to be distracted by what I want for me right now.

This shit just needs to be over because I'm beyond exhausted of constantly stressing and living with an enormous amount of guilt.

"Come here," he grunts, tugging me toward a group of four people.

They're all female, and that's probably intentional.

"Sara, Jodie, Lindsey, Lorri, this is Bella." He turns to me before they have a chance to open their mouths. "They all work at the diner."

Wow. He's picked the only people here who are probably above board and not druggies, prostitutes, or general lawbreakers. I don't want to meet those types of people.

"Hi," I say, giving them a polite smile. "It's nice to meet you."

They mutter a collective, "Hi," move in a bit closer together, and look back at Rocco like they have no idea why he's introducing me.

I hear ya, ladies.

I'm not in their diner club, so I'm not welcome in their fold, and they're making it obvious. I won't be losing any sleep.

He's either proper shit at social cues, or he just doesn't give a damn because he doesn't move us on. It's getting awkward. I bite the inside of my lip as the diner crew stares at Rocco.

Someone needs to say something.

Why is he just standing here?

I nudge his arm, and I'm probably not that subtle, but I don't care. We *need* to go and talk to someone else.

"What?" he says, looking down at me.

Really?

"Great meeting you," I say to the girls.

I walk off toward the fire, and Rocco is right on my heels, like I thought he would be.

"Where are you going?"

I spin around and narrow my eyes so hard that I almost can't see. "What was that? Introduce me to people who aren't so…cliquey."

"Click what? You're not even making sense right now. I'm doing what you asked."

"Oh, yeah, course you are," I mutter, my voice dripping with sarcasm.

"Isabella," he hushes. "You are fucking ridiculous."

"Don't be a knobhead. Let's go talk to"—I bite my lip as I look around—"him."

He raises his eyebrow, not even looking at who I'm pointing at. "That sounded an awful lot like you wanting me to set you up."

"Is he as aggravating as you?"

"Go home," he growls. Then, he looks over his shoulder.

My God, Rocco is the most frustrating man on the planet.

One minute, he's happy to have me here, and the next, he's acting like I just murdered his puppy. Today is definitely the puppy thing.

"No, I don't like him."

One thing I could totally get on board with right now: Alcoholism.

I take a breath as he makes my blood boil…and not in the good way.

Prick. Prick. Prick.

Folding my arms, I glance around again. "Fine."

To the side of the bonfire, closer to the water, is an older woman who seems to be a bit of a mother hen. She makes eye contact and smiles. Rocco is too young to have known Celia, but this woman isn't.

The only problem I have is that everyone here, who isn't Rocco, looks more likely to stab me in the face with a broken bottle than start a conversation.

I'm an outsider, and they don't like outsiders. I was kind of hoping to be accepted by them because I keep showing up with Rocco, but he's too preoccupied with keeping me away from them to make them think I can fit in.

"Look, just stay here, okay?" Rocco orders before walking off to the large coolers.

What's up his arse tonight?

Stretching my arms around my back, I look around and try to pretend like I'm not a total loner right now. I'm surprised he left me even though he's only gone a few metres, but the cooler is near a big group of men.

"Hello," the lady who smiled at me says.

I jump when I see she's made her way over. She's probably in her forties with a short, curly bob and heavy fringe. Her hair is bleached far too light, and her eyes are too heavily framed with eyeliner.

Although she looks stuck in the eighties and a little scary, I smile. At least she's making the effort to talk to me.

"Hi."

"I've seen you around a couple of times, but he's been keeping you to himself, huh?"

I roll my eyes. "You could say that."

"How long have you been with Rocco?"

"Erm, well, we're not officially together. I've not known him long...and he's pretty moody." *Though it feels like we've been close for years.*

Laughing, she nods, the permed bob nodding along with her. "That's Rocco! I'm Faith," she offers.

"Bella. It's nice to meet you."

"You, too, sweetheart. Have you moved to the area?"

"No, but I have family close by. How about you? Have you lived here long?"

She looks to the sky and theatrically shakes her head.

Weird.

"Oh, you could say that. I was born 'ere."

Good. Do you know Celia?

"I've heard that about a lot of people," I say.

"Yeah, it isn't easy to get out."

"Here," Rocco snaps. He steps so slightly in front of me that it could be accidental, but it's not. He's putting himself between me and Faith.

I flinch at the acidity in his voice. All I've done is said about five words to someone else, so I don't know why he's so pissed and being rude.

Miserable wanker.

I take the beer he thrust at me and scowl at the venom in his glare. "Thank you," I say tightly.

I want more time with Faith, but Rocco's presence has her taking a step back.

Why?

"Uh, I'll let you get back to it. Lovely to meet you, Bella."

Giving her a smile, I lift my hand in a short wave. "You, too."

She walks away, taking another look at me over her shoulder.

As soon as she's gone, I lob the beer on the ground. "What. The fuck. Was that?"

Rocco's knuckles turn white around the neck of the bottle he's holding. "What're you doing?"

"Nothing! My God, Faith was just saying hello, and you made her feel so unwelcome."

"Why're you making friends?"

"Why wouldn't I? Seriously, what's going on with you today? Has something happened?" I ask.

There has to be something; no one gets this upset over nothing. He has no bruises, so he's not lost a fight or anything like that.

"Nothing is wrong with me. Come on, I'm taking you home."

Usually, he'd say to his, so I know he means to my grandparents'.

"I don't want to go."

"Ugh!" He throws his hand up. "Why do you have to be so impossible all the fucking time?"

"Not convinced I'm the one being impossible here."

"We're going, Bella."

Yeah, we are. I don't want to be out here with him right now. All he's doing is making me want to come alone without him knowing.

I spin on my heel and stomp back toward the road. *Stupid arsehole!*

Rocco follows but leaves a few paces between us. Smart of him because, right now, I want to punch him between his legs.

Before the river disappears out of sight, I look back. Faith is talking with the young girls Rocco didn't know, and they're laughing. I should've stayed with them rather than leaving with the grump.

If Faith is the mother-hen type—and the way she is with those girls makes me think she is—she might have known Celia.

SIXTEEN

ROCCO

Since my behaviour at the river last night was "so appalling"—Bella's words—I've promised to take her out again. She wants to walk. I really need to buy her a fucking treadmill. That way, I could sit on the sofa while she did all this active shit.

She is taking everything in like she's going to be quizzed on it after. Something is going on with her, and although I usually mind my own business, I want to know hers. The way she acted yesterday was suspicious. The people she wanted introducing to were older. I thought I was onto a winner with the girls from the diner.

My girl isn't looking for friends here.

Ellis is bored out of his mind. This isn't how either of us wants to spend our weekend. We've both seen these parts a million times over, and there's really nothing special about any of it. So far, we've seen the pub, two closed pubs, a sports field, park, two schools, and a few shops. In all of that, I think the only place that's still playing on the right side of the law is the primary school.

"Are we done?" Ellis asks, pressing his palms together and looking directly into Bella's eyes, pleading.

"Bella?" I ask on his behalf.

Her eyes dart to mine. "Is there anything else?"

Now, she looks like the one pleading.

What are you looking for specifically? I would kill to know that.

"There's a scrapyard up ahead. That's it. You've not seen the river properly in daylight yet."

Either of those what you want?

My heart thuds as I wait for her reply. I'm desperate to know what she's really doing.

"Scrapyard first," she replies.

I don't know why I feel compelled to do what she asks. I could've sent her on her way earlier. I'm not a tour guide or anyone's lapdog. Anyone else, and I would've told them to do one long before now.

"Nah," Ellis says, throwing his arms up. "I'm out. See you dickheads later."

Bella watches in amusement as he walks off, shaking his head. They seem to get along well, despite all their differences and Ellis's general dislike of any woman who isn't either his mother or someone willing to get naked with him.

Although she's crazy, Bella is surprisingly easy to get along with—for Ellis anyway. She drives me to drink. To be fair, Ellis is probably drunk now. His eyes did look a bit glazed.

"I guess it's just us," she quips, stating the obvious.

I step closer, and she tilts her head up to watch me. She's not intimidated, and that's honestly not what I'm trying to do right now. I bend my head and plant a quick kiss on her lips.

"Hmm, what could we do now that we're all alone?"

Her hazel eyes twitch, and although she stands her ground, her breathing is faster. Shit, she wants to get naked, too. That is not helping. I said it as a joke—sort of—but if she's game, then I'm definitely in.

"I would like to go to the scrapyard," she whispers. Her voice is rough, like she swallowed gravel, and her eyes are wild.

Taking a step closer, I lean in. "Is that really what you want to do with me, Bella?"

Her lips press together, like she's trying to stop herself from using them in a way we both want. Her breathing still isn't something she's gotten control of; it's coming thicker and faster.

"Admitting you want sex is nothing to be ashamed of."

"I know that. I'm not stuck in the fifties, but I'm not going to sleep with you to prove a point."

"So then, sleep with me because you want to."

She rolls her pretty eyes and folds her arms. "Lead the bloody way to the scrapyard, Rocco."

Since I first met her, there have been so many moments when I've wanted to tell her to fuck off, but something stops me every time. I don't know if I'm just bored or if there's more to it. Her reaction to me just then and the way my body is responding to her being turned on are exactly why I can't walk away anymore.

She's intriguing. I love the mystery even if it drives me up the wall. There are few people around this place who still have mystery. I've peeled back the layers of everything around here, and it's just rotten to the core. Although I don't know what she's up to or why, I know she's good inside.

"Right this way," I say, taking a step back and gesturing for her to walk on.

She blinks out of the trance she was just in and starts to walk, stumbling over the first step.

Looks like we're fucking each other's brains out in her mind, too.

Bella keeps close as we walk along the road. Every wall beside us is covered in graffiti. Occasionally, there's something good enough to pass as art, but apart from that, it's just a lot of swearing.

"Did you do any of this?" she asks, wiggling her fingers at the wall.

"A long time ago. My contribution has been covered since then. Let me guess; you've never done it."

"Are you trying to make me feel inadequate because I've never drawn big words on a wall?"

Tilting my head back, I laugh. I properly laugh and for the first time in a damn long time. I fucking feel alive.

Is this what it feels like to be normal?

I love that she gives as good as she gets—better even most of the time.

"We'll try graffiti sometime," I say.

She could do with relaxing. Her eyes hold so much responsibility.

"You want to take me on a vandalising spree?" she says in disgust.

My God, the tone in her voice then almost makes me ashamed that I suggested it. She has never sounded so private school before.

"Yeah, why not? Are you worried we'll be caught?"

She screws her nose up. "Would the police even care around here?"

"Not really. They tend to only turn up if someone has died or is about to."

Her body jerks, and her eyes turn cold and distant, but she doesn't stop, and we carry on walking.

All right, what was that about? She scared or something?

With a nervous laugh, she nudges me with her elbow, like she thinks I was kidding. That was either her trying to cover up her fear or there's more to that reaction.

It's anyone's guess.

"Don't worry, Snow White. You'll be fine with me."

Narrowing her eyes, she stops and folds her hands.

Uh-oh, I think I'm in trouble.

Cocking my eyebrow, I smirk. *Let's do this.*

I crave the arguments with her. Every time she's being challenging, I get harder than a rock.

"Why are you referring to me as a Disney princess? Either you really don't know me *at all* or you have a thing for little girls' movies."

I could fight with her all day.

"We both know it's the first one," I reply to Miss Cryptic.

"You've hardly shared your life story, Rocco."

"Look the fuck around. This is all there is. This is all I am."

She blinks and slowly shakes her head. "No, this is where you live, not who you are."

Same difference.

"Do you want to see the scrapyard or not?"

"I do." She nods.

Why?

We start to walk again, and she keeps her eyes on everything, taking it all in. She really must not get out much if she wants to remember all this.

"It's up there," I say when the half-rusted chain-link fence comes into view.

There's not much need for the seven-foot fence. No one would dare steal because Hugo would kill them; it's to keep the cops out more than anyone else.

"Okay," she replies. She's already looking ahead.

What the fuck is she searching for?

"You need a car?" I ask.

"No, I have one. You know that."

"Daddy buy it?"

Gritting her teeth, she seethes, "Yes. Fuck you."

"Lighten up, sweetheart, yeah? Not many people wouldn't take a free car from the 'rents."

"I do share it with my sister, you know," she grumbles, as if that makes her any less of a princess just because it's not completely hers.

We stop outside the fence, and I give her time to commit the place to her memory. Battered old cars hide the true nature of the business—drugs and firearms. Of course, I don't feel the need to share that nugget of information with Cinderella.

"Did you get your car here?" she asks.

Along one side is a car sales. Secondhand and mostly chop shop.

"Well, I didn't get it from the Mercedes showroom."

I can't be one hundred percent sure who the legal owner of my car is, and I don't particularly give a flying fuck either. I got papers that say the car is mine, and whether they're the legal ones or not, it doesn't matter to me. There's not much Hugo can't counterfeit.

"Right," she mutters. "Okay, where to next?"

"My place," I reply.

"And what's at your place?"

"All my shit. What do you think's there?"

She rolls her eyes.

"Come on, Bella. I've spent the best part of the day being your fucking tour guide. I'm hungry and bored."

"Fine, I'll leave you to it. Thank you for showing me around."

"Where are you going?" I question.

If she thinks she's walking around on her own, she's mistaken.

"Well, I'll just head back to my grandparents' house. I don't want to take up your whole day."

I thought I wouldn't want her to either, but actually, I don't want her to leave. She's too amusing for me to let her walk away. I want to spend time with her. We're not done here.

"Come back to mine?" I find myself saying.

"Erm, that's okay. I'll leave you in peace."

"That was my fault," I say, snatching her wrist and tugging her flush against my chest. "I made it sound like a question, and it wasn't."

She tries to look pissed off, but her breathing is coming out a little bit harder, and her body is melting against mine.

"Isabella…"

"All right, fine. But I'm not sleeping with you."

"Maybe not yet."

"Maybe not ever," she fires back.

I lean my forehead against hers, and her eyes burn.

"Don't say things you *know* are untrue; it's embarrassing. We both know it's only a matter of time."

"You bastard!"

"Cut the offended shit, Bella. I'm cool with giving you time, so you can justify it to yourself, but don't ever deny the inevitable."

"I'm torn between wanting to shag you to shut you up and bashing you around the head with that crowbar," she says, nodding to the discarded tools on the other side of the fence. "And you think *I'm* entitled? What makes you think you can just click your fingers, and I'll strip off?"

"Experience."

"Ah, but you have no experience with *me*."

That's fucking true; I'll give her that. If she were a typical girl from around here, I'd have bedded her already. Truth is, I don't really know how to handle her. She wants me—I can tell that much—but for some stupid reason, she's resisting.

Why wouldn't you give in to something you want? Especially when it comes to sex.

"Are you telling me that you don't want this?" I ask.

Her eyes flutter closed when I move my mouth closer.

"No, I'm telling you that, when and *if* we have sex, it'll be when *I* want, when *I'm* ready."

"Looks like you're ready now. I can feel your body, Bella. I feel how hard you're pushed up against me, feel how hard your chest is rising and falling. You want this as much as I do."

Her body shudders, and I grow stiff. I want her so bad; it's painful. My body is burning with the need to be inside her. I'll never need time. If she let me, I'd take her against the fence right now.

"Rocco…" My name is a plea, and I groan, gripping her wrists tighter. "Please, not here."

I let her go and take a step back.

"My place," I say through gritted teeth. "No funny business, I swear." Right now, I'll just take her being with me.

"Erm, yeah, okay," she whispers. "I can really do with a coffee right now."

And I can really do with a fight since I'm not getting laid.

I take her back to my flat, and again, I make no apologies for the tiny, cheap pit it is. I'm not ashamed. Bella has never cared that my place is probably the size of her car.

She slumps down on the sofa in the tiny kitchen/dining/living room.

"I need coffee, Rocco. Tell me you have coffee."

She's treating my place like it's her own.

This is fucking weird.

"Um," I say nervously. *What is going on with her, with me?* "Yeah, I got coffee. I'd say, *Make yourself at home,* but you've got that down."

She shrugs, kicks off her shoes, and curls up on the sofa.

I like it.

I need a JD. Straight.

Flicking the kettle on, I grab the jar of coffee.

"Actually, wait!" she shouts as she jumps up.

There's really no need to shout. My kitchen is about three steps from the living room area.

"I'll do it. I'm fussy with coffee."

"Just with coffee?" I ask sarcastically.

"Piss off. Tosser," she mutters. "Coffee, one sugar and milk in first. Stir, add the water, and then stir again, both ways."

Is she for fucking real?

"Don't look at me like that. I said I was fussy."

"Yeah. Well, you *really* didn't lie."

"Just let me make it. What do you want?"

"JD," I reply, dropping the spoon in the mug and opening the fridge. "And you don't think the princess nicknames are justified."

"Liking your drink a certain way isn't—"

"No," I snap, cutting her off. "Let's not do this, Bella."

"What are we doing, Rocco?"

My skin itches all over. A part of me wants to run for the door at hearing those words, but a bigger part of me wants to know what we're actually doing.

"I don't know," I reply honestly.

"We're friends, right?" she asks, stirring her fucking coffee granules into the milk and sugar.

"I s'pose."

"Okay," she replies as she nods. "That's a good start. I could really do with…"

Her head whips around, so I can't see her. She doesn't finish her sentence, but then she doesn't need to. For some reason, she doesn't have many—or any—friends. The girl is certifiable, but she also has an addictive personality and plenty of independence and attitude.

"Yeah, me, too," I admit.

I've got Ellis, and he's solid, but round here, you don't have the type of relationship where you confide in other guys.

"We're pretty unlikely friends," she says, looking back up with a smile.

"I dunno. Two screw-ups—"

"You think I'm a screw-up?" Her mouth drops, and she narrows her eyes.

"Well, something's clearly wrong for you to *want* to be here all the time."

She laughs humourlessly. "I'll give you that."

"Fuck this," I say, slamming the booze cupboard door shut.

She doesn't have much time to look shocked before my mouth covers hers, and I lift her up. Her legs wrap around my waist, and her hands attack my hair.

"Rocco," she moans into the kiss.

I almost fucking come in my jeans.

SEVENTEEN

BELLA

When Rocco puts me down, I'm breathless and still teetering on the edge. My body is buzzing, but I know that it'd be a mistake to jump into bed with him.

I step back, putting some much-needed distance between us. I had to slow things down even if I'm regretting that dumb decision right now.

Rocco takes deep breaths, grabs JD from the cupboard, and closes his eyes tightly as he takes long gulps from the bottle. I want some, too, and I don't even like it.

Calm down, Bella.

Composure is hard to regain when your heart is trying to free itself from your chest. I go back to making my coffee as my insides squirm in need. My body is aching.

This not-shagging-him thing sucks.

"Erm, shall we go through to the living room?" I say, picking my mug up.

The sofa is against the other wall of the room, and it's the only place to sit.

He shrugs and adjusts himself in his jeans.

That's surprisingly hot.

He's not said anything since before the kiss, and it's getting weird. We sit on the sofa side by side because he only has a three-seater. We're entirely too close. I can still feel his lips, hard and demanding, against mine, his erection pulsing against my stomach.

I take a deep breath and sip my boiling hot drink. I don't even care that it burns the inside of my mouth.

Think of something else.

The moment after a kiss can be awkward sometimes. This isn't awkward; it feels more like unfinished business, like we're just pretending that stopping is what we both think is best when, in reality, neither of us can delude ourselves or each other.

Coming out tonight was a mistake.

"When do you have to go home?" he asks. "Your proper home, I mean."

"Erm, I'm going back tomorrow. I'm on study leave now, but I have to go to school tomorrow and check in."

"What exams are you taking?" he asks. It's a forced question, but he's trying to take his mind off the cracking, sparking sexual tension between us.

"A-Level English Lit, Drama, and Sociology."

"You'll ace Drama."

I glare. *Dick.*

"I won't ace any of them. Livvy will."

"Your sister, right?"

"Yeah. My twin actually."

His eyes widen like saucers. "Fuck. There are two of you?"

"Ha-ha. There's definitely only one of me. She's the *together* one."

"Sibling rivalry?"

I shake my head. "No, nothing like that. I don't resent her. I love her. I love that she's not like me, and I want her to do well. I'm just stating facts here. Whatever happens and wherever I end up, I'll be all right. I'm just not Cambridge material like she is."

"She got in?"

"Yep, if she gets the results, which she will. She's brilliant."

"And you?"

"I like the idea of uni, but I'm not cut out for it just yet."

"Why not?"

Well, I can't go with the truth.

"I'd like a gap year first at least. I want to travel a bit, and after that, I'll see if I want to go."

Lies, lies, lies. I couldn't give a shit about a cop-out gap year.

"Yeah, where do you want to travel to?"

Screw him and his questions.

"America, Australia, a bit more of Europe, Thailand, Japan, and then wherever else I fancy."

"Uh-huh," he replies, cocking his eyebrow. "Why do you look like you're not sure of your own plan?"

Motherfucker.

How transparent am I?

"I don't know what you mean."

"Sure you do. If you just don't want to go to uni, Bella, that's fine. I'm sure your parents would understand."

"Oh, of course they would," I mutter sarcastically.

"Are they pushy?"

"It's not what you're thinking."

They just don't want me to piss away opportunities that Celia never got a chance at. When your older sister's life ended in her teenage years, it makes your parents come down hard when you're not "living up to your potential."

I get it, and I hate that I'm not achieving what I should be right now, but *nothing* is more important than giving the best shot I can for finding justice for Celia.

"All right," he says, narrowing his eyes at my vagueness. "What are your parents like then?"

"They…normal. They want the best for me. I'm naturally academic, so they don't understand why I don't put in even a tiny amount of effort to get further and achieve more."

"Why don't you? No offence, but if I had the opportunities you have—"

"Because life isn't that simple."

"That's it?" he asks. "That's your whole argument?"

I shrug one shoulder. "What else is there? I don't have to justify anything. Sometimes, things aren't what they seem. We both know that life isn't fair and equal for all. There can be a person who has everything and a person who has nothing, and they can both be the same fuckups or high achievers."

"Right. But what about those people who have everything and *choose* to be fuckups?"

Why the hell can he read me so easily? It's irritating.

Also, I might not be together like Livvy, but I'm hardly 2007 Britney.

"Again, life isn't that simple."

Chuckling, he swigs his JD. "Right. I get ya."

He doesn't get me. He has no idea what I'm talking about, but he's either annoyed that I'm not being clear or he's bored.

"What about you? Did you go to uni?"

The bottle freezes midair in his hand, and his eyes slide over to me. "Does it look like I went to uni?"

"Who knows? You could've gone to Cambridge but are now down on your luck."

He lowers the bottle and rests it on his thigh. "Right. Well, shocker here, but I didn't. I left school at fifteen. Fucking *hated* it. Moved out of my mum's flat and I've been here ever since. Jealous of my life?"

Cracking a smile, he turns his body, so he's facing me. Our legs touch, and my blood rushes to the surface. My breath catches, and I want to reach for him.

"You're regretting pushing me away in the kitchen, aren't you?" he says, smirking in a cocky manner. He takes a long swig of JD.

"You knew that the second I did it. Not the point though. I'm not jumping into bed with you."

"Have you ever had casual sex?"

"Yes," I reply.

"Ah, bad experience one or two?"

I'm not answering that. "It wasn't that bad with either of them—besides them not really knowing what to do with me. It was just pointless and forgettable and not something I'm in a hurry to repeat."

"I won't be pointless and forgettable, Isabella." The way his rough voice wraps around my full name makes my stomach heat.

Oh, I already know that.

"That'll be for me to decide…and I'll let you know."

"When?"

"When I'm ready."

"You're either testing my control, or you're torturing us both," he says.

Somewhere between is about right. I'm not a bunny-boiler, so it's not about knowing I have all of him, but I do want to know that he wants me for longer than one night. And the more I hold off, the more I'll know if I still want him.

"I'm insulted that you think I'm doing either. And, if you're desperate, I'm sure there are a lot of women around here who wouldn't mind giving you a hand…literally."

"There are. I'm not interested."

Don't ask why not. Bunny-boiler territory. Do. Not. Ask.

"Can't say I blame you. I've seen some of them." Better to be a bitch than a cling-on.

He laughs, takes my mug out of my hand, and puts it on the coffee table. I know what he's doing, so when he tugs on my hand, I move myself onto his lap. He's still rock hard.

This is a bad idea.

My body aches to rub against him. I'm throbbing, and all I want is the sweet release that arching my hips would give. Rocco feels it, too. He takes a deep breath and tenses under me as he tries to refrain from moving. His hands are fisted on the sofa beside his legs.

Why did I have coffee and not alcohol again?

"What're you doing?" I ask. My voice shows how much I want him, which is a lot.

"Move," he demands.

Yeah, that does sound like a good idea.

139

"Rocco…" I want to say more, but words mean nothing right now.

"Shut the fuck up. I get the no-sex thing—well, I don't, but I'll run with it—but right now, I *need* you to move your fucking hips as much as you do. Ride me, Bella. Now."

Bloody hell. Who knew his ordering around could be so sexy?

I do what I was told and grind myself against him. My eyes roll back as he moans loudly and raises his hips in time with mine.

Rocco grips my arse and hisses. His eyes are wild, and he looks like he wants to devour me. Actually, he looks like he wants to fuck me, and I'm seriously reconsidering my stupid no-sex rule.

He grinds around in a circle while holding me in place, and I cry as the friction makes my whole body pulse.

Oh my God!

"Rocco," I cry, my body breaking into thousands of pieces as I come so hard I feel my heart pounding against my ribcage.

He stops suddenly, fingertips digging into the flesh of my butt. "Isabella," he growls through gritted teeth. His eyes are tight, and his chest rises and falls too fast with his heavy breathing.

Rocco hasn't come, and he doesn't want to like this. He is asking me to let him take our clothes off and slip inside me, and there is no way I'm going to say no.

I lift my leg and flop over onto the sofa. My body is limp and satisfied.

If he can do that through clothes, what is going to happen when he gets them off?

The thought alone has me burning.

With shaky post-orgasm hands, I take off my jeans and throw them on the floor.

Rocco closes his eyes and takes a breath. I would be offended that he's shut them, but he looks like he's holding on by a thread. I love knowing that he wants me as badly as I want him.

By the time he opens his eyes, I have my top off. I'm just in a pair of matching—*thank God!*—lacy underwear.

"Fuck me, you are perfect, Bella," he breathes.

Though I don't hate how I look, body confidence is never something I've excelled in, but Rocco's words and the way he's staring make me feel beautiful.

I'm so bloody lucky to have him.

"I really think you should take off your clothes," I say.

God, it will be the first time I'll see all of him, too.

Eek!

Rocco hops off the sofa, grips the bottom of his T-shirt, and whips it over his head. I laugh at his eagerness. I'm surprised the material didn't rip.

"Impatient much?"

"I know we've not known each other long, so it can't feel like it's been forever…but it feels like it's been forever."

"Right," I say, grinning up at him.

His words just about make sense, so I do understand. I've never wanted anyone so quickly or this much. It kind of scares me. After the last two disasters, I didn't want to jump into anything, but with Rocco, I'm leaping headfirst.

"You still have your underwear on," he says as he unbuttons his jeans.

Biting my lip to stop myself from squealing at his latest action, I nod. I haven't taken my underwear off yet because I'm enjoying the show.

Rocco's muscles ripple as he shoves his jeans down. No boxers on.

Score.

I take in a breath. He is beautiful.

The V! Oh, that V. Come to mama.

His legs are nicely defined. Chest is basically carved from stone, and—*oh, sweet Jesus*—his thick cock is standing to attention.

"When you're quite finished objectifying me, you should get fucking naked."

I blink up at him. "Um…"

Damn it. Words, Bella. Think of some.

"I'll take off my underwear," I mutter like a bloody idiot.

Rocco's mouth curves into a smirk. "You do that."

Try to think coherent thoughts!

Sitting up, I pop my bra strap open behind my back, not caring that my usually flat stomach doesn't look its best in a seated position. Rocco certainly isn't judging. Or maybe he just hasn't seen it because his eyes are glued to my breasts. At a size B, they're not huge, but again, Rocco sure isn't worried about that.

"Oh my God, woman, you're killing me."

He reaches out, and his hand cups my breast. I'm not at all prepared for the bolt of electricity to my groin that gives me. I breathe in hard.

I want his hands all over me. I crave his touch everywhere.

"Rocco. Rocco, please," I pant, squirming at the overwhelming need to have him inside me. Right the fuck now.

He reaches over, grips my hand and tugs me roughly to my feet. I slam against his solid chest. Air rushes from my lungs, and I think I might pass out.

Rocco doesn't let go of my hand as he walks forward, forcing me back. He's breathing thick and heavy. Desire pools south as he takes us into the bedroom.

"Lie down," he orders, coming to a stop by his bed and dropping his hand.

My eyes are fixed on his as I raise my leg on the mattress and flop back. My head hits his pillow with a soft thud. Rocco grips my thighs, and I almost fly off the damn bed.

Chuckling, he pushes my thighs back down and runs his thumbs up toward where I *really* want them.

I'm breathing like fucking Darth Vader, but I can't control it. I'm needy and so damn turned on that I could implode.

"Rocco," I whine.

I try to push my thighs together to relieve some of the throbbing, but he tightens his grip and holds my legs apart.

"Patience, Isabella."

"Fuck patience!"

With the biggest grin I've ever seen, he slips his thumbs on the top of my thong and pulls it down. I lift my butt to help, and he slides them over my knees and finally past my ankles.

"I have never seen anything so flawless before," he says, staring at me like I'm a meal.

"Less talking and more..." I arch my hips rather than finishing my sentence.

"Five minutes ago, you didn't want to have sex."

"Things change. Please tell me you have condoms."

He raises his dark eyebrow and leans over me.

Hello, chest.

I lift my arm while he's rummaging in his bedside table. His skin is so soft, but the muscles make him hard. Rocco groans as I run my hand down the centre of his chest, splaying my fingers over the bumps of his six-pack.

"Okay," he says, sitting up and ripping the condom wrapper open.

Impatient again.

I'm not going to say anything this time in case he slows down to prove a point.

I watch him slip the condom over his erection and turn his eyes to me. Without a word, he leans over me, supporting himself with one hand. Neither of us speaks, for once, and the only sound is our heavy breathing.

Rocco bends, and his lips press very lightly against mine. My brain short-circuits. His tongue brushes mine, and I moan as my body pulses.

It feels too good already.

He lowers himself more, and I feel him pressing against my entrance.

Hell yeah.

"Oh God," I murmur against his lips.

Rocco bears a little weight on me at the same time when the kiss evolves. He slowly slides inside me while his mouth devours mine. I wrap my arms around his neck, legs around his butt, and I kiss him back with as much passion and need.

I take Rocco's bottom lip between my teeth, and he drives into me hard. He grunts as he picks up the pace, and I tighten around him. His hips slam against mine.

Oh, shit!

He's too good. This is too good.

"Rocco, I'm getting close," I mutter against his lips as his mouth plays with mine.

My body is building so agonisingly slow. With my pulse jackhammering in my ears, I cut my nails into his shoulders.

"How close?"

"Close!" *Like really close.* I arch up, meeting every toe-curling thrust in desperation. Breaking away from his lips, I throw my head to the side and close my eyes. "Rocco, please."

He bears more weight on me, and the orgasm slams into my body, vibrating all over. I cry out his name and tear my hands down his back.

"Fuck, Bella," Rocco snaps, thrusting harder and then burying his head in my neck. He stills inside me, his breath out of control, the same as mine.

"We should have done that ages ago," I whisper. My legs feel like jelly.

"Yeah, we should have," he replies against my skin as he kisses my neck. "I'll be good to go again in five."

Rolling my eyes, I playfully slap his shoulder. "You'll have to sort yourself out in five. I'm light-headed, and I don't think I can walk yet."

"You don't need to get up, and you can't faint while lying down."

"Down, boy," I say, shoving his shoulder.

Laughing, Rocco pulls out of me and rolls onto his side. He's smiling and staring. It makes my heart ache in the best way.

"You look happy."

"I am, Bella."

Good.

I'm happy, too. Happier than I can ever recall being. It's an incredible feeling, and I don't want it to end. But it's also damn terrifying.

EIGHTEEN

ROCCO

When Bella got over her control issues, she gave herself to me, and I loved every damn second of it. Actually, it was less about her control issues and more about the orgasm I gave her when her clothes were on. Then, she practically demanded I do the same, minus all the clothes in the way.

I'm lying on my bed, waiting for Bella to come back from the bathroom. My cock is hard again, and with my mind flicking back to being inside her every five seconds, that's unlikely to change anytime soon.

She was incredible. Hands down, the best sex I have ever had. No one can get to me the way she does. My back stings from the scratches she gave me. It's a very satisfying, dull pain.

She walks back in from the bathroom with my discarded T-shirt on.

Fuck. Me.

I don't usually like to share, but she can wear my clothes any day. Her hair's a mess, and her lips are swollen. No one has ever looked so sexy before.

"Are you going to take that off?" I ask.

Her lip quirks. "No. Why?"

"You look good in it—don't get me wrong—but I prefer what's underneath."

"I have things to do, so you'll just have to get your libido in check."

"Or you can do that for me."

"Sure," she says with a shrug. "I'll leave now, and you'll have no choice but to cool it. Or you could give one of those girls a call. I bet one would rush right over."

"They definitely would, but in case you haven't noticed, I like you," I say, dipping my chin toward my rock-hard erection. I'm ready for her. Again.

"So I see."

"Do you need to be somewhere?" I ask.

"No."

"Why are you trying to leave?"

"The sex is over, so…" She purses her lips and picks her top off the floor.

"Ah. You're running out."

I don't want that.

Wow, first time for everything.

"Not running." She wriggles two fingers back and forth. "Walking."

"You should stay. We could go get some food."

What am I saying? What the fuck am I doing? I shouldn't get her to stay.

This is bordering on *something*, and I shouldn't let anything happen. Being her friend is a stretch, but taking her out again is far too much.

She looks surprised as she reaches down for her clothes. "You want to go out?"

"I'm hungry," I reply tightly.

We both know this is more than eating out together; we've done that before. We just had sex, and it wasn't dip-and-then-slip sex either. No, I definitely don't want to slip away after shagging her. I want to take her out to fucking eat.

"Okay"—she tightly grips her jeans in her hand—"we can do that."

She looks about as convinced as me that this is a good idea.

We both know that we can't be anything. Cinderella will be going off to uni, and then she'll marry her rich prince and live in a castle. I'll still be here, fighting for money and taking what I need. I can't be anyone's Prince Charming. The best I can do is the Beast, and that would get old for her really fucking fast. And, apparently, he owns a library. I don't even have one book.

"Where do you want to go?" she asks, chucking her clothes down on my bed and taking my T-shirt off.

Every inch of her glorious body is on show.

"I changed my mind."

"Get your head out of the gutter, and put some clothes on. You're buying me food."

I watch her get dressed while I pull on my jeans and the T-shirt she just took off. It smells like her. I'm half-tempted to take it off so that I'm not one of *those* people, but it's my fucking shirt.

Once we're ready and out the door, Bella gets in my beat-up Jeep and kicks a few cans out of her way. She doesn't care that my drive is a banger and that I've not cleaned it since I acquired it.

"Where are we going?" she asks absentmindedly while checking her phone.

"Not too far away."

Tilting her head, she glares. "That wasn't the question. I didn't ask the distance."

Here we go. I love this.

"Well, that was my answer."

"Why can't you give me a direct reply?"

"I did. It just wasn't the one you wanted."

"Whatever. Whatever, Rocco," she says, holding her hand up.

"Checking in with Mummy and Daddy?"

"Piss off," she grumbles.

That's a yes. I've not had to check in with someone since I was about five. I can't understand why she needs to at eighteen. She's legally an adult.

"Where do they think you are?"

Her eyes slide to the side and glower.

"I'm just askin'. Fuck, you're touchy."

"And you're judgmental. You don't need to know where my parents think I am. Why do you care anyway?"

I don't know why I care.

"I'm only making conversation."

"No, you're being condescending and kind of a prick."

"I'm taking you out for dinner, aren't I?"

"Only because we had sex."

"I think we should have some quiet time," I say. Talking to her is like taking punch after punch to the head. Repeatedly. And, still, I crave it.

"You started the conversation." She shakes her head and looks out the window.

And I suddenly feel like I'm married.

"My parents think I'm at a friend's house. They're happy, thinking that I'm finally fitting in."

"You don't fit in," I say sarcastically.

Instantly, I want to kick myself. She's sharing willingly, and I'm being a dick.

"Sorry, I didn't mean that."

"Nah, it's fine. I've never been one of the popular people, and I really couldn't care less if people liked me or not. I have no time to be fake or pretend to like what I should be interested in."

"Good."

As frustrating as she is, she should never change for anything.

"Why do you care what they think? You don't have to tell them where you are."

"I live in their house, Rocco. They're my parents, and they're very protective of me and Livvy." She looks away again and takes a deep breath.

What else is going on?

"Why?"

"Because…they're our parents, and they love us."

"Obviously. But I want the answer you're holding back."

"I'm not holding anything back."

"Bullshit!"

"It's not bullshit."

"If you're going to lie, Isabella, at least make it convincing."

"Oh my God," she growls. "You're such a dickhead."

"And you're a liar."

"They're protective because our other sister is dead!" she shouts. Her eyes immediately widen.

Fuck.

Oh, shit, I didn't expect that.

I look at her and glance back at the road now and again. Thinking of her being in pain sucks.

"Bella…I'm sorry."

She shrugs and tilts her head. "It's okay. It was a long time ago." Her voice is weak.

It's not okay, and maybe it has been a while, but she's not over it.

"Yeah, but something tells me that doesn't just go away."

Dipping her head, she wraps her arms around her stomach. "No, it doesn't."

I pull into the car park of the only half-decent restaurant on the border between her side of town and mine.

"Do you want to talk about it?" I ask.

She shakes her head. "I would really rather not. Can we just eat, please?"

"Sure."

After looking out the window, she turns to me and asks, "Why did we come so far out? Are you scared we'll be seen?"

"People have seen us together dozens of times. Get out of the car. I'm starving."

I want to talk about her family. I want to know more about the sister who died, but I don't want to push her. It's not like I don't understand what it's like to not want to talk about your past. I don't exactly start my conversations with, *Hey, my mum overdosed.*

Bella gets out and follows me into the restaurant. It's not posh here, but it's definitely a few hundred steps up from the cafés we've eaten at before. We're seated straightaway at a table in the corner.

"This place is nice," she says.

The server takes our drink order and gives us some time to look over the menu.

"You sound surprised."

Rolling her eyes, she laughs. "Well, I'm used to you taking me to greasy dives."

Everything is different now.

I want to spend more time with her. I want to treat her like—

Oh God, don't even think about wanting her to be your girlfriend.

"We can get back in the car and—"

"No," she says, kicking me under the table. "I like it here. I like this."

Me, too.

"What're you getting?" I ask her before this conversation goes somewhere I'm not ready for.

She purses her lips and hums. "The barbeque chicken sandwich sounds good. Do you know if it is?"

I shrug. "Never been here before."

"Really? Why did you decide to come here then?"

"Ellis once mentioned it and said the food was decent."

"Ah, you want to take me to decent places," she teases.

"I'm not a complete wanker, Bella."

"No," she says, shaking her head. "Not a complete one."

"I'm real close to dragging you out of here."

She wiggles her eyebrows. "Oh, yeah?"

"Not what I had in mind, but I'm open to suggestions."

"I bet you are," she says dryly.

We place our food order—her going for the sandwich and me a big, fat steak.

"Bella…"

She narrows her eyes and stirs her Coke with the straw. "You've already asked if I wanted to talk about it, and I said no."

I love how she knows what I'm going to say before I say it.

"All right, I'm sorry. If you ever want to, I'm here."

With a small smile, she dips her head. "Thank you."

The whole weight of the world is on her shoulders, so I hope she does talk to me someday.

NINETEEN

BELLA

Rocco is mad at me.

But then, when isn't he mad at me?

We had such a lovely time last weekend at the restaurant and, you know, the sex we had before and after. This last week, he has been messaging me more and more. It's because I told him that Celia is dead. Thank fuck I didn't let any details slip. I have to be more careful.

It's Friday night, and I'm back at his house. Being with him is addictive, and as much as I know I should put some distance between us now that I've spilled more than I wanted to, I can't actually make myself leave. Talking to him is the best part of my day. I already miss Celia more than I can ever say; I'm not ready to miss Rocco, too.

He paces from the small kitchen into the even smaller living room, and I sit back on the sofa and sip his beer, which probably isn't the best start to making nice again. I'm not sure what I've done this time, but I have no doubt, I'll find out soon enough.

"*Soooo,*" I say, "want to share why you're in pace mode?"

He stops for a second to glare in my direction before picking up the pacing again.

I guess that's a no.

"Are you mad at me because I didn't come here last night? I told you I couldn't get away."

"No," he snaps.

"Are you mad at me because I wouldn't watch your fight?"

"No."

"Because I have better hair than you?"

This time, he stops again and looks at me like I just started stuffing Cheerios up my nose.

"I'm not mad at you, Isabella, okay?"

The use of my full name says otherwise, buster.

"Then, what's going on? Because this behaviour isn't normal, even for you, Rocky."

"I don't box. I street fight, so drop the *Rocky* shit. And I really don't think you have any place, lecturing me on normal behaviour. Who's Adam?"

"What?"

"Look, I personally don't give a flying fuck who's shagging who and if they're single. But I don't like being lied to, Isabella."

Did we just enter the twilight zone?

Shoving off the sofa, I slam his beer on the coffee table and glare. "Who the hell do you think you are? I *never* lied to you about being single, not that you ever asked. Adam is a sort of *friend*, and we've only spent time together to revise. One, why don't you grow a damn pair and ask me rather than pacing the flat, being a miserable shit? And, two, how do you know Adam?"

I've been faithful to you, you fucking idiot!

His jaw tightens. "He's not your boyfriend?"

"No! Again, how do you know him?"

"I followed you."

"I'm sorry. You what?"

"I. Followed. You," he says slower, like I didn't hear and not because I'm stunned at the creeper in him.

Seriously, how have I not killed him by now?

I'm too shocked and too pissed off to speak. Inside, I'm burning with anger. My fists clench, and my jaw locks.

How dare he follow me. And how the hell did I not notice?

"Rocco!" My voice is about a million octaves too high.

Sighing, he sits down, and I follow. We've never really had a deep conversation, not for long, but his stalking of me is bound to be about as personal as you can get.

"I know next to nothing about you, Bella. You come here a lot, but you're not always here, if you know what I mean, and besides arguing and some pretty intense sex, I get nothing. You don't talk about what happened with your sister. All I know about your parents is that they're protective, and they want you to go to uni. Maybe this fucking place has made me paranoid, but I like to know who the fuck is in my bed and my life!"

"All right, that makes no sense when all you've ever had is one-night stands."

I'm not buying that bullshit. He couldn't care less who he was shagging as long as he got off. Before me, I hope anyway. We've not said we're exclusive, but we both know we are.

"You know what I'm getting at. If you're hanging around here regularly, then I need to know who you are."

"Isabella Hastings. Student at Ickworth Grammar School. Short. Twin. There. Happy?"

"Not really. I knew all that before, and I don't like *not* being able to figure something out."

"What do you want to know?" I ask, knowing I'll have to lie if he asks the wrong questions.

Running his hands over his face, he shakes his head. "I don't know. There's just…something."

"Oh, right," I say sarcastically.

"Something about you that I can't put my finger on."

"Everyone has secrets, Rocco."

"It's not that."

"Then, what is it?"

Laughing, he shrugs. "I dunno."

Fuck, this is so unhelpful.

"I'm not really sure what you want from me right now."

"You're not the only one, Bella. It's driving me crazy."

"My favourite colour is orange. I love Chinese food. My favourite film is and always will be *Jurassic Park*."

Rocco laughs. "Really?"

"It's a classic. I challenge you to find someone who doesn't like it."

"You're crazy."

"Have you not watched it?"

"Once, a long time ago."

"Once? You've only seen it once?" I ask. "Okay, come here."

"You want sex?"

I roll my eyes and get my iPad out of my bag. "No, I want you to watch this. Come on."

"We're watching a movie on that tiny screen?"

"Unless you have the DVD…"

He gives me a flat look and shuffles over to my side of the sofa. Slinging one arm over the back, he leans closer. His side is plastered against mine, and for the first time since I arrived, he relaxes.

I don't want to be one of those obvs-he-loves-me girls—and, yes, I heard those words being spewed from a twat's mouth at my school—but I have a feeling that his obsession with knowing me and his inappropriate stalking aren't about checking me out. Rocco's made it clear that he doesn't do the commitment thing, but his actions speak of the contrary.

"You have *Jurassic Park* on iTunes," he states in the most judgmental tone I've ever heard. "You're such a geek."

I don't even care.

"Yep, get used to it," I reply as I hit play.

"I can't believe I'm fucking watching this. Aren't dinosaurs for kids?"

"You have no soul."

He snorts. "Don't I know it?"

Wincing, I open my mouth to apologise, but he shakes his head. Damn, I'm stupid. Rocco has such a low opinion of himself, and I hate feeding into it because I happen to think a hell of a lot about him. Although it's ridiculous because I've known him only a couple of months, he's pretty much the only guy I *really* trust.

There's something about him, too.

"Rocco?"

"Hmm?"

"You can't follow me again."

"Yeah, I know. I'm sorry. That was a mistake."

His apology is all I need. He knows it was wrong, so we're cool.

"It's okay."

I snuggle into his side and enjoy the feeling of being safe. He and his place make me feel at home, like I'm supposed to be here. This really isn't a smart idea.

The film starts, and Rocco sighs sharply, but I know he's just acting bored. Even if he's genuinely bored, I don't give a damn. He's watching this, and we're spending proper time together that isn't out on the streets where I have an ulterior motive or in bed where I can't even form a coherent thought.

"How could you ever think a park with dinosaurs was a good idea?" he says two minutes into the film as he kicks his feet up on the coffee table.

I've not seen him this chilled out—ever. It's nice, and I'm *totally* picturing us as a couple right now.

"It's a fabulous idea. The problems stem from having one employee in charge of all the little things—you know, like the *security* of the park."

"So, you think it's fucking stupid, too?" he asks, smirking and nuzzling my neck. "We could do something that's not stupid right now."

My slut body arches to give him better access. "Rocco," I say, laughing and pushing him away, "stop." *Stop* has never meant *carry on* to me before. "Okay, fine, don't stop."

I shove him away, but he grips me around the waist and takes me with him. We end up lying on the sofa with him below. I can tell that he likes the position as much as I do.

The iPad is somewhere on the floor now, but I don't care as we begin attacking each other's clothes.

TWENTY

BELLA

I *hate exams.*
Hate. Them.

To my right, Livvy is powering through the A-Level English Literature paper, and I'm looking at it like it's written in Latin. If I don't pass my A-Levels, I have no chance of going to uni. Now, I don't want to, but, you know, I want the option next year.

This is stuff I know, too. Reading, escaping to another place, is my vice. I actually like the English class, but my mind has shut down, and all I can think about is Hugo.

I read Celia's diary again this morning. It was such a stupid idea because I knew the outcome would be me stressing about it, and I need to concentrate right now.

If I could just be tested on obsessive behaviour and throwing your education down the toilet, that would be ace, and I'd get all As.

The clock above Mr Branson's head ticks by. Eleven minutes have passed, and so far, all I have written is my name.

Concentrate.

I can't fail. My parents can't afford for me to repeat the year. The school won't offer a scholarship for a repeat of year twelve, and eighteen grand is a lot of money. I doubt I'll even be allowed to come back if they did pay full price. Failures don't look good on a private school's stats.

Maybe I can pretend I'm sick, so they'll let me take it later. But I doubt I'll find Hugo and solve Celia's murder in the next few days, so it's pointless to delay the inevitable.

I read the first question again and zone in on what I'm supposed to be doing.

Focus.

It takes a lot more effort than usual, but I finally manage to finish the exam and on time. Hopefully, I didn't fail.

"Front row can leave first. Everyone else remain seated until it's your turn," Mr Branson orders, pushing his frameless glasses further up his nose.

Waiting for my turn is torture, but it's worth the relief I feel when we're finally outside the gym.

It's over.

Livvy is all smiles when she looks at me over her shoulder. She links her arm under her friend's as they chat.

Girls still do that linking thing at seventeen and eighteen? I thought it died off mid-teens.

"How did you do?" she asks, pulling her friend to a stop so that she can talk to me.

I shrug. My future in picking up litter on the street is pretty secure. "We'll see. What about you?"

"It went really well," she replies. "I'm sure you did fine. You're way more academic than me."

Of course she did fine. If she gets anything below an A, I'll be shocked. If I get anything above a C, I think everyone will be shocked. And I'm not necessarily more academic than her. I'm just fortunate that a certain amount of smarts comes naturally. The person marking my exam might not agree.

"Good. Cambridge is looking great then."

She suddenly looks terrified. "Oh God, I hope so."

"You'll get the results for sure, Liv. There is no way you're not going to Cambridge. Don't stress; you've got this," I say.

Smiling, she lets go of her friend and gives me a hug that's only awkward for one of us—that one being me.

"Thanks, Bells. You always know how to make me feel better."

Good.

I take a small step back, aware that she's still too close to me. "Are you coming home with me now or…"

"Yeah, I'm coming. I'll see you guys tomorrow," she says, hugging her friends.

I don't know why I find hugging friends so weird. And the way they get all overly vocal when they see each other. *OMG, it's been, like, three minutes since I last saw you.*

Who fucking cares?

Actually, maybe I do know why I find it so weird. I'm not equipped to be around people, especially when I have to talk to them. My tolerance for bullshit is permanently on low.

I give her friends a weak smile and leave with my sister.

"So, you don't think you did well?" she asks.

"Not well enough. I'll be ecstatic if I get a C."

Actually, I'll be shocked if I did that well.

"You're underestimating yourself, Bella. You've never had to try very hard to get good grades. You're incredibly intelligent without even trying."

She's only saying that because she doesn't know what I get up to when I go to Nana and Grandad's. Intelligent, that is not.

"I guess I'll find out soon enough."

More importantly, Mum and Dad will. When they made the decision to send us to private school, I promised myself that I wouldn't mess around, and even though I haven't, I've let something get in the way. If I fail, I'm going to owe them *a lot* of money. Even with the scholarships, they've still paid a crapload, plus extracurricular activities, uniforms, and trips on top of fees.

"You'll be fine," she replies. "Are you doing anything tonight?"

"No plans. Want to watch a movie?" I find myself asking the question before thinking.

It's rare we spend much time together. When we're getting along though, it's nice to plan something.

Her brown eyes widen in surprise because I've suggested we spend time together. "Sure…your choice."

"Thank God! I don't think I can sit through *Dear John* again."

"It's a classic," she argues.

"How is it a classic? *Psycho* is a classic."

She laughs. "I think your movie choice says a lot about you."

She is absolutely right.

"Yours, too," I reply. I think I'd rather be crazy than romantic.

"My movie choices aren't concerning though, Bella. That's the difference between us."

There is absolutely more than one difference between us.

"Fine. How about we watch…*Magic Mike*?" I suggest, wiggling my eyebrows, identical to hers. "You know you can't say no to that."

Livvy grins, and it's like looking in a mirror. We do have a similar about-to-be-perverted smile.

"I'm in. Good pick, Bells!"

We head along the path toward home. Parking at school is usually nonexistent, so unless it's pissing down, we don't use the car, as it only takes a few minutes. I don't mind walking, but walking and getting wet is a no.

My phone pings with a WhatsApp message. Not many people text me, so Livvy eyes me as I dig my phone out of my bag. She doesn't know about Rocco.

Ellis wants you to come to a BBQ tomorrow.

Ellis wants me to. Not Rocco, too? I tap back a quick reply.

I'm in.

"Everything okay?" Livvy asks, her voice heavy with suspicion. She's looking at me far too closely.

You have the same face. Fuck off!

"Yep, everything's fine."

There's no way I'm going to tell her about Rocco yet. She'll want to know everything about him, down to the damn deodorant he uses, and I can't tell her how we met or where he's from.

She doesn't know everything. No one does.

Livvy is Miss Safe and would flip if she knew I was sneaking out and walking the streets at night. Then, she'd tell our parents.

"Okay," she says, clearly annoyed that I'm not telling her who the text was from.

She overshares, and I share the bare minimum.

"Are you all right, Bells?"

"Yeah. Why?"

"You've been more distracted than usual."

"In case you forgot, we have our exams."

She narrows her eyes. "It's not that, and you know it. We've all grown used to the fact that we have no idea what's going on in your head, but it's getting worse. We were super close until…"

"Until Celia died," I finished.

When we were younger, we did everything together. We could waste hours playing Barbies. Well, Livvy would play, and I'd be the evil villain who pulled their heads off, but we still did it together. When Celia died, it stopped. By the time Livvy dealt with what'd happened, I was lost, and we didn't play anymore. Since then, we coexist but never really spend quality time together. Unless you count sitting in a room, being silent, and watching TV. I don't.

We did that nails thing, but I mostly sat quietly, feeling like a third wheel.

"Well…yeah, until she died. I don't want that to affect us. I mean, I understand that it affects every aspect of your life when you lose someone, but can we please try and get back to how things were?"

"Sure. You got a magic wand?"

"Bella, I'm being serious. If you don't want things to change though…"

"No, sorry. I do. I don't know *how* to change things."

"Talking is always a good start."

"Erm, all right," I say. "What do you want to talk about?" *This is weird. So very, very weird.*

She smiles and flicks her dark hair behind her shoulder, like she's about to get serious. "The message. Do I know him?"

Fuck's sake.

"No, you don't know him. I know you want to talk more, and that's…doable, I guess, but can we not talk about this particular subject? Please!"

Pouting, she shakes her head. "We're teenage girls, Bells. We're supposed to have these particular conversations. It's like *the* subject."

"Well, I'm not your typical teenage girl, Liv."

"Oh, we're all aware of that. You said you'd try, so I'm holding you to it."

"Fine. Again, no, you don't know him, he's not my boyfriend, and, no, you can't meet him." *Like, ever.*

"Early days. I get it. I didn't want anyone to meet Harry when we were first talking."

Unfortunately for me, I go to school with the little wanker, too.

"It's not like that with him. We're…friends, and that's all it'll ever be." *Lie.*

"Uh-huh," she teases in a voice that makes me want to trip her up. "Doesn't seem like it."

I'm not sure Rocco is the type to have a proper girlfriend. He's a bit of a loner, and I don't get the impression that he likes having ties to people or places. He doesn't want anything in his life that he can't walk away from in a second, and I want someone permanent.

Sometimes, when we're together, it feels like a lot more than a friends-with-benefits arrangement. I don't want to get my hopes up though because I'm starting to really, really like him. If he stopped wanting to see me, it would hurt. A lot.

If he's just a very nice chapter or paragraph in my life, depending on how long he wants to hang out with me, then I'm going to enjoy it.

"We're friends," I repeat. "Now, let's go perv on Channing Tatum."

"Ooh, yeah! I'll just call Harry first and let him know I'll be over a little later."

"Have fun with that," I mutter, widening my eyes.

"Bella," she chastises, "he's not as bad as you think."

I hold my hands up.

While she calls Harry, I send Rocco another message.

> This weekend needs to hurry up.

> Horny, are ya?

I roll my eyes at his reply. Obviously, that's what he thought I meant.

> Channing is about to take care of that.

> Who the fuck is that???

Oh, yeah, oops.

Rocco doesn't really know many current actors or movies.

> Tatum. The actor. Livvy and I are going to watch *Magic Mike*. I'll have to bring the DVD over.

> Don't bother. Sounds shit, and you'll be too busy sitting on my lap to watch anything.

Shaking my head, I laugh and put my phone away.
I miss him.
Yeah, the end of us is definitely going to hurt.

TWENTY-ONE

ROCCO

I still don't know why Bella keeps coming here as often as she can. We hang out, have a lot of sex, and walk around seemingly aimlessly. She doesn't seem to be bored yet.

Shouldn't she have woken up and realised that she could do better by now?

It doesn't make sense. Not that I'm complaining. I can't get enough of her.

I'm an exciting person, but I'm not sure how long I can make that excitement last for her.

I've felt her and tasted her now, and that's usually about the point when I walk away. I'm not walking. Bella is different. I'm not stupid enough to believe that she's different in a happily-ever-after way, but there's something that keeps me going back for more. And more. And more. Neither of us can help ourselves.

It's almost eleven o'clock on Friday, and I'm at the river with Ellis and a few others. Bella is coming tomorrow—tonight, she's studying—and I kind of just want to go to bed now because there seems to be no point in being anywhere.

"Your girlfriend's back then," Faith says, stepping in front of me and giving me a knowing smile.

I jump slightly at her sudden appearance.

Did she say girlfriend?
Bella.

I turn and see the beautiful brunette walking toward me from the road. She's wearing black skinny jeans and a plain white fitted T-shirt. Simple but—*fuck me*—it's effective. She's a day early, but I have never been so relieved to see anyone before.

A smile touches her lips as she makes her way over to me, which I return. How can I not? Bella is stunning. Her eyes are big and warm and completely fixed on me.

"Hi," she says, stopping so close to me that I can feel her breath.

She tilts her head, and I just want to grab her and haul her off to my flat.

"Hey. What're you doing here?" I whisper breathlessly.

Her eyes narrow. "Same thing as you," she replies.

I doubt that very much. I'm here because there's nowhere better; she has plenty of better options. She's here to do something specific…and not just me. It pisses me off when she lies.

"Right. Wanna head to my place?" I ask. "We might as well skip ahead." *Please, let's skip ahead.*

Having her here around drug dealers, druggies, prostitutes, loan sharks, and fuck knows what else has me on edge.

I'm always ready to fight and defend myself, but Bella brings a weakness in me that I didn't know was possible.

"And what makes you think I came to sleep with you, Rocco?"

I laugh and dip my head. We're now only an inch apart.

"Because we've been at it like rabbits on ecstasy."

"Yeah, I get it," she snaps, slapping my chest. "So, last weekend, Ellis mentioned a fight at the scrapyard tomorrow."

My jaw tightens. *Fucking Ellis.*

"And?"

"And I want to watch."

No, she doesn't.

I raise my eyebrow as a few things settle into place. There's something at the scrapyard she wants to see. Or someone. Since the first fight, she's actively avoided The White Rabbit on a Friday night, and now that the fight's been moved, she's suddenly all over it.

Maybe her reaction to the fight and the location and the people there will give me another clue.

"Okay," I reply, "we'll go."

"You weren't going to go anyway?"

Grabbing a beer from the cooler beside me, I pop the lid and hand it to her. "Nope. Fights between Lonny and Hugo never last long. Waste of time."

Her eyes widen, and she stiffens. Her reaction tells me a lot. I just need to figure out which one of them she is looking for.

They're both about ten to fifteen years older than her and have lived here their entire lives, so I have no idea how she would know either of them. But I want to know. I want her to unravel and spill every last secret.

I'm pathetic.

"Well, if it doesn't last long, I guess we'll have time to do something else after." Her voice is uneven and low.

The mention of one—or both—of them has left her shaken. After the fight, I'll be taking her home and not for the reason I usually do.

"What time does it start?" she whispers.

"Midnight," I reply.

She purses her lips. The fight is over twenty-four hours away, and it's clear that she wants it to be sooner. Fights in the day tend to attract unwanted attention.

Bella's mind has only ever been half here, but right now, she's completely somewhere else.

"You okay?" I ask. "You look pale."

"I'm fine." She breaks a smile and takes a sip of beer. "So, why are fights between Hugo and Lonny always over so soon? They both crap?"

"No, they're both good."

171

"They beat you?"

I give her a flat look. "They're not that good, Bella."

She rolls her eyes and relaxes. I have about a quarter of her attention.

"Of course not. You're practically Rocky."

"Sweetheart, you need to give up the boxer thing. I'm much better than a man with padded gloves."

"I'm kinda thinking it'd still hurt."

Lifting one shoulder, I reply, "No doubt it would, but there's something more real about fighting with all you have on you. I don't see the point in protection or weapons."

She deadpans. "You don't see the point in protection?"

"Rubbers, yes. Knives and guns, no."

"You enjoy fighting, don't you? It's not just for money."

I don't know why, but admitting that I do to Bella leaves a nasty taste in my mouth. "No, I don't just do it for money." I love the power. I love walking into a ring surrounded by people, knowing I'm going to win and the other guy is going to lose.

"You don't ever think about what could happen to you when you're fighting? You could be seriously hurt, killed even. I read about this guy who was killed with one punch to the head."

"If people stopped to think about everything that could go wrong, no one would do anything."

She tilts her bottle in my direction. "Not the point. This is dangerous, Rocco. One bad punch, and you could be dead."

"It's hardly like I'm going to come up with the cure to cancer," I reply.

Her face falls, and she lowers her beer, like it's suddenly too heavy for her to hold. "So, that means your life is disposable? You don't have to just do something, like cure an illness, to be worthy of having a long, happy life."

God, I love how idealistic she is.

I might not be a murderer, but I'm definitely not a good guy.

"I hope you always have that opinion, Bella."

172

"I hope, one day, you change yours."

I laugh and sip my beer. There's not much chance of that unless I end up winning the lottery…and I don't even play it.

Bella looks over the other guys. She's here more and more, but she still doesn't really interact with many people, mostly just Ellis and me. Occasionally, she'll engage in conversation with Faith but not often.

"You want to head over there?" I ask.

We're standing off to the side with the beer cooler, and everyone else is now around the fire.

"Nah, I'm good here. Want to sit?" she asks.

Good. I don't really want her with them anyway even if Ellis is there, too.

I drop to the floor and kick my feet out in front of me. She joins me.

The river ripples gently in front of us, and Bella stares at the water as it touches the shore with the wind. She tries so hard to look calm and peaceful, but I can see the panic and urgency lurking under the surface.

"I can't believe I used to go in the water as a kid. It's disgusting," I say.

Bella turns her nose up. "Yeah, you're gross. I won't even go in the sea."

"Why not?"

"It's full of pee and whale sperm."

Laughing, I turn my body to face hers. "You have a unique way of looking at the world."

She shrugs and leans against my side. "So do you."

"I call it as it is."

"So do I."

Yeah, maybe we're similar in that way, but that's about it.

"Why did no one stop you from getting in the dirty, pissy water then?" she asks.

My arm hooks around her shoulders, seemingly of its own accord.

What the fuck is that? Why did I do that? We're not in my flat now.

173

She settles in closer, and I take a deep breath.

Shit. I don't want anyone to know she's my weakness.

They probably all know anyway. Faith has called her my girlfriend.

"Everyone did it. There were no parents around. We all hung out on the streets and by the river from a young age. I don't remember the last time I had to follow rules set by an adult."

She sighs. "Sounds fun. Growing up, I had a lot of rules and restrictions. They're still trying to enforce them."

"You have parents who care. Don't ever underestimate how amazing that actually is."

"I guess," she replies. Her mind is elsewhere.

"What's wrong? What else happened when you were younger? Or is it about your sister?"

Blinking up at me, she stills. "What makes you think something else happened?"

"Bella, I *felt* the walls go up just then. Something bad happened, other than your older sister dying, and that's why your parents are strict with you."

She licks her lips and drops her eyes. When she glances back up, they're filled with tears. "There's nothing else. It's just…everything changed when Celia was killed. I was only six, but in that moment, my childhood ended. There was no innocence left, and my parents couldn't pretend the world was perfect anymore. The hood had been lifted, and I saw everything for what it was. My parents became so overprotective that I could barely breathe. Even now, I can pretty much only sleep over at my grandparents' house, nowhere else."

"Killed? God, Bella, I'm sorry she died," I say, pulling her tighter against my side until her body relaxes again. "What happened to her?"

She looks away, and the walls go higher. "Can we not talk about it, please?"

"Yeah, sure." I don't want to push, so I'll be patient and wait until she's ready to tell me.

Please talk to me sometime.

174

I don't know what it's like to have siblings, but I can imagine how hard losing one would be.

It's the absolute wrong time, but I lean down and kiss her. She tastes like beer and chocolate.

Kissing Bella is like free-falling. Every fucking time. I can't get enough of her.

She moans and twists her body until her chest is pressed against mine.

We're still not close enough.

Gripping her firm arse, I haul her onto my lap. She smiles against my lips, and her fingers find their way to my hair. I love it when she tugs deeper into the kiss.

Everyone is still around, but right now, I don't care.

TWENTY-TWO

BELLA

I wake up beside Rocco, and it's officially another one of my favourite mornings ever. The weekends are so much better than weekdays and not just because there's no school revision sessions. Every time I'm here, it gets harder and harder to leave.

Right now, my parents think I'm at my grandparents' again, and while it could so easily go very wrong if they called, I can't bring myself to care. If Rocco and I want to do this more often—and that will be a big, fat yes—then I have to tell my family I'm with him. Livvy sleeps at Harry's, so they can't kick up a fuss.

Ha! Of course they can kick up a fuss. And they will.

It's not like I have to ask permission to be out anymore. I'm a bloody adult! Not that they'll see it like that. They'll focus on the fact that they don't know exactly where I am and freak that something could be wrong.

I could be killed, like Celia was.

Rocco's still sleeping, his arm resting across my waist and his leg thrown over mine.

Ah, I'm fucking crazy about him.

"Morning!" I yell.

Rocco jumps and bolts up, gripping the quilt and shouting, "Fuck! Jesus Christ, Bella!" His eyes are wide and alert, like he's looking out for a man with a gun.

I double over, laughing and replaying it in my head over and over. "Oh my God, your face just then!" Biting my bottom lip, I try to stop myself from laughing.

What did he think was going on?

He looks mad. Real mad. His eyes narrow, and his nostrils flare. Closing his eyes, he chants, "You like her, you like her, you like her. She's good in bed. You like her, and she's good in bed."

I throw my arms above my head and lie there, watching him struggle in not retaliating. I'd give anything to hear what he's actually thinking. As juvenile as it might be, I really love to argue with him.

"I'm sorry. I couldn't resist."

His eyes narrow further until I can barely see them anymore. "What the fuck is wrong with you, Isabella?" he growls. "My first instinct is to fight. You are so fucking lucky I didn't hurt you!" Shoving the cover off him, he gets out of bed and storms out of the room. "You're fucking insane!"

I can't help laughing again. It's funny, even more so after his little rant. Rocco would never hurt me. I wasn't worried about that at all when I decided to wake him up in the best way…for me.

"Payback is going to be a bitch!" he shouts from either the living room or kitchen.

"Bring it…" *Oh*. I want to use his surname here, but I don't know it. *Shit, how can I not know that? I'm sleeping with a man, and I don't know his surname!*

Wow, Livvy is the together twin, and I'm the slutty twin.

"Rocco, what's your surname?" I call out, sitting up to look for my clothes. I'm pretty sure we made it to the bedroom before our clothes were off.

"I'm not telling you any-fucking-thing you want today. Get out of bed. I'm making coffee." His flat is so small that you don't have to shout to be heard in different rooms. But he is.

Angry Rocco is sexy Rocco.

"Why does you making coffee require me getting up?"

"Because you woke me up, and if you want a caffeine hit, you've gotta get up. I'm not bringing it to you, Cinderella."

I'm not even getting into the whole Cinderella-was-the-servant thing; he wouldn't get it.

"But I don't want to get up yet, Rocco."

This is backfiring.

"Well, I'm not bringing it in after you almost gave me a heart attack, so get your arse out of bed!"

Damn it.

"Fine!"

If I'd known he wouldn't bring it to me, I wouldn't have scared him.

Ha! Yes, I would have.

I roll to the end of the bed and get up. He'd better make a really, really big cup of coffee.

What time is it?

Before I go find him, I check my phone.

Ew. It's not even eight in the morning yet. On a Saturday.

"Why is it so early?" I ask, walking out of the bedroom and into the kitchen.

I love it so much at Rocco's place. My parents would probably be horrified if they knew who Rocco was and where he lived. They're mostly nonjudgmental, but they so wouldn't like how dodgy his lifestyle is.

He turns to glare at the same time I walk into the room. "Don't even fucking talk to me about the time. I could still be asleep now."

"You could go back to sleep," I point out, leaning against the doorframe.

"No, I can't. I'm very awake."

"Sorry."

He smirks. "Are you?"

"Well, no, not at all actually. If you had a sense of humour, you would have laughed."

It's then I realise that we're both still naked, and Rocco might have been scared, but his dick certainly isn't.

"Face is up here, Bella."

So, he might have just told me to look him in the eye, but he's certainly not taking his own advice. Unless my face is suddenly on my boobs.

I hold my hand out and take the mug he passes to me. "Thanks," I say. "I need to drink quick and get home."

"What time do they think you'll be back?"

"I told them I would leave Nana and Grandad's at nine, so I have an hour and ten minutes before I need to go."

"What if they call your grandparents?"

Shrugging, I sip my coffee. "They never have so far."

He suspiciously eyes me. Or he's just trying to figure out if I'm all there.

"Stop looking at me like that. I fully understand that shit and fan might meet, but…" I shake my head. "I don't care enough to stop seeing you."

I don't. Rocco means a lot to me, and if my parents find out, then so be it. They can't prevent me from coming here.

"Rocco, you are my sanity in a world full of crazy."

His chest expands as he takes a big breath.

I've said too much, and I sound so desperate. Shit.

"You know, we're friends, and the sex is really good and—"

"Bella!" Rocco says, cutting me off.

I can feel that my cheeks are on fucking fire. *Thank God he stopped me!*

"I don't want you to stop coming here either. Never stop. I should want you gone, but I don't."

"Good," I reply, gripping my mug tighter as warmth spreads through my chest.

We stare at each other, and if he were anyone else, it would be awkward by now. His eyes look so much darker, and the expression on his face tells me he wants to do some things that would make me very late in leaving here.

I clear my throat and put my mug down. "As much as I would love to go back to bed, I really can't be late."

"I thought you didn't care if your parents found out where you were?" he challenges, lifting his eyebrow.

"That doesn't exactly mean I welcome it either. Things are so much easier with them not knowing about us."

He blinks, like he's testing out the idea of us being an *us*. Bringing his mug to his lips, he takes a mouthful. I guess it's a good sign that he's not sprinted for the door.

Could he really want more, too?

I never had him down as the settling type, but our relationship is definitely changing. Maybe it won't be anything epic or lasting, but we've moved past casual.

"So, we keep it quiet," he grunts.

I'm not sure if that's what he wants. He's not said he wants us to be official and public, but the tension in his shoulders kind of makes me think he's considering it.

Are all men headfucks?

I'm glad I've never had a proper relationship before. I'm not even in one with Rocco, not really, and I'm second-guessing what we are, what I want us to be, and what he wants.

This having-feelings-for-someone crap is exhausting.

"For now," I add.

Rocco dips his head in what I assume is a nod of agreement. He's hard to read sometimes, so I can't be sure.

Ugh!

"Right," I say, "I should get ready to leave."

Rocco leans back against the counter, watching me. He doesn't say anything or protest, so I walk out of the kitchen and head to the bathroom to freshen up before I get dressed.

There isn't much in his bathroom, so I comb my hair with my fingers and splash water on my face. It's ice cold.

Fuck!

I hop between both feet and wave my hands because that always helps. Cold water is supposed to be better for your pores, right? I press the towel over my face to dry it. Once I'm finished in the bathroom, I put yesterday's clothes back on and go looking for Rocco.

He's still in the kitchen, leaning against the counter, like some sort of model. He'd laugh at me if I suggested he should apply to an agency, but he would absolutely get signed.

My bag is over my shoulder, and it catches his attention first.

"You're leaving right now?" he asks, frowning.

"Yeah, I should. If I'm late, my parents will start checking up on me."

"Right." He nods. "You're back tonight?"

Bless him, he seems nervous, looking anywhere but directly at me.

"I'll be back tonight."

There's no way I'm missing this fight.

I'll probably have to sneak out because Mum and Dad are not going to be thrilled with the idea of me going to Nana and Grandad's again.

Rocco steps forward, and because his kitchen is tiny, it takes him only a second. He presses his naked chest against mine, and I feel like I'm drunk.

My God, the man is gorgeous. And he smells really, really good. I want to strip my clothes off again and take him back to bed.

"See you later then," he rasps, dipping his head.

"Yeah," I whisper. "Later."

Rocco chuckles under his breath and then plants his lips on mine. My skin buzzes at the contact.

Hell yeah.

The more time I spend with Rocco at his place, the less I like home. I can relax at his; there are no horrific memories. Everything here is happy.

I pull out of the kiss and smile.

My shared car is parked outside Rocco's place. I don't turn around as I walk to it, but I know he's watching me leave.

I get inside and start the engine. Glancing in my mirror as I pull onto the road, I see Rocco smirking at me in the mirror.

I'm going to miss him.

Once home, I park in the drive and get my key ready. My legs carry me to the door at a snail's pace. My stomach drops to my feet. I'm dreading going inside. It's getting harder. The closer I possibly get to finding the man who killed Celia, the more I see her around the house.

"Isabella?" Dad calls.

"Yeah, it's me."

"Come here. We have coffee if you can fit any more in."

Obviously. But this kind of feels like an ambush. They're both sitting on the same side of the table, which they don't do unless they both want to be looking at me.

"Okay," I say, smoothing my hair at the back as I walk further into the kitchen. "What're you two doing this today?"

"Possibly decorating the dining room. I'm so fed up with the red," Mum says.

Riveting stuff. I'm looking for your daughter's killer.

I could never tell them what I was doing. They want justice badly, but they wouldn't ever let me risk my safety for it.

Mum shakes her sleek hair, fluffing it up again. "So, all of your exams are over now?"

"Yeah, last one was Friday."

"That's good. Do you have any plans for the summer before university?" Dad asks.

"I'm going to LA to try and make it as an actor."

Dad gives me a flat look. Whatever. I don't care. I've had this same conversation with them over and over again.

My parents and Livvy are planners. I'm not a planner. I like not knowing every single thing I'm going to do up until the day I die.

"Isabella," Mum scolds.

"I don't know what I'm doing over the summer yet. And I've not made a decision on uni." *Again, I'm lying.*

"You need to go even if you decide to change your degree."

Oh, yeah, makes sense. Not.

Right now, uni feels like a filler for three years. I don't want to go and spend thousands on a degree that will do nothing for me because I won't be able to concentrate. When I go, I want to be focused and ready for it.

And, yes, I might well regret that and think I'm an idiot later on in life, but at the minute, I can't think about anything but finding Celia's killer. And, obviously, I can't stop thinking about my sort-of boyfriend.

TWENTY-THREE

BELLA

Rocco is taking me back to the river because I pestered him until he gave in. Then, we'll be watching the fight later. I'm nervous as hell because I think Celia's killer will be there, and if he's not Hugo, I have no idea who it is. I could've spoken to him already.

Don't think about that.

"So, do you do anything else there?" I ask as he drives along the abandoned road out to the river.

We could have walked, as it's really not far from his flat, but I get the impression that he wants to be able to make a quick getaway. He's not happy that we're going. I don't know why, as I've been to the river a few times now, and nothing has happened besides people standing around, talking.

He grips the steering wheel harder. "Nothing."

"Are you going to mope all evening? Because, if you are, maybe you should drop me off at the river and then go home."

"Yeah, that's happening," he grunts.

"Can you please cheer up? I don't know why you don't want me to meet more of your friends."

He cuts me a look. "You've met Ellis. He's *it*."

"Am I not included?" I pout.

He rolls his eyes. "Right now, no. You're pissing me off, and I don't know why you want to spend your time at a 'sad little river beach that doesn't even have any sand' over being home with me." He uses my previous words against me.

"Ah, you're jealous that I don't want you all to myself tonight."

"Please, I'm not that pathetic," he says.

"Yes, you are."

"Bella, shut the fuck up!"

God, if he meant that *shut up*, I would punch him in the gut.

"You're getting mad because you know I'm right."

"I'm getting mad because you're being fucking impossible. I don't know why I thought it was a good idea to have a girlfriend."

My breath catches.

He totally just dropped the G bomb!

I never thought I'd hear him say that. I'm so bloody obsessed with him, and I literally would've killed to be official. Well, maybe not *literally*.

"Hmm, I'm your girlfriend?"

"You know what I mean," he growls.

"I sure do," I reply, grinning at him like a moron.

Rocco grits his teeth. I'm surprised when he doesn't reply with something witty or sarcastic. I've obviously worn him down again.

We pull over at the side of the road, and he cuts the engine. "Can I *please* just take you home?"

"I'm staying at my grandparents'."

Sighing in exasperation, he whacks the steering wheel. "You know what I fucking mean. My place."

Home.

I like that.

Don't get too ahead of yourself, Bella.

Yeah, it's too late for that. I already know our kids' names.

"Come on. I'll let you drink tonight, and I'll drive *home*."

He starts to laugh. And then he laughs harder. Well, at least he's not being a miserable shitbag anymore. I kinda love his laugh.

"Bella, you're perfect." He laughs again, shaking his head.

I don't let the *perfect* comment go to my head because I know he doesn't mean it in the way I want. But I kinda love that, too.

I have it bad.

"Can we just go and have some fun?" I shove the door open, rolling my eyes with the biggest smile.

I head down to the river.

Rocco soon catches up, throws his arm around my shoulders and kisses the top of my head. "If it's fun you want, we definitely should leave."

"I want to meet your friends…or acquaintances."

"When do I get to meet your friends?"

Looking away, I bite my lip, embarrassed to admit that I don't have any. When Celia died, I was too young to understand what was going on, but as I got older, it consumed me. I have no time for friends, and the few I had, I pushed away. No one bothers with the girl who couldn't care less about them.

It's fine. It's just the way it is.

"Bella? Hello? When do I get to meet your friends?" he repeats.

"You can meet Livvy one day."

"Your sister? You don't always get on with her. I want to meet your *friends*."

"Well, that'll take all of two seconds. I don't like many people."

Rocco stops and grips my wrist, turning me so that I'm facing him. His eyes bore into mine, searching for the thing I can't give him—the truth.

"You don't have anyone?"

"That's not true. I have you…" I don't look directly at him because I can't bear to see sympathy.

Having friends isn't important. I don't have time to pretend I'm interested in which guy is the latest squeeze and which girl we're hating on next. It's boring.

"Yeah," he murmurs, lifting my chin with his finger so that I'm forced to look at him, "you have me."

Swallowing a truckload of emotions that I don't have the capacity to work through right now, I reply, "We can leave if you want." I no longer care about meeting these people tonight.

Shit.

What is Rocco doing to me?

I never want to take time out of going through a million possibilities of the night Celia was killed, especially not for something I want, and I'm hit with a pang of guilt. A pretty big one.

She's my sister, and I shouldn't prioritise spending time with my boyfriend over continuing to search for her killer. I owe her.

"Where have you gone?" he asks, stroking the side of my face.

"What?"

"You look miles away, babe. What's going through that head of yours?"

You don't want to know.

I shake my head. "Nothing. Now, come on, let's stay and you can introduce me to everyone. Please."

"Fine."

"Rocco? Is that you?"

We both turn toward the female's voice.

"Faith, hey," Rocco says.

"Hi, guys," she replies, sighing and flattening her curly bob. It doesn't work. She looks flustered.

"You okay?" Rocco asks. His voice is rougher than usual.

I'm not at all convinced he wants her talking to us, but he doesn't want to be rude to her.

Faith laughs while shaking her head. "Yes, I just got back from the youth centre. We had the plumbers in to fix a leak."

"You have a youth centre?" I ask her.

Faith gasps. "Rocco, you've not told her? It's one of the things around here that provides a positive atmosphere. My husband, Keith, and I saw so many young people wasting their lives, so we decided to try and do something. I hope we help the few who use our facilities."

"That's pretty cool."

Faith smiles. "We're proud of it."

"You'll have to take me one day, Rocco," I say, looking up at him.

He grunts a reply, which sounds like a yes. It's probably not.

"Absolutely do." We fall into silence, and Faith stares at me for a second. "Well, I'll let you two go. Beers are in the cooler, as always."

I wait until she's gone. "Does she organise these…whatever it is we're doing here?"

"No, she likes to think she's in charge of the whole town. Nosy bitch."

There's some hostility, but Rocco doesn't really like anyone here besides Ellis, so it's not surprising.

"Why don't you get a beer?" I say.

"Don't want one," he grumbles under his breath.

"Fine, whatever. I'm going to talk to Ellis since you're a miserable arse."

I stomp off toward Rocco's one friend—one more than me—and leave Mr Miserable behind.

"Hey," I say, nudging Ellis's arm.

"Bella, hi." He looks around, probably for Rocco.

I follow and see my boyfriend grabbing two beers from the cooler without taking his eyes off me.

"What's up his arse?" Ellis asks me.

"Ugh, he's being a baby about bringing me here again."

Ellis nods like he understands completely.

He's standing with a girl.

His girl?

She rolls her eyes at him. "Since Ellis is being rude, I'll introduce myself! I'm Izzy."

"Bella."

Rocco shoves a beer at me with a scowl.

I give him a sickly-sweet smile. "Thank you, dear."

"You're seriously trying my fucking patience, Bella."

I know, and I love it.

"Oh, you need to get laid, man," Ellis says. "I've not seen you this uptight in a while."

Rocco glares at him. "I tried. She wanted to come here."

While the three of them talk, I take a second to look around.

Okay, you're looking for someone over the age of thirty.

There are about four people here who look old enough. And I don't really know where to go from there. I think my actions have made it clear that I'm so completely out of my depth. I should've watched more *Homicide Hunter*.

"Bella?" Ellis waves his hand in front of my face.

"Huh?"

He laughs. "I was just asking if you're coming to the fight?"

"Yeah, we are."

Izzy smiles. "At first, it feels weird to watch two people kicking the crap out of each other, but you harden to it. Just a way of life here."

Yeah, sounds fab.

"Not sure if I'll get used to it, but I'll watch…through my hands probably."

Ellis chuckles. "You're such a princess. You'd be fine watching Rocco; he doesn't lose."

"I don't care; it's never going to happen." The thought of watching someone I care about getting punched and kicked makes me feel physically sick.

"I'm with Bella here," Izzy says. "I wouldn't like to watch someone I love getting hit."

Oh, she did not just say…

God, I'm not going to look at Rocco. Why the fuck did she out me like that?

Beside me, Rocco tenses.

Well, that's just great.

Now, I feel like I should watch him fight to show them that I don't love him...which is ridiculous and would be a complete lie because I love him. A lot. Yeah, I can't lie to myself, and I don't even have the energy to try to deny it. I've fallen for him in the short space of time I've known him. It was inevitable really.

"What do you do, Izzy?" I ask.

Ellis grins and throws his arm around her shoulders. "She's at uni. One of the few people around here who is."

He's so cute when he's proud of this girl who isn't his girlfriend but might as well be—according to Rocco. I can see it, too. Ellis and Izzy are adorable together.

"Cool."

"What about you?" she asks.

"Yeah, I'm not in uni."

Rocco raises his eyebrow. "You're going."

"Oh, am I?" I challenge.

"Isabella, drink your beer."

Ellis and Izzy laugh. I don't really find Rocco's bossiness very funny tonight; he's being a bit of a knobhead.

"You think Lonny or Hugo will win tonight?" Ellis asks Rocco.

Hugo.

My heart sinks at the sound of his name. I need to see him, but the thought of it turns my stomach.

"My money's on Hugo," he replies before taking a long sip of his beer.

I don't want to drink mine now. I want my mind one hundred percent clear. I still don't really know what he and Celia were since her diary reads a little like a bunny-boiler stalking a guy. Hugo clearly wasn't as into her as she was into him, if at all, but she didn't see that. In my sister's mind, they were going to happen.

I wish I knew if she was right.

"I can't believe street fighting is an actual thing. What's the point?"

"Because, Cinderella," Rocco says sarcastically, "not all of us have wealthy parents."

Whatever.

A few other people stop by, and our circle of four gets bigger. Rocco doesn't introduce me. I don't think he's being ignorant; he just doesn't like that I'm integrating into this part of his life.

"So, are you coming tonight?" Faith asks, joining our ever-growing group.

"Yep. I'm not sure if I'm looking forward to it."

She folds her arms and thins her lips in disapproval. "It's barbaric—men hurting each other for money—but there aren't many opportunities around here, and a fight pays well."

"It does?"

Rocco has never told me how much he makes, but then I wouldn't expect him to.

"People come from out of town to watch, and they bet. You can easily make a few thousand in a night."

"Really? No offence, but…er…" *How do I put this without sounding like a mega bitch?*

"But why do they live here if they can make thousands in one night?" Faith adds, correctly guessing my question.

"Well, yeah."

"The people who bet big are the ones who travel from out of town. The money isn't guaranteed. You might not win, and you can't fight daily. If you win, you do well, but it's not enough or frequent enough to get you out."

Okay, that makes sense.

I wish Rocco would get out. He deserves so much more.

"Will you be going tonight?"

She shakes her head. "Not tonight. I have a young girl staying at the youth centre tonight until we can find her something more permanent."

"Is she okay?"

"Her father was abusive, so she ran. I'll speak with social services tomorrow and see if there's anything they can do for her, though there rarely is. She's a flight risk, so I don't want to leave her alone for too long."

God, I can't imagine being in that poor girl's position. The longer I'm in this place, the more I appreciate my family, no matter how fractured we are. Still, I can't seem to be able to get along with them.

I really wasn't always a massive brat.

"I hope she gets help soon."

"I'll make sure she does. So, anyway, how did you meet Rocco?"

"We ran into each other, and it kind of went from there."

"He seems happy with you."

I lift my eyebrow. "Really? How can you tell that from his moodiness tonight?"

She laughs. "Well, he's less moody than usual."

Jesus, they must all have a right laugh with him on a normal night. Not.

"Glad I'm toning down the grumpy. I really kinda like him, and my family has started to notice something's different with me."

"Would they like Rocco?"

"They won't like me being with him. My twin, Livvy, is perfect and has the perfect boyfriend. They'll be off to a great uni together, and he's so respectful that it makes me feel ill. He's boring as hell, but that seems to be what they want for their daughters."

"Ah, the opposite of Rocco."

"Pretty much. I won't be able to keep them away from him forever."

"I don't envy you that. Thankfully, my parents accepted Keith when we got together at fifteen. Do you not have a great relationship with your family?"

"Not really. I'm nothing like Livvy."

"I'm sorry to hear that. I've dealt with a lot of young girls who fell out with their parents, and it's a horrible situation. If you ever want to talk about it, you can always find me at the centre, near the diner."

"Are you a therapist?"

"Unofficially. We've helped a lot of young people at the centre. I think I've just about heard it all."

I doubt that.

"Bella," Rocco says, cutting across the circle of people to reach me.

My heart beats faster, the closer he gets.

"Are you ready to go?"

"Go?"

His arms wrap around my waist, and he loses some of his tenseness. "You wanted to see the fight," he says like *duh*.

"Oh, yeah, I'm ready."

It's that time already?

My stomach is in knots, as I know I'm about to come face-to-face with Hugo for the first time.

Faith smiles and takes a step back. "I'll see you soon, Bella."

"Bye," I say, swallowing a lump the size of a golf ball.

My heart is racing off the charts, so much so that I feel light-headed and have to hold on to Rocco's hand super tight.

Don't faint.

TWENTY-FOUR

BELLA

Rocco and I follow his friends to the scrapyard. I've managed to force my jelly legs to keep moving, but I sure as hell don't feel like going anymore. I half-want to turn around and run away from all of this. Things would be so much easier if I could forget what I know and what I've seen.

I love my twin, but sometimes, I envy Livvy for getting to be the normal one.

"Tense?" Rocco says.

He's not really asking; even I know I must look like I'm walking to my own death.

"Just nervous for the fight," I reply, staring ahead because I'm too scared of giving it all away if I look him in the eye.

"If you don't want to go—"

"No, I do," I answer a little too fast. "This is kind of big around here, right?"

Please don't pick up on my nervousness.

He snorts. "And you love it here so much that you want to adopt our pastimes. If you're going to lie, Bella, make it believable."

Bugger.

I don't know what to say to that.

He obviously knows I'm lying, but I can't really tell him the truth. I don't know who I can trust completely. Since my sister was murdered, trust is something I find ridiculously hard. People are capable of some pretty nasty shit.

"When are you fighting next?" I ask.

His eyebrow lifts, but he doesn't say anything about my change in subject. "Not sure. Why? Do you want to watch?"

"No, thanks." I would quite literally rather watch reruns of *Jersey Shore* and/or *Geordie Shore* all day.

"Strangers are fine?"

"Yes. I've decided I don't like the thought of you getting hurt," I admit.

His eyes flick down, and he takes me in for a second. His step almost falters, but he pulls it back in time. I don't really know if he likes that I worry about him or not. I was never supposed to fall for him.

How things change…

"I don't lose, Bella."

"So I've heard, but that's not really what I was talking about. It's hard to watch someone you care about get hurt."

My mind flashes back to my lifeless and bloody sister on the floor, and it's like a massive kick in the stomach.

Hard *doesn't even begin to cover the pain.*

"I might take a few punches, but I never seriously get hurt."

"Not the point. You could."

"Anything could happen then at anytime. I could cross a road and be hit by a car or fall down stairs and bash my head."

"There's a difference between accidents and putting yourself in danger."

"Is that not what you're doing by sneaking out, not telling *anyone* where you're going, and wandering around the bad part of town in the middle of the night?"

Okay, he has me there.

I can't really preach about safety when I'm putting myself in danger every time I come here. Celia is worth it though. I

196

don't think money or boredom is worth risking your life, but justice is. Rocco is worth it, too.

"Touché. But you know you're walking into a fight. I—"

"Don't have a clue what you're walking into," he finishes. "I'm not convinced that's smarter, Bella."

"Fine, we're equally stupid."

He laughs, and my heart lifts.

"Maybe we are."

As we approach the scrapyard, I start to feel the buzz in the air. But I'm not sure if the buzz I'm feeling is a good one. A lot of people with a crapload of excitement and anticipation are milling around. I just kind of feel sick about the whole thing.

Hugo is here somewhere.

Will he recognise me?

I might as well be Celia's doppelgänger, as all of us sisters look alike. So, if he knew her as well as she obsessed over him, he'll for sure realise I'm related to Celia.

Shit, what do I do if he recognises me as a relation of Celia?

I did not think this through.

"Um, can we stay back a bit?" I ask.

As we walk through the rusted, tall metal gates, I can taste bile in the back of my throat. I want to go home, get a boring boyfriend, and go to uni. Maybe I should be more like Livvy. It certainly seems like a good idea right now.

Rocco shrugs. "Yeah, whatever. I thought you wanted to watch though?"

"I'll be able to see."

"No, you won't. You're little."

Rude.

"I'm not that short."

"You come up to my shoulder."

"All right, BFG, not my fault."

His eyebrows pull together in a frown. "What?"

He's never read The BFG. *Of course not. Jesus, he had no childhood at all.*

"Never mind," I say. "If I get splattered with blood, I will freak, so I need to be far, far back."

He smirks, and I'm not sure if that's because he thinks I'm ridiculous or because he doesn't believe me.

I tried so hard not to react when he mentioned Hugo, but it was hard. The guy is the only link between Celia and this place since her friends are absolutely not talking about it. All I've ever gotten from them are lies. Who lies about that? They're either scared of someone or covering for someone.

"Sure, Cinderella. We wouldn't want to dirty your shoes now."

"You bastard," I snap. I want to storm off, but I don't feel safe here without Rocco, so I'm stuck.

The clouds above us shift to grey, and rain is about the last thing I need right now. They're not the kind of people to call off a fight because of some water, but my nerves are already fried, and standing in the cold rain would only piss me off.

Rocco laughs, and as annoying as it is, he makes me feel a little bit better. I definitely like him too much.

I'm rubbish at detaching my emotions when it comes to him and Celia.

How do I manage it with the people who made me and my twin—the other half of me—but not my deceased sister and a practical stranger?

In my pocket, my phone starts to vibrate.

Shit, this can't be good.

No one but family calls me because I don't really have friends.

Rocco glances down at me. "You gonna get that?"

I don't even dare to look at who's calling. If it's Nana or Grandad, I'm screwed.

Swallowing, I reach into my pocket.

Please, please be a cold caller.

Mum. It's Mum. Fuck.

"Oh God," I mutter.

"Busted?" Rocco asks. His eyes glitter with amusement.

I dash off to the side farthest from people, accept the call, and hold the phone to my head. "Hi, Mum," I say.

"Bella, are you okay? I couldn't get an answer from the house phone."

Crap, she's been calling Nana and Grandad!

"Oh, yeah, sorry." *Say something better.* "They're asleep, and I just got out of the shower." *Good. Much better than a rambled apology.* "Is everything okay?"

"Livvy is unwell."

My stomach bottoms out. "What? What's happened? Is she going to be okay?"

"We had the on-call doctor out, and he thinks she's dehydrated. We're taking her to the hospital now."

Fuck.

"Should I wake them? Which hospital?"

Rocco's expression is no longer one of pure entertainment. He looks concerned.

"No, that's not necessary. She's been sick today, so we think she'll just need to stay the night, so they can get some fluids into her."

Harry had better not have knocked her up.

"Why is she sick? Can I talk to her?"

"She can hear you, love. You're on speaker in the car."

"Liv, are you all right?" I say immediately after learning she's listening.

"Yeah, I'm fine."

She doesn't sound fine; she sounds exhausted.

"What's going on?"

"The doctor thinks it's a bug. Maybe you should stay with Nana and Grandad an extra couple of days."

I want to say, *You can't catch pregnancy*, but that would make me a bitch, and it probably is just a bug. Livvy is on the pill, and she's too perfect to miss one.

"Okay. Make sure you call me when you know what's going on."

"I will," she replies.

"Darling, I'm going to go now. We're just pulling into the entrance," Mum says. "We'll get Olivia settled, and then I'll give you a call."

199

"'Kay, love you guys."

"Love you, too," they reply all at once before the call is disconnected.

I'm uneasy as I put my phone back in my pocket. I want to rush off to the hospital, but I also want to stay here and find Hugo. I've been looking for months, and now, I've finally found him. But my twin is in the hospital.

How do I possibly choose between my sisters?

"What's going on?" Rocco asks.

"My parents are taking Livvy to the hospital. She's been sick, and the doctor thinks she's dehydrated."

"Do you need a lift over there?"

"They pretty much told me not to. Livvy thinks it's a bug and doesn't want me to catch it, and my mum said she'd ring when there was news."

"So, we're staying?"

I frown as guilt settles in my stomach. "Yeah, we're staying."

Livvy is okay. She has our parents. Celia has no one. Her file is stuffed in a cold-case drawer at the police station, and as of right now, I'm the only one still looking.

Three years ago, her file was pulled, and another detective attempted to find the person responsible. Celia's killer's prints and DNA had been lifted at the scene but never brought up a match. Mum cried for hours when we were told that. She'd hoped the bastard would have been arrested for something, so his details would be on record. It was pretty much the only hope my family had. But the only evidence has been locked inside me, and I can't talk until I know who he is and what the danger is to my family.

I won't watch another sister be killed.

"All right. Let me know if you change your mind."

I've changed it about a thousand times since I hung up the phone.

"When does this start?" I ask.

Rocco checks his watch and shrugs. "Shouldn't be long now."

I arch my eyebrow. "You look beyond bored."

He wraps an arm around me and tucks me into his side. This is new. I like it.

"I'm good," he replies, looking over the crowd.

Oh, screw it.

I extend my arms and lock them around his waist. He started it, so he should be able to handle the amount of clinging I'm going to be doing. I kind of feel like I need something physical to hold on to. Shit is about to get real.

The crowd morphs into a circle, and I know that means it's showtime. Rocco angles us, so we can both see without having to uncouple. Behind us, the gates are closed, and two bangers are being driven in front of them.

I awkwardly crane my neck to see what they're doing. I don't like being shut in. "Er, Rocco…" I say nervously. Yeah, I definitely don't like those gates being barricaded.

He follows my line of vision and explains, "If the police come, they'll have to get through the cars and gates, in which time we'll have made it out of the side gate."

"And they won't just go to the side gate because…"

"They don't know it's there. It changes often."

"The gate changes?"

"Position, yes. It's a chain-link fence, Bella. They cut the connections in a different place each time."

What the hell else do they do here to have the need to change quick exits for every fight?

"I suddenly really, really want to go to the hospital."

"It's fine." He laughs. "I know which one it is."

And how does he know?

"Right. Now, I feel much better," I mutter sarcastically, tightening my death grip around his middle.

He jogs my arm to get my attention, and when I look up, he says, "I promise, you'll be fine."

Wow. He's promised me something.

The way he's staring at me makes the skin on my arms pebble. His promise tears right through my heart. He's not just talking about tonight. Whether he wants to or he knows it, Mr

Detached is getting attached. And I'm as emotionally attached to him as I am physically right now.

Neither one of us planned this.

Why can't things just fucking go as planned?

"I trust you," I whisper, getting lost in the intensity of his eyes.

I should walk away. I should absolutely walk away right now, but I can't.

I'm completely in love with him.

TWENTY-FIVE

ROCCO

Lonny and Hugo are announced, and all eyes are pinned to the centre of the ring we've created. My eyes, however, are pinned to the fucking spider monkey stuck to my side.

I don't even have the energy to tell myself that I don't like it.

Lonny and Hugo are similar in appearance. Their heads are closely shaven, both have dark eyes, and they are the same height. They're not related although it's possible. Lonny's dad was a dog and impregnated whatever woman thought sleeping with him was a good idea. As far as I know, Hugo isn't aware of who his dad is.

Bella's eyes flit between the two. Her body is stone underneath mine. I can't tell what's she's thinking because she has her poker face on. It's fucking annoying.

"So, who is who?" she asks. Her voice breaks.

She had every intention of sounding casual, but it was anything but.

"Hugo's the one facing us."

She takes a hard intake of breath.

Bingo. He's the one she's here to see. But why?

"You look like you recognise him," I press.

"No, I've never seen him before in my life," she whispers.

Truth.

Although I have very little idea of what goes through her mind, I know she's telling the truth. But that just leaves me with even more questions.

"Why are you so jumpy then? How do you know *of* him?"

"Please, not here, Rocco," she hushes when Faith turns to look at us.

She lingers on Bella for a few seconds and walks off. It could be a perfectly innocent look. Bella does stick out here, and when someone new arrives, we check them out pretty hard.

"Where then? I'm tired of Cryptic Isabella."

"Whoa, full name. You sound like my parents. Let's go to yours."

"Now?"

She nods her head and swallows, totally on edge. "Yeah, right now."

"But they've not even thrown one punch yet."

"I've seen everything I need to."

Okay, what the fuck is going on?

"All right, come on." I lead her around the outside of the circle and toward the seventh chain-link panel from the end—this week's escape route.

Ellis laughs and wiggles his eyebrows as he spots us sneaking off.

Tosser.

I stick my finger up and then push the edge of the fence, so we can slip through.

Bella is silent as we walk back into town, toward my car. This doesn't seem like a conversation to have out on the street though, so I don't push her to talk yet. It can wait until we're completely alone.

She doesn't say a word as we get in my car. I watch her out of the corner of my eye as I start the engine and drive off. Bella's lips are pressed together, like she's trying really hard not to talk. It must be excruciating for her.

I should say something, but what?

The silence between us makes me nervous. I'm not down with this relationship thing, so I don't know what's normal, but I don't like this. I'm cool with us being okay and shouting, but this nothing is shitty.

My flat comes into view, and I sigh in relief, gripping the steering wheel. The silence is grating on me. I hate that she has secrets, which pisses me the fuck off even more. She's not mine, and she doesn't owe me anything, but I want everything.

Before I've come fully to a stop, she's out of the car.

What the fuck is up with her?

Scowling, I follow, but her eyes stay fixed in front of her. Even when we argue, I still feel her close, but right now, she might as well be on a different continent.

I unlock the door and shove it open. Bella immediately goes inside and heads to the sofa where she flops down, as if standing is just too much effort.

She looks so right and so wrong while curled up in my flat. She deserves so much better than this, but I feel like she belongs here. Too much fucking confliction.

"Start talking," I order as I sit beside her. I'm tired of half-truths.

Meeting my eye, she says, "I found Celia's diary, and it mentions Hugo. A lot. Shortly before she died, she met Hugo. She knew him and used to sneak here when she stayed with our grandparents." Her shoulders sag, like she's had the weight of the world removed.

I feel sick. She's here on a fucking mission. A risky one that I should just send her home because of. This is a bad idea. Hugo isn't a good person, any more than I am. He's a fighter and a drug mule.

"What do you think finding Hugo will do?"

Does she think he killed her sister? Do I think that?

If someone told me that Hugo took someone's life, it wouldn't surprise me but not a teenage girl's. I don't think he's that sick.

She shrugs, and her eyes fill with tears. "I don't know. There are too many questions with too few answers. Someone knows what happened to her. Her friends won't acknowledge any part of the secret life Celia led. Hugo *must* know. There are people here who knew my sister. You've probably seen her."

"Excuse me?"

"No, I don't mean it like that. You were young when she was here, but she used to go to that pub you took me to."

Fuck.

I exhale long and hard. "Jesus, Bella."

"I know. I know it's a lot. I just want answers. Celia deserves justice."

"You think finding Hugo will achieve that?"

"Not sure. I think it's one step closer though. He is the only person she mentioned. She fancied the arse off him, and by the way she wrote, he knew her, too."

"You think they were together?"

"No, she only wrote about her feelings for him. Nothing happened there—that she wrote about anyway."

My mind is spinning. Bella is playing a dangerous game, one that can get her seriously hurt. I'm torn between telling her parents what's going on so that they force her to stay away and offering my help.

"I don't think he would've hurt her," I say.

"I don't know either way, but I have to find out."

"How? Shit!" I explode as I stand up. I don't know what he would do if she accused him. "Do you have any idea how unsafe this is? Do you even have a plan? Fuck's sake, Bella, do you have a death wish?"

I've lost it. She's made me fucking lose it.

What the hell is wrong with her?

"Calm down!" she snaps.

"Calm down? Are you joking? You're risking your life!"

"It's worth it!"

"What?" I shout, throwing my hands up.

Not much gets to me, but her life does. She is everything. My fingers itch to wrap around her neck and choke some sense into her.

Right behind me, she's on her feet, face like thunder. "She's my *sister*. Wouldn't you do the same for your sister?"

"I don't have one," I shoot back, glaring at her stupidity.

"Well, for someone you love then, idiot! Oh, but wait. I forgot big-man-with-a-heart-of-steel Rocco doesn't love anyone!" she shouts.

"Well, I fucking love you!"

Shit.

I've shocked myself as much as her. The words just spilled out, and the second I said them, the enormity of it hit me.

I *love* her.

I've never been in love. I didn't even realise I was until I said it.

Warmth spreads through my body. I feel like I was frozen, and Bella just lit a fire.

Bella stares at me with her mouth hanging open. Well, she doesn't look pissed off with me anymore.

"You what?" she asks.

But I know she heard every word.

I can deny it now and tell her I didn't mean it. I *should* do that. I *can't* do that.

"You heard what I said."

"Yes," she replies as she waves her hand at her stunned expression. "This isn't the face of someone who didn't hear."

"Then, why say *what*?" This is a ridiculous argument, but I'm biding my time because I know she wants me to repeat it.

"Rocco!" she snaps. "Oh my God, you're *so* frustrating!"

"You're no picnic either, sweetheart."

She sighs sharply, shoves her hands on her hips, and closes her eyes. After a few seconds, she breaks the silence with, "I love you, too."

"I know."

Her eyes open, and she's glaring at me. "Okay, I love you a little less."

"No, you don't," I reply.

"Are we done arguing about why I'm looking for Hugo?"

"We're not even close to finished, but right now, I need to take you to bed."

Smiling, she steps forward and into my embrace. I pick her up and carry her through to my room.

Bella's legs, wrapped around mine, tighten, the closer I get to the bed. When my leg hits the wooden frame, I lean forward and let go.

Laughing, Bella unwraps her arms from my neck and falls onto the mattress. She bites her lip, looking up at me like I'm some fucking god, with her dark hair fanned over my pillow.

How did I ever get this lucky?

Bella pushes herself up onto her elbows and raises her eyebrow, daring me to act.

I lift my leg and crawl onto the bed. Bella takes a breath as I get closer, and I stop when I'm right above her.

"What do you plan on doing to me?" she asks.

Hooking my fingers over the waistband of her leggings, I tug them down, not needing to answer her question with words. Her underwear comes, too, in the interest of saving time. With a giggle, she pulls her legs, helping me remove the clothing in the way.

The bottom half of her is naked. Soft, smooth legs drop back down on either side of mine.

"Fucking hell, Bella," I breathe.

She's stunning.

Her beautiful body still makes my heart stop, no matter how many times I've seen it.

"That top needs to go."

Without hesitation, she sits up, whips her top over her head, reaches round her back, and pops her bra undone. She's damn fast when she's horny.

"I think it's a little unfair that I'm naked, and you're fully clothed," she says, chucking the bra at me.

I don't move as it hits my chest and falls. For a second, I'm can't move. My eyes won't leave hers.

How can anything be so perfect?
Move, Rocco, for fuck's sake!

I grab her knees with each hand and pull them up. Bella's hazel eyes widen before she groans, realising exactly what I'm about to do to her.

"Oh, shit, Rocco," she pants. Her voice is thick with need, and it's all I have to hear to get me going.

I lean in and flick my tongue between her legs. She cries out and bucks her hips, pressing herself against my mouth.

"Yes!"

I smile as I flatten my tongue and hold her still. Nothing feels better than the way she reacts to me.

"Let go," she orders, trying to move.

Shaking my head against her, I take her clit into my mouth and suck. My erection is straining against the denim, and I have no idea how I've not come just at the sound of her so turned on.

"Motherfucking hell!"

What?

Bella tries to arch, but I press down on her thighs, feeling the resistance, as she desperately works on wriggling that body.

"Rocco, stop. I can't take it. Please. I'm close," she whimpers, fingers digging into the quilt.

All right.

I sit up, still fully clothed, but I only need my jeans off for this. "Condom," I order.

She rolls to the side and yanks open my drawer.

I rip the button on my jeans open and shove them down. "You're on top. Ride me, babe."

Bella wastes no time in rolling the condom over my cock and climbing over me. I watch her hover herself above my erection. My instinct is to close my eyes and focus on how fucking amazing she feels, but I can't look away.

Her chest rises and falls a little too fast, and her eyes are hooded. She stares at me like I'm some sort of king.

I love her. I love her so much that I'm surprised my heart hasn't fucking exploded by now.

She places her palms on my chest and lowers herself. I slide inside her, and my hands instinctively grab her hips as I push up.

"Jesus, you feel incredible, Bella," I groan.

"Yeah, back atcha," she says. "Oh God, you're everywhere." Her eyes snap closed as she starts to rock back and forth.

Yes.

"Yeah, just like that." I lay my head back, moving my hands back to grip her pert arse.

I still can't believe this girl is mine.

She moans my name, and my dick pulses.

"Bella, harder. I need you to come because watching you ride my face earlier—"

"Oh my God, Rocco."

I'm not sure if it's my words or the way she's jumping up and down on my dick like her life depends on it, but she tightens around me in a death grip, and my eyes roll back.

"Fuck," I hiss, coming hard and pulling her down against me. Throwing my head back, I close my eyes and ride out her second orgasm.

"Damn," she mutters, circling one more time.

Chuckling, I wrap her in my arms, and my eyes flick open. "You good?"

"Yeah. Obviously."

Smiling, I hold on tight, knowing she will have to go back to her parents' house soon.

I can't get enough. No matter how much time I spend with her, I always want more.

TWENTY-SIX

BELLA

Livvy spent one night in the hospital, but she's fine. Right now, she's sitting on the sofa, staring at the TV. That wouldn't usually be strange, but the TV isn't on.

It's Saturday morning. I've been away from Rocco for six days, and I miss him like mad.

I'm so, so close to the door and being with him for the weekend. A few more steps, and I won't have to worry about my family for two days. It'd be so easy to leave, but she looks sad and...

Can I leave without being a mega bitch?

No, I can't.

Damn.

Sighing, I turn and head to the sofa. "What's up, Liv?" I ask, dropping down beside her.

"Harry and I had an argument." She sniffs and wipes her nose on her hoodie sleeve.

Yuck.

"I suppose that makes you really happy," she adds.

She's refusing to look at me, probably thinking I look smug. I'm not. I don't like her being upset. But, yeah, okay, so it does make me happy that she thinks he's a bit of an arse. Gloating is a dick move though, so I won't.

"No, I don't like it when you're all depressed like this. You do know that the TV isn't on, right?"

She gives me a look and folds her arms.

"Fine, I'll bite." Rolling my eyes, I ask, "What happened with Harry?"

"Why are you doing this?"

"You like to talk about things," I reply.

Livvy is the talk-it-out ambassador. "Yeah, *I* do, but you don't," she says.

"Well, I'm not the one who will be doing the talking…"

This is weird. I pull my feet up and hug my legs. Livvy looks equally as uncomfortable, tugging on her hoodie. We don't do this; we don't talk to each other. I was fine with that. I still am actually, but look what's happening.

"We had an argument about uni. He wants us to rent a flat off-campus."

Of course he does. How would he keep an eye on her if they lived in the halls and got assigned different buildings? Ugh, he's such a wanker.

"Why don't you? I assume you'll be getting a mortgage and having all those kids eventually."

"Don't be funny, Bella. If you don't want to talk, then just go wherever it is you were going."

"No, I'm sorry. No more smart-arse comments, I promise." *To your face anyway.*

"I want the full uni experience. I'm already in a serious, committed relationship, which I wouldn't have any other way, so I can't have the casual side of uni. Not that I want it anyway. Do you think it's unreasonable of me to want to live separately the first year?"

"Not at all. If you're going to be together forever, then what's the point in rushing?"

"That's exactly what I said to him. To which he hit back with, 'There's no point in waiting because we're going to be together forever.'"

Touché, dickhead.

Shrugging, I let go of my legs in a bid to force myself to relax. She's my damn twin; this shouldn't be odd.

"You don't actually need an explanation that he agrees with. If you want to have the full experience, then you can have it. I mean, you're already missing out on experimenting, so live where you want."

"Yeah, I know he'll come around. I just hate when we're in the middle of a fight. It doesn't happen often, like once every six months, and it sucks."

Wow, Rocco and I argue once every few minutes.

"It was horrible, Bella. He *raised his voice.*"

Obviously.

"Huh? How have you argued before?"

She frowns. "Don't judge how we argue."

"Can you even call it that if you don't shout?"

"You're getting off track, and it's not making me feel any better."

"I'm sorry…again. How did you leave it with him?"

Looking up, she blinks, like she's trying to stop herself from crying. "He said, 'Clearly, you're not as into this relationship as I am,' and walked out. I've tried calling for the last two hours, and he's not picking up. Should I go and see him?"

"No! You're not in the wrong, so don't go running to him with apologies."

She will probably end up telling him that she's at fault. I hate that. And I hate him.

"Seriously, Liv, you can't back down on something you really want. You said yourself, he'll come around, so leave him to cool off and contact you."

"You think I'm pathetic."

"No, I think you love him, and you want to make things better."

"When did you get so rational about relationships? Especially mine. Is there a boy, Isabella?"

Don't smile, don't think about him, don't give it away.

"Bella, tell me!"

"There's no one. Maybe I'm just growing up. Who knows?"

She raises her eyebrow, not believing a single word, but she doesn't press any further. "All right. Where are you off to anyway?"

"A friend's place for the weekend."

"Yeah? Do I know her?"

"Nope."

"Hmm, do I know *him*?"

"Livvy…"

Raising her hands, she laughs. "Fine, I give up. You know, if you ever want to talk about anything, you can talk to me, right?"

Okay, it's weird again.

"Thanks, but I'm all good."

"You're always all good, but I worry about you as much as Mum and Dad do. You don't ever seem…happy."

Her eyes well up, and I'm seconds from running out the door.

"Are you sad, Bella?"

"What, like, at this second? No."

"Do you have someone who makes you happy? You don't have to tell me anything or give any details. I won't even question where you're going or when we can meet whoever it is. I just want to know that you're not doing all of this alone. I know that finding Celia was horrific and shaped your future, but—"

"Livvy," I say, cutting her off. *Stop talking.* "You need to breathe. Look, I appreciate the concern, but I'm really okay. I promise you, I'm not always sad."

I don't want to touch the *someone* subject because it will get back to Mum and Dad, and they'll want to meet him. I'm not ready to share Rocco with anyone. I love that I have him all to myself.

"Right. That's good. Anyway, I don't want to keep you from wherever you're going."

"Are you okay though? I don't want to leave if you're still upset." *And I want to make sure you don't bloody call him again.*

"You go. I'm going to put on a movie, eat chocolate, and ignore Harry's first three calls."

I smile. "Good girl. See you later."

"Bye."

Once I hit the road, it doesn't take long to get to Rocco's. I feel emotionally lighter, the closer to him I get, which is bizarre, considering going to this part of town is what used to mess with me.

This isn't just about Celia now. It's about me, too.

Realising that is difficult, and guilt wraps itself around my neck, making it hard for me to breathe sometimes. But I'm slowly becoming okay with accepting that I'm allowed some happiness, too.

There isn't one thing in this world I wouldn't do to change what happened the night Celia died, but as I was a young child, I know it's not all my fault.

I park outside his house and cut the engine. I practically dive out of the car and sprint to his door.

Before I knock, the door is open, and Rocco is standing in front of me. I breathe a sigh of relief. This is my happy place.

"You okay?" he asks, frowning.

"I am now. Livvy and I had a proper conversation."

"That's bad?"

"Er, no, I don't think so."

Unless she tries to talk to me more. I'm cool with being there for her when she needs me—I want to do that—but I'm so not up for daily deep talks.

"She had an argument with Harry about uni, and I think I stopped her from running to him."

"You convinced her to break up with him?"

"Oh my God, I wish! Not break up, just wait until he realises he's being a twat and then apologises to her. She was upset that they'd had an argument, and he'd actually raised his voice this time."

"This time? They've never done that before? Haven't they been together for years?"

"Yeah, I know. I don't know if they're the freaks or if we are."

"Are you kidding me? They are! And do you plan on standing in the doorway all weekend, or can we go in the living room?"

I roll my eyes and push past him.

Holy. Sweet. Jesus.

The living room is lit with candles, and a blanket on the floor is covered in rose petals. So, he's totally taking the piss right now because I joked the other night about how cheesy it is when guys do that for sex, but it does look really romantic.

"Really?" I say sarcastically, looking at him over my shoulder.

"Clothes off, Bella."

"No, that's not how you're supposed to do it. First, you need to put on some Lionel Richie, and then you ask me to dance. We kiss, and you gently lay me down on the blanket where you make sweet, sweet love to me."

His forehead creases in a frown, and he folds his arms. "Yeah, I just wanna do you doggy-style on the floor."

Romance, meet grave.

"How have you managed to bed around fifteen women?"

"They weren't the type of women who wanted Lionel."

"Poor Mr Richie. Well, you need to learn to step up the *real* romance because I want some, baby!"

"You, Isabella Hastings, want romance?"

"Yes, I do. Not all the time because that would make me want to throw up, but sometimes, yeah, I do. God, you've turned me into a girl."

"Well, if you make me do the romance thing, you'll be turning me into a girl."

"Shut up, idiot. Men do romance. So…romance me."

"Right now?"

I nod.

"But I need prep time. And by that, I mean, I need to Google it."

Laughing, I walk closer to him. "You would Google romance?"

"I need to if you want something other than me fucking you on all fours."

"Fuck's sake!" I slap his arm, making him chuckle. "Stop ruining this, you wanker."

Grabbing my hand, he tugs me a few steps closer until I'm against his chest. He's lucky he has a nice chest, or I'd hit him again. His eyes are alight with humour, and it makes me swoon. I love seeing him like this.

"I don't know how to do the romance thing well, but I do know that I'm crazy about you. I love you, Bella."

He seals his lips over mine before I have a chance to tell him that I love him, too. It's not like he doesn't already know anyway.

I kiss him back, melting into him, and he leads the kiss into something hot and heavy. Rocco walks forward, forcing me to go back. His arms snake around my back, and one of his hands finds its way into my hair. And I'm lost.

TWENTY-SEVEN

ROCCO

Bella wants *real* romance.

Does that mean chocolate and flowers? I have fucking chocolate in the cupboard, and there are petals on the damn floor. That counts for something, right?

God, I don't have the first clue on how to do this. It's a miracle she's still here with me, and the longer we're together, the more she is going to expect from us.

Growing up, I saw my mum with a string of different men, and not a single one did anything nice for her. Mum's relationships taught me what not to do, but that doesn't mean I know what to do.

Bella sighs and snuggles into my side, tightening her arm around my chest. I love it when she can't get close enough.

I love her. I might not know what to do with her outside of the bedroom, but I won't give up.

How hard can it be to turn on the romance?

Yeah, good luck.

"You okay?" I whisper.

"Mmhmm," she mutters in her usual post-sex sleepy tone. "I like the candles."

"Good, because it's fucking boiling, and I feel like I'm going to pass out."

"Ha! That's not from the candles; that's from my awesome on-top moves."

Chuckling, I kiss her forehead. "Not gonna lie; I've never had better than you."

"Would you even remember?"

"Ruin the moment, Isabella, why don't you?"

Giggling, she pushes herself up and leans on my chest. "I'm sorry. I really don't think I need to say that you're the best I've had."

"No. After all the moaning and the, 'Oh God, yes, Rocco,' you definitely don't need to tell me."

"Now, who's ruining the moment?"

She leans down and bites my collarbone. My dick starts to stir again. When she sits back up, she's pouting. I want to take that bottom lip between my teeth.

"We're not good at moments, are we?" I ask.

"No, pretty horrible at them actually. We should definitely stay together, so we can contain our failures."

Not arguing with you.

I'll be with her for as long as she'll let me.

"Not planning on going anywhere," I reply.

The smile I get back makes my heart race. Her eyes are fucking smiling. Her *eyes*! I've never been around happiness like this before, and to know that I'm responsible for it is completely indescribable.

She's very quickly thawing my heart.

"I think I have about a thousand rose petals stuck to my body," Bella says, brushing a few off her arm.

"Want me to remove them with my teeth?"

"Are you ever satisfied?" she asks.

"With you? Every time. But I like to be satisfied multiple times a day."

"We've had sex twice in the last hour."

"I said, *multiple*."

She tilts her head, and I know what she's about to say is going to be sarcastic or cocky.

"What's your definition of *multiple*?"

"Nine. So, buckle up, sweetheart, because you need to service me another seven times."

Bella's eyes narrow, and she slaps my chest. "Keep talking like that, and you won't get *serviced* again for a very long time."

That's a lie. She loves it as much as I do, and the girl is practically a nympho.

"What do you want to do this afternoon?" I ask her.

"I don't know."

"Anything, Bella. I want to take you out."

She bites her lip, frowning, as she thinks of something. Bella's not really one for venturing out among people that often, so I can tell she's struggling.

"I want to go shopping."

"You do? Really?" That's not exactly what I wanted to hear.

"Yes, I need new underwear."

I sit up, almost knocking her over in the process, and I think I pulled a muscle from moving so fast. "Come on then. Get dressed."

Any type of shopping is something I do as little as possible, but if she's going to be choosing underwear for me to peel off that perfect body, I'm all up for it.

Bella laughs and stands up, brushing petals from her legs. I'm not laying those out ever again even if it is to prove a point that I can do romance. Fucking things just get in the way. When I did it, I just wanted to see her reaction. I didn't think about having to clean the damn stuff up.

Twenty minutes later, we're free of petals and ready to leave. Bella's excited. She hasn't stopped smiling since I agreed to go shopping. Thank fuck I took that fight and won because, now, I have a couple thousand to spare.

I've always had enough money. It's probably because, besides rent, bills, and food, I don't buy anything. My money stash is growing, but it might never be enough to move somewhere really nice. My cut for the fights I win are decent but nowhere near the amount the organisers and bettors receive. The more I win, the more I can demand though.

Bella tugs on my arm. "Let's *go!*"

She can't get out the door fast enough, and my heart sinks. This is going to be one of those things where I stand, bored out of my head, while she goes in every shop. I just want the underwear one and then to go back to mine.

"All right! Fucking hell, Bella."

I slam my door shut behind us, and she's already dragging me toward my car.

"Where's the fucking fire?"

Looking over her shoulder, she grins. "I'm excited. I never thought I'd get you to go *shopping* with me. It's so...normal."

"I can do normal."

"Apparently so. You're not allowed to moan."

"You're not allowed to get any underwear I can't see through."

She turns her nose up. "Ew. Tacky."

"I really don't care. I want to be able to see your—"

"Let me stop you there," she says, backhanding my chest. "I love you, Rocco, but not enough to wear see-through undies."

Laughing, I throw my arm around her shoulders. "Please, you're obsessed with me. I've seen your screen saver."

"Get over yourself. That's just a really good picture of me."

"Uh-huh," I mutter.

She can't lie. I can see how she feels whenever she looks at me.

"You know what? You can piss off."

"You're doing nothing to convince me. In fact, you're only making your case worse."

She walks to the passenger side of my car and folds her arms. I stay at my side and mimic her actions. When she can admit how she feels, then I will take her to the mall. Until then, it looks like we're going to stare at each other.

Bella sighs sharply. "I don't want to play Who Can Outdo Who right now."

"Then, get in the car."

"Rocco! Come *on*."

"I'm not stopping you, Bella."

"Yes, you are!"

"No, your stubborn nature is stopping you."

I love messing with her. When she gets angry and her eyes turn deadly and her posture is hostile, I get so excited. She's perfect in every way, and I don't know how I got so lucky, but I'm glad I did.

"Fine, but if you don't get in the car, we can't leave…and if we don't leave, you don't get to see me modelling my slutty new underwear."

"Well, hold on a second. How slutty are we talking?"

It might be worth letting her win this one. My girl is beautiful in everything I've seen so far, but I *really* want to see her in slutty underwear.

Her eyebrow lifts. "*Very* slutty."

Shit.

"Fine."

Happily admitting defeat for the first time in my life, I rip my car door open and get inside. Bella gets in next, and as I look over, I wish I hadn't conceded. She's smug. *So* smug.

"To the shops, Batman," she says, pointing out the window.

"Batman?"

"Oh my God, please tell me you've heard of Batman?"

"Yes, of course, I have. But I don't know why you're calling me it."

"Jesus," she mutters, widening her eyes. "Forget it. Let's go."

I start the engine, still fucking clueless, and pull onto the road. Some of the shit she talks about has me scratching my head.

"Ugh, Livvy texted me."

"Everything okay?" I'm not letting her go. I don't care if her sister is still crying over her dickhead boyfriend.

"Yeah, she just said that Harry's tried calling three times already."

"What's wrong with him? Why is he blowing up her phone?"

Bella rolls her eyes. "He's an idiot. I'll deal with Livvy later. It'll only wind me up because she'll bitch about him, take nothing I say on board, and apologise for whatever crap *he's* done."

"Relationships are fucking stupid."

She smirks and nudges my arm. "'We're all mad here.'"

"What?"

With a sigh, she slowly shakes her head. "Jesus. Don't worry about it."

Ah, it's from a TV show or a movie.

I don't see why she can't use her own words rather than stealing shit from movies or TV or books or wherever else the fuck she gets it. I know of certain films and characters, but I wouldn't have a clue where any quotes were from.

We park at the shopping centre, and Bella leads the way.

"Here first," she says, stopping dead and almost pulling me over as I'm still walking.

I look up at the shop. Ann Summers. Right, never been in here before. It looks full of ladies' underwear though, so I'm down. We step inside, and I want to buy it all. She's gorgeous, and I know she could rock anything on these shelves.

Bella starts to look at different sets, touching the fabric and reading the labels. She would look amazing in everything in here.

Curling my arms around her waist, I whisper in her ear, "Something see-through. There's a couple over on the other side of the shop."

She laughs and shakes her head. "Nope."

"Crotchless?" I say just for the reaction I know I'll get.

Immediately, she tries to get away, probably so that she can whack me, but I hold on tight.

"I don't think so."

"You're disgusting, Rocco."

"I was kidding, Bella."

"I don't believe you. But you want to come to the special room with me?"

What?

"They let you do that here?"

What kind of shop is this?

"Seriously? It's not like that!"

She grabs my hand, and I drop my arms.

"You're going to like this."

We go through a door, which has an eighteen-plus sign on it.

This is looking positive.

"Ah," I say as all the fun stuff comes into view. There are a lot of toys, and I think I would like to pretty much use every single one with her.

She smiles, and her eyes are heated. "See?"

"Pick up whatever you want, and if you think you're leaving my flat for the rest of the weekend, you're very fucking mistaken."

"Shh!" Bella hushes, slapping my chest with the back of her hand. "Whisper! We're in public."

Before I can tell her that I don't give one fuck about who's listening, she grabs something.

"Ooh, this!"

Er...

I give her a look. "We're not buying a vibrator that's bigger than me." The thing is fucking massive, easily the size of my forearm.

"I'm kidding. That'd hurt like a bitch, and you're—" She bites her lip, her cheeks turning the lightest pink.

"Whoa, hold up. I'm what?"

"You're...not going to want to use that either."

"No, tell me what you were really going to say."

"I don't want you to get a big head."

I step closer to her, completely taking over her personal space. "You think I'm big?"

"Maybe. Now, choose some toys, and let's go home."

Home.

Bella calling my place *home* should scare me. It doesn't. Damn it, I need to be more realistic about this. I can't get myself out of the life I have, and she deserves much more.

What can I do? I love her too much.

TWENTY-EIGHT

ROCCO

I lead Bella back to my car because, by the way she's looking around, it's clear that she's forgotten where we parked. Good thing she didn't come here alone, or she'd never find her car and get home. Especially with that pointless tiny thing she drives.

I walk to the driver's side, open the door, and chuck her bags on the backseat. Bella looks at me over the roof, on her tiptoes, and raises her eyebrow.

"What?" I ask.

"You know, if you were a gentleman, you would open my door for me."

"Just get in the car, Isabella."

Laughing to herself, she opens her door.

Does she say shit like that just for a reaction?

She must because I've made it abundantly clear that I'm not the fluffy gentleman type.

I get in and turn the engine on.

"Let's get home, sunshine," she says, dropping down in the seat and slamming the door shut.

Her sarcastically sweet smile makes me grit my teeth.

She's definitely doing it on purpose.

I tear out of the car park, gripping the steering wheel like my life depends on it.

Why do I let her wind me up?

"You'd better change into one of those sets the second we get in," I mutter. The more I think about her in that underwear, the more my frustration with her melts away.

"Okay, but first, can you stop at the supermarket?"

"Why? I have food."

I've started shopping now that I have her. When she's hungry, she's a fucking nightmare.

Her eyes flicker with heat. "Uh-huh. I was going to get whipped cream though."

I grip the steering wheel harder and almost crash the damn car in the process. "What?"

"We've never done that before."

"No, we haven't. I'm down," I say. Whacking the indicator, ready to turn right at the light, I head to the supermarket near home.

We both go in and get the whipped cream—two cans. I'm pretty sure, from the smirk on the guy at the counter, it's obvious what we're about to do.

Bella leans over while I shove my card in the machine and whispers, "We should've bought a cucumber and condoms, too."

I cut her a look and take my card back. She would absolutely do that, too.

"Cheers, man," I say to the guy as he hands me the receipt.

We head back out to the car.

Bella's smiling like it's Christmas as we head along the side of the building to the car park.

Out of the corner of my eye, I see a man dressed entirely in black with his hood pulled over his head. He raises his hand and—

Bang.

Bella gasps and grabs ahold of my arm. She's scared.

Fuck.

I shove her between the supermarket and a block of flats next to it while looking over my shoulder. The shooter dives into a beat-up Ford and takes off.

"It's okay," I whisper to Bella.

We're not going to get shot at. The shooter has gone, and people are already gathering around whoever is now on the ground. I don't know his name, but I've seen him around before. Now, he's dead.

"Wh-what the hell was that? Why did he do that? Why do people do that?" she mumbles, stumbling over her words. Her fingers are cutting into my biceps.

I take her face between my hands and press my forehead to hers. "Hey, you're okay. It's done now. He's gone. You're safe, I promise."

"But…why?"

"I don't know why, Bella. There's not always a reason…or not one you would understand."

She shakes her head, eyes wide with fear. "There has to be. It doesn't make any sense. Is the person he shot dead?"

I nod. Middle-of-the-forehead shot isn't something you survive.

"How do you just decide to take someone's life?"

"Whoa, Bella, breathe."

She takes a breath, and I see tears well in her eyes.

Shit.

Her head snaps around, following something.

A car?

"That's the one," she says.

The one what?

She really is in shock.

"I see it everywhere."

"Huh? See what, Bella?" I look off in the distance. "You mean, the car?" It's just a dark Volkswagen Passat. "I don't know whose it is, but most young lads drive round and round."

When she looks back at me, her eyes are wide and filled with terror. "I want to go back to your place now. I don't like it here. Can we go?"

This is getting weird.

"Yeah," I reply. I tuck her into my chest as much as I can as we hurry back to my car.

The people who don't want to be around when the cops turn up have left, and only two people are now with the dead guy on the floor.

To Bella, this is horrifying, but to me, it's business as usual.

I drive back to mine, and the second we come to a stop outside my flat, Bella is out of the car and running to my door.

Is this the part where she leaves?

It should be. I should make her if she doesn't.

I let us in the flat after locking my car, and she heads to the living room.

Shit, I'm losing her.

The thought makes me feel sick.

Closing the door, I follow her. Bella's sitting on the sofa, staring into space.

This is why I should've ended things between us before it really began.

I crouch down in front of her and stroke her hair from her face. "Hey, I'm so sorry you had to witness that. It doesn't happen often, not murder."

"Is he *definitely* dead?"

Unless he's immortal…

"I think so, babe. Are you okay? I know it's a shock the first time you see something like that."

She looks down and whispers, "I'm okay."

That's a goddamn lie. Clearly, she is not okay. Her hands are shaking, and she looks like she's seen a ghost—or a fucking *murder*. I don't really know what to do to help her.

"When did you first see something like that?"

"Er, I think I was about four."

She presses her lips together and nods. "How many times have you witnessed someone dying?"

"I'm not sure." I've not kept count, but it's probably around five. "Why do you want to know?"

"I…" She licks her lips. "No idea. Sorry."

"Don't be sorry, Bella. Tell me what you need. Do you want me to drive you home? I'll understand if you don't want to be here right now."

"No. Despite what just happened, this is the only place I want to be."

How can she mean that? Some guy just got *shot* in front of her.

"Really?" I ask, unable to hide the surprise from my voice.

"You make me feel safe," she whispers.

"Jesus, Bella," I say.

Cracking a small smile, she leans forward. "I'd really like it if you took me to bed now."

"You would?"

She looks sure, but I'm not feeling it. Something happened back there, and she's using sex to distract herself from it. Now, I'm no stranger to meaningless sex, but I refuse to do it with her.

I hold her gaze, and her eyes twitch.

"Bella, talk to me."

"I'm sorry. I'm just a little shaken up. It's not every day you see someone get shot."

I push off the floor and sit beside her. She curls into my side and buries her head in my chest.

"It's okay not to be strong and cocky all the time," I tell her.

"Yeah, maybe you should tell yourself that once in a while."

I want to tell her that I'm fine and that, in the past, I've never had anything to lose, but that seems like rubbing it in. Growing up here has hardened me. I don't get scared when shots are fired. And I always thought that was the best way to live, but being with Bella is making me question that.

Maybe the happiness someone can bring is worth having a weakness for.

Though I can't see that being true if anything ever happened to her. It would break me if I lost her for good.

"Maybe I should," I agree. "Let's make a deal. In front of each other, we don't always have to be strong. Okay?"

The deal is for her. I want her to open up and tell me everything, and I still want to know what she's holding back, but I have no intentions of offloading any of my shit on her.

Tilting her head, she looks up at me and cracks a beautiful smile that makes my heart thud. "Okay, deal."

"What?" I ask when a frown steals the smile.

"I don't know. It's just...I've never had someone to talk to. Not someone I feel like I can talk to anyway."

"You'll always have me, Bella."

No matter how long always is.

"I'm holding you to that. I've never been this close to someone before, and I don't want it to end."

"If I'd known it'd only take a guy getting shot for you to open up more, I would've paid a hit man."

Her mouth falls open, and I wince.

"Sorry, babe. Too soon?"

"Yes, too soon, dickhead!" She slaps my chest and glares.

I know that, if I keep looking at her, she'll smile, but I don't think I'm done with her being angry yet. I fucking love her angry.

"Sorry, I wouldn't really hire a hit man. I—"

"Don't even finish that sentence."

"It's nice to see that your fire is back."

She bites her lip. "I didn't mean to act like a little girl."

"Shut up."

Her eyes narrow. A darkness is still there, but she's doing better. "Did you just shut me up again?"

"Mmhmm. What are you going to do about it?"

Oh God, please do something kinky.

"I'm going to withhold sex."

"Oh, because that's going to happen. At least threaten something you have a chance at following through with."

"Fine. I'll make you meet my parents."

I wait for the fear as her words sink in. That should make me want to run for the hills...but it doesn't.

"Isn't meeting the parents inevitable? We should get it out of the way."

She sits up straighter, so fast that it startles me. "What the hell, Rocco? Are you joking right now? Because I feel like you should be joking. Why doesn't your face look like you're joking?"

"Wow, someone's a commitment-phobe."

"I'm not. I'm with you exclusively, aren't I? You're just crazy to think that meeting my parents is a good idea."

"First, you'd fucking better be exclusive with me. Second, why are you freaking so much? You think they'll hate me?"

"Er, I *know* they'll hate the thought of me being with you. They're not like normal, supportive, and accepting parents. They worry too much, and they want me to be with a boring, safe guy with a full rest-of-life plan. And a good pension."

"Who has a pension in their early twenties?"

"Harry has one at eighteen."

"Fucking hell." My mouth falls open.

That ain't normal. There isn't much I wouldn't do for Bella, but getting a pension is one of them.

"Exactly. Let's keep the parent meeting until we absolutely can't put it off any longer."

Yeah, they're going to hate me.

"Sure. You mean, like after the birth of our first child, right?"

She arches her eyebrow. "I mean, like after the birth of our second child."

Works for me.

If Ellis had overheard this conversation, I would never hear the end of it. I don't plan things with people, especially having children.

"I feel like I need to drink a lot of beer," I say.

She grins and nudges my arm. "Children talk?"

"Yeah."

"Yeah. Grab me one, too, please. Actually, grab me, like, four."

Well, at least we're on the same page about kids, too. For now anyway.

If I can't get away from here, there's no way I'm bringing a baby into this place. It's too dangerous.

I had Bella around *gunfire* today. Somehow, I need to find a way to give her the life she deserves. A life that is far from here.

TWENTY-NINE

BELLA

If Rocco finds out I'm at the scrapyard alone, he'll flip. So, it makes sense that I'm not going to tell him.

Hugo is here. His face is messed up. His right eye is about twice the normal size, his lip is sporting a long gash down the centre, and he has bruises all over his jaw. Still don't know who won, but Rocco was definitely right about it being a close fight between them.

Being here is beyond stupid, especially after witnessing a murder yesterday, but I can't let a silly little thing like sense get in the way. Rocco barely left my side after it happened, but he fell asleep, so here I am.

Hugo looks up and stops whatever it is he's doing under the bonnet of an old Ford Escort. "Can I help you?" he asks.

I bloody hope so because I'm tired and drained, and I want justice.

Every step I take closer to him makes my heart thud. He could either be Celia's killer or just someone she used to know.

I tilt my chin up and straighten my back. *You can do this. For Celia.*

"Yeah, I'm looking for a car stereo. Mine's had it." Lies roll off my tongue so easily. They have done so ever since I was six years old.

"What car you got?" he grunts.

"Fiat 500."

He lifts an eyebrow. "That's not a car."

I roll my eyes. *Is he related to Rocco?* "It wasn't my choice."

He's right; it's more of a go-kart than anything else, but Livvy wanted it, and at the time, after sneaking out of my parents' house, missing the family meeting, and getting caught, I wasn't allowed to be a part of the decision-making process. Not that I give many fucks since it gets me away from the house faster than walking.

"How'd you break the last one?"

I shrug. "It just stopped working."

"And you just assume you need a new one?"

"Okay, well, do you know how to fix them?"

He straightens his back and suspiciously eyes me.

Fuck, does he recognise Celia in me?

"Yeah, I know how."

I need to leave, like *now*.

"What's your name?" He's looking too hard.

Please don't see my sister.

It's game over if he figures it out.

Damn it, damn it. Fuck.

Celia probably didn't mention her sisters' names to him, but I still feel the need to lie out of my arse. Only I can't really do that because if he's around when Rocco or Ellis says my name...

"Bella," I reply. "Yours?"

"You know mine."

Double fuck.

He tilts his head. "You were here the other day, right?"

Oh God, he saw me.

"Erm, yeah." I fidget on my feet. "The fight was...good." Not that I was there long enough to witness much of it.

Smirking, he leans his hip against the car. "Good? You don't sound convinced of that. You Rocco's girl?"

"Yeah, I am."

So, he just recognises me as a mate's girlfriend, not Celia's sister. I think. I hope.

I really, really hope.

Chuckling, he shakes his head. "Didn't think he'd ever settle down."

I don't want to know why…because I can guess.

"Believe it. Are you not the settling type?" I ask, not entirely sure I want to hear what he and Celia were…or weren't.

He turns his nose up, like he just smelled something gross. "No fucking way."

"Really? But you've had girlfriends before, surely?"

"Depends on your definition of girlfriend."

"Someone you spend longer than one night with."

Laughing, he kicks the dusty ground. "Then, yes, I've had a girlfriend."

Celia?

"Hmm, what happened to her?"

Oh, nice one, Bella. Like he's going to come right out and say, Actually, I murdered her.

"Why do you think something happened to her?"

The pulse in my neck starts to drum, and my palms sweat. "No, I just mean, what happened to you guys since you're not together now?"

Stay calm.

He studies my face, searching for something that I don't ever want him to find. He's looking for recognition, like that feeling you get when you're sure you've met someone, but you can't think of who they are.

I shake my head. "You clearly don't want to talk about it. Sorry, I shouldn't have pried. It's none of my business."

"I don't mind talking about her."

Good.

He shrugs. "We just didn't work. I'm not good at monogamy."

Did you cheat on my sister, you prick?

Though, in the grand scheme of things, cheating isn't the worst thing he might have done to Celia.

"Where's Rocco?" he asks, looking behind me like he expects him to be standing nearby.

"Home," I reply. "Hey, have you and Rocco ever fought?" I know this, but I need to quickly move on from him asking me questions.

"Nope. I'm not really into it much anymore. Getting old. Lonny just had it coming."

Right.

Okay, so my plan isn't as solid as I thought because I don't know where to go from here. If he offers to take a look at the stereo, I'll have to actually break it when I get home. Seriously, I don't know why I even open my mouth sometimes.

"Rocco likes fighting. Is it that way for you? Or was it that way?" I ask, genuinely interested.

Enjoying getting punched is the dumbest thing I've heard, and Livvy talks some crap.

He lifts one shoulder in a lazy shrug. "Suppose."

"Wow, you're a real talker."

Why do I keep getting the watered down version of everything here? No one can be bothered to talk for longer than five seconds.

He takes a step closer to me, and I suddenly wish Rocco were here, too.

Hugo glares, and he's built like The Hulk. "Around here, you do what you've gotta do."

So, what does he feel he's got to do right now?

I stand my ground even though every instinct is screaming at me to run. "Even if surviving meant doing something that would seriously hurt or even kill another person?"

His head tilts to the side, and his eyes darken. "What do you mean?"

"Yesterday, a man was shot outside the supermarket. I saw it happen."

"And you think it was me behind the trigger?"

"No!" I force myself to laugh. *Was it you? Did you murder my sister?* "Of course I don't think that."

"Good. I didn't murder him."

I hold my hands up. *This is so not going the way I want.* "That's not what I was suggesting, I swear!"

Though I did notice that he'd said he didn't kill *him*, not that he wasn't a killer.

"There's a lot that goes on here that's completely alien to me. People don't seem to care much about the lives of others."

"You don't belong here, Bella. It never ends well when a girl from the right side of the tracks tries to play happily ever after with a guy from the wrong side."

What does he mean by that? He's speaking from experience. Was that a confession?

Did you kill my sister, you son of a bitch?

"Isabella!" My name is snapped from somewhere behind me.

Oh, crap.

I look over my shoulder and see Rocco stalking toward me with a heavy, pissed off frown.

He's mad.

Don't think I've ever seen him look so angry before, and he's hardly the most cheerful person.

"Rocco, man, did you lose your girl?" Hugo says.

Not helping.

Rocco seethes, and his shoulders tighten, as if he's preparing for a fight. But it's not Hugo he addresses first. "What're you doing?" he growls at me. His hair is a little messy from where he was sleeping.

"I couldn't sleep, so I went for a walk. You were out of it, and I didn't want to wake you."

It's not a flat-out lie. I did walk here.

"She snuck out of your place?" Hugo asks, his voice laced with humour.

Okay, why is he still here?

"Apparently, she can't help it," Rocco spits through his teeth.

So, maybe I regularly sneak out of my grandparents' house, but I didn't want to with Rocco. It's just that he would have been less than supportive if I'd told him what I was doing. He's a bit over the top when it comes to my safety.

Also, I'm a terrible fucking person for making him worry, which he clearly was since there are only two people in his life that he cares about…and I'm one of them.

"Get in my car. Now."

Man, he's extra bossy when he's pissed.

Arsehole.

Gritting my teeth, I salute him and stomp off toward his car. I might be acting a little childish, but he's treating me like one, so screw him.

"Bella!" he snaps.

I hear his footsteps gaining. I don't look around.

It only takes him a few seconds to fall in line. His eyes are fixed on me. I can feel them burning a hole in the side of my head. There's no way I'm engaging yet. I'm too bloody livid. Not only did he interrupt a potentially pivotal conversation about my dead sister, but he also made me look like an idiot in front of Hugo.

Not that I care what Hugo thinks of me, but he's unlikely to want to talk to me again after that.

Great. That's just fucking great.

Tears sting behind my eyes.

What if that was my chance to find out what Celia and Hugo really were, if anything?

He could've given something away.

After twelve years, I'm so tired of this, and I just want the truth.

"Are you going to tell me what that was about?" he asks through his teeth.

I stop on the spot and narrow my eyes. "Oh, hell no! You don't get to be the pissed off one, not anymore, you twat!"

"Excuse me?" His voice is cold and quiet.

I'm still burning inside. *How dare he treat me like a kid back there!*

"Ugh! You made me look like a real dickhead in front of Hugo. I'm not seven. Sorry I didn't tell you I was going for a walk, but that doesn't give you the right to—"

"Oh, shut the fuck up, Bella. I have every right to come and find my missing girlfriend! What are you doing out here?"

"I actually can't believe you just told me to shut the fuck up."

Who the hell does he think he is?

"Well, believe it. You're acting like a spoilt brat."

"I went for a fucking walk. How is that spoilt?"

He throws his arms up. "You know why!"

"I don't have to check in with you." Turning around, I rip the passenger door open. "You're being completely unreasonable."

"*I'm* being unreasonable?" he scoffs, slamming his hand down on the roof of his car.

I hope he dents it.

"Er, yeah. You tracked me down, like some sort of stalker again, and now, you're yelling at me and acting like *I'm* the crazy one."

"It's dangerous for you to wander around here at night. I know you want to find out what Hugo's relationship with Celia was, but this isn't the way."

"Then, what is the way? How else am I going to figure it out?"

He roughly runs his hands over his face. "Why don't you get it? This isn't for you to figure out. Go to the police, Bella. Don't put yourself at risk."

"He killed her, and no one knows who he is," I say.

He rounds the car and takes a step closer to me. His eyes soften. "Yeah, babe, I know that. It sucks, and it's unfair, but you getting hurt isn't going to help."

"I won't be able to forgive myself if I don't at least try."

"My life would be so much simpler if I hadn't fallen in love with you."

I laugh, closing my eyes and sinking into his embrace. "Ditto, buddy."

THIRTY

BELLA

Rocco stares up at his bedroom ceiling. His arm is around me, and he's not let go of me since we got home. But I can tell he's angry. It's not like he can get all high and mighty though. We both put ourselves in potential danger.

"I love you," I whisper against his skin as I kiss the curve of his neck.

"I love you, too," he replies. "But I still think you're fucking crazy, and you need to stop."

He doesn't get it, and he probably never will.

"How can I stop, Rocco?"

"Your sister was *murdered*."

"Yes, surprisingly, I haven't forgotten about that! Come on, that's exactly why I *can't* stop. Someone out there took her life, and they should be behind bars."

"You don't know that they're not."

"And you don't know that they are. I need answers. Hell, my whole family does."

"Why does it have to be you? I don't understand why you can't go to the police."

"Seems rather odd—*you* telling me to go to the police."

He roughly rubs his hand over his face and sighs. "I'm not getting into that with you. It's different. I don't want you pursuing this anymore."

Why not?

All I want to do right now is get to know Hugo and then maybe find out if he knows what happened to Celia or at least if he knows someone who hated her.

"You can't ask me to stop."

"I fucking can."

"You're not my dad. Not that he could either. Believe me, Rocco, I'm not the type of woman you can order around."

"Oh, I get your reluctance to do what the fuck you're told and what you know you should do. This is your safety, your *life*, that you're playing around with here. I'm sorry Celia died, but this won't bring her back. Do you think she would have wanted anything to happen to you?"

"Of course not, but that's not why I'm doing it. When you love someone, you do what you need to do. I know you worry about me, but you won't ever change my mind. I'm sorry, but I'm doing this. I will find out who killed her."

"Well, that's great. First girl I've ever loved, and she's on a suicide mission."

"I promise you, I won't get killed."

Closing his eyes, he shakes his head. "You can't promise that."

"Can and did. Please, Rocco, I really need you behind me on this."

He turns his head, and his eyes open. I see the worry etched into his face. I hate myself in this moment because I know that I can't back down. I could stop that look, but I won't.

My eyes begin to sting, and I hold my breath. *Shit, I'm a horrible person.*

"I'm sorry," I whisper.

"Don't be sorry. I get it, Bella. You started this long before me. I swear to God, if you get hurt…"

"I'll be careful."

"Too right you will. You won't go anywhere on your own, and you'll tell me everything. If you're determined to do this, we're doing it together."

Pushing up onto my elbow, I shake my head. I should've known he'd say that. Even though I would feel a hundred times safer with him beside me, I don't ever want to put his life at risk.

"No, you can't," I say.

My heart splinters at just the thought of him being hurt.

"Then, stop what you're doing."

"Please don't do this," I plead.

"We both have terms that we can live with. This is mine. Leave this, or let me help."

"Is there a third option?"

"I walk," he replies. His voice is sharp, and it cuts through my chest, leaving me bleeding.

He'll leave me. If I don't let him help me look for the murderer, he'll leave. I know I should take him up on it. If we're done, then there won't be any risk of him being harmed. But I don't know how to say good-bye.

Do it.

I can't put him in harm's way.

"Walk, Rocco," I whisper. The words feel like razorblades cutting into my flesh as they leave my mouth.

He laughs and pulls me onto his chest until I'm almost square on top of him. "I love you so much more, Bella. I was never going to walk. You mean everything, for fuck's sake! You're not someone I could leave. Ever."

"So, that was a test?" *Who does that?* "Would you ditch me if I'd told you to stay and help?"

His eyes are laughing. "What part of *I'm never going to walk* don't you understand? You're never getting away. I won't ever let you leave."

Oh.

"Er, you know stalker is so last year, right?" I joke, trying to be cool when I feel like my heart is going to fly right out of my chest.

He rolls his dark caramel eyes.

"You're a real headfuck sometimes, Rocco. You don't think we'll have forever, but you won't ever let us break up. How does that work?"

"You know my lifestyle and where I live. Folks around here don't usually live happily into their seventies."

"So, you think you'll die young?"

"Well, not tomorrow. I'm just saying, there's a good possibility I won't make it to my seventies."

I can't believe he just said that. You're supposed to plan for forever.

"I don't want to talk to you when you're being a prick."

"They teach you words like that at a posh school?"

I roll my eyes. "The school isn't posh. I'm definitely not posh. My family is not posh. Liv and I got in because we each had fifty percent scholarships," I defend.

I would literally rather cook my own head than be like a few of the students who think they're better than everyone else because Mummy and Daddy are minted.

"All right," he says as he runs his hands up my bare back. With a quick kiss, he brings us back to our original discussion. "We'll find out what happened to Celia together, but I need complete honesty from you."

No.

My legs are ready to run and get me the hell out of here. I can't give him that. Every part of me aches when I think back to that day. It hurts beyond anything I ever thought possible, and I don't think I can physically talk about it.

He doesn't seem to notice my inner turmoil, which I'm thankful for. Telling him isn't an option. I can't go there.

"What do you want to know?" I ask, praying that he'll only ask questions I can give him straight answers to.

I will lie if I have to.

"When and how did she die?"

"The carnival was in town. It was May and a gorgeous, sunny day. Everyone was out in the street—eating, dancing, watching the parade, and playing games. Celia was in the house when she was killed. No one heard a thing because of the noise outside. She was stabbed eleven times."

"I'm so sorry," he says, running his hand through my hair. His voice is softer than I've ever heard it before.

God, I love his soft side as much as the hard.
I wonder if he'd still love me if he knew the truth.
Probably not.

"I just want someone to pay for what they did to her, Rocco. She deserves that much."

"She does. We'll try, okay?"

I nod my head and cover his lips with my own.

"Did you bring the diary?" he murmurs against my lips.

"Yeah."

"Can I see it?"

It feels like a betrayal. The entries are Celia's, and they're private. It's bad enough that I've read it. But I can't deny him when he's helping me.

"Um, okay."

"You're not comfortable with that at all, are you?"

"It just feels strange, but I'll get over it."

"Good, because I need to know everything. I don't like this. I'll be digging into the lives of people I shouldn't. That's not how things work around here. You have the back of your own."

"You've never felt like these people are your own though."

"That's not the point, and you know it. *You* are the one I'm concerned about. I love you and want you to start living your life again, so I'll do whatever is necessary to make that happen. I don't care what I have to give up."

Oh, shit.

My heart practically implodes. His words bring tears to my eyes. I know my family loves me, but I've never felt it as strongly as this. Rocco makes me feel safe and secure, and that's not something I've felt in a very long time.

"And I promise you, as soon as this is over, I'll do everything I want to do."

"What is that?" he asks.

That's the question I avoid like the bloody plague.

"I really, really have no idea. I think I want to work with animals, but I'm not sure what I want to do specifically."

"Vet?"

I shake my head. "I don't like blood."

He laughs and rolls us over. I adore the feeling of his weight on top of me.

"You don't like blood. What are you going to do with animals then?"

"I'm not sure. I thought about animal rescue, but I don't know if I could stomach seeing the abuse side. Maybe I'll find something I can do at home, so I don't have to see anyone."

He kisses my forehead. "Hermit."

"Or I'll just marry rich."

"Right," he says, his face falling.

I grip his upper arms as he goes to leave. "No, Rocco, I didn't mean that. You know I don't care about money. I was just messing around. Honestly, I don't know what I'll do, but I'm looking forward to finding out *with* you."

"You're so sure we'll last?"

"Yes," I reply without hesitation. "I don't care where either of us came from. We're here now, and that's all I care about. Kinda thinking that you see us as temporary now though…"

"Everything in this world is temporary, beautiful."

"That's very deep."

"It's very true. My time with you is limited, and as long as I get every part of you, I'm okay with however long that is. I'll take what I can get because nothing has ever mattered to me the way you do."

"You're going to make me cry, Rocco."

Rolling his eyes, he stops me from thinking and even breathing by kissing me until we're clawing at each other.

THIRTY-ONE

ROCCO

Bella is still asleep, mouth open, matted hair everywhere.
Fucking beautiful.

There's still sadness around her eyes, but at least now, I understand why. She lost her sister in one of the worst possible ways.

On my bedside table is Celia's diary. There's fuck all in there other than the ramblings of a lovesick teenage girl. I'm not sure if I want Bella to think about me the way Celia thought about Hugo or not.

I turn over and watch her. She looks peaceful right now, but I know, when she wakes up, her sister and her mission will be on her mind. I have no idea where to start with her little crusade. The people I waste time with are dodgy as fuck, but I just can't picture one of them stabbing a teenage girl to death. None of them are that screwed up.

But she is convinced that Celia's killer is from here, and that seems a hell of a lot more likely than someone from her side of town.

I make a mental list of the people I feel could take a life without giving a shit. At first, I couldn't think of anyone, but the more I think, the longer the list gets. I might spend most evenings with these people, but I don't really know them. Ellis is the only one I'm sure wouldn't do something like that. He's too young to have killed Celia anyway.

Bella's sister was murdered by someone I have potentially spent years in the company of.

How do I even begin to sort through the list of shady characters? And how do we get a confession?

We can't exactly go around, accusing people. I'm surprised Bella's gotten this far with no help. She's just as clueless as I am.

She stirs and pouts in her sleep. I'd love to know what she's dreaming about.

Her stunning hazel eyes flick open seconds later, and she whispers, "Hi."

I can't help smiling like a lovesick idiot. "Hi." The way Bella looks at me is indescribable. I would literally do anything for her, no matter how dangerous. I'd lay down my life to protect hers. "So...I was thinking I could go out alone tonight and listen a bit more when people are talking to me."

She looks at me like I've lost it. I kind of have if I'm entertaining this crusade she's on.

"Huh?"

"People talk about all sorts of things in front of me, but I've never really listened. Maybe if I do, I can find out something."

"Yeah?" Her eyes widen in hope, and she rolls onto her side. "Really? Rocco, that would be awesome. Though I'm not looking forward to not seeing you."

"I won't be gone all night. Stay, and I'll do you real good when I get back."

Rolling her pretty eyes, she replies, "We say *I love you* to each other, and you're still calling it *doing me?*"

"I'm not ever calling it *making love* if that's what you're hoping for."

With a laugh that has me smiling, too, she splays her fingers out over my chest. "I think I would be extremely weirded out if you ever said that."

"What are you going to do while I'm out?"

"Netflix," she replies.

"You watch too much TV."

"Netflix isn't TV. Netflix is life."

What the fuck is wrong with people?

"Bella, find a hobby that doesn't include staring at a screen."

She gives me a flat look. "I'm sneaking away from my family to find a murderer. I have a hobby."

Hmm…

"Most people collect stuff or draw or something like that."

"I'm not most people."

No, she really is not.

At ten at night, when Bella is engrossed in whatever shit she's watching, I head out the door. Ellis is already at the river, so I make my way down.

Tonight, I have to talk to people. I've been hanging out here with these guys for years, but I know very little about any of them. They could all be killers, and I wouldn't know.

I walk toward the fire, and everyone around it looks dodgy. Bella's sister was older than her, so her killer would be at least a similar age. If he's even here.

Right now, I feel like an idiot. There's no evidence that someone here did anything to Celia, but if I don't snoop, Bella will continue to do it, and that's too risky.

Ellis turns as I approach and lifts his eyebrow. "So, what gives?"

"What?" I ask.

"When Bella's over, you usually try to keep her to yourself. She go home?"

I walk around him and grab a beer from the cooler. Next time I come, I really need to pick up a few bottles beforehand to donate. "She's at mine."

"Then, why are you here?"

Fuck. Think things through!

I pop the cap off the beer. "She's binge-watching TV, so I thought I'd come for a drink."

He watches me, his dark green eyes brimmed with suspicion. "Rocco, I know you don't share much, but I do know you. What's really going on?"

"Is Bella okay?" Faith asks, stepping closer. She smiles. "Sorry, I overheard."

"She's fine. Everything's cool."

Taking the hint that she shouldn't be a nosy bitch, Faith nods and retreats. I know she's struck up some sort of friendship with Bella, but that doesn't mean she needs to know our business.

Ellis nods to the edge of the grassy area, and I walk in the direction, so we can talk without people listening in.

"Come on, what's happened?" he asks.

This isn't my secret to tell, but honestly, I'm out of my depth, and Ellis is much more involved than I am. I trust him more than I thought because I'm considering this. Groaning, I run my other hand over my face and then down a quarter of the bottle in one long gulp.

"Rocco, I'm not getting any younger here," he mutters.

"Bella's looking for someone."

"Right now?"

"No."

"Who?"

"I don't know."

Ellis tilts his head. "I'm confused."

I look over both shoulders. Everyone is out of earshot.

"Twelve years ago, her older sister was killed in their home. Bella is trying to find out who did it."

"Are the police not doing that?"

"She told me they put it down to some home invasions that had been happening, called it a burglary gone wrong," I reply.

"And the thief was never caught?"

"Apparently not. After finding out her sister knew Hugo, she's convinced the guy is someone who lives or lived here."

Ellis's back straightens. "Okay, that is weird. Why has she been coming here if she thinks there's a killer? Surely, she wouldn't want to be anywhere near him."

I shrug. "It's a mess, Ellis, and I don't know what to tell her."

"How is she trying to find him? Just by hanging out here?"

"Pretty much. That's why she's been so keen on seeing everything and watching fucking fights. I mean, do you think Hugo could've killed a teenage girl?"

Ellis thinks for a second and blows out a breath. "I don't know, man. He's kind of a recluse, and I've not spent much time with him. I have heard things though…"

"Things?"

"About how he used to be."

"Like brutal when he was fighting? Yeah, I've heard that, too."

"Yeah, but not just organised fights. According to Kane, Hugo would get hired for his muscle. Someone didn't pay a loan, and Hugo would be sent."

I know a lot of muscle for hire, Ellis has done it, but I didn't know Hugo used to be one.

"Is Kane a reliable source?" I don't know him well, same as everyone else around here, but he works with Ellis and seems decent enough.

"I trust him."

"Fuck's sake," I groan, looking up at the sky. "Bella could be right about this."

When I lower my head, Ellis is looking at me with all the sympathy in the world.

"She's not going to let this go, is she?" he asks.

"Nope, I've tried. And I have no idea where to go from here. I don't want her putting herself in danger."

"So, don't tell her."

I laugh. "Yeah, that's what I was thinking, too. If she thinks it's a dead end, she might stop looking. It's safer than her trying to prove it was Hugo."

Because how would we even begin to do that? It's not like he's going to admit it.

"But then if she finds out herself and knows you lied…"

"Great. So, I can't win?"

"You're in a relationship, Rocco. What made you think you could ever win?"

True.

"I need a plan," I say.

"Keep her out of it for now. I'll do some more digging."

"You don't need to get involved, Ellis. I—"

"Fuck off," he says, cutting me off. "You're a mate, and I like Bella. Besides, people don't tell you their deepest, darkest secrets because you've never shown any interest in their lives—ever."

That does make sense.

"Why do you want to help just like that? No thousand questions, no wanting to talk to Bella."

"I don't need to know any more than your girl's sister was killed, and we might know by who."

"Right." I scratch the back of my neck. "Er, thanks."

Ellis laughs. "Man, it's worth it just to see how uncomfortable you are. It's not a bad thing to ask for help and rely on someone else, you know."

"Isn't it?" I've never had help, not even as a kid. I practically learned how to take care of myself before I learned to fucking walk.

"Leave it with me. I'll see what else I can get from Kane."

I give him a nod and look away to take another swig. I want to leave because this is awkward as hell, but I can't go home too soon because Bella will be full of questions. Lying to her isn't going to be easy, but if I go home and tell her what Ellis said, she won't leave it alone. I want proof before I tell her anything.

If Hugo is the reason Bella is broken, I'll fucking kill him myself.

THIRTY-TWO

BELLA

I'm in Rocco's kitchen, drinking coffee because I need to be a functioning human. He's standing opposite me, and so far, he's only said that he found out nothing last night.

Celia's diary is now in my bag on the counter. There's nothing new to learn in there, but I can't let it go. It's like getting a piece of her back. When I read it, I hear her voice in my head.

"What? Not a thing? Wasn't Hugo there?"

"Babe, I'm sorry there's not more to tell yet."

I shrug. "Not sure what I thought would happen anyway. It's not like he was going to come right out and tell you what he did."

"If he's even done anything. I'll keep my ear to the ground, but for now, I think you should take a massive step back."

"What?" I literally jump back from him and knock my back against the counter. "I can't do that. You said we'd figure this out together."

"And we will, but you can't go bulldozing in and expect—"

"What happened last night?" I demand. "You've changed your damn tune, and it's not cool."

"I've not changed anything. I just think you need to be smart about this."

"I *am* being smart about it."

"No, you're not."

"You're being a prick! I'm not giving up on my sister, and I'm sure as hell not stepping back when I feel like I'm getting closer! If you don't want to help, that's fine, but don't ever think you can tell me what to do."

"Oh my God, you're blowing this way out of proportion. What's going on, Bella?" he snaps. "There's more to this. You're completely obsessed to the point where it's scary and unhealthy. What the fuck happened to you?"

"Get out of my way, Rocco," I reply calmly, stepping to the side and attempting to walk out of the room. Under the surface, I'm seething, but right now, I just need to get away from him.

He leaps forward. His arm shoots out, and his fingers curl around my wrist. "No."

I yank myself free. "Don't touch me! Just let me leave."

"Tell me what happened. Why're you so fucked up? What happened to you that made you so cold? Why are you constantly running around, poking your nose into everyone's business, following my friends like a damn stalker? What's. Going. On?"

I shove the palms of my hands into his chest and sob. Pain slices through my heart. I need help. I cover my mouth with my hand to try and stop myself from crying.

Fucking get ahold of yourself!

Rocco steps closer and places his hands on either side of my face, the way he does when he kisses me. Only this time, his lips don't reach for mine. He looks into my eyes and asks one last time, "What happened to you?"

And, this time, I don't lie. I'm too tired of it. I feel like I'm suffocating because I have to watch what I say all the time. "I watched him kill my sister."

Rocco stills, and his face falls. He slowly lowers his hands. "You what?" he whispers.

"I was in the house when he killed her." I'm shaking. This is the first time I've ever admitted it. No one knows but me and Celia. "I've never told anyone else that."

"Fucking hell. God, Bella. Why haven't you told your parents? The police?"

I couldn't tell.

"Bella, talk to me," he demands, folding his arms over his chest.

I glance up and meet his eyes. "She told me not to."

"Celia?"

I nod in confirmation, but that only makes him look more confused.

He scratches his jaw. "She didn't die straightaway?"

"No, she did." *Thank God she didn't suffer.* "But she knew who he was before he broke the door in. She knew what he was going to do, Rocco."

He shakes his head. "Start from the beginning."

I wrap my arms around my stomach, feeling sick.

How can I do that? I constantly relive that day over and over. I don't want to talk about it. If I could erase it from my memory, I would.

"Bella! For fuck's sake, you can't tell me something like that and then close up. Baby, tell me what happened."

Baby is more of an affectionate term than he's used before, and he's not the fluffiest person. But I like it. I *need* it right now. I need him more than I've ever needed anything, and if I'm going to properly have him, I have to let him in.

Rocco moves closer and wraps me in his arms. Then, he waits. I feel strength in his embrace, so I cut myself open and let my past bleed out.

"It was the street carnival. Everyone brought food and drinks, and we had games and stalls up and down the road. The stall where my parents were was outside a neighbour's house. Celia was at home, getting ready. Olivia and I were playing that stupid game where you have to hook the duck to win a crappy prize. I needed the toilet, so I went home."

Rocco pulls me closer. He knows where this is headed now.

"So, I went inside and used the toilet. When I finished, Celia was in the living room, still putting on her lip gloss. That was when we heard banging on the back door. I knew the instant I saw Celia's face that something was very wrong. I'd never seen her look so scared. When I think about that day, I can still *feel* the fear."

"What happened, Bella?"

I take a breath. *God, I don't want to say it.*

"She leaped up and grabbed ahold of me so hard that I thought my arm was going to snap. I didn't understand what was going on, but I was terrified because she was. Celia told me that I had to hide and that, whatever happened, I was to *never* tell what I saw. The banging on the back door was getting louder, and she kept looking back. He was going to get in soon…"

"Go on," he prompts softly.

I swallow sand. "She said he was a 'very bad man,' and she didn't want him to hurt our parents, me, or Olivia, too, so I had to promise to stay hidden and not tell anyone.

"She said it over and over, Rocco. 'Don't tell anyone about this because our family will be in danger.'

"I planned on telling my parents as soon as he left.

"I had no idea what he would do. Celia hid me in the cupboard, told me she loved me, and made me promise again not to tell and to forget what was going to happen."

I take a deep breath and press my face in his chest. Images of that day flash through my mind.

"The door was kicked in. I heard a struggle and a loud bang, like something heavy had been knocked over. Celia was begging him to let her go. I was in the dark and terrified, but I still did the stupidest thing and opened the door a little."

Rocco's body tenses. "Did he touch you?"

"No, he never even saw me. He was too busy tightening his hands around my sister's neck. Celia saw me looking on in horror. Her eyes widened as she clawed at his hands and gasped for breath. Even though she was fighting a losing battle for her life, she still gave me the look that told me to shut the door and stay quiet. I did what she'd ordered and heard my sister gasp for a few more seconds…and then he stabbed her. Eleven times in the chest.

"It took me ages to finally come out. Her eyes were open, and even though I was little, I knew she was gone. The end table was on its side. I think she'd knocked it over to try to stop him from getting to her. I don't know. My parents walked in seconds later and screamed. They assumed I'd just found her, and I was so shocked and so scared that I didn't correct them."

"No one heard anything?"

I wipe my eyes. "No, not with the carnival music. That's obviously why he chose that day to kill her. He must have been stalking her. I mean, she knew he might come, so she must have been threatened by him, right?"

Rocco frowns. "Why did he do it?"

I shrug. "I don't know. I doubt she would've told a six-year-old even if she'd had time."

"Jesus." He takes a breath. "You've carried that around all this time?"

Rocco runs his fingertip under my eye, wiping a tear.

"I know I'm a horrible person for not telling, but I fear for my family's safety, and I've been confused about the whole thing. Every time I want to tell, I remember what Celia said. So, now, I have to make it up to her. She hid me so that I wouldn't get hurt. She made me keep this secret to protect the rest of us. I can't let this go on forever. Celia deserves justice, and that's all I want right now."

He sighs, and I know he likes the idea of me searching for a killer even less.

"I understand it's dangerous, but you don't get it, Rocco. This is my *sister*. I let her down, and I have to make up for it."

He pulls me into his arms and cups my cheek with his hand. "You were a *child*, Bella. You didn't let her down. She made the right decision when she told you to keep quiet. It's what anyone would have done if they were scared the same man would harm their family."

"No. I should've done more, and I'll always regret that."

His eyes harden. "There's nothing you could've done. Do you think he would've spared your life because you were six? People like that don't give a shit. If he'd seen you, there's no way he would have let you live and risked getting caught. Celia was right. You would have done the same thing if the roles were reversed, and keeping your end was the right thing to do, too."

"No, it wasn't. The older I get, the more I realised that. No one has been held accountable for her death, and more people could have died at his hands. How is that the right thing? I'll never forgive myself for sitting back that day, and I'll never forgive myself if someone else has lost their life because of my silence. Please appreciate that I need to make this right."

"Okay, I get that, Bella, but shit happens. You're responsible for your actions, no one else's. This isn't on you. The blame lies with the killer only."

I do believe that to an extent as well, but this is different. It's not okay to think, *It's not my fault*, if you think someone will do wrong again. Not to me anyway.

How am I supposed to sleep properly, knowing something I've done or not done has directly resulted in someone being hurt?

So, maybe I'm insane, and maybe this will all end badly, but drowning in guilt is no way to live. I don't want to just exist anymore.

"Rocco, I need to do this. Even if he never touches another person, my sister deserves for her killer to be behind bars."

He sighs long and hard. "Fucking hell. I really don't like this."

"I'm not asking you to put yourself in danger."

Frowning, he cups my chin. "I'm not thinking about myself. My life doesn't mean shit to me. Yours does."

My heart aches at his confession. His life means so, so much to me, and I hate hearing him talk about it like he's dispensable.

"Don't, Rocco. Please don't say that."

"It's the truth. I'm not going anywhere, Bella—never—but you are. You have so much potential, and I'm not letting you gamble your future—*your life*—for some scumbag piece of shit."

I shouldn't have told him. Celia's death flipped my world upside down, and I can't have that happen again. If Rocco is injured while helping me...God, I don't know how I'd get through losing someone else I love.

"You might not think you're anything special, Rocco, but I do. If you don't want to live here, then leave. You can get out."

He sceptically lifts an eyebrow. "And do what?"

"Whatever you want."

"I love the world you live in," he says, as if I'm living in a fucking fairy tale.

We're not going to settle this, and I'm not stepping back and letting someone else I...*love* be harmed again.

And I do really love him. Despite our differences, the fact that we can't go a day without some argument, and that we've known each other only a couple of months, I love him. A whole lot.

"Rocco," I whisper, feeling a wave of emotion wrap around my throat.

"It's okay. We'll figure this out together."

That wasn't what I was talking about. He thinks I mean Celia's killer. I don't. Well, I do, but right this second, it's about me and Rocco.

"I don't want anything bad to happen to you," I say.

"Back atcha. It'll be fine, baby. I promise you that I'll help put your sister's killer behind bars if you promise me something in return."

"What's that?"

"When this is all over, when he's gone down and you have justice, you'll start living for you. Whatever you want to achieve, you'll go out and get it."

I've not told him my life is on hold, but obviously, he knows. I've tried a few times to not allow it to consume me, but it never lasts longer than a few days. The plans I made fizzled out as quickly as I set about realising them.

It's hard to move on when you're chained to the past.

This isn't some small thing that I need to take care of before I can move forward. This is so fucking huge that it chokes me.

But I love my sister, and not having my life all about me is a small price to pay her back for saving me. Because that's what she did. Celia saved my life when she hid me away and made me swear to never tell.

"Promise me, Bella, when this is done, everything becomes about you."

I kiss his lips and whisper, "I promise."

THIRTY-THREE

BELLA

I get home late, and I'm exhausted after baring my soul to Rocco. It feels good to have told my story though. I didn't realise how heavy a secret like that had weighed until I let it out.

Now, I get to worry about Rocco in this, too, though. He's much better than me at this who's-dodgy-and-who's-straight street shit, so if this all goes horribly wrong and anyone is going to get hurt, it's going to be me. I can live with that outcome.

I turn out of Rocco's road and head toward home. Ed Sheeran is singing on the radio, and I join in for a little "Castle on the Hill." The shittiness of Rocco's part of town gives way to greenery and houses that aren't boarded up and covered in swear words and penis drawings.

Behind me, a dark sedan breaks heavily to avoid a collision.

Shit. What the fuck are you doing, you dickhead?

Frowning, I rhythmically check my mirror and the road.

What a knob. He's too damn close. Back off!

I can't see the make of the car, but—

The Volkswagen? Could this person be purposefully following me?

The hairs on the back of my neck stand, and a shiver runs down my back. I grip the steering wheel and try not to react. Easing off the accelerator, I slowly drop from sixty to fifty. He does the same but keeps a tiny gap.

What does he want?

Am I being totally paranoid here?

I am. I probably am. That's what I do sometimes, right? Just calm down because it's just a bad driver. There are a billion of them on the roads.

I press the call button in the car to ring Rocco because he will either calm me down and make me see sense or get in his car and follow me. Either one is good with me at the minute. The second my finger leaves the button, the car makes another sharp break and takes a hard left, leaving the road I'm on.

Sighing, I sink back into the seat and shake my head.

See, you're a paranoid idiot!

Fifteen minutes later, my heart rate is back to normal, and I'm pulling into my drive. I really need to take a break from obsessing about a killer because it's doing my mental health no good. I can't see everyone and every situation as a threat; that's not healthy.

I park the car, get out, and let myself into the house. Dad is sitting on the sofa when I walk in. Seems like he's alone, and there's no other noise in the house.

"Hi, Dad."

"Hi, Isabella. Can you come and sit down, please?"

My heart is instantly in overdrive, hammering away, as I imagine the worst.

"What's happened?" I ask, the blood draining from my face.

Is it Mum or Livvy? Not my twin, please. Is Liv sick again?

"Nothing has happened. I'm sorry I made you fear the worst."

Sighing in relief, I sit at the end of the sofa and angle my body toward him. "Good. What did you want to talk about then?"

"You finding a job."

Oh.

"All right," I reply, giving a nod. "I'll ask around in town."

"Your mum and I have. There are jobs going at Ted's Diner, Another Chapter bookstore, and Bernie's DIY. If you're not going to university this year, you will work and contribute. You're eighteen, and we are only willing to financially support you and Olivia while you're in education."

I shrug. "Yeah, seems fair."

Dad takes a breath through his nose, and his jaw hardens.

Ah, I see; this is to scare me into going to uni. He thought, when it came down to it, I would rather study than work. Now, he's not happy because I've agreed.

On the coffee table is a pile of newspapers. The top one is open on the Careers page, so no doubt, the others are, too.

He's thorough; I'll give him that.

"I like the idea of the bookstore."

There would be less people, and I know what books are. Ask me a question about DIY though...

"I could get Livvy a discount on her course books."

Dad's eyes darken, but he nods, trying not to give it away that he's hating the idea of me working. "I bet she would like that."

She won't. She's just as nuts about me following her path as Mum and Dad are.

"Well"—he clears his throat—"take those newspapers, and have a look, go online. Then, make a CV to take to the bookstore. If you need help with the CV, let me know. You want to make it professional and to the point as much as you can and tailor it slightly to each job you're applying for."

Okay, I just forgot all that.

Picking the newspapers up, I smile. "I'll get right on it."

This is going to suck.

I have enough in my savings account to survive for a while, but I should be earning. Besides, I don't think it's optional if I want to continue living here, and it's not like I have enough to move out.

Dad reaches for the TV remote and focuses on that rather than me now that his plan has backfired. I don't want to piss him off even though I'm clearly very good at it, but I can't follow a path that he wants. What I do from here has to be for me.

I sit on my bed and dig in my bag for my phone to message Rocco.

> Is women's fighting a thing? Dad wants me to get a job. I'm looking at them now.

While I'm waiting for him to message back, I start to flick through the Careers page. My phone beeps seconds later.

> Two words: Pole dancer.

I roll my eyes at his obvious reply. Honestly, you would think he'd at least try to be more original.

> Already had an interview for that, but the guy's dick tasted rank.

> NOT AT ALL FUCKING FUNNY!

Why, why, why are we having this conversation through WhatsApp? I really want to see his face right now.

> You started it. Hey, when you look at me, do you see Head Chef?

> Can you cook?

> Not really. That's why we usually get pizza or go out.

> Be prepared for rejection.

Once I've finished messaging Rocco, I head downstairs because I can hear *Catfish* on TV. We all love that show, even Dad. Mum and Livvy are home now, sitting on the sofa with Dad. I drop down on the single seat near it.

The girl on the screen has been talking to this dude for *five* years, and he makes excuses every time she asks to meet.

You're obviously being catfished, you moron!

I'm sorry, but anyone who talks to someone on a computer for five years can also work a web chat.

Livvy glances at me and gives me a fleeting smile. My phone beeps, and she looks at it like it's a discarded bag in an airport.

"You okay, Liv?"

"Mmhmm." Her eyebrows rise with interest. "Who's texting you?"

Translation one: I didn't know you had friends. Translation two: Who are you shagging?

"A friend," I reply.

"Oh, yeah?" Mum says, suddenly interested.

This gets Dad's attention, too, and I know the game is up. They'll never believe I'm constantly texting a *friend*. Firstly, I don't like talking to people at the best of times, and secondly, I don't really have friends.

Bugger.

"Who is he then?" Dad asks.

His back has straightened, and he looks ready to tear Rocco apart. He'll be even more ready when he meets him. Rocco's physique is a billion miles away from Harry's scrawny body. And Rocco's older.

They don't like me and Livvy knowing people who they've not met. Celia was killed by a stranger. Possibly not a stranger to Celia though if I'm right about Hugo.

"He's no one."

"Isabella," Dad warns.

I roll my eyes. Pretending is not going to get me anywhere. "Fine. His name is Rocco."

"Rocco," Mum repeats.

I know she's picturing either a tattooed biker or a coke addict. If I didn't care about things working with Rocco, I'd indulge in that a little.

"Yes."

"Well, what's his surname, how old is he, where does he live, and what does he do for a living?" Dad asks, sitting up even more. Any further, and he'll go straight over and face-plant on the floor.

"Twenty-two. Not too far away." *And I don't know his damn surname!*

And I say what to the career question? Illegal street fighter isn't going to cut it here even if he is undefeated.

"Do you have a picture?" Livvy asks.

Oh, I have many. Most of them are in my Photo Vault app, never to be seen by anyone else. I bite my lip. Since our first flirty sext, Rocco sent me a few naked pictures, too.

"Sure," I say.

They can see a safe one from the regular photo album. I get up a recent one of me and him together. He's really not into having pictures taken, not that I let that stop me, but on this one, he's smiling and holding me close. Makes a nice change to me catching his middle finger.

"Whoa," Livvy says. Her eyebrows shoot up, and her eyes widen.

I'm not sure if I should be insulted or not. *Did she think the best I could do was an ogre?*

"Bells, he's well nice."

"Yep," I reply.

I'm very aware of Rocco's good looks and the muscles on that body that'd make Hercules weep.

I'm such a lucky bitch.

"Hand it over," Mum says, eagerly reaching out for the phone. Her fingers wriggle impatiently, as she is desperate to see the guy her daughter is shagging.

I won't bring up that part.

Dad's mouth is pressed into a grim line. This is hard for him.

He gave that look to Celia when she kept going out, giving them lies in response to, "Where are you going?" and constantly stressing them.

I hate that I'm doing the same thing. They'll understand when this is all over though.

"He looks very nice, Bella. When can we meet him?" she asks.

I go to laugh but catch myself before. *How about never?*

"We're really not at the meeting-each-other's-family stage, Mum."

Dad scowls. "Isabella, if you are seeing someone, we want to know who it is. All I know about this person is that he's four years older than you." He said *person* like it's a dirty word.

Dad instantly hates boys. There's no first chance with him. They have to win him over so that he'll give them a second one.

He also knows Rocco's name, too. I don't bring it up because it'd be a dick move, and it would only aggravate him.

"Your dad's right," Mum says, siding with him. "Is there a particular reason you don't want us to meet him? Or does he not want to meet us?"

I look to Livvy to help.

"We haven't discussed meeting anyone yet; that's all. It's still in the early days."

Not that it means anything to my parents.

"We're not going to become emotionally involved in your relationship, Isabella. If you two don't work out, it won't be a problem here," Dad says.

"Yeah, thanks."

"That's not how I meant it, and you know it."

I know they would hate to see me upset, but, bloody hell, he could've put it a little better.

"If you're going to be leaving this house to see him, we need to meet him." Dad uses his no-nonsense tone.

His dark eyebrows knit together, and his jaw clenches. He looks like a strict head teacher, and I feel like a misbehaving student.

I haven't even done anything wrong!

"Fine," I concede. "I'll see if he can come over sometime."

"Tomorrow. You'll invite him for lunch tomorrow," Dad demands.

This is why I don't like authority. Except when I'm all needy and Rocco is ordering me around. Then, I like it a lot.

Livvy gives me a sympathetic smile. "I'll invite Harry, too. I'm sure they'll get along."

Yeah, she really doesn't know Rocco.

"Sounds good," I reply.

In reality, nothing has ever sounded worse. I am intrigued though. I wonder what his reaction is going to be when I tell him that he's coming over for lunch. It's almost worth it.

"I'm going to my room," I say in defeat.

"Make sure you call him!" Dad shouts when I'm halfway up the stairs.

I don't bother to reply. There is nothing nice I want to say right now.

I dial Rocco's number and sit on my bed. My door is shut, and I flick the TV on just in case one of them decides to listen in.

"Hey," he says gruffly, answering just before it went through to voice mail.

"My parents want you to come to lunch tomorrow."

Better to rip the plaster off.

"What? Bella, what the fuck?"

I can see how he was taken off guard, but he's usually a bit more together, even with surprises.

He's going to say no.

I mean, I want him to decline, but my parents are not going to like it. I'm too tired for that argument today.

I groan. "They kept asking who was texting me."

"And you told them?"

"I tried to lie! They guessed."

"And, now, they want to meet."

"Pretty much," I say, chewing on my lip.

"Fuck's sake. Fine!"

I wish I were there to see his grumpy face. I love it when he gets like that. I love it more just after—when he pounces and we have pissed off sex.

"Come over now," he demands.

His voice is rougher than usual and does things to my insides that makes me wish I were already there.

"You're not off, being busy and important?" I tease, meaning bloody street fighting.

That's the one thing I hate about him. He can be cocky and sure of himself when it comes to winning, but there are no guarantees. One bad punch, and it's all over. He could lose more than his pride.

I can't lose him.

"Just hurry the fuck up." He hangs up.

I laugh. Such a smooth talker.

Someone knocks on my door and opens it before I have a chance to say anything. I could have been changing in here.

"Hey," Livvy says. "Can I come in?"

"You're already in."

Rolling her eyes, she walks across the floor and sits on my bed. "You okay?"

"Yeah, I'm good. Dad's going to make tomorrow real awkward, isn't he?"

"Oh, yes. Remember how he questioned Harry?"

I do remember. That was a fun evening. Completely different now that I'll be the one going through it. I did not have nearly enough compassion for Livvy that day.

"Perfect," I mutter sarcastically.

"Are you worried that Rocco can't handle it?"

I do laugh at that. There's not much he can't handle, if anything.

"Nope. He'll be fine. He doesn't scare easy."

The guy voluntarily enters into fights where the *only* rule is *no weapons*. I can't see a middle-aged couple making him quiver.

"Well, that's good then. If you get anything from tomorrow, Bella, it'll be the knowledge that he really wants to be with you. If a guy can make it through the first meeting with Dad and then still wants to be around, you know it's love."

I already know that.

"I'm going to need a lot of wine," I say, bending my head and groaning into my hands.

"Have you called him yet?"

"Yep." Sitting up straight, I smirk. "I've never seen him flustered before."

"I can't believe you never told me about him. How long have you been together?"

"A few months."

I'm not going to address the first part of that. Why would I have told her? We're not close. It's not worth going there though.

Livvy claps. "What's he like?"

"Intense," I reply with a smile.

"What else?"

Sighing, I look up and wonder why the fuck I didn't think of a decent lie. "You'll find out for yourself tomorrow."

Shit.

THIRTY-FOUR

ROCCO

I've never met the parents before, and I don't particularly want to now. They're not going to approve of their eighteen-year-old daughter being with the twenty-two-year-old fuckup from the dodgy side of town.

It's a good thing I don't give a shit about what anyone thinks.

"You look nervous," Bella says as we walk along the path to her house.

Yeah, well, I feel like I'm walking the plank.

But I can't tell her that.

"I'm not."

If her parents hate me, it's no skin off my nose. Bella isn't the type of girl to ditch someone because of another person's opinion, so I have nothing to worry about there. *Right?* I need to believe that.

"Okay, okay."

"Are you going to knock on your own door?" I ask.

She looks up at the fuck-off huge solid wooden door.

"Bella, are *you* nervous?"

"Fuck off, Rocco," she snaps, reaching into her bag for the key.

"No, wait." I grip her wrist before she can open the door. "Why are you still worried about this? If they hate me, will it change anything for you?"

"No," she replies.

"Then, where's the problem?"

"Nowhere," she replies.

Fuck.

Every time we have these stupid arguments, I want to bang her brains out and strangle her at the same time.

"Isabella, tell me."

"Ooh, you pulled out the full name." She rolls her eyes. "Fine. Not only is it a big step, but it's also a first for me. Livvy has her long-term dickhead boyfriend, and I've never brought anyone home before."

"Why is her boyfriend a dickhead again?"

"Ah, you will see soon enough. Let's get this over with. I'm staying at yours tonight." She sounds sure, but she looks bloody terrified.

Tugging on my hoodie, she pulls me in close.

"You know you're welcome to sleep with me anytime."

"Don't you mean, *stay* with me?"

"No," I say, shaking my head. "No, I really don't think I do."

"Your brain is in your penis."

She lets me go, and I take a breath.

Showtime.

Bella unlocks her front door. A door that is attached to an impressive house. She said her family lived in a modest home, not some mansion. Or mansion to me. My whole flat is about one-twentieth of the size of this.

Taking a deep breath, she shoves the door open and tugs me into a grand entrance hall, which actually is the fucking size of my flat.

Jesus.

Maybe they're not rich, but they're certainly not living month to month.

"Mum, Dad," Bella calls out.

I wasn't stressing about this meeting because I knew it wouldn't matter to her whether they liked me or not, but I fucking am now. I don't have a steady job, and what I do for money is hardly going to be welcomed by her family.

Four of them slide around the corner from what I assume is the kitchen since it has tiled flooring.

Bella is an almost perfect mix of her parents, but I can see more of her mum. Her sister obviously looks similar, but there's no mistaking the differences between the twins—and the fact that I've got the pretty one. The guy behind Livvy must be Harry, the dickhead boyfriend, who Bella hates.

"Rocco, these are my parents, Karl and Erin. That's Livvy and her boyfriend, Harry."

Her dad looks me up and down, his expression hard.

Her mum is much more welcoming. "It's lovely to finally meet you, Rocco. We've heard so much…and it's all good, I promise."

Yeah, Bella's not likely to tell you the bad.

"Good to meet you, too."

She's told me the bare minimum about you.

Livvy steps closer. "Thanks for coming, Rocco. I wasn't sure if Bells would share you with us when we asked."

Bells?

"Are we going to stand in the hallway all afternoon?" Bella asks sarcastically.

I see why she's got a reputation as the difficult twin.

Erin's mouth thins, but she moves back. "Come through. I'll put the kettle on. Would you like a tea or coffee, Rocco?"

"Or something cold?" Livvy adds.

I don't know her, but she seems too nice. I don't like too nice. I like Bella and her bratty mouth.

"He likes coffee," Bella answers for me. "Rocco, sit." She tugs me to one of the eight stools around a long granite breakfast bar. It looks like it has flecks of gold melted into it.

"You cool?" I ask her, keeping my voice low so that no one else can hear.

She gives me a side-glance that screams, *Fuck off.*

Not sure what I've done, but I'm enjoying it. I love her when she's mad.

"So…Rocco," Karl says, trying my name like he's not sure it's even a real word, "what do you do for work?"

Illegal fighting and the occasional car theft.

"I work at a friend's garage."

Out of the corner of my eye, I see Bella raise her eyebrow. *What did she expect me to say?*

"Ah, I might have to get you to look at my car—"

"Really, Dad!" Bella cries.

"It's fine, Bells," I reply, purposefully goading her by using the nickname Livvy called her.

It works. Her eyes turn cold as steel, and I hold back a laugh.

Karl continues his list of questions, "Where do you live, Rocco?"

"Baker Street."

He and Erin exchange a look that I know all-too well from telling an outsider where I live. I've managed to screw this up in less than five minutes. I'll never be good enough for their daughter.

"It's a nice place, Dad," Bella says, seeing her father's disapproval. "It's right between a brothel and a crack den."

What the fuck?

Coughing on a dry throat, I open my mouth to protest, but I don't really know what to say.

"Isabella!" Livvy gasps.

My fucking idiotic girl rolls her eyes. "Clearly, I'm joking. But I can see the judgment, and it kinda sucks."

Fuck. Awkward doesn't even cut it.

I laugh even though there's nothing funny here. I want to bolt for the door. "Bella, baby, what're you doing?"

She shrugs and looks away.

I knew she didn't have the best relationship with her parents and sister, but I didn't think it was this bad.

Bella seems angry with them, and I have no idea why.

Erin puts my coffee in front of me.

"Thank you," I say, seriously considering pouring the whole thing over my head.

Why did I think this would be a good idea again?

I'm better off as a loner, but there was absolutely nothing I could do about Bella. She exploded into my life, and there is no way she's going anywhere, but I didn't have to involve more people.

"Thanks, Mum," Bella mutters, looking at her coffee like she's up for joining me in scalding my face. She bites her lip, avoiding everyone.

She's supposed to be the buffer, the person talking to everyone to prevent uncomfortable silences.

Step it up, Bella.

Karl clears his throat. "Are you hungry, Rocco? Erin makes a mean roast beef."

"Ew, did you really just use the word *mean*?" Livvy says, laughing at her dad.

Harry joins in and puts his arm around her. I feel like they should be wearing matching trousers and sweatshirts around their necks.

"Hey, I'm still young, I'll have you know."

"Roast beef is one of my favourites," I reply.

Erin smiles. "Good. Bella said you liked it, and I'm glad to hear she wasn't just having me on."

Why does Erin think Bella would lie about that?

Bella rolls her eyes and looks at me for help.

What the hell happened?

It's almost like Bella is a stranger here, too.

I want to know why.

Was it because of Celia's death?

Whatever it is, Bella seems almost uncomfortable around her family, and I want to help.

THIRTY-FIVE

ROCCO

Bella gives her parents a tight, awkward smile and turns to me. "I'm going to show Rocco around in a minute." She gives me a side-glance and mouths, *Drink up.*

I do as I was told because I have a lot of questions, and she's going to answer them. Or I'm going to ask a lot, she's going to avoid, we'll argue, and then we'll have make-up sex.

I'm fine with either.

Actually, I prefer the latter.

We leave the living room, and Bella stops near the stairs to feed two fucking goldfish in a bowl on the windowsill. I didn't know she had fish.

"They yours?" I ask.

She nods while dropping a small amount of food into the water. "Uh-huh. Ben and Jerry."

Of course.

Harry and Livvy hover close behind us. I don't look at them—my focus is on Bella—but I make sure I can see them in the corner of my eye. They're not going to do anything, but the part of me that knows the dangers of turning your back on someone needs them in sight.

"So, Rocco, are you at uni or…" Harry asks, knowing full fucking well I'm not.

"No, uni isn't for me." Mainly because I never finished high school, and universities are very judgmental over that shit. Plus, I'd hate it.

He nods his head. "That's a shame. We can't wait, right, Liv?"

Fuck me, this guy is boring.

Bella lifts her eyebrow, and, yeah, I know what she means. Harry's dull, a bit of a Mr Perfect. If Livvy weren't so similar to Harry, his future wife would cheat on him and lie about the paternity of their children.

"Harry and I are going in September. Hopefully, Bella will decide to go, too."

"God," she groans. "I'll fail at uni."

"No, you won't. Why do you think that?" I ask.

For someone so cocky, she doesn't have the healthiest opinion of herself.

Grinning, she shrugs. "Because I already can't be bothered to do the work."

I chuckle, despite suspecting there's a lot more to it than that. "Yeah, they don't like that. You can do it though, and you know that."

"Whatever. Let me give you the tour."

I look back at her parents still in the living room, whispering to each other. "Er…"

Erin looks up and smiles. "Go, please. We'll call you when lunch is ready."

Bella waves at her mum over her shoulder without looking back, and we head up the stairs. I have a feeling this tour is just going to be of her room.

I'm very okay with that.

"Okay, who has a roast for lunch?" I ask once we're upstairs.

"Ugh, my family when they're trying to impress."

"I wonder what they would've made if they'd known where I lived in advance."

Snorting, she rolls her eyes. "Cheese sandwich and possibly crisps if they were feeling generous."

"They hate me already, don't they?"

"They don't hate you. Even if they do, I really don't care."

Yeah, I know she doesn't.

We stop outside a door.

"This room is mine. Celia's is at the end."

"Which one we going in?"

She hesitates a second before replying, "Mine. I don't go in hers when they're home."

"Why not?"

"They never go in."

"Are you not allowed?"

"They've never said not to. It's kind of an unspoken rule."

"That you break?"

She looks up and grins. "Yeah. Quite often actually."

Just like sneaking out and falling for a guy from the wrong side of the tracks. No wonder she thinks they prefer Livvy.

I walk into her room, and it's just as I imagined. Pale green walls, band posters everywhere, notebooks and sketchpads stacked on an overflowing desk, massive bed literally in the middle of the room.

"The bed?"

"It's a thing you sleep in."

I stare at her. "Hilarious. Odd place for it."

"Yeah, I moved it out to paint and then kind of liked it. Mum and Livvy said it was ridiculous, so I kept it there."

I'm not surprised.

"Do you like it there?"

She narrows her eyes. "No, it's ridiculous."

Laughing, I shake my head. "You're impossible."

"So I've heard. We don't have long until lunch."

I step closer. "And what would you like to do while we wait?"

"Don't be coy, Rocco. It doesn't suit you."

I dig my fingers into her hips and pull her against me. Gasping, she hits my chest and runs her hands up my body and around my neck. I love how quickly she catches on.

"But what if my parents hear?" she whispers.

From the mischievous light in her eyes, it's obvious she doesn't give a shit about who hears.

"You'll have to exercise self-control and be quiet."

"I don't like being quiet."

"Believe me, I've noticed."

Someone knocks on Bella's door, and she pulls away from me, glaring.

"What?" she snaps.

"Can we come in?" Livvy asks.

Is she fucking serious?

I shake my head, but Bella's already taking a step back and telling them to come right in.

Livvy's smiling when she opens the door, and Harry follows her like a good little puppy dog. I wanted to make Bella come, not make small talk with her sister.

"Do you support a team?" Harry asks.

Shrugging, I sit on Bella's bed. "No, not really."

"Ah, Livvy and I are huge Manchester United fans."

We live nowhere near Manchester, but all right.

Livvy sits on Harry's lap once he's settled on Bella's desk chair.

Bella slumps down beside me.

"Bells hates football, too," Livvy says. "It's really is lovely to meet you, Rocco. My sister seems happy again."

When she said *again*, it felt like she meant that Bella's not been happy in a long time. I know she's stuck in her obsession with finding Celia's killer, but surely, she's been happy at times since her sister died.

"I am in the room, Liv!" Bella exclaims.

"I know. I'm just saying, it's nice to see you happy, and I want nothing more than for you to move on and start living. Celia would have wanted that, too."

Bella tenses, dipping her head. If only Livvy knew just how much *Bells* hasn't moved on.

"Leave it, Olivia. I'm fine. I've always been fine."

"Hey, she's not attacking you," Harry cuts in.

I give him a look that people back home know means that they need to stop what they're doing or run fucking fast. Bella tucks herself into my side when I wrap my arm around her. I think I'd rather talk about football again.

"How long have you two been together?" I ask.

They act like it's been fifty years.

Livvy beams. "Four years."

"It seems like forever though, right, Liv?" Harry turns to us. "We have our differences, but we never really argue. Not for long anyway."

I laugh until I realise he's being serious. Bella rolls her eyes.

"Jesus, Bella picks a fight at least three times a day."

"I do not pick fights! It is not my fault that you're unreasonable."

Raising my eyebrow, I tilt my head her way. "Oh, come on. You love fighting."

"So do you."

Grinning, I dip my head and press against hers. "Maybe a little."

"I'm kinda wishing I hadn't let them in now," she whispers.

"I don't need to say I told you so."

Harry and Livvy can probably hear, but neither of us cares.

"Lunch!" Erin shouts from downstairs.

Livvy and Harry leave first, and I suddenly don't want to get up. Eating with her family and getting to know them seemed like a good idea, but now, I'm not sure. I don't do this shit.

Bella gets to her feet, and I force myself to follow.

What am I supposed to talk to them about? I can't tell them the truth about myself.

"Just keep smiling," Bella mutters, looking at me over her shoulder as we go downstairs.

That's hardly encouraging.

My girl leads me into the dining room, which is three times the size of my kitchen and living room, and we sit down. Bella's dad is already sitting at the head of the table, and her mum is fussing over serving plates of food that could feed about twenty people. Harry and Livvy are opposite me and Bella.

This scenario is a million miles away from anything I've ever experienced. The only time I eat at a table is if I go out with Bella or Ellis. My mum bought food but never served it.

"This all looks amazing," I say.

"I hope you enjoy it," Erin replies. "Dig in, please."

Bella reaches for the plate of sliced beef. She drops one on her plate and then a couple on mine. The rest of her family and Harry start helping themselves. I pick up the massive bowl of mashed potatoes.

This is all fucking weird.

"Where did you and Bella meet?"

"The café Nan and Grandad take us to," Bella says. She looks from her mum to me.

I'm sure as shit not going to correct her. Erin and Karl wouldn't like knowing the truth—that their daughter showed up in a rough part of town alone and at night.

Erin sits a little taller. "Have you met my parents, Rocco?"

"I haven't." Not properly anyway, we didn't speak at the café.

Bella takes the bowl of mash from me. "I was alone, Mum. You're not the last ones to meet him."

"What's your plan then, Rocco?" Livvy asks.

"My plan?"

Bella rolls her eyes. "Livvy loves a plan."

"Right," I say. "No plan yet."

"Well, that's okay," Livvy says.

I know it is.

"You know, I so admire people who kind of go with the flow. Bella is like that. She's happy to take things as they come. I wish I were a little more like that."

I don't miss the look Harry gives her. The prick doesn't want Livvy to be more like Bella. I dare him to say it.

"Liv, you've planned your outfits for the rest of the week. You'd be lost without your lists," Bella says.

"You could do with planning a bit more, Isabella," Erin says.

Is this about her life after she's finished sixth form?

She's done with her exams and school. Soon she will get her A-Level results, and she will be forced to do something. I don't care what she decides, but her parents sure do.

"Yeah, yeah," Bella mutters, loading some vegetables onto her plate. "I'm going to stay at Nan and Grandad's tonight."

Erin raises her eyebrow. "Is that code for, *I'm staying with Rocco?*"

Shit.

I pour some gravy over my plate and ignore Erin's comment.

Bella doesn't. "Are you saying you won't lose your shit if I stay at his?"

"Language, Isabella," Karl scolds. "We appreciate that you're eighteen, but tonight, you need to stay home."

I cut her a look that says, *Shut up*, and to my absolute shock, she does.

I'm not bothered if her parents don't like me, but it would be easier on Bella if they did. It's not unreasonable that they want to get to know me more before they're comfortable with their daughter being with me. Besides, she sneaks away to stay at mine anyway.

"Why?"

"You know why," Erin says quietly. She avoids looking Bella in the eye and instead cuts into a slice of beef.

I don't know why. Is anyone going to tell me?

Bella sighs. "Fine."

I carefully watch her, hoping this will be one of the rare occasions where I can read her. Nope.

Why can't she go out? She's a fucking adult!

The rest of lunch is awkward and seems to drag on forever. Bella barely says another word to her parents, and I spend the hour answering a few questions and desperately trying to think of things to say.

THIRTY-SIX

BELLA

Rocco's car disappears out of sight, and I know, as soon as I go back inside, my family is going to say things. They don't think we're better than anyone else, but they definitely won't like that I'm with a bad boy.

I bet Mum calls him that at some point.

"Isabella, kitchen!" Dad shouts.

"What's up?" I ask, walking into the room and pretending like I don't know what's going on.

They're going to be shitty about him, and I'm already pissed off about it.

"Rocco seems like a nice person, love, and we know you like him, but I'm not sure he's right for you," Mum says.

"He doesn't really live near a brothel." *I think.*

"Isabella, be serious."

"Fine. You don't think he's right, but I'm eighteen, an adult, and it's not actually any of your business."

"You're our teenage daughter, living under our roof, so it's entirely our business," Dad chimes in.

"Well, there's nothing we can do about me being a teenager or your daughter, but I can move out."

Dad folds his arms. "And go where?"

"Rocco's."

Mum's eyes widen, knowing I'm bloody stubborn enough to do it if they force my hand. I might well be living in their house, but that doesn't give them the right to control who I'm with or be a dick to him.

"Let's all calm down a minute. Isabella, we're not telling you what you can or cannot do. We're merely raising an issue," Mum says.

"What's the issue with him then? Because he was perfectly polite, and he's never done anything wrong. Do you honestly think I would be with him if he didn't treat me right?"

"You've always liked a bad boy."

Ding, ding, ding.

"But you're not going to want one forever, and you have university to think of," Mum says.

"I don't want uni, Mum. I'm sure you know that by now. Rocco won't be influencing my decision either way, but just so you know, he's on your side of the argument. And I'm not going to listen to him either."

Dad shakes his head. I know he's found it hard to deal with me growing up, so he pretty much leaves me to my own devices unless it's absolutely necessary.

God, I turn into a five-year-old when I'm around my family.

They make me angry most of the time. I don't remember being angry before Celia died, but after she was gone, everything inside me changed.

Do I blame my parents for her death, too? I certainly blame myself.

It wasn't their fault, but I can't help thinking that, if they'd just come inside with me…

"Where do you think you'll be if you don't go?" Dad asks.

"There are plenty of successful people who didn't go to uni. Do you really think Richard Branson is sitting on his private island right now, wishing he'd gone to Cambridge?"

"Don't have a dig at Cambridge just because Livvy is going there," Mum snaps.

Jesus, she's crazy.

"Oh my God. You know what I meant, and this has nothing to do with Liv."

"So, you're not jealous of—"

I click my fingers, effectively cutting her off. "Don't even go there. I'm *really* not jealous of her life. I want her to go to Cambridge and do whatever else she wants, but you have to stop comparing us. You have the same goals for us both, and it's unrealistic."

Stomping off, I head to my room.

I'm so done.

———————

"Are you seeing Rocco again today?" Mum asks as I walk into the kitchen in the morning.

When I see her, my anger is renewed and burning in my stomach. She pushes a coffee toward me like it's a white flag.

"Yes. Why?"

She licks her lips. "I'm concerned; that's all."

"About?"

I know what about, but if she's going to be difficult about me being with Rocco, she can bloody well come out and say it.

"His age. His lifestyle."

"He's four years older than me, and he fixes cars for a living."

Well, he kind of helps Ellis fix cars…when he's not fighting.

Best not to mention that.

"You're about to go to university."

Did we not have this conversation yesterday? Because I seem to remember telling her I'm not going. Does she have amnesia?

"I'm not going, Mum."

"Isabella," she huffs on an exasperated sigh. "You have to go to university. You're only eighteen. In a few months' or years' time, you might not be with Rocco, and you'll regret this decision."

I roll my eyes because this conversation is old. "Mum, seriously, my decision has nothing to do with Rocco. Before I even met him, I knew I wasn't going."

Her jaw tightens. She brushes her shiny hair over her shoulders. "You're making a huge mistake. What will you do?"

"I don't know. Get a full-time job, I suppose. Dad has already spoken to me about it."

"Oh, brilliant, Isabella. You have so much potential, and you're throwing it away for a man you barely know. I don't understand why you can't see what you're doing," Mum says.

"I know exactly what I'm doing, thanks."

Whoa, massive lie.

I mean, I know the basics, but as far as having a plan goes, like Livvy, I'm walking around blind here. But I'm fine to go with the flow. If I never get into uni when all this stuff with Celia is over, it'll be all right. I'll make it work.

There's nothing wrong with going straight into a job.

Maybe I'll be Rocco's manager because I bet his cut of the fights is nothing compared to what the organisers get. I should suggest that to him just to see his reaction.

"Do you?" Dad mutters, walking into the room. He's been listening in then. His eyes glower, and his face is red as he tries to hold it together and not shout.

My parents aren't shouty people and believe talking is a better way of communicating and sorting out problems. They've always tried to drill that into me, Livvy, and Celia.

I bet they're kicking themselves right now.

"Just because I'm not following the path that *you* want doesn't mean my life is going to suck."

Mum sighs in frustration, being a bit dramatic, like I just said I'm moving to LA to pursue a singing career. I can't sing for shit.

"We're not trying to force you to follow in our footsteps, but we're older and wiser. You can't see the mistake you're making, but we can."

"But it's *my* mistake to make. I can't have you making all my decisions for me."

"That's not what we're trying to do," Dad says, backing Mum up.

"Then, back off a bit."

Mum practically growls. "We can't. You don't get it. You're not a parent."

Fuck's sake.

"Actually, I do get it. I'm not going to die like Celia did."

Mum looks away, taking a breath.

There. It's been said. I've finally addressed my parents' biggest fear and the reason we clash so much. I can't go out there and find my own way and make my own mistakes in case something bad happens to me like their eldest daughter.

"Is that..." Dad trails off, shaking his head. "We worry more—of course we do—but we're not trying to hold you back."

"Maybe it's not intentional, but even Livvy can't argue that you're OTT restrictive."

"We're not restricting you, Bella," Dad says, frowning, as he defends his and Mum's actions. "Everything we do is in your best interests and to protect you."

"I don't need protecting against Rocco. You've written him off already, and you've only spent a couple of hours with him."

"We're not here to argue with you, Isabella," Dad says.

I grit my teeth. "No, you're just here to try and tell me what to do. Keep pushing all you want, but I'm not giving him up. You're going to have to get used to the fact that you can't micromanage every aspect of my life."

With nothing more I can say without yelling at them, I dash out of the room and upstairs.

Fucking parents.

I dive in my room, slam my door for effect, and reach for my phone. Rocco was quite clearly uncomfortable during dinner with the judgmental stares and Harry looking down his nose at him.

I dial Rocco's number.

"You okay?" he asks, answering on the first ring.

"No. You?"

His chuckling down the phone puts a smile on my face, something I didn't think was possible right now.

"Still pissed off with the family, huh? Don't fall out with them on my account. We knew they wouldn't be thrilled."

"Not the point. My parents are so unreasonable. They don't know you, Rocco."

"They don't need to know me."

"Before they fucking judge you, they do! I'm so mad, I can barely look at them, and the longer I think about it, the angrier I get."

My hands shake, and I want to cry on his behalf. He's not bad. He's amazing, and I hate that they can't see that. They're not even willing to try. He deserves that much.

"Bella, calm down. There's nothing you can do right now. Unless…are you wound up because their opinion of me changes something for you?"

"Fuck off. You know it doesn't! Ugh! Why the hell are you even saying that?"

"Because it'd be understandable if it mattered to you."

"Okay, I'm going. Call me later when you've stopped being a dickhead about this."

"Come on, Bella, you don't—"

"Bye, Rocco." I hang up because I can't talk to him right now either.

The rational part of my brain is taking a break, and I know my reaction is over the top, but I'm pissed off. Getting my period very soon, too, so everyone can actually fuck off.

Rocco calls straight back, but I end the call and send him a quick message, asking for space until later. Of course we both knew that my parents wouldn't react well to me being with him, but we were supposed to be solid. When he asked if something had changed, he basically took a mallet to that and left behind cracks.

Rocco doesn't have a high opinion of himself, and I *hate* that. With the way they were acting toward him, it's like my parents were backing up his dumbarse theory that he wasn't worth much.

And I'm annoyed beyond words because a little part of me is hurt that they're not even trying to get to know him. I wasn't supposed to care what they think, but I do. It does matter.

THIRTY-SEVEN

BELLA

No one is at the river when I arrive, which is fine because I need some time to think. My parents are making it so hard for me to be at home right now. Their disapproval of Rocco has hit me surprisingly hard. I didn't know I cared what they thought.

The last few days have been tense, and Rocco and I haven't spoken a whole lot.

Rocco's name flashes up on my screen again. I tap End Call. He's pissed off that I'm letting my family come between us, and he's right, but it's not so easy to cut them off. We've argued over them, too.

I've spent so long pushing my parents away, so I didn't think I would want to hold on to them. My parents won't accept Rocco through fear of something happening to me. If it comes down to it, who will I choose? The question is in Rocco's eyes every time he looks at me. He would never ask though.

"Bella?"

I jump, leaping to my feet, as I realise I'm not alone. Well, that was a nice reminder to never let my guard down here. Thankfully, it's just Faith, and she's holding her hands up.

"I'm sorry. I didn't mean to scare you."

My heart starts to slow back to normal. "No, it's okay. I was in my own little world."

"Is everything all right?"

I look up to the sky and sigh heavily. My mind is spinning at a hundred miles an hour, trying to figure out what to do. "Not really, no."

"Bella, sit back down and talk to me. Maybe I can help you get some clarity."

Oh, I wish she could.

But I sit anyway because, at this point, I'm willing to try anything.

I look at her and smile. "My parents don't approve of Rocco, and it's putting a massive strain on my relationship with them both. I have no idea what to do. Losing any of them isn't an option."

"I'm sure it won't come down to that. Your parents are only worried, and that's understandable, given where you're each from. They don't want to lose you."

"No, they don't, but they seem determined to make me break up with him."

"I'm sorry, Bella."

I shrug. "It's fine. I'll figure it out."

"Can you bring them to Rocco's place, so they can see that it's not that bad? He's not too deep into this area that your parents' car would be jacked. Probably."

That's true. Rocco lives in the most decent part of the broken side of town, but it still wouldn't be good enough. I still worry about my car.

"I think what they're looking for is someone who lives a whole lot closer to me. My sister's boyfriend is perfect—*their* idea of perfect. He's definitely not mine. Anyway, they measure every guy against Harry, and Rocco will never live up to him in their eyes."

She raises her eyebrows. "Is he that great?"

"Wealthy family, A-star student, off to Cambridge University, and has the next fifty years planned out. Rocco doesn't have a conventional job, he dropped out of high school, and he doesn't plan what he's going to have for dinner that day."

"Does that bother you?"

"No, not in the slightest. I actually like it—besides the fighting part."

"Bella, your parents can have aspirations for you—that's normal—but the only person who gets a say in your life is you. I speak for everyone around here when I say, we've never seen Rocco so happy before. I don't want to see him barely existing again."

The thought makes me feel sick. I press my hand to my stomach. Imagining him lonely hurts.

I know how that feels. I'm constantly surrounded by family, but I've always felt alone.

"I don't want him barely existing either. I hate that he's gone so long, having nothing. What if my parents never accept him, and we have to do separate...everything? It'll be awkward, and I don't want to have two Christmases."

She looks at me like I'm crazy.

Am I overreacting?

Running her finger under her heavily lined eyes, she says, "I don't think it will come to that."

"Well, I hope not. I want him to be involved in my family stuff, like Harry is." I frown and add in a grumble, "He spends some of Christmas Day with us."

"Rocco will be spending Christmas with you, too."

Does Rocco even do Christmas?

I doubt it since he doesn't have any family, and I can't see him and Ellis exchanging gifts and pulling crackers.

What if he's never done it, even as a kid?

"Did you know Rocco's mum?" I ask.

If he's never celebrated any holidays, it will hurt me, but I want to know.

"I did."

"What was she like? I mean, was she ever sober? Did she ever give him normal childhood experiences?"

"She was lost in her addiction most of the time. As far as I know, she was too baked to do much with Rocco. I could be wrong though. I didn't know her that well."

"So, he had no Easter egg hunts, no summer holidays, no trick or treating, and no Christmases?"

Faith tilts her head, and her curly bob sways. She curiously watches me. "I don't think so."

My God, that is so sad. Every kid should have a happy childhood.

I wonder, if I do all those things for him, will he hate it? He'll probably hate it and think I'm crazy. But he always thinks I'm crazy, so…

"Oh," I reply soberly.

"He's a toughie, Bella. He's not damaged because of it."

"No, I know that. It's just hard to think of him as a kid missing out on so much."

"Well, now, he has you."

He does have me. I'm going to make sure he's so goddamn happy that it will erase his whole childhood. And, really, all I have to do is get naked.

"Can we talk about something different?"

With a smile, she replies, "Of course."

"Will you tell me more about what you do? You help people, right? All I hear about is how bad this place is, but you do good."

Her light-green eyes light up when I mention her work.

"We help, yeah. There are a lot of people in need and at-risk here, particularly teenage girls. The number of runaways is at an all-time high, and we do what we can for them. They can stay at the centre. It's not fancy, but it's a warm place to sleep. We do our best to help them find legitimate employment or get back into education."

"How do you fund that…if you don't mind me asking?"

"We own the building. We pay water, electric, and heating bills and rely heavily on fundraising for the rest."

"That's awesome that you're giving people a second chance. Everyone deserves that."

"I agree; they do. I grew up in this place, so I understand how hard it is to survive. Keith and I were never able to have children, but I consider every young person we help ours."

Wow, it's nice to hear that she's so passionate about helping people who need it the most. She's completely different to my parents; they're not willing to give Rocco a chance because of where he's from.

I'm not at all close to my parents, but right now, I've never felt so much distance between us. They're not doing it intentionally to hurt me, but everything they do keeps us apart. At no point in my life have I made a relationship between us easy, but neither have they.

I'm not sure if that can ever be fixed now; the cracks keep on growing.

"What are your parents like?" I ask Faith.

She shakes her head. "My mum could be a bit flaky from time to time, but overall she was great. My dad loved me and did what he could, but he was in and out of prison."

"Oh," I say, wishing I'd not asked. I sort of want to know what her dad did to land himself behind bars, but it's rude to ask. "Sorry."

"No, it's okay."

"Despite what I assume was a difficult childhood, you've done some real good. A lot of people use the past as an excuse to do bad."

Faith smiles. "Thank you. I tried to be stronger than that. I want to help people and perhaps prevent young women from going through some of the things I did. If you ever have some time to give, we can always use volunteers."

"Sure," I reply. "What do you need volunteers to do?"

"We've raised enough money to decorate the communal areas, but we need anyone who's handy with a paintbrush."

"Er, I'm not *handy*, but I'll definitely do what I can."

"You're one of the good ones, Bella. Do you mind me asking why you started coming around? It's unusual for someone who clearly lives in a nice area to be here."

Faith has such a kind, giving heart that she makes me want to spill everything. But that would be dumb as fuck since I don't really know her. Rocco already knows the truth about what happened with Celia.

"Well, like I said, I don't get along with my parents and sister much. I love my grandparents, but there's nothing going on where they live, just lots of old people! So, I started exploring, and my first night here, the first person I came across was Rocco. I don't believe in fate—there's too much bad for that—but I was definitely meant to find him."

She frowns, but her eyes light up. "You don't believe in fate?"

It's all bullshit.

"Nope. You do?"

"Oh, I definitely do. I think there are too many coincidences for them to be coincidences."

"We're going to have to agree to disagree here."

Faith laughs. "All right. Perhaps you'll change your mind one day."

That's unlikely. How, at sixteen, was it Celia's fate to be murdered?

"Anyway, what are you still doing here with me when you have a man who adores you living five minutes away?"

"You're right," I say, getting up. "Thank you for the chat."

"Anytime, Bella." Faith gets to her feet and hands me a scrap of paper. "This is the address of the centre. You are welcome whenever you like."

I take it and shove it in my pocket. "Thank you. Let me know when you need help there. I'd like to do something for you in return for letting me vent and making me feel a whole lot better."

"You're never in debt to me, but some help would be appreciated. Have a good night," she says before walking in the opposite direction of Rocco's place.

"Bye," I call out. Then, I power walk to my man's flat.

I'm done being mad at him now, and I just want to make up with him.

THIRTY-EIGHT

BELLA

After speaking with Faith, I spent the night with Rocco. For once, we ignored the elephant in our relationship and focused on each other. But I had to leave in the morning, and walking into my house made me feel so uncomfortable that I wanted to turn straight around again.

I'm in my bedroom, reading Celia's diary.

> *This bitch is sniffing around Hugo again, but he doesn't seem interested in her. I'm sure he's just worried what people will think about us because I'm supposedly a POSH GIRL. I don't care if my family is well-off. I want Hugo. Love doesn't care about money or social class! I just need to get Hugo to realise that we're perfect for each other.*

I drop the diary and shake my head with my hands over my face. *Oh, Celia.*

That's not the first time I've read that particular little entry either. I'm embarrassed for her still. Hugo must know something about what happened to her though. She obviously made herself known to him, and he's fully immersed in this world.

For Celia's sake, I hope he wondered what had happened to her when she stopped coming around. If he doesn't already know, that is.

Unable to take reading another word, I slip the diary under my cover and head downstairs. The house is quiet. Dad is already at work, but Mum has the day off today, so she must be around somewhere. Livvy is probably crying down the phone to Harry about how much she missed him overnight.

Mum is in the kitchen, drinking coffee. She looks up and smiles. Her lips are a light pink today, and it really suits her fair complexion. "Morning, darling. There's coffee in the pot." She's smirking since it's 11 a.m. so hardly early.

Oh, I'm already going there.

"Morning," I reply as I grab a mug from the cupboard. I pour the coffee in and take a gulp. It's fucking hot, and I wince, but it's so good.

"Are you free today?" Mum asks.

I freeze. *Oh God, she wants something.*

Lowering the mug from my mouth, I reply, "Yeah. Why?"

"I thought we could have a girls' lunch. Well, breakfast for you."

Shit, what's going on?

"Why?" I ask slowly.

"We haven't done it in so long," she replies. "Livvy will be there, too."

"*We* haven't done it ever."

Mum dips her head. "I would like to change that."

Is she trying now?

Her motives are suspicious, but if we can work something out and I can get rid of this constant little worry, then I'm all up for it.

"Okay…"

She smiles and stands up. Her hair and makeup are perfect, and she's wearing a red summer dress. I wish I cared enough about my appearance to think spending an hour a day wasn't a waste. I don't think I'm bad-looking, but I'm definitely not perfect like my mum.

"Great. Are you ready to leave now?"

I put my mug down. "Sure…"

"Stop making everything you say sound like a question. There is no need to be so wary. You're my daughter, and I want to take you to lunch."

I hold my hands up, still suspicious as fuck but whatever. "Sorry. I guess this is strange. Or new. New sounds better than strange."

Mum laughs. "Get in the car, Isabella."

I do as I was told because, frankly, I'm totally weirded out and wondering if there's some ulterior motive here. But, mostly, I want a relationship with my mum, so I'll give this a chance.

I go outside to get in Mum's car. It's summer and bloody hot today. I'm wearing jean shorts and a long vest with *Tom Hardy* written across it. Livvy looks a bit more like a proper grown-up in a floral skirt and white vest.

Mum drives, and while she talks to Livvy, I look out the window, not knowing what to say. Today is, I think, about getting closer and sorting out our differences, but right now, I'm just reminded of how little I have in common with both of them.

"We're here," Mum says, pulling into a parking space outside a cute little bistro in town.

"What are the portion sizes like?" I ask, getting out of the car.

Mum rolls her eyes with a smile. "They're decent. You won't leave hungry."

We walk across the car park and are halfway when I see something. Someone. A dark figure in the distance, looking my way.

What the hell?

Whoever he is, he's tall, and his shoulders are wide set. An old red phone box hides the left side of his body and makes it difficult to see him properly.

His dark hood is up, disguising his face.

303

The hairs on the back of my neck stand up, and I miss a step. If it's someone connected to Celia's killer, he's seen me with Mum and Livvy.

"I'm really looking forward to this," Mum says, drawing my attention.

I smile. "Me, too."

When I turn my head, he's gone.

That was fucking creepy. But, honestly, he could have been looking at anyone and anything. It's probably innocent. I'm getting more and more paranoid.

Calm down. It was nothing.

Livvy holds the door open, and we don't have to wait long before we're seated near the window. I pick up the menu and scan. It'll take me at least three times to properly read what they have.

Mum and Livvy have been here before, I think, as they've not even picked up their menus.

I glance out the window, but the person is gone. He was probably waiting for someone and found them.

Forget it.

Once we order our drinks, Livvy steers the conversation to her and Harry. She is animated, talking a hundred miles an hour about the flat she will be renting with Harry when they're at uni. She hasn't told me she backed down, despite not wanting to live with him the first year.

"Wait," I say, shaking my head. "When did you let him get his way?"

She tilts her head from Mum to me. "Don't start, Bella. Harry and I talked it through, and I'm happy to live with him now."

"You mean, he sweet-talked you, and you're too dumb to see through it."

"Isabella," Mum scolds.

"What? Come on, like you can't see what he's done, too. How are you not mad at him for making her change her plans? You taught us to be strong and independent, not to back down to any man."

"That's enough," Livvy hushes. "It's really none of your business. I'm perfectly happy with my choice, so get off the girl-power bandwagon and be supportive, like a normal sister does."

"Okay, fine."

"Plus, I really don't think you should judge."

Oh, she did not.

"Meaning?"

"Really? Your criminal boyfriend."

"He's not a criminal." *Kind of.* "Those charges were totally bogus, and the guy survived."

Mum's head snaps up, and Livvy's eyes bulge.

"Ha!" I point at her. "Kidding. Rocco's not a criminal...and he wouldn't even try to pressure me to live somewhere I didn't want to." *So, fuck you.*

"That's not funny, Isabella. We worry about you," Mum says.

"Well, don't. You have nothing to be concerned about with Rocco, okay? I really like him, and he feels the same, so I would love it if you could give him a chance before you wrote him off."

Livvy raises her eyebrow and says, "You kept him a secret from us after meeting him in one of the shittiest parts of town. What do you expect?"

"Language, Olivia," Mum scolds.

We both ignore her.

"I expect you to be nice and, like I just said, give him one chance. Everyone's given Harry a chance, and for all we know, he's using prostitutes behind your back."

"You're being a cow, Bella!" Livvy snaps.

"So are you! God, you're supposed to be the together, levelheaded one. You know you're being unreasonable."

She grits her teeth. "Tell you what. If you lay off Harry, I'll give Rocco a chance."

Ugh, really?

There are so many people I'd rather give a chance to, like Hans from *Frozen*. Technically, I have given Harry a chance before, so she's actually asking for a second one for him.

But I bite my tongue because, as much as I love to win a fight, I'm not dumb enough to not know which battles I should pick.

"All right, that seems fair." So, yeah, the words practically hurt, but it would be nice not to bicker with her all the time. About Harry and Rocco anyway. "Mum, what deal do I have to make with you?"

"My reservations can't be eradicated with a deal, Isabella. I don't know him, and that concerns me."

"Obviously, you don't know him because you're not willing to get to know him."

I bet she's still super glad she invited me along today. She and Livvy probably have lovely lunches together when they come alone.

Make more of an effort, Bella.

Mum's pink lips purse the way they do when she knows she's in the wrong. "That's a fair point, Isabella. Perhaps we have been too hasty in judging him. Do you think he would come to the fair with us tomorrow?"

"I wasn't even going to go, but I'm sure we can arrange something."

Since Celia died while Mum, Dad, and Livvy were all preoccupied at the summer fete, I've avoided things like that. Mum and Dad didn't go to any for a few years after, but when Livvy and I were around ten, they started going again. I've refused and stayed with my grandparents.

"Good. Now, can we please enjoy lunch?" Mum says, raising her eyebrows and looking between me and Livvy. "What are you both having?"

Livvy pushes her menu away. "I'm going for a chicken Caesar salad. Bella?"

"You're having a salad? We're at a restaurant."

Livvy rolls her eyes at me.

"Whatever. I'm going for a grilled chicken sandwich with chips and onion rings."

Mum laughs. "You've always had a healthy appetite."

That sounds an awful lot like, *You're fat*, but I'm not, and my mum would never call me that, so I let it go.

"I have Dad's metabolism."

"Are you definitely going to invite Rocco to the fair?" Livvy asks.

"Er, I will."

"It's tomorrow. You should give him some notice."

Why is she suddenly so interested?

I pull my phone out of my pocket and send him a message.

> Fair tomorrow with my family. You in?

> Fuck no!

I look up at Mum and Livvy and smile. "He's in."

> Awesome. They can't wait either.

> Do NOT agree to this, Isabella.

"That's great," Mum replies.

I can't quite tell if she's being sarcastic because she's shit at it.

> Surprise, too late. We're going to have so much fun!

> What the fuck is wrong with you? Have you lost your tiny mind?

> Love you, too! See you tonight.

> ISABELLA!

"Did you decide what you want, Mum?" I ask, ignoring my phone vibrating with another message from Rocco.

"The salmon, I think. Is that Rocco messaging you?"

I smile and put my phone back in my pocket. "Yeah, he's really looking forward to the fair."

She laughs again. "He's dreading it, isn't he?"

"Can you blame him?"

"No, I guess I can't. We didn't act properly when we first met him, and I'm sorry for that. Will you tell him that when you go there tonight?"

"I will. It's cool anyway. He doesn't hold a grudge."

My phone buzzes again. He's definitely not looking forward to this.

THIRTY-NINE

ROCCO

"I would rather boil my head than do this," I moan as we walk toward the entrance of the fair.

Bella's parents, Livvy, and Harry are meeting us by the Ferris wheel.

"I would rather take a bullet in my dick."

"Oh my God, will you shut up? You're like a little baby."

"I'm spending the night with four people who hate me."

"And one who loves you, so suck it up, buster."

I throw my arm around her shoulders, and she smiles.

"You'd better be *really* nice to me when we get home."

"And by nice to you, you really mean…"

"Nice to my dick." *God, please be nice to my dick.*

"Good thing you didn't shoot it off then," she says sarcastically, nudging my ribs.

"Ha-ha. Shit, there they are. Bella, are you sure you want to do this? I'll take you anywhere else you want."

"It'll be fine."

"*Anywhere.*"

"Grow a pair, Rocco."

"Fuck off, Bella."

She slaps my chest as we approach her family. Thankfully, they've not seen us yet. A few more seconds…

"Just act normal, and relax, will you? You're tense."

"These people make me tense."

"Grow up with them, and then come and talk to me." She hushes me as we reach them.

Her mum sees us first, and she's all smiles. "Rocco, I'm glad you made it."

"Me, too," I reply, holding on to Bella tighter.

Her dad shakes my hand. "I hope we can put our last meeting behind us and move on. You are important to our daughter, and we would really like it if we could all get along."

Bella looks up at me with fucking Bambi eyes.

"I'd do anything for her, so I'm willing to forget the past and move on."

That seems to please them. They exchange a look, and it's not, *Get this scummy wanker away from our daughter.*

"Are we going on the Ferris wheel?" Livvy asks. "Rocco, do you do rides?"

"I don't do fairs, but I'm up for this," I reply.

Bella smirks. "If you get scared, we'll get the man to stop."

I glare at her. "Thanks. I think I'll be okay."

"Well, just saying."

"Hey, after that, you can join me and their dad and see who can shoot down the most cans," Harry says. "It's tradition, and I always lose."

"Sure," I reply.

"Dad, prepare to have your arse kicked because Rocco is an awesome shot. He doesn't get paid as much when he misses."

"Isabella!" I snap, staring at her, open-mouthed.

Aren't we trying to get on and show her parents that I'm not a fucking criminal?

She starts to laugh and nudges my arm. I'm not laughing. And neither is her family.

"I'm not a hit man," I say, holding my hands up.

Her mum shakes her head. "We know that, Rocco. I'll never understand her humour."

"You're not the only one." I pull Bella closer and kiss the top of her head even though I want to strangle her right now.

This was her idea. I'm only here because she wants us all to be friendly and have Christmases or something together, yet she's cracking jokes like that.

We get on the ride. Thankfully, it's only two people to a car.

Bella lays her head on my shoulder. "I think it's going well," she says.

"Oh, do you? After that stunt, there's definitely time for it to go to hell."

"You know what? That's what I love about you the most—your upbeat, glass-half-full attitude. You should volunteer as an elf at the town's Father Christmas grotto."

"Sarcasm again. And it's your fault. *Why* would you joke to your parents about me shooting people? They already think I'm bad for you."

She sighs. "Rocco, you don't understand."

"Too right I don't. So, why don't you explain it to me?"

"It was funny."

"*That* is your explanation?"

"Why else would I have said it?"

Sighing, I rub my hands over my face. "God, you are fucking crazy. If I wasn't so in love with you, I'd throw you off this ride."

She tilts her head in my direction and smiles. "Aw, you love me."

"No more joking about me to your parents."

Smirking, she salutes. "Yes, sir."

Bella must be one of the most sarcastic people I know.

"I mean it, Bella. You're the one who wants this to work. I've never done the parent thing before, and it doesn't bother me if I don't see them."

"I know. I'm sorry. It means a lot that you're here and that you're willing to give them another chance."

"Thank you. But, if you think I'm wearing a fucking Christmas jumper and singing carols…"

"Wow, I would pay to see that."

"Not enough money in the world, babe."

I throw my arm over the back of the car, and she leans in, snuggling back against my side.

"Are you enjoying yourself so far? And, just so you know, if you say no, I'm jumping." The only reason I'm here is to make her happy.

"I am. Spending time with my family usually sucks big time, but this isn't painful at all. I like having you with me."

"If that was all you wanted, we could've gone to mine."

She looks up at me with a frown. "With my family?"

"Fuck no. We can never bring them to mine. Though I would like to see their faces when they walked in."

They'd have to take it in turns, as I genuinely don't think we'd all fit in the living room.

"One day. I'll film it."

"Bella!" Livvy shouts just as I'm about to lean in and kiss my girl.

Bella laughs at my frown and gives me a much quicker kiss than I was going for.

"What, Liv?"

"This is so cool. Do you remember doing this as kids? You would always rock the car and scare me."

"I remember," Bella replies, looking behind us to see Livvy.

"You like this ride then?"

She shrugs. "We were only allowed to go on the Ferris wheel for two years before Celia died. I did rock it a lot, and Livvy was such a bitch about it."

"It was probably the fear of you rocking too far and her falling to her death."

"Probably, the massive baby."

"You're not scared to die?" I ask. For some reason, I'm nervous to hear her reply. I want to hold her closer.

"No, not anymore," she replies in a quiet voice that slices through my heart.

Bella is willing to die for her cause.

How can her life mean so little? How can our relationship mean so little? Fuck.

"Mmhmm," I mutter, withdrawing.

We have to spend the entire evening with her family, and right now, I want to be alone.

"What?"

"Nothin'," I reply.

"Come on, Rocco, that's not your *nothing* face. Spill."

"No."

"*Please.* Did I say something wrong? Isn't it better not to fear death? I mean, no one is making it out of here alive."

I snap my teeth together in a bid to stop myself from saying something I might regret.

"Rocco, please. Jesus, you can't expect me to believe that you're scared of dying, so why are you making such a big deal out of this?"

"Maybe I changed my mind. I've never been scared of anything before, but…" I shake my head. There's no point. "Never mind."

"No, tell me. You can't get mad and then not tell me why. That's not fair."

"Fine." *Shit, am I really about to tell her this?* "I'm scared now, Bella. I could take anything, handle anything. Then, I met you, and suddenly, I'm fucking terrified. I'm scared that I'll lose you. I'm scared that you think so little of your own life that you'll lay it down for something that will ultimately change nothing. And I'm scared of how I feel about you because I've fallen in love with you. I'm still falling, and I can't stop. I can't even slow it down."

All right, I said too much.

"Rocco," Bella rasps. Tears fill her eyes, and she grips my hand, threading her fingers through mine. "I…I didn't know. God," she mutters, "I'm scared of not being with you, too. I love you so much, and nothing will ever compare."

There's still a *but*.

"Go on," I say.

"I don't know how to stop what I'm doing. How can I give up on something like that?"

"You just do. Look, I'm not asking you to stop looking, but I don't want you risking your life. I know you love your sister, but finding who murdered her isn't worth it."

She shakes her head. "That's not...God, stop confusing things! This was so simple before you."

"Right back at ya, Cinderella."

"Do you want to break up?" Her voice is quiet and unsure.

"Don't be so fucking melodramatic, Isabella. You make me want to put a bullet through my own head, but we're not temporary, all right?"

Giggling, she snuggles back in my side. "So, we make each other's lives more complicated and frustrating, but we're not ever breaking up. We would be perfect candidates for *The Jeremy Kyle Show.*"

"The what show?"

"TV, Rocco, watch it!"

"Are we ever going to make it off this stupid ride?"

We've only just gone over the top, and we're about to start back down again. It's still hot, and Bella is wearing shorts and a T-shirt, which is a win for me. Her legs are incredible.

She looks out at the view and sighs. "You can see the whole town."

I give her a look. "What the hell else did you expect?"

Her head snaps to me, and she glares those pretty eyes. "Yeah, you should do that shooting thing now...tosser."

When we get back down, Harry tells me that we should play the game where we have to shoot down the targets to win a crappy fire hazard of a stuffed animal.

"Let's do it," I say, picking up a gun.

Harry nods and grabs another one.

Karl gets his.

Before we can start, Bella grips my forearm and tugs.

"What?"

She pulls me closer and whispers, "Okay, dilemma." Her beautiful eyes are full of humour. "Do you shoot really well and beat my dad and Harry *or* let them win so that my family doesn't think you really are a hit man?"

"What part of you thinks I'm going to let anyone win?"

"Ah, that's what I thought. Kick their arses, and win me a huge stuffed Minion."

"Er, is that one of those big yellow things?"

She takes a deep breath. "TV, Rocco!"

I laugh.

"Are you sure you're ready for this?" Harry says.

Ten cans are stacked up on a shelf at the far end of the tent.

Bella leans against the stand where the guns are lying. "I want a Minion, baby."

"It's not coming home with us."

Her smile takes my breath away. I love the look she has whenever I refer to my place as ours.

Fucking hell, she is beautiful.

FORTY

BELLA

Harry goes after Dad's pitiful attempt of shooting down four. Harry gets five cans and grins triumphantly. I turn to Rocco, and the face I'm pulling is what I'm hoping looks like Puss in Boots from *Shrek*. Rocco rolls his eyes and holds up the gun.

Hello.

I never thought watching a man shoot a pretend gun would be so sexy.

FYI, it is.

He pulls the trigger in quick succession and knocks down eight.

"Yes!" I cheer, jumping up and down.

He hasn't won me a Minion because you have to get all ten down to get the big one.

"Well done, Rocco," Dad says, giving him a nod and smiling at me.

"You beat Dad!" Livvy sounds genuinely impressed.

I don't know what to make of that.

"Shall we move on to the ghost train?" I ask.

"I'll be sitting that one out," Mum says, walking off with Livvy.

Dad and Harry follow them.

I link arms with Rocco, and we make sure we're a little bit behind.

"Only eight, huh?"

He raises his eyebrow and smirks like I'm missing something.

"What?"

Chuckling, he pulls his arm away and wraps it around my waist. "I didn't really miss the last two."

"Huh? Yes, you did."

"No, I aimed to the side. I could have easily gotten them all, but I knew you would try and bring that fucking yellow teddy to my flat."

"Oh my God, you dickhead!"

Rocco full-on laughs and catches my arm as I swing my fist toward his chest.

"I'm offended you thought I missed two stationary cans."

I think Mum can hear our conversation because she looks behind and smiles.

See? He's not that bad.

Lowering my voice, I say to Rocco, "I think you're winning my mum over."

"It's hard not to fall for me eventually."

Cocky twat.

True though. We were inevitable.

"Oh, obviously."

"You don't really think I'm going on a ghost train, do you?"

"It's more manly than the Ferris wheel."

"I'm not biting, Bella."

Mum turns, slowing down so that she falls in line with me and Rocco.

Great.

We're so close to the ghost train. She had better be nice.

"I'm in no way telling you to ignore my daughter, but with Isabella, selective hearing is often required," she jokes.

Rocco chuckles. "Yeah, tell me about it."

Well, fabulous.

"You're so getting on that train," I say to him, narrowing my eyes.

I don't hear his reply because I see someone in the distance, watching me, staring like they're trying to kill me with a look. He or she is wearing a grey hoodie and dark jeans. My blood turns cold. When I turn to Rocco to get him to look, I see a flash as the person—probably more likely a male since the build is tall and broad—dashes off behind a stall, and then he is gone.

My heart is in my throat. I think I've seen this person before at the river, but I can't be sure. He was looking at me like we'd crossed paths before.

Who is he?

Rocco pulls me closer. "Bella? Hey, are you okay?"

I snap out of it and look around. Mum is concerned, and Rocco looks like he's about to kill someone. My lungs have deflated, but I force myself to look up.

"Sorry, I was in a complete daze there."

I add a smile for Mum's benefit, but when she looks away, satisfied that I'm okay, I widen my eyes at Rocco. He immediately knows I lied to Mum and that something is wrong.

Something is so wrong. I don't feel safe.

"Do you want to get something to eat instead of going on the ride?" he asks.

"Yeah, sounds good. Want anything, anyone?"

They decline, and Rocco and I walk off.

"What was that?" he asks as soon as we're out of earshot.

"Okay, the other day when I was out with Mum and Liv, I thought I saw someone watching me, but I figured I was just being paranoid. I saw him just now. I think at least. He was definitely wearing the same dark hoodie. I think I've seen him around the river."

Rocco tenses and stands taller. "What did he look like? Did you recognise him?"

"He was too far away. I don't even know if it's a he."

"What was he wearing?"

"Or she. Dark hoodie pulled up over his head. It's probably a guy, as he was tall and stocky."

"Where did he go?"

I point back toward the direction. "Behind the hot dog stall. He's probably long gone now." Grabbing Rocco's wrist to ground myself, I step closer. "I'm kinda scared here."

"Hey," he says, lifting my chin and smiling. "Nothing is going to happen to you. Not ever."

"Why are you happy?"

"Because you're worried."

What the fuck?

"Okay, *dick!* Uncool."

He shakes his head and does a sweep of the area. "No, I just mean that you're concerned about your safety. I like that."

Of course he does.

I never thought I'd be scared, and I don't know if that's just because there is no turning back now or because Rocco has given me something good to focus on.

Perhaps a little of both.

"Glad you're happy. What are we going to do about Greg Portman?"

"Who? You said you didn't know him," he asks.

Closing my eyes, I shake my head at myself. "Stalker in *The Bodyguard.* I really don't know why I thought you'd get it."

"I'll take you to your family, and then I'll do a quick sweep."

"But I want to come with you."

"Isabella," he says, sighing in exasperation.

"Fine, I'll stay with them. But we need to get doughnuts, or it'll look suspicious."

Rocco takes his wallet out of his pocket and grabs a five-pound note. "We'll take ten, please," he says, handing the guy behind the stall the money. "Anything else you want to do to waste time, so this guy can get away?"

"Um…" I purse my lips and pretend to think.

Rocco's eyes narrow.

"I think I'm good with the doughnuts, thanks." I give him my best smile, pretending I'm okay.

Rocco practically snatches the bag of doughnuts from the guy and grabs my hand. Before I can tell him to calm down, we're power walking back to my parents.

"I'm just going to find a toilet," Rocco says, giving me a look and handing over the bag.

Mum takes a doughnut I offer, even after she said no.

Rocco leaves, and she waits a few seconds before saying, "I'm glad you both came tonight."

"Me, too. I think Rocco is having a good time as well, despite this really not being his thing."

"I think he likes it because you do."

"Yeah, he has to; it's in the contract."

She laughs, and her eyes warm.

"So, you don't think he's too bad anymore?"

"We just don't know him, Isabella. Let's join your dad," she says.

We walk toward him at the other end of the ghost train. He's just hung up his phone.

We're almost there when someone bumps into me. I'm thrown a step and turn to confront the person.

I swear to God, if you try to run off without apologising…

"I'm so sorry. I didn't see you," the guy says. He holds his hands out and grimaces. His hair is blond and shaved close to his head, and he's really, really tall. No wonder he didn't see me from all the way up there. "I wasn't looking. Are you okay?"

"Yeah, I'm fine. I'm sorry, too."

"Hey, you didn't run into me. No need for you to apologise."

"I'm British, so…"

He laughs, nodding his head. "Well, again, sorry, and maybe I'll see you around…"

"Oh. Bella."

"Bella." He grins without telling me his name, and then he backs off.

I don't find it cute and mysterious that he didn't give me his name; it's rude and annoying. But he apologised.

"Okay?" Mum asks.

"Yep, I'm good."

Where is Rocco?

He's been gone ages. Or what feels like ages.

FORTY-ONE

ROCCO

The fair yesterday ended up being exactly what I thought it would be—a big fucking mistake. When I left to try and find the guy Bella thought was watching her, it all kicked off. I was gone fifteen minutes, scouring the whole damn field the fair was on, and her parents seemed to think that was me messing around.

We couldn't tell them why I was gone, but fifteen minutes was too long for a piss, so an accusation of cheating was thrown around. I don't know if I was more insulted that they thought I would ever look at another woman or that I could be done in fifteen minutes.

I couldn't find the guy she'd described, and she eventually calmed down and admitted that she had just felt spooked and that it could have been random. He might have been looking at someone else entirely. Fucking perfect.

She folds her arms. "I don't know what to do now. Mum apologised, but—"

"Your parents are unbelievable, Isabella!" I snap, slamming the kitchen cupboard.

Erin has just tried to call Bella again, but she cancelled the call and switched her phone to silent. It's currently lighting up with another phone call.

How fucking dare they assume shit just because I was longer than expected.

She sighs. "I know. I'm not exactly jumping for joy here either. Hey, do you think you could stop slamming things and pacing, so we can talk?"

"No," I growl.

I'm pissed off, and I want to fucking punch something.

Why can't I have a fight today? I would win big.

"Rocco," she pleads.

I close my eyes and take a breath and then another. "I'm sorry, Bella."

When I open them again, I see her eyes are filled with tears.

Jesus.

"You don't need to be sorry. They do. I don't want to go home."

"I don't want you to go home either, but you don't have much here, so you should pack a bag. I can make some space, not that my stuff is taking much room."

Her mouth stretches into a big smile. "Are you asking me to move in?"

"I don't see where else you're going to go."

"My grandparents'."

"Would you rather live with your grandparents?" I ask, calling her bluff.

"Maybe. They have Sky TV."

I roll my eyes. *Damn telly addict.*

"We can get Sky TV."

"Ah, you want me to live with you."

My God, she really thinks she's being cute when she's doing this shit. Never did I think I would have a relationship, but I always figured, if I did, it would be with someone easy. Isabella is the definition of difficult.

"Yes," I spit through my teeth, glowering at her.

"Aw. Well, since your proposition was so beautiful and heartfelt, how can I resist? I'll go to my parents' place tomorrow and pick up a few things. For tonight, I'll need to borrow a T-shirt for bed."

"You're not wearing anything in bed, and when you get up, you steal my clothes anyway."

"Yeah, and I kinda hate myself for that. I never wanted to be one of those women, you know?"

Shaking my head, I reply, "No, I really don't know."

I wonder what it's like to be her, to be inside her head twenty-four/seven. How fucking exhausting.

To think, in the beginning, I wanted to know her mind better. *How naive was I back then?*

"Well, it's dumb, and now, I'm one of them."

"Then, don't wear my T-shirts!" *Why is this even an issue?*

She pouts and bats her eyelids. "But I want to."

Don't kick her out. You love her. You love her, and you want her here.

Maybe as time passes, I'll get more used to the constant flow of crap that comes out of her mouth. Or I'll just learn to switch off to it.

Either of them will do.

"Isabella, I'm going to have a shower."

"Want a hand?" she asks mischievously, wiggling her eyebrows.

I walk off, but my body responds to an offer that I'm almost sure wasn't a joke, and I start to get hard. Stopping in my tracks, I shout over my shoulder, "Get your clothes off, Bella!"

Three months. That is how long I've known Bella for.

Shouldn't you take your first relationship slowly?

In three months, we've met and fallen in love, and today, she's moving in. That's fast, potentially too fast, but I have no experience of what an appropriate time line is. And I don't think she does either. So, fuck it.

We'll figure it all out as we go, or we'll kill each other. But dying together is considered romantic now, based on some of the shit Bella watches.

I'm going to have to put up with a lot more TV as well as the unstoppable talking of whatever random crap she's thinking at the time.

I can't bring myself to dread it. I want her with me permanently. In three months, she's become everything, and I love her so fucking much that, sometimes, I feel like I'm suffocating.

God, I've been watching too much of her shitty TV programmes, too.

Before I can go get a beer, because I need to do something manly, my doorbell rings.

"It's me, dickhead. Open up!" Ellis shouts.

I open the door. "What do you want?"

"She's moving in?"

"What? How do you know that?" I ask, moving aside, as he decides he's coming in.

I follow him into the kitchen where he opens my fridge and grabs two beers.

You read my mind, man.

"She called me."

He hands the beer over, and I almost drop it.

"She did what?"

"Don't have a heart attack," he replies. "You know she's only got eyes for you."

"Why are you two talking on the phone?"

"We're not allowed to be friends?"

I frown. "No."

Ellis laughs and drains about a quarter of the bottle. "Suck it up, buddy. You can't have her to yourself all the time. She told me her parents are dumb fucks, and now, she's living with you. What happened?"

"First time I met them, they made it clear that I wasn't good enough," I say.

"We know that. What else?"

I give him the middle finger and continue, "We all decided to give it another go, and long story short, they accused me of cheating on her. They want her to be with someone like her sister's boyfriend."

Ellis smirks. "Is he better than you?"

"I'm close to wrapping this bottle around your fucking head."

"No, you're not. Did you think meeting parents of a girl like Bella was going to go well?"

"Nope. Bella's not like her parents though—lucky for me. I don't know what's going to happen now. She can't cut them out of her life, despite how angry she is and what she says, but they're never going to approve."

"If they want a relationship with their daughter, they're going to have to learn how to back off."

"Her mum will, I'm sure, but I'm not convinced about her dad. He *really* doesn't like me."

"You are sleeping with his daughter."

"And that preppy prick is sleeping with his other one, but he's accepted him with open arms."

Ellis raises his eyebrow. "Ah, but you said it yourself, he's preppy. If you're really worried, you could pick up a few knit vests and—"

"Not happening!"

"Thought not. You're going to have to live with your bad boy rep and accept that her mummy and daddy will always think you're not good enough."

"I don't give a shit what they think of me."

"Well," he says, putting his beer down, "mark this date on the calendar. Rocco's in love, and he can only think of his girl. I'm proud of you, bro. It's a beautiful thing to see."

"You should go now."

"I don't think so." He picks his beer up and downs another quarter. "I want to talk about my problem now."

"Put cream on it."

He rolls his eyes. "Izzy wants us to be exclusive."

"So do you. Where's the problem?"

"Am I too young?"

"You're almost a year older than me. You've been fucking around with Izzy for years, and the girl I've known for three months is moving in with me. Fuck off."

"When you put it like that...hey, do you think maybe you and Bella are moving too fast?"

"Yes, but I don't care."

Putting the bottle down again, he runs his hands over his head and grips the back of his neck. "I thought it would be a long time before we had women troubles."

"Yeah, I thought it would be never."

"I thought you would be never. If it wasn't for the shagging around, I would've thought you were gay," he says.

"Whatever. Are you done yet?"

"I can't go, man. You only have a few hours of freedom left before you're *living* with your *girlfriend*."

I wonder how she's getting on at her parents' house. If they're in, they're going to freak out. They will try to convince her to stay. I don't think she will. She's committed to this as much as I am.

"And what do you think we're going to be doing? I'm not really gay, you know."

"Funny, dickhead. I thought we could go out of town a bit to Bleu."

"I'm not getting married, and I don't want to go to a strip club." And, since Bella, I've not wanted to look at another woman in that way.

"What're you saying? Everyone wants to go to a strip club."

Why won't he just leave?

"Ellis, I'm not going anywhere. If I want to see someone dancing around naked, I'll give Bella a drink." One, because that's all it takes.

"I don't think it's cute anymore—how loved up you are. Who's going to go there with me now? I love it at Bleu."

"There are plenty of single guys around here. And attached or married guys with little to no morals. You'll find someone, I promise."

"But I don't like any of them."

"You should stop talking to Bella. You're starting to sound like her."

"So…strip club?"

"Fucking hell, Ellis!"

Chuckling, he holds his hands up. "All right, I got it, you miserable fucker."

Good.

Hurry up, Bella.

"Besides, Izzy would have your balls if she found out."

Ellis frowns and takes a swig of beer. He's clearly struggling with his obvious feelings for her. Honestly, I never thought I would be happy to be with someone, but there is no comparison. The prick just needs to go for it.

"When's your next fight?" he asks, finally changing the subject.

"I don't know. Soon, if you don't stop being a dickhead."

"That's the second time you've threatened violence toward me tonight."

"Keep it up, and there will be a third," I say, smirking. "Right, we have a couple of hours, so I say we get fucked up on JD, and I kick your arse on the Xbox."

I might not watch TV, but I do occasionally kill people on the console.

FORTY-TWO

BELLA

When I get home—or rather, to my parents' house—
Mum's car is gone.

It's good they're not here because they wouldn't leave me
in peace to pack, but I do have to wait for them to get back
before I go. Leaving a note is a coward's way out, appealing
though. There is probably going to be more shouting.

I head straight for my room where I pack clothes, makeup,
toiletries, a hair dryer, and a phone charger. Anything else, I
can get another time.

I'm just zipping up my suitcase when Livvy walks into my
room.

"Bella, I'm—" She stops talking as she notices what I'm
doing.

Great. I was hoping I would only have to do this once.

"Where are you going?"

Standing the case up, I pull out the handle. "To Rocco's. I
don't want to be here after what Dad's done. Mum even had
the audacity to defend him. How dare they. I fucking hate
them for what they said about Rocco, and I would rather sleep
on the streets than be here."

"Bella, I agree they made a really bad decision to accuse him of cheating, but you can't just leave like this. Stay, and we can all sit down and talk. It's not too late to repair this."

"Yes, it is too late. They promised to give Rocco a chance, and look what happened. They've made it very clear that they'll never be okay with Rocco. Despite not wanting to go to the fair after the way they treated him the first time, he went because it was important to me. He didn't have to give them a second chance, but he did, and I think that was pretty big of him. What did he get in return, Liv?"

"I understand that, and I'm with you. They behaved appallingly, but they're your parents, and you can't just leave."

"Oh, I can."

"And you expect me to tell them for you? That is so typical of you, Bella."

I roll my eyes. "Calm down before you hyperventilate. I'm not running off. I'll wait until they get home and explain face-to-face."

Shaking her head, she groans. "You're making a big mistake."

"No, I'm not. The only mistake I made is thinking they would be supportive of something I wanted."

"They love us both the same."

"They don't like us both the same though. If it were you with Rocco, they would have gotten to know him. They would have been polite even if they hated him. Why not for me, too, huh?"

"Come on, Bells, I think that's obvious."

I glare.

What does that mean?

"I'm not so sure it is. Enlighten me."

"Well, your attitude to begin with. You're moody and withdrawn. You act like you're constantly bored in our company. You make no secret of the fact that you'd rather be with Nana and Grandad—whose house you should be running off to by the way—and you keep a serious relationship from us."

"And?"

She rolls her eyes. "And that makes you hard to trust. Not to mention, you're throwing your future away by not accepting a uni place."

"Get a grip, Liv. You act like I should just die now and get it over with if I'm not attending uni. I really think you need to have a word with yourself."

"Don't do this."

"I've made my decision, and there is nothing you can say to make me change it. I don't want to be here."

"How long will you be gone? Dad already feels terrible, and he knows he's made a huge mistake."

"I'm not coming back. I'm moving in with Rocco. That's where I'll live."

"Jesus, Bella! You can't move in with someone you barely know. What the hell happened to you?"

"Mum and Dad happened. I would've moved in with him eventually anyway, so it doesn't matter."

Livvy folds her arms. "Really? You sound so immature right now. It's only been a couple of months!"

"You can talk. When you and Harry first got together, you were going to die of old age together at the seaside...or something like that."

"It's different. Harry and I don't live in different worlds."

"Well, neither do me and Rocco. Now, we're about to live in the same flat."

She laughs without humour. "I cannot believe you're doing this."

"Believe it. Now, if you'll excuse me, I need to get my suitcase downstairs and wait for the parents."

She steps aside, shaking her head in disapproval. Good thing I've never cared about her opinion of my life.

"This'll kill Mum and Dad after Celia."

"You would think that, after Celia's death, they would be more pro *as long as my kid is happy* rather than only thinking about what they wanted for said kid."

Her mouth closes and thins. She has nothing to come back at me with because she knows I'm right. They know Rocco is in my life to stay, and Dad still chose to try and come between me and Rocco.

I'm done.

Livvy follows me downstairs, watching me struggle with getting the heavy case to the ground floor. It comes as no surprise that she doesn't offer any help. I wheel my belongings over to the sofa and sit in the seat closest to the door. A quick getaway will be good.

I'm so nervous that my stomach is churning over.

My twin sits opposite me, waiting.

I look everywhere but at her.

How long have we had that stupid glass swan ornament on the fireplace?

The harder I look around the living room, the more I notice. When Celia died, I tried not to look too hard. It really hurt.

I've missed a lot of changes.

I still see her dead body on the floor though. That's one thing that will never change.

I sit back and wait impatiently.

Finally, forty-nine minutes later, I hear Mum's car.

Livvy sits up straight. I stand and grab my case.

Showtime.

"Good luck," Livvy mutters.

I smile sarcastically at her. "You're about to be left with them. It's not me who needs luck."

She's going to have to listen to Mum and Dad going on and on about how stupid I am and how it won't be long before I come crawling back.

Liv says something else, but I don't hear because the front door opens. Mum notices me straightaway, and her face falls. Dad takes a few seconds. He closes the door and kicks off his shoes. But, when he does look up, he stills.

"Isabella, what's going on?" Mum asks cautiously.

"I don't want another argument, but I couldn't leave without telling you face-to-face."

"Leave? Where the hell do you think you're going?" Dad snaps.

He knows where I'm going, but I reply anyway, "To Rocco's. I can't be here, not after yesterday."

Walking closer, he pins me to the spot with his stare. "Don't be ridiculous. You're not going to that man's house."

"*That man?* Are you serious, Dad? My God, why did I bother staying? I should've left a note and taken off as soon as I was packed."

Lesson learned.

"Take your bag upstairs, Isabella."

"No."

Keep your cool.

"Let's calm down for a minute," Mum says, pleading with Dad, fearful that he will drive me away.

Too late; it's already happened. I can't believe I used to be close to Dad. The man standing in front of me is nothing like the Dad I used to know.

"There's no point, Mum. We can't agree. He won't listen, and he'll never give Rocco a fair shot. That's a deal-breaker for me. I don't want to live here anymore. It's toxic, and I'm worried something will be said that we can never come back from. I love you both, but I can't be around you."

Mum walks closer, almost stumbling, as if her legs are weak. "Don't be silly. This isn't irreparable. Tell her," she says, demanding for Dad to back her up.

She wants him to back down, but he's not going to do that. In his eyes, he's right, and Rocco is the worst person in the world for me. Dad won't accept him, and he will watch me walk out of this house.

"I tried to tell her how insane I think this is," Livvy says, butting in where her opinion is not fucking wanted.

"Liv, you're already the golden girl shitting glitter and making them proud. This doesn't concern you, so sit down."

"Is that what all this nonsense is about?" Dad asks.

"No. God, I'm not jealous of Livvy, and I definitely don't want her life. I like my life. It's just unfortunate that you hate it so much."

"That undesirable man isn't your life, Isabella. You're *eighteen*, and right now, you're making so many mistakes that it's hard to pick the biggest one."

Like he doesn't think me moving out is the biggest one.

"You need to take a step back and think about what you're doing and where you're going. You've been with him a matter of months."

"I need to take a few steps that way," I say, pointing to the front door. "Then, I need to get to Rocco's. See? I know what I'm doing."

"Yes, you sound like you have it all planned out."

Dad's not sarcastic often. I'm almost proud.

"I have enough planned out, and the rest, I'll deal with as it comes. Sorry that's not good enough for you, but I'm not like you, Mum, and Livvy. If you would stop trying to force me into that mould, maybe we'd get on better, and maybe you wouldn't be losing me right now."

"Isabella," Mum sobs. She turns to Dad and points at me. "Do something! You can't just let her walk out. It's not worth this. Can't you see that? I don't think he's the best match for her, but I'm not willing to risk my relationship with her over it."

She pleads a good case, but it's hopeless. He's as stubborn as me, more so probably. He's right, and I'm wrong, and that's all he'll ever see. Fucking hurts.

"Mum, I'll call you tomorrow," I say.

She's so upset, and it doesn't feel good at all. At least she can see sense. He's making me choose, and that's completely unfair. Rocco has done nothing wrong to warrant this treatment, and I stand with him.

"I can't sit back and watch her make a mistake with him," Dad says.

He's willing to lose me over this, and it makes my heart ache. This isn't how it's supposed to go.

But this is getting us nowhere.

I don't ask Livvy if I can take the car because I still have the key, and I need to go. I'll get it back to her, and she can have it to herself. I've got savings, so I can get something else.

"Isabella," Mum says, panicked, as I walk toward the door. "No, please don't go, not like this. Talk to me. Tell me what you need, and I'll make it happen."

"You can't, Mum. Look, I'll speak to you tomorrow. We can meet up sometime, okay?"

She grabs my hand. "Don't do this."

"I can't stay. I love him, Mum, and I shouldn't have to give him up because you and Dad have decided you don't like him."

"I know. I'll try harder, I promise. He's not a bad person. We just don't know him yet. Invite him over, and we can all have a big discussion. We'll clear the air and—"

"Mum! That's not going to happen."

What planet does she live on?

I understand she's desperate, and that kills me, but every person in this room knows I'm not staying, and Rocco's not coming over for a fucking chat.

"Bells, listen to Mum," Livvy pipes up as I'm reaching for the door.

"I'll text you when I get home, Liv, okay?"

Mum presses her hand to her mouth and sobs, and my heart falls out of my chest.

I need to leave.

Turning the handle, I shove my case out first, and then I'm free. Dashing to the car, I yank the boot open, shove the case in, and get in the driver's seat.

I take a breath.

Bugger. I've moved out.

FORTY-THREE

BELLA

When I get home—*God, that feels weird*—Rocco is in the kitchen with Ellis. They're both glossy-eyed. Little drunks. I lift my eyebrow at them.

Rocco is on his feet and in front of me the second he sees me. "Are you okay?" he asks, bending his head to look me in the eyes better.

He wraps his arms around me, and I didn't realise how much I'd needed that until he was touching me.

I close my eyes and sink into his embrace. "Yeah, I'm okay," I whisper.

"Mmhmm. Truth now, please?"

"It sucked. Mum cried, Livvy snapped, and Dad was not backing down. He let me walk out of there. He would rather I move out than admit he was wrong and try to make amends." I know we don't have the typical father-daughter relationship, but I never thought he'd willingly let me walk out of his life.

"I'm sorry, baby."

I snuggle my head against his shoulder and sigh. "It hurts. He's my *dad*."

Damn it, I shouldn't be saying this. Rocco's dad walked away from him and died.

"He'll realise. One day soon, he'll come running to you, full of apologies."

"It'll be too late," I mutter against his T-shirt.

Rocco kisses the top of my head. "No, it won't."

"Drink, Bella?" Ellis offers, cutting in.

Laughing, I pull away from Rocco and wipe my eyes. "A really strong one, please."

Ellis grins. "Now, that, I can do."

"Yeah, I can tell. How many have you two already had?"

"Not been counting," Rocco replies. "I'm not drunk though."

"Have you ever been drunk? Like properly drunk?"

He's told me that he doesn't like being that vulnerable because he doesn't trust anyone, but I find it hard to believe he's never been off-his-face drunk.

"He has once. We were twelve and in school."

"Twelve?" My mouth drops. "Rocco!"

One of his shoulders lifts in a lazy shrug. "School was boring."

"Yes, but, Jesus, you were a child."

"Everyone gets drunk."

"Sure, but not usually just after they've watched cartoons."

He frowns. "I never watched cartoons."

"I swear, you've lived your whole life under a rock," I say sarcastically. I take the glass of…something from Ellis. "Thanks."

I don't ask what it is. With him, it's probably best not to know.

Rocco seems more concerned about what Ellis is giving me as he asks, "The fuck is that?"

I take a sip, and, my God, I should've waited for Ellis to reply. The unidentified liquid burns on the way down.

"Jesus," I say, pulling a face and shaking my head. "That's foul, Ellis."

"It's not supposed to be nice. It's a bit of everything Rocco has…including a previously unopened bottle of sherry."

"I'm sure that was here when I moved in."

"Ew!" I slam the glass down on the counter. "That's so gross."

"It was unopened!" Ellis defends. "Anyway, I'm going to head out and let you two talk since Rocco clearly has some questions he doesn't feel he can ask in front of me."

"Fuck off, man," Rocco says, sighing.

Ellis chuckles, salutes, and then leaves.

I really like him. He's a good friend to Rocco, and he rarely takes himself seriously. He's the type of person you can be around all the time and not get bored of.

"Has anyone tried to call you?" Rocco asks.

I pull my phone from my pocket and check. "Mum and Livvy. They've sent messages, too."

He pushes my hair behind my shoulders, preventing me from hiding behind it. "They're not the ones you want to get in contact, are they?"

"I don't think Dad is going to be calling anytime soon."

"Maybe I can try talking to him?"

That's going right to the top of the list of things I never thought I'd hear Rocco say.

"You want to talk to my dad?" I ask, needing confirmation that I heard that correctly.

I don't even want to bloody talk to him right now. He let me walk away. I swallow a jolt of pain and consider drinking more of that disgusting concoction Ellis made.

"*Want* might be stretching it. I will if I can help."

"I don't think it will help. He's made his decision, and I want him to come to me. He's acting like me being with you is the worst thing ever—no offence—and I find that insane after what happened to Celia. He's so scared of something happening to me and Livvy that he's pushing us away. Well, just pushing me away actually. I bet, if she suddenly left Harry and got with some *undesirable*, he would be fine."

Rocco's eyes light with humour. "Did he call me an undesirable?"

I grimace. Bugger, I didn't mean to let him know that. "Kind of."

"Yeah, maybe I won't call him."

"Something is wrong with him, and I want no part of it until he realises how stupid he's being. I still want to see Livvy though. My mum, too. When it came down to it, she was willing to be very accepting of me and you. I know that doesn't excuse what she did the first time you came over, and she's not faultless for standing up for Dad, but—"

"Hey, take a breath," he says. He presses two fingers to my mouth, very effectively shutting me up. "You don't have to justify having a relationship with your mum to me. She might not be my number one fan, but she loves you. I'd never stand in the way of that, babe."

So…he's totally perfect.

"Thank you."

"Don't thank me…just take your top off."

Oh, of course, that was going to follow. Charming.

Rocco holds his hands up. "I'm joking. Is there anything I can do though?"

"Not right now. I'm emotionally done, so I need to lie down."

Pulling me closer, Rocco seals his mouth over mine and gives me a long kiss. It's not madly heated and urgent. It's sweet, and it makes my heart hurt in the best way. I grip his back, my nails cutting into his T-shirt, and his hands find my hair. He twists a chunk around his hand, and he holds me exactly where he wants me while his mouth drives me insane.

"You taste like booze," I say when he lets me up for air.

"Yeah, Ellis is a fucking bad influence."

Shoving his chest, I put my hands on my hips. "So, this is all Ellis's fault, huh?"

He lifts his shoulder, and his whole body tilts.

Drunk.

"All his fault. I offered him tea."

I laugh because that's bullshit. He doesn't even buy tea, so there's none in the house. He's a coffee drinker, and so am I.

"Yeah, all right, Rocco."

"You getting that?" he asks as my phone vibrates with another text.

Since I left the house, Mum has been messaging me.

> Isabella, come home, so we can talk about this.
>
> Isabella, this is absurd. You cannot run away!
>
> Call me, Isabella!

Great. I fire a response to Mum and then text Livvy.

> I am home. Once things settle down, maybe we can talk.
>
> Liv, all's okay. I'll see you soon. x

Mum is the first to respond.

> Playing house with that man is not going to get you anywhere. THINK about what you're doing.

Her use of *that man* makes me want to punch something. I grit my teeth and look up. Rocco is watching and waiting.

"My mum is impossible again," I growl. My blood is boiling in my veins.

"Yeah, I'm not a massive fan."

"I don't know what to do. She's done a complete one-eighty. I can't exactly cut her off, but right now, I would love to."

He snorts. "Well, I vote we cut her off. For a couple of weeks anyway."

"Oh, that'll help. I'm all for getting some space, but I can't fall off the face of the planet for that long. She's still my mum."

"I saw your reaction to her text. You're upset, and that pisses me off. Your mum's being a twat."

"Rocco!" I snap. "Stop."

"Why are you shouting at me? I've done nothing wrong. Your parents are the ones who've made this impossible. You *moved out* today because of them."

"Is that the problem? I don't have to stay here if it's too soon."

I mean, I have no fucking idea where else I'd go, as I don't want to run off to Nana and Grandad's and make things awkward with them and my parents. But I don't want Rocco to feel forced to have me here.

"We're together. It's permanent," he says, like it's the most stupidly obvious thing.

"That doesn't mean we have to live together. We've only known each other for two minutes!"

His jet-black eyebrows rise. "That doesn't bother me, but from your tone, I'm wondering if it bothers you."

"Don't be ridiculous, Rocco."

He takes a step back. "*I'm* not. The way you're reacting is childish."

What the hell is going on?

My head is spinning.

Why do we always do this?

I'm not even sure anymore why we started arguing, but I'm so tired and emotionally drained after this shitty day.

"Okay, I need to leave for a while."

I turn around, but Rocco grabs my arm, preventing me from going anywhere.

"Bella, stop."

Tugging my arm from his grip, I spin around. "I need you to give me some time. Things are tense, and we're both going to say stuff we don't mean." I'm coiled too tight and about to blow any minute.

"Where are you going?"

"I'll just go to the café and get a coffee. I'll be back in a little while."

Rocco frowns, and he looks so lost that I almost give in. But I can't because I'm angry, stressed, and hurt, and I feel like I'm about to explode. My relationship with my parents has taken a nosedive, especially with Mum back on Dad's team, and I don't want the same to happen with Rocco.

He needs to sober up, and I need to clear my head.

"Bella…"

"I won't be long."

"You're coming back? Nothing's changed, right?"

"Nothing at all, but when I'm in this mood, we're not going to get along. I need to calm down, so I don't snap, and you need to calm down, so you're not slagging off my family."

His mouth thins, but he chooses not to reply. I take his silence as agreement and leave.

I'm not going to the café though. I know exactly where I want to be.

FORTY-FOUR

BELLA

I close the front door and walk toward the road. My car is still outside. *Thank God.*

The street Rocco lives on is somewhat safe. It's deeper in where you have to really watch carefully.

I take a left and walk along the path. A car drives past from behind. I hear it first and look out of the corner of my eye, keeping my head forward so that I don't appear nervous. As it passes, I miss a step. The Volkswagen. Inside is a man with light hair behind the wheel, and a girl is sitting beside him.

I stumble forward.

Don't read too much into it, you paranoid freak! Teens with nothing better to do, remember?

I clench my fists and carry on walking. Up ahead, Faith is walking toward me. She raises her hand in a wave and quickens her pace.

"Hi," I say as we stop in front of each other.

"Bella, are you okay?" she asks softly.

Her choice of words and tone confirm that I look like a mess.

"I've had a proper rubbish few days."

She tilts her head in sympathy. "Fancy a cuppa?"

A coffee. "That sounds good actually."

Around here, the only people I talk to besides Rocco are Ellis and Faith. Ellis isn't brilliant at giving advice.

"Come on. The youth centre is just around the corner."

She turns, and I follow her down the road. Now that I'm living here, I'll have to get more involved, so the youth centre is a great place to start. Faith said that teen girls use it most, so I could possibly meet people my age there.

Faith punches in a key code on the large green door. The building is one-story and pretty big. It's grey and ugly, but I love what it stands for.

We walk into a large game room. There's a pool table, two arcade games, massive beanbags, a TV, and a wall stacked with books and DVDs. I'm surprised this place doesn't get robbed.

Faith leads me into the kitchen, which is a bit like a school cafeteria. There are about a dozen tables, a food service area, and bins.

"I really appreciate you letting me come here," I say.

It'll only be an hour or so, and then I'll go home and sort things out with Rocco. I hate the arguments and how it was left, but we all need a bit of time to cool down.

"Anytime you need to, Bella; you know that," Faith says, flicking on the kettle to make us a drink.

"Rocco's not a bad person. I don't understand why they won't accept that. I mean, they don't even want to talk; my dad doesn't anyway. How can you judge a person without really knowing them?"

She turns around and folds her arms. "I know what you mean, love. I'm judged for where I live."

I turn my nose up. "It sucks."

"Yes, it does."

My parents are overprotective and strict. Livvy and I have always been allowed to make our own decisions, but they certainly let us know when they don't agree. We've not chosen to do anything they don't like...until I turned down uni and got together with Rocco.

"I don't know what to do if they don't come around."

"Can you give up Rocco?"

I'd like to think that I could give him up over my parents, but *they're* the ones asking me to choose.

"Bella?" she presses.

"No, I can't. But, at the same time, I can't cut my parents out of my life."

"You don't have to."

I tilt my head. "How's that?" Right now, I'm not seeing many options.

"They'll come around."

"I hope so."

"Well, you're welcome to stay here for as long as you want, whenever you want. It's not luxury, and it's home to a few other girls in similar situations, but it'd give you the space you all probably need."

"There are other girls living here?"

"Yes, three boys and two girls. Larissa and Tamara are sisters, and they've had a lot of problems with their parents. Both alcoholics, neither worried about whether their daughters had food in their bellies or clothes that fit."

"Are they okay?"

"They are now. Been here about a year, I suppose. Got jobs and planning their next move. I'm not saying you need to leave home forever, Bella—that's not my decision—but I think you know something has to change if you're going to have Rocco and your parents in your life."

She's right. I can't stay home for another year if they're going to bitch at me nonstop about ditching him. Rocco and I had very different childhoods, and I understand why they're concerned, but he's nothing like the people you hear about from this part of town. He would never hurt me. Plus, I wouldn't move back now. I'm committed to Rocco.

"Maybe I'll stay a little bit longer today if that's okay?"

I like it here. It's strangely peaceful, and I love the idea of doing something to help someone else. I constantly feel like I'm failing Celia because I have no real leads, so at least here, I can be of use.

"Of course. We could really use your help in the main house actually."

"The main house?" I frown.

She's not mentioned another place before. Unless it's just her house...but then what can I do there?

"Yes," she replies as she pours boiling water into two mugs.

The smell of coffee fills the air, and I suddenly feel like a druggie desperate for the next fix.

"We live not too far from here, on the outskirts of town. There's an outbuilding housing three young women."

What the fuck?

"Okay..."

That's weird, right?

She laughs. "I didn't make that sound too good, did I? These young ladies have had a particularly bad time, and at the minute, they aren't ready to be here. We do everything we can to ensure this place is safe and secure, but people are free to come and go as they please."

"So, the girls at your house were abused or scared of men? I mean, they're there, alone, right?"

That's basically what I'm getting from what she said. They can't stop guys from using the centre, so the best option is to have those three girls somewhere else.

"You read between the lines well, Bella. Some of the things Eliza, Penny, and Yasmin have been through are indescribable."

"Why are they with you, if you don't mind me asking? Wouldn't social services get involved and find them somewhere to live?"

"They all had involvement from social services at home over the years, but they all ran away. I can't send them away, knowing what they would be going back to." She places my coffee in front of me and takes a seat. "I understand this is unusual, but the help we get around here isn't adequate. You've seen the lack of police involvement."

I think it can't help that no one speaks out.

"I have to do something," she says with passion.

"That's admirable."

"Thank you."

"What happens to those girls then?"

"We give them a safe place to stay, listen to their stories, and help them plan for the future. I'm no rival for professionals, but I'm here, and I won't turn them away. I think they feel safer, being among their own rather than with some fancy therapist."

The steam coming off my coffee swirls in front of Faith's face. I watch it for a second and try to figure out how I feel about this. On the one hand, what she's doing is amazing, but they're at her house, and they clearly need professional help.

Is she just doing more harm than good?

Her intentions are honourable. She's a good person.

"What do you want me to do?" I ask.

"We're having a fundraiser, and we need help on the stalls. I want the girls to join in, so they're not just sitting around the house, thinking. I'll be there, too, of course, along with Keith and a few other volunteers, but I think it might be good for them to have someone their own age around."

I shrug. "Yeah, sure. The fundraiser is this afternoon though?"

It's two o'clock all ready.

Surely, if it was today, she would be there by now?

She laughs. "No. Sorry, the fundraiser is tomorrow. We've always had more success on a Sunday. But we need to set up the tables and stalls today."

"Okay, I'm in."

"Thank you, Bella. I'll drop you off at Rocco's once we're done. It shouldn't take more than an hour or two."

"That's fine. I might be ready to apologise for overreacting, but that doesn't mean I can't leave him to sweat a little longer."

Once we've finished our coffee, we get in Faith's car, and she drives in the opposite direction of Rocco's flat. I know she's more on the outskirts of town, but I have no idea exactly where that is.

"That car is everywhere," I say, looking behind me as the dark Volkswagen saloon goes past.

When I turn back, Faith is looking at it in the mirror. She shrugs. "I don't recognise it. How do you mean, everywhere?"

"I just see it a lot. At first, I thought it was following me, but that's definitely irrational."

"Have you seen who's inside?"

"Not really."

She gives me a smile. "I can see why you jumped to that conclusion, but it's probably some teen who hasn't had a car long. They tend to drive round and round and try to impress."

"Yeah, they do that where I live, too. It felt strange that it was around almost every time I was here."

"Most people are, Bella. There's not a great deal to do here."

That's the truth. Even the basketball courts are broken and covered in graffiti. There's not a decent park or cinema around.

"They should go to your centre."

Laughing under her breath, she makes a right at a set of lights, and we're almost out of town. "It stops being cool after a certain age, I think. Cars suddenly become more fun than playing pool or card games."

Yeah, I can see that. Even though she seems to be right in the middle of the community here, she can't know everyone.

"This is your house?" I ask as she pulls onto a dusty road.

Ahead is a brick house, three metal outbuildings and what looks like a couple of sheds. It has an industrial feel to it rather than a homely one.

"This is home," she replies.

She told me it was one outbuilding.

"You have a lot of space here." *That you do what with?*

"We like our space. Keith's parents and grandparents lived here before us. They ran a car garage from the warehouses."

The buildings are old, but if two generations of people ran a business from here, wouldn't there be evidence of that over the large doors? The sun would have faded the metal and left a new-looking strip where a sign was.

Unless it wasn't a legit garage.

Like one with stolen cars given new details. Cars cut about and stuck back together.

I probably don't want to know. Faith has it now, and she's using the place to do good. I'm almost positive.

She parks in front of the warehouse closest to the house, the one I assume has the girls living in it. When she told me about it, I assumed it would be a proper habitable building but, from the outside, it looks run down and unused.

"Here we are," she says. "Let's go in, and you can meet the girls."

"Okay. Are the supplies in here for the fundraiser? I didn't see anything outside." My stomach gets heavier, and I begin to regret coming here.

"Yes. We have it out back on the field. I prefer having a large amount of people away from my home."

I put my hand on the door handle and nod. My stomach turns a little. Faith speaks so genuinely, and everything she says makes me think she's an awesome person, but I can't shake the feeling that something is off.

I want to trust my gut, but I've overreacted in the past.

Watching Celia be killed when I was at a very young age left me cynical. Obviously, I know good people are out there, but it's not always mega easy to tell them from the fake ones.

Is Faith fake good?

What possible reason could she have for bringing me here if it wasn't to accept help that I'd offered though?

Shit, I'm the fake good person. I'm here because I want to know everyone and be involved in everything I can, so I can find my sister's killer.

"Bella?" Faith says.

I look up, and she's frowning at me from outside the car.

"Sorry," I reply.

I get out of the car. Shutting the door, I take a quick glance around. It really is in the middle of nowhere. I can't see another house at all. We're surrounded by fields, and further on is a splatter of trees.

I follow her into the warehouse, and the second she closes the door, I want to run back out. It's dark, and the interior has been divided into rooms. It's very DIY, and you can see the joins between plasterboard. There's a large open area with sofas, a TV, and a small kitchen, but everything else is behind closed doors.

What is the everything else?

Taking a quick look, I count seven doors.

A bathroom can count for one, so what are the other six?

I don't like this anymore.

My breathing hikes.

"Penny, Yasmin, Eliza?" Faith calls out.

They're real at least.

I lick my lips and clench my fists. *Stay calm. Everything is probably fine.*

One of the doors opens, and three girls walk out.

The air is kicked from my lungs.

Fuck.

They look awful. They're thin, their eyes are sunken in, and their skin is dull. Shuffling forward, they walk toward Faith…but none of them look at her.

I need to leave.

"This is Isabella. She's going to be staying with us."

Staying?

My head whips around, but before I can speak, someone grabs me. A scream rips from my throat, but it's cut off when a dirty, large hand covers my face. Strong arms cage me against an unknown chest.

Fuck. Fuck, fuck, fuck. This isn't happening.

I thrash around as best I can, but the guy holding me is too strong. He chuckles, and it sends shivers down my spine.

"You're right, Faith. She does look just like her."

No.
It's him.

FORTY-FIVE

BELLA

He—the man who stole my sister's life—holds me so tight that I can barely breathe.

Is this it then? Is this where it ends for me?

I look to the girls behind Faith while my lungs set on fire. *Help!*

"All right!" Faith snaps. "Let her go. She's our guest after all."

He digs in my pocket, taking my phone, and then lets go. I stumble forward and gasp for air. Placing myself in front of a corner so that no one is behind me, I try to think. The one time my mind is completely fucking blank is right fucking now! I need to get out of here.

Stay calm.

Running won't do any good. There are five of them, more hidden away possibly. And the arsehole who murdered Celia is by the door.

Look at him, I demand of myself.

Faith is staring at me, and it's the first time that she looks harsh and ugly.

It was all a lie. She's known who I am this whole time.

Wow, I'm a real idiot.

I ignore her because, in the grand scheme of things, she is nothing. With my heart in my throat, I raise my eyes, and there he is. Standing before me is the man who took so much from my family and everything from my big sister.

Blond hair.

Oh my God, it's the man who bumped into me at the fair. He was around my family! He's the same build as the one watching me at the restaurant, too. It was the same person. It was him all along.

Bile hits the back of my throat. I swallow, not willing to give him the satisfaction of knowing how scared I am.

I didn't get a good look at him when he was hurting Celia. I was young and petrified, but now that I see him, I'm thrown back to that day. The terror comes flooding back like a fucking tsunami, and I want to cry.

Don't let him see you cry, for Christ sake!

His stare makes my stomach bottom out. He's looking at me like I'm a meal, but I won't allow myself to react.

I steady my shaking hands. Every moment since Celia died has been leading to this point right here. And I have no bloody clue what to do next.

It's not exactly looking good.

I need you here with me, Celia.

"Why?" I ask. My voice is calm, and I surprise myself because I feel anything but calm. My body burns in anger and the desire to kill him. Before I laid eyes on him, I wasn't sure if I could take a life, but, my God, I wouldn't even hesitate.

Hate engulfs me and courses through my veins.

Everything is there again—Celia hiding me, her screams, the smell of wood from inside the cabinet before it was overpowered by blood, the sound of her choking, and then the knife cutting through her flesh.

Pain rips through my body as I relive every aspect of that day. I feel and smell it all again, and I want to die.

Celia was so, so scared. She knew she was going to die at the hands of this animal.

Oh God, why did I start this?

"I've thought about Celia many times over the years."

"Don't you fucking say her name!" I spit, glaring at him. I couldn't hate him any more than I do. "Why? Answer me!"

His cold stare scratches at my skin like sandpaper.

Answer me, you bastard!

"Isabella," Faith says.

I don't want to take my eyes off this piece of shit in front of me, but the way she just said my name makes me think she's going to explain.

I've waited too long for this. Celia's death was so senseless, and Faith will never validate it, but there had to be a reason.

"What?" I seethe, turning my attention to the bitch.

How stupid am I to have trusted her?

"Look around, Bella, and tell me what you see."

I don't because I've seen it already, and I'm still clueless. Obviously, she's not here to help those girls, but I don't know what she's doing with them.

Wait.

Oh, fuck.

Young women. All those rooms…

"You're fucking sick," I mutter. My ears are ringing.

This is a brothel. She sells those girls to men for sex.

No. No, no. Did she do that to Celia?

My body goes light, and my head feels like it's floating.

Don't pass out. Breathe!

Oh God, my heart aches for my sister. *Did these arseholes make her sell her body?*

Faith laughs. "I can tell what you're thinking. Celia found out too early what was going on. She ran, but we couldn't let her speak out."

No. I don't want to hear anymore.

I pinch the bridge of my nose and take a breath. That's what she was running from. They killed her. Jesus, now, I understand why she didn't want me to tell anyone what I was about to witness.

I drop my hand. "You sent your lapdog to kill my sister before she could tell anyone what sick fucks you were."

"Watch your mouth!" Lapdog snaps.

359

I flick my hand at him. "Fuck you!"

"When I saw you, I immediately knew who you were. I don't forget a face, and you're a dead ringer for Celia. It couldn't have been more perfect. Initially, I did worry that you would figure it out too soon as well, but you didn't," Faith says.

"Who *are* you?" I ask her.

How can someone do that to another person?

The three girls behind Faith cower and look to the floor.

"I do what I have to do to survive."

"No, you do what you do because you're evil and rotten and selfish."

She slowly shakes her head. "I don't expect you to understand. This is what Keith and I inherited. This is how we stay alive in a place like this."

"That's bullshit. This might not be Disneyland, but you don't have to do this. You don't have to be this person. You can let me go."

"Oh, I can't do that. I'm owed."

Lapdog laughs, and the crass sound makes me want to vomit.

"Everyone in life has a fate, Isabella," Faith says.

"Right. So, yours is to be a pimp, and my sister's was to be a prostitute. You're a fucking fruit loop!"

"Watch your mouth," she spits.

"Seriously, you want to sell me for sex, but you're offended by swear words? Wow."

"Tank, take her to the back. When you're done with your turn, get the girls to brief her. Business as usual."

I turn ice cold.

When he's done? When he's done with what?

"No!"

I take off, but Tank—the bastard—is faster and catches me, covering my mouth with his disgusting hand. He laughs as I frantically thrash around to get out of his grip. Digging my nails into his hand, I rip down, and he lets out a deep scream.

"Fucking bitch! I can't wait for this!"

He shoves me through a door and launches me at a bed. My shoulder blades scream at the force he used to push me. I land in a heap, bouncing on a mattress I'm sure is filthy and covered in things I don't even want to know about.

Faith said he'd get his turn.

What does that mean? What's he going to do to me? Is Faith planning on letting him kill me? Oh God.

I flip over and scrub my hands over my face to try and clear my panic and think rationally. I need a plan. And a miracle.

Think, Bella!

He's still standing in the doorway with both hands gripping the frame like he's holding himself back from ripping me apart. His eyes are void, and his yellowing teeth are bared. Everything about him is evil to the core.

"What to do with you…" he says, tilting his head forward and stepping into the room.

He grabs the door, and in one swift movement, he slams it shut. I'm trapped with him. Ice wraps around my heart.

I push myself up and stand beside the bed. The room is basic with just a bed, a small side table, and a bin. I don't want to know what is in the drawer. The mattress is covered in a white sheet. No quilt and no pillows.

There are so many questions I want to ask, so many things I want to say, but it makes no difference. I don't want to give him the power of denying me answers, and I don't want to give him the satisfaction of seeing me upset.

Whatever you do, show no fear.

"Has any encounter with a girl ever been consensual? Or do you always have to force them?"

He snarls, and the sound cuts through me. I swallow.

Don't react.

My heart is going a hundred miles an hour. I can hear it thump.

I put my arms behind my back and grip my hands together. It's an act that's trying to make me appear more confident and casual so that he doesn't know I'm bloody terrified while concealing the fact that I'm shaking.

"Are you trying to end this sooner? Faith wants to keep you a while, but don't think I won't go against her if you push me."

How long is she planning on keeping me then? Days? Weeks? Months?

She has to know that Rocco would find me eventually though.

My head is spinning with so much information, confliction, and fucking terror.

"You *murdered* my sister. If I'm going to die, too, don't think I won't take you with me, you sick fuck!"

Tank laughs, and it's horrible. "You can't stop me. We both know I can do anything I like to you, and there's nothing you can do to prevent it." His footsteps echo through the room as he plants his chunky black boots down on the floor.

He's getting closer. I want to back up or leap over the bed and have something between us, but that's what he wants.

He got what he wanted with Celia. It played out exactly how he'd envisioned, but that won't happen with me.

I can feel her with me right now more than I ever had over the years. When I was little, I used to lie in bed at night and pretend she was beside me. I felt close to her then, but that was nothing compared to this moment. She's here, and we'll do this together. That thought gives me so much strength; I know I won't back down. Whatever happens, whatever he does, I will face this and see it through with my big sister.

Tank tilts his head as he comes to a stop about a meter away from me. I raise my eyes to meet his and let go of my hands behind my back.

"You're going to die, and I'm going to watch," I say. I'm running on adrenaline, anger, and stupidity. Thank God, because if I wasn't, I'd be begging and trying to run.

He doesn't get to win. Not this time.

"You have no idea who you're dealing with. Your sister didn't have that problem."

I frown. "Except she did because she figured out your disgusting little scheme and ran."

His mouth spreads in a sickening grin. "And look where that got her. I took her life, Bella." Closing his eyes, he breathes heavily through his nose. "Oh, it was good. My best kill by far. She tried to fight." His dead eyes open and pin me to the spot. "The skin on her neck was so soft and so warm under my hands as I squeezed."

Shut up!

I press my mouth together as my stomach goes on a fucking roller coaster.

How scared was she when he was strangling her? I should have interrupted, ran for the door to spook him.

I did nothing!

Tank takes another step, and I can feel his breath across my face. He smells gross, like cigarettes and stale beer. Without warning, he snaps his knee up and ploughs it into my stomach.

Fuck.

I cry out, gripping my tummy, as I fall to the floor. Pain rips through my middle, making tears well in my eyes. I double over, my knees and elbows hitting the wooden laminate floor.

"See? I can do what I want."

"Go to hell," I hiss, lifting my head and coughing through the agony.

Tank chuckles. "One day. You'll be there sooner. You can say hi to your dead sister."

Screw you.

I don't care when he threatens me, but when he mentions Celia, my blood boils. He took her life and changed mine forever. I despise the animal.

"What you're doing isn't working. Say what you want about her, but I don't care." It's a massive lie, but he doesn't need to know that.

Planting my hands on the floor, I stand up. My stomach is so tender that I don't even want to stretch it out by being upright, but I have to. "You act so tough, like you do whatever you want and no one can stop you. You killed Celia because

Faith had told you to. Well done for listening to *Mummy*, Tank."

Oh, shit, what if she's actually his mum?

With a guttural growl, he flings his head forward and smashes his forehead against mine. A scream rips from my throat, and I stumble sideways, hitting the side of my head against the wall. I grip the plasterboard and lean against it for support.

My head feels like it's splitting. I blink and turn around again.

You can take it. Don't back down.

He tilts his head to the side. "She begged, but you won't, will you?"

"Why don't you hold your breath and wait for it?"

"Oh, I'm going to enjoy this." He stands taller and puffs out his chest; it makes him look twice the size. "Your skin is so fair, so soft."

His hand slips into his pocket, and I resist the urge to watch what he's doing. I keep my eyes firmly on his.

Though I'm not looking, it's hard to miss the bright reflection on the window from the *knife*.

"This is the one I used on Celia."

Motherfucker.

I feel like I've been kneed in the stomach again.

It's fine, it's fine, it's fine. Don't stop looking at him, and don't react!

Gulping, I fight hard to stay in control and not look at the weapon that was once covered in my sister's blood. "Bit old now, isn't it?"

The corner of his mouth lifts in a snare. "It still works," he whispers.

Oh my God, how many other people?

I roll my eyes. "This is getting boring now. Why don't you leave and let Faith get on with whatever she's planning? We both know you're going to be called out there soon." *I hope.*

Tank's eyes turn black, and he lunges. I shove my hands out to protect myself, but he's too quick. His fist slams into the side of my head, and I drop to the floor.

Pain radiates through my skull, and it instantly starts throbbing. My ears ring, and my vision blurs. I feel him before I see him. A heavy weight lumps down on my legs, pinning me to the floor. My head is spinning, and I try to lift my hands, but it hurts too much.

Two rough, large hands cling to my neck, and my eyes fly open wide.

Fuck, he's going to kill me.

I claw at his hands, scraping my nails through his flesh. He growls, but he doesn't move. He squeezes harder until I can feel my windpipe close completely. I can't breathe. Panic takes over. I thrash my legs and frantically tug at his hands while I gasp for breath that doesn't come.

This is where it ends.

I've never been that scared of dying, and I didn't think I would be massively scared when the time came. But I am.

I open my mouth and try to suck in air, but it doesn't work. His grip is too strong, and I can feel myself weakening. My legs kick seemingly of their own accord, and it takes so much effort to dig my nails into his hands.

I'm tired. My heart is working overtime, and my lungs deflate in the most painful way possible. The corners of my vision turn dark, like I'm approaching a tunnel.

My legs still.

I'm sorry, Celia.

Suddenly, the pressure is gone. I cough loudly, sucking in air, my arms flying up to gently cover my now-naked neck. The weight from my legs disappears, and my lungs inflate.

I look up, and Tank is standing above me, smirking. He lifts his heavy boot above my head and then…darkness.

FORTY-SIX

BELLA

I wake up, and I'm in a different room. I'm momentarily disorientated, but the second I realise what's going on, my heart stops.

Faith. Tank. He killed Celia.

This can't be the end. I have to get out.

My head is pounding so much that it makes my eyesight blurry. Groaning, I push myself up, so I'm sitting on the bed, and I hiss as my ribs scream at the movement. I wince, holding my chest with one arm.

The three girls, who are probably a couple of years older than me, stare at me. I want to ask for help, but I'm paralysed by fear. Everything hurts.

How long was I out for?

The last thing I remember is lying on my back on the floor and seeing the sole of Tank's black boot above my head.

"Are you okay?" a voice says.

I can't tell which one of them spoke, as my vision is still impaired. I rub my temple, and it feels wet.

What the hell?

As I pull my hand from my head and down in front of my face, my eyes widen. Red blood covers my fingers. I look up and meet the eyes of the person who spoke. She comes into focus a little more now. Her hair is light and super long.

"I'm bleeding."

"It's okay. I think it's stopping," the tall, skinny one says.

I blink, and it improves my vision. The world is sharp once again. Pressing my other hand to the wound near my temple, I check again. There is less blood this time. She's right; it is stopping.

The littlest one, the redhead, takes a tentative step closer to me and repeats her friend's question, "Are you okay?"

No, I'm really not.

I have cuts and bruises and a possible broken ribs, but worse than that was thinking he was going to kill me. It was hearing what he said he wanted to do. And the very worst part was him talking about my beautiful big sister like she was a piece of meat.

"I'll live," I reply. *If I can get away, I might anyway.* "How long was I unconscious for?"

"About forty-five minutes," Red replies.

God, I must have been gone for at least two hours then. Rocco will be looking for me by now. I said I would be quick, and he would have given me about an hour, ninety minutes at most, before he started to worry. He won't have a clue where I am, and he doesn't know I left with Faith. But he won't stop until he finds me.

"Who sleeps in here? We need to get out of this place."

The room is much bigger than the one Tank had me in. There is a double bed complete with cover and pillows, a wardrobe, and a chest of drawers. This must be one of their rooms.

They look between each other with an is-she-serious-about-escaping expression.

I'm deadly fucking serious. I'm not staying here. I'm not having sex with anyone. And I'm not going to be killed by Lapdog.

"Hello?" I snap, clicking my fingers. If I didn't feel like I might throw up, I would stand.

"He does. You really don't want to run. We've seen what he does to the women who try."

So have I.

"Where are the exits?" I ask. "Do the windows open?"

"There's only the front door. The windows don't open wide enough to slip through. I've tried the windows," Red replies.

She doesn't make eye contact, and her head is tilted down enough that her red hair cloaks her face.

Damn it, she's tiny as hell, so if she can't squeeze through, then I definitely won't.

"Okay. We go out the door then."

"The men will arrive in an hour and thirty minutes."

That's not happening. It's not. There is no way in hell I'm letting anyone touch me.

"No," I snap. "We're leaving before they arrive."

"I don't see how you're going to achieve that. Honestly, it's best to go along with it. If you do what you're told, life isn't so bad," the tall one says.

"Which one are you?" I ask.

"Eliza."

"Eliza, never in the definition of the phrase, *Life isn't so bad*, does it include human trafficking and prostitution."

That's what this is. Faith gets girls and sells them like they're possessions.

"Now, I'm trying to get out of here. Are you three in or not?"

Red shakes her head, and her friends take a step closer to her. "I don't want to die."

"Fine, that's your choice. Don't get in my way though, and please don't tell them."

Eliza's pale blue eyes light with fear.

"I need your help to distract whoever is in the building. Who is that anyway? Just Faith and her lapdog, Tank? Does Keith spend much time here? Does Hugo?"

"Keith doesn't come out here. He stays in the house. The only time we see him is when they bring new girls. And I don't know Hugo." The third girl, a pretty blonde with killer green eyes, smiles. "I'm Yasmin."

No Hugo. At least Celia wasn't betrayed by her obsession.

I return the friendly gesture. "Where are the other girls?"

"Some are sold. Others work the streets for Faith and stay in the other outbuildings."

"Jesus." I take a breath.

How could no one else know about this?

Rocco and Ellis certainly didn't. It sickens me to think that some probably do, and they say nothing.

"I will help you," Yasmin says.

"You will?"

"No, she won't!" Eliza grabs Yasmin's hand and tugs. "You can't get yourself killed for a stranger."

She shakes her head. "I won't. All I need to do is go out there and pretend like I'm feeling unwell again. That will give Bella the chance to escape. You and Penny have to stay in here, so they think Bella is with you. Come on, I would do this for anyone wanting a chance to escape."

"Thank you, Yasmin," I say.

"Don't thank me until you get away."

I can see in her tired eyes that she doesn't think I'll do it, but she won't take hope away from me. She'll never know how much I appreciate her help.

Eliza sighs, looks up to the ceiling, and shakes her head. "All right. They'll be checking the rooms and any bookings, so they'll be distracted anyway."

Closing my eyes, I press my fist against my mouth.

Oh, what the fuck?

They take bookings for men to come here and have sex with teenage girls. I know why Celia ran. Yasmin, Eliza, and Penny might stay to keep alive, but I'm with my sister.

What's the point of living when it's in hell?

Taking a breath to regain my composure, I drop my hand and look at them again. "Are you sure none of you wants to come, too? If we all go, it could be safer. You deserve better than this."

"We're staying," Penny says. Her dark eyes look exhausted and void. She's given up. "We stay together."

God, I'm not going to convince them.

They're not going to allow a stranger to potentially break their bond to each other. I don't even know what to think about that.

This probably isn't something I want the answer to, but I still ask, "How old are you?"

"Penny and I are seventeen. Yasmin is sixteen."

Her words are like a punch in the stomach.

They're all younger than me.

"And how long have you been here?" My voice is barely a whisper.

"Two years for us all, give or take a few months. They usually keep five of us here, but over the last four months, the other two tried to escape." Eliza pointedly looks at me.

"How do you know they didn't escape?"

"We heard the screams," Penny replies. "You're a fool to attempt this."

I want to tell them that they're the fools for staying, but all things considered, that seems a bit too bitchy, even for me.

"I'm not afraid to die."

That's not entirely true. I didn't used to be afraid. Since meeting and falling in love with Rocco, I've cared more. I want a future and a life with him. But Celia has been the centre of my everything since the second she hid me in that cupboard before being killed. Once I grew up and properly understood and pieced things together, I made her a promise that I would bring her justice.

Yasmin looks up at the clock on the wall. A clock that's probably counted in hours until the next disgusting arsehole arrives.

"It's time," she says. "Look, I don't know how this is going to play out, but I do know that you're going to need some help. Do you have a phone? Did he take it?"

"He took it," I confirm.

Eliza says, "I saw him put it on the side table near the door. It might still be there."

"If you get out there, call someone who can be here quickly."

"She means, not the police. They don't care about what happens around here. We're disposable people," Penny adds.

"Yeah, I got that impression the second I arrived."

Yasmin continues, "Go around the back. Behind the warehouses are a couple of sheds; you can hide behind them. Don't do what the others did and run for it. Be smart and hide. Until the men arrive, there is only Faith and Tank here. Keith is away."

"Thank you, Yasmin."

She gives me a weak smile that screams, *You fucking idiot*, but sanity has never been a strong point of mine anyway.

"They're out there. I hear them talking," Penny says with her ear against the door.

No turning back now.

FORTY-SEVEN

BELLA

This is it; I'm going to escape. Hopefully.

Without hesitation, Yasmin strolls past Penny, who quickly gets out of her way, and goes out into the living room. I bolt to the door and peer through the small slit. Penny and Eliza are close behind me.

Yasmin walks toward Tank and Faith, hunched over and holding her stomach. Faith looks immediately concerned, but I no longer think it's because she cares about Yasmin's welfare. She's worried that the girl won't be able to sleep with fuck knows how many men tonight.

Please let this work without Yasmin getting hurt. She's only fucking sixteen!

She places herself so that Faith and Lapdog have their backs to the door. They crouch down as Yasmin bends over further and makes a sound that's a bit like a growl.

This is it. This is my opportunity.

With my heart beating so hard that I can hear my pulse, I slip out of the door and hold my breath. My Converse sound like high heels as I gently lift my feet up and tiptoe toward the door.

Faith stands up straight, and I freeze. I'm out in the middle of the hallway, still about five feet from the door.

God, this is it. Don't turn around. Please. Please!

I can see my phone.

"So, you can't work tonight?" Faith asks.

She sounds pissed off, and I wish that I could take Yasmin with me.

I take a longer stride and reach behind my back, picking my phone up. Tucking it in my pocket, I sidestep one last time, and I can finally reach the door handle. My heart is racing, but I have to try.

Faith puts her hands on her hips as she listens to Yasmin's apology.

Fucking bitch. I hate her so much. But not as much as I hate him.

I need to do something about him, but right now, I have to get out and call Rocco.

Oh, crap, he's going to be livid.

"She gets ill a lot," Lapdog says.

I wonder why.

Yasmin glances at me through her hair while she leans over. It's all I need; she's telling me to go. I carefully take the final step and wrap my hand around the handle. I twist, and the door opens. Relief floods my heart. I didn't want to acknowledge it, but I was scared that it would be locked.

Why isn't it locked?

Whoa. God, no.

They don't lock it because they know the girls won't try to escape, and the ones who do are killed.

I burn in anger for these girls.

Stepping out the door, I give Yasmin one last look. *I'll get someone to come for you.*

Then, I'm out. With the gentlest of touches, I turn the handle, and the door is closed again. I've done it. I take a breath, and tears well in my eyes.

Out the back.

Yasmin said to go around the back and hide near the sheds. The warehouses are all quite close together, so I can run between them if I need to. Sticking close to the wall, I sprint for the back. My heart is absolutely pounding, and I'm not entirely sure if I'm of sound mind or operating on shock. Or a mixture of both.

My legs collapse and go down in a lump when I get to the back of a warehouse. A sob escapes, but I clamp my mouth together.

Shut up!

You're okay. You can do this.

I press my palm to my chest in a bid to slow my breathing.

Shit. It's a miracle that I escaped in the first place.

I can't stay hidden long. As soon as they notice I've gone, they'll come looking for me. But I have no idea where I am or which direction I should go in. There's one road, and the rest of my surroundings is fields, light forestry, and a river I can now just about see in the far distance.

Don't think about your lifeless body being chucked in that river.

And hide really well.

Running is so very tempting; it's instinctive. But Yasmin is right; I need to hide. She's seen other girls being killed because they couldn't get away fast enough. There are plenty of little buildings here to hide behind. And there are only two of them.

With my hands shaking worse than a basic white girl trying to twerk, I fumble with my phone and call Rocco's number.

The call connects after only a second.

"Isabella, where are you?" he growls.

It's only been about two and a half hours, but he sounds like he's not slept for days.

"I don't know exactly," I whisper, half-sobbing at hearing the mixture of anger and concern in his voice.

Why didn't I memorise the way we came?

I know the general direction and turning left at a set of traffic lights, but that's about it.

"I'm at Keith and Faith's house. There are other girls. And *him*. You need to come and get me, Rocco. They're human traffickers, and I'm fucking scared! They wanted me to—"

"They're what? Jesus, what the fuck is going on? What did they want you to do?"

"Human trafficking. They have a goddamn brothel and were trying to make me work there. They had Celia! It was *them*, and now, they want me to replace what they lost! I ran when I had the chance, but there's just one house and a few old buildings. If I run for the road or forest, they might see me. I need you to come."

"What the fuck?" he roars.

I don't really get what he says next because it's just a bunch of expletives.

"Rocco," I hiss, gripping the side of an old shed door. "For fuck's sake, come and get me. I...I'm scared."

"Bella?"

"Ellis? Where did Rocco go? I need him to—"

"I heard. He's pacing and looking for his keys, but we're coming. You need to put the phone on silent and get into a position where you can see all around you but where you can only be seen from one direction—or better still, not be seen at all. Tell me where you are. Can you send your location?"

"I only have signal to call. No Wi-Fi or cellular data to send anything or connect to the internet. I don't know where I am either! Their house!"

"Okay, calm down. We'll figure it out. Can you hide anywhere?"

"Yeah, there are three warehouse-looking buildings, sheds and farmland. We went to the centre first and then came to wherever I am now. We didn't drive for long, maybe twenty minutes. No longer. There are some trees in the distance but not enough to be a proper forest and a river running the opposite side of the road."

I need to get to a place where I can see but not be seen.

"Okay, I'm getting the laptop out now. We'll find you," he says.

"Shit," I whisper, hearing movement from the house. "Someone's outside."

"Are you hidden?"

"Kind of."

"Phone on silent, Bella. Now."

"It already is. I can't hear footsteps, so I don't think they're looking for me yet. Listen, the battery on the phone is low, so I'm going to go in case I need to speak to you again. I'll hide, but please hurry."

"Stay safe," Ellis orders.

In the background, I hear Rocco shout, "Don't fucking hang up," but I end the call.

Six percent left, and I might need every one of those. I won't use the phone again unless I need to call them in twenty minutes if they're not here.

They'll be ten minutes, tops. Rocco won't be giving a shit about any speed limits—not that he usually does. All I have to do is hide for ten minutes.

I can do this.

I look up to the sky as I feel a tear roll down my cheek. *I'm making a bit of a mess of this, Celia.*

Until now, I've not had much chance to dwell on what happened in there, but I have finally done it. I have found the man who took my sister's life. His handprints are still on my wrists.

Closing my eyes, I think about Celia, and I've never felt as close to her as I do in this moment. She could have run out of the house when he arrived, but she was scared that he would come for her family. She hid me and died so that I would be protected.

Sleep easy, Celia. I've found him. I love you.

My sister will have the justice she deserves.

And maybe I'll get to have the life with Rocco that we both want.

"Isabella!" Tank roars.

My eyes fly open, and I launch to my feet.

No, they've realised I'm gone.

I creep to the end of the shed and slow my breathing, so it's light and so fucking quiet. Heavy footsteps get louder, and I know Tank is coming this way. I can only hear one set though, so Faith probably isn't there. It's one against one, and all I have to do is stay hidden until Ellis and Rocco arrive.

Piece of cake...

Biting my lip, I tune everything out and really listen. The footsteps are coming from my right, so I go left and tiptoe to the other end of the shed. Twisting my neck, I slowly look down the left side of the shed. No Tank. I step around the side.

"Bella?"

Oh, crap, he's close.

His voice sounds like it's right on me. I check out the ground, watching carefully, as I sidestep down the shed to the other end. I don't know exactly where he is, but I think he's on the other side of this small wooden building.

I put one step across the other and take a breath. I'm at the end, and I need to look around the corner again. Tank has gone quiet, and I'm terrified of seeing his face when I make my next move.

My body is buzzing with the rush and the fear. This needs to be over soon because I don't think I can take much more of it.

Please hurry, Rocco.

"Come out, come out wherever you are," Tank calls.

His voice isn't close. He's still on the other side. I safely round the corner and lean my head against the wood. My pulse is thumping.

Hang in there.

Rocco will be here any second.

I close my eyes.

Please stay with me, Celia.

FORTY-EIGHT

ROCCO

Ellis wrenches the steering wheel around the bend, almost ploughing into a tree. We narrowly miss death and screech into a vast space filled with a house and outbuildings. This has to be it.

I'm already looking in every direction, desperate to find my girl. "Where is she?"

"Shed at the end, furthest away, in the corner. Best place not to be seen."

Shoving the car door open, I leap out and sprint toward the shed. "Bella!" I shout, not caring who fucking hears me. In fact, I welcome it. I want them all out here, so I can rip their sick fucking heads off.

Ellis is hot on my heels, his feet stomping into the gravel as hard as mine.

"Isabella!" I shout.

She runs out from behind the shed.

Good girl.

She launches herself at me, and I catch her, stumbling backward.

"I'm sorry, Rocco. I'm so, so sorry. I had no idea who she was, or I never would have gotten in that car. Obviously. I'm sorry."

She starts to sob, and it rips me apart. There's blood on her face and the start of a bruise.

My hands clench into fists as I hold her tight. "Shh, it's okay, baby. I got you."

"Rocco, we're not alone," Ellis says.

"Good," I growl. Letting go of Bella and positioning her behind me, I turn to meet the arseholes who took my girl. "Tank."

Motherfucker.

He cocks his head. "Well, this just got interesting. I was a little upset when I noticed Bella had gone, but this is actually perfect. I thought we were going to have a repeat, and I'd have to make the trip back to Casa Hastings." Looking up, he shakes his head with a grin that makes even me feel uneasy. "Now though, you get to watch me rape and kill your girl, and Bella will know exactly how her sister felt."

"Fuck you, you sick bastard!" Bella screams from behind me, losing it at the end because she starts sobbing.

Did Tank rape Celia?

"Shh, he's goading you."

I'm absolutely going to kill the wanker for threatening Bella, but I'm not going to let him know how much his words are affecting me. It's good actually. The more pissed off I am, the more it's going to hurt him, and right now, the wanker is going to be in a fuckload of pain.

"He hurt her. He…"

I ignore her and concentrate on Tank. My eyes lock on his.

"You're Keith and Faith's little bitch, huh? Hurting young girls because you're a weak prick who can't fight a man."

He laughs. "You have no idea what's going on here. We're partners."

Ellis looks at me and rolls his eyes. Pointing to Tank, he says, "You hear this knobhead?" He turns back to Tank. "I'm sure you think that. I'm sure they encourage you to think that, but deep down, you know the score. They knew you would be easily manipulated, and all they had to do to get you to be their lapdog was let you believe you held some power."

Bella grabs my arm. She's still behind me, so I can't tell what's going on back there, but I think the enormity of the situation is hitting her. She's face-to-face with the man who murdered her sister, and I need to end this and get her out of here.

"Shut the fuck up," Tank spits. He shoves his hand under his jacket and pulls a gun from his jeans.

Oh, shit.

I freeze for a nanosecond before gripping Bella's hand tighter and holding her against my back. He wants her, and he has a gun. Gritting my teeth, I stare at the fucker who has me scared. I don't get scared of other people—I can handle myself—but he wants to kill my girl, and it would be so easy for him to do so.

Ellis has a gun on him, but it's too risky for him to use it while one is pointing toward us. Bella could get caught in the crossfire.

"Put that down, and fight like a man for once," I growl.

"I don't think you're in any place to make demands, Rocco. Now, move aside, and give me the girl. I'm owed a Hastings."

"You're owed nothing, you sick fuck!" Bella shouts.

She squeezes the life out of my hand, and I have to shove her back behind me to stop her from running at him.

I tilt my head, so I can see both her and him. "Stop!"

She's angry because she's finally met the man who killed her sister—I get that shit—but she's really not helping the situation. I need him to put the fucking gun down.

"You know I'm not handing her over, Tank, so put that down, and let's settle this properly."

I'm going to rip his head off.

His eyes narrow, and with my heart in my stomach, I watch his finger flex on the trigger.

"Do it, Tank," Faith says as she steps around the corner, witnessing what's going on. "Shoot them all."

I would rather spend the rest of my life with Bella, but if I die tonight, that would be okay. I can accept that…if I can somehow get her out of here.

"I want the girl," he replies, stepping from side to side and eyeing Bella like she's a piece of meat.

"Put the gun down," I say.

He's not listening to Faith; thankfully, his attention is on Bella and me.

Faith bares her teeth and steps closer to him. "Tank, end this. Now. We don't have long."

"Long until what?" I ask.

"Shut up!" she snaps.

"Men will arrive soon to rape the girls they've kidnapped," Bella says from behind me. "Faith's a fucking psycho."

"Shoot the bitch!" Faith orders. "Or I will." She pulls a gun from her back pocket and aims.

Fuck!

For the second time, my world stops spinning.

"I know you want her, Tank, and I'm all for it, but I swear to God, if you don't do it, I will."

Tank looks at her, and that second is all I need. His distraction gives us a chance. I let go of Bella's hand and launch for him. My shoulder slams into his chest, and we both go down like a sack of shit. His head cracks on the ground with a sickening thud that I hope kills the bastard.

I look up, and Faith is now pointing her gun at me. Tank is still down, so at the very least, I've knocked him out.

"If you want to hurt her, you're going to have to use that," I say, nodding at her gun.

She brings her other hand up and holds it steadier. "What makes you think I won't?"

Using my hands, I push myself up onto my feet. I feel Ellis close in, keeping Bella behind him, the way I did. He'll never know how much that means.

"You're holding it like it's a bomb. You're unsure. You don't do the dirty work; that's why you have Tank in your pocket. Now, put it down before you hurt yourself. I'm leaving with my girl."

She laughs but lowers the gun. "You have no idea what I'm capable of, Rocco. I don't need to pull the trigger to pull the strings. Right, Tank?"

Fuck.

I swing back around, but he's awake, alert, and aiming.

"No!" Bella screams.

Bang.

Fuck.

FORTY-NINE

BELLA

I hear my scream ringing in my ears long after I've closed my mouth.

Tank shot the gun.

He shot Rocco.

"No! Oh God. Rocco."

Rocco drops to his knees, and I leap forward, going with him.

One more shot is fired from behind me.

Ellis.

I think he shot Tank, but I don't look. I'm too focused on Rocco. My world narrows until there is only me and him. I can't bring myself to care about anything else.

This isn't happening.

He can't die.

His words come back to haunt me.

"Folks around here don't usually live happily into their seventies."

He planned for this all along. He knew he would die young, but he wasn't supposed to be right. I was going to show him that he was only being negative and that his life didn't have to end the way so many others had around here.

Hissing through his teeth, he collapses further and falls down on his back. I hover over him, in shock and terrified that I might lose another person I love.

Shit, there's blood.

"Fuck me," he growls. "It fucking stings."

Stings?

"Put pressure on the wound, Bella," Ellis says, walking back and forth with one hand gripping his gun and the other on the phone to the emergency services.

I don't know where Faith is, but she's probably ran.

I jump at the sharpness of his voice but push down and apply pressure to the bullet wound in Rocco's abdomen. I'm almost instantly covered in his blood. The hot red liquid seeps through my fingers.

Rocco groans in pain and frowns, giving me a look.

I swear, if he says anything sarcastic right now…

"Stay with me. Please stay with me," I beg, my voice sounding weak.

I lean down closer, still making sure I'm applying the same amount of pressure to the wound.

Please let this help him hang in there until the paramedics arrive.

He smiles and reaches up to cup my cheek. His hand already feels cold. "God, I love you, Bella. Never forget how much."

"Don't!" I sob. "Don't do that. Don't you dare say good-bye. I can't lose you, Rocco. I love you, and I need you. You're not allowed to leave me."

"You don't need me. You're so strong. You can do this," he whispers. "The only thing you need to do is keep the promise you made."

I know instantly what he's referring to. Back when I told him what had happened when Celia died, he made me promise that, when this was all over, I'd start living my life for myself.

If I lose him, how do I start living?

"Please fight. Ellis is on the phone, and the paramedics will be on their way. You're good at fighting, remember? It's what you do."

His eyes are glazed, and he's just looking at me so intently, like he's taking every millimetre of me in…because he thinks this is the last time he'll see me.

My stomach coils. It hurts so, so bad to think that he's giving up.

"You can't die, you twat!" I snap.

He laughs, sucking in a breath straight after, as the action probably hurt a lot. "Everyone dies, baby. I'm not scared to go if it's my time. I know you'll keep your promise. You're the only person on this planet that I trust completely."

No.

"Rocco, *please* hold on. You can't die because of me."

"Isabella," he rasps, "I would die for you a thousand times over."

Fuck.

His words make me want to curl up beside him. I cry, and it feels like I'm the one dying. He's still here, but I feel the loss stabbing deep.

"Please don't," I plead, keeping the pressure while lowering my head to his. "Listen to me. You do know that I won't break a promise to you, but that doesn't mean you can leave me. We're only three months into forever."

"That doesn't matter to me. Three months with you is all the forever I need. It's more than I ever thought I'd have."

My heart tears apart at his words, and I feel the ache grow and take on a life of itself.

He has to be okay, or I won't be. Rocco is the one thing in my life that I'm sure of. We're a team, and despite our different backgrounds, we work. He is the other half of me, and I need him to function.

"I don't mean to sound selfish or ungrateful, but I was kind of hoping for the kind of forever that lasts until we're old."

He would have gotten a forever, too, if it wasn't for me. I shouldn't have called him. I should have just run.

This is all my fault.

"Oh God, Rocco, I'm so sorry. What have I done? If I hadn't dragged you into this, you wouldn't have been…"

This is so much blood. Oh my God.

His thumb presses down on my lips, and I sob.

"Shh, no guilt. I *chose* this, and if I had the time again, I wouldn't do a single thing differently. I wouldn't change meeting you and falling in love with you. I would rather die here right now than live into old age, having never met you."

His voice is broken and drifting, and his breathing is getting more laboured by the second.

Where is the fucking ambulance?

"No, please," I cry, shaking my head and blinking tears down my face.

This is worse than Celia. I caused this. Rocco is the best person I know, and he's going to die.

Fuck.

The guilt and crushing pain of facing a life without Rocco…it leaves me breathless in the most excruciating way I've ever experienced. I cry out as every inch of my body is encased in agony.

Don't die. Please, please don't leave me.

"Rocco…" I whisper as his chest struggles to rise and fall. "No! You can't go."

Groaning, he brushes his fingers across my cheek. "I need you to know that I will always love you. Don't you dare fall apart, Bella. You're stronger than that. Live, baby. Live for us both. Live for *yourself*, and go out there and do whatever you want. I'll be there, right beside you, every step of the way. You gave me everything I never knew I wanted. I couldn't love you any more than I do."

God, I can't listen to him saying good-bye. I want to beg him to hold on, but I can't talk.

"I love you so much, baby," he whispers.

"No. Rocco…"

"It's Carson."

"What? What's Carson?"

He takes a ragged breath. "My surname."

Oh God, he's finally told me.

Smiling, I brush the side of his face. "Well, Rocco Carson, I need you to fight for us right now because, one day, I want that to be my surname, too."

With the most beautiful smile on his face, he slowly closes his eyes.

"Rocco?"

No, don't do this.

I gently nudge his shoulder, but he doesn't move. His chest is still.

Fuck no.

I shake him harder. "Wake up! Rocco!" I scream.

No, no, no.

I lay my head on his and fall into oblivion.

EPILOGUE

BELLA
TWO MONTHS LATER

Rocco's headstone is cold under my fingertips despite the warmth of late summer. My heart swells. Being here hurts so much, and I still feel the overpowering pain as fresh as the day he died, but I come every day to feel close to him.

I feel his absence every second. He was only in my life for a short time, but he changed so much.

He changed me.

When he died, I wanted to give up, but I couldn't let him down. Rocco wanted me to live, and there was no way I wouldn't honour his wishes.

I love him so much that I'll live for us both. Whatever I do and wherever I end up, I'll take him with me. He gave me the opportunity to move on from Celia's death, and whatever I decide to do next, I will give it everything.

I will never stop loving you, Rocco.

Dropping my hand, I take a breath. The grass above him is such a vivid green. He might not have been the most fun-loving person, but he brought a lot of colour to my life.

He would be proud of my progress. I got good grades, and next year, I'm going to uni. I'll do something epic in his name.

I'm determined not to give up.

And it helps that Faith and Keith are in prison. They both got life. When I learned of their fate, I cried my eyes out. It was such a bittersweet moment. They took so much from me, my sister, and Rocco, but they'll never hurt anyone else again.

Tank is buried somewhere here, too. I've not looked for him, and I don't plan to. He's nothing.

"I thought you'd be here." Ellis's voice booms behind me.

I smile as I look over my shoulder.

"Hey," I say.

I scoot over, so he can sit on my blanket, too.

"Thanks. How're you doing?" he asks, brushing his hand over his blond hair.

That's a very good question and one I'm still working on.

I shrug. "Today is better than yesterday."

But there's no telling what tomorrow will bring. There is no *easier* with each passing day. Sometimes, I wake up and feel Rocco pushing me on, and other days, I miss him too much to leave my bed.

"I miss him, too," he replies, taking my hand.

I squeeze, taking comfort from Rocco's only friend.

Since he died, Ellis and I have been hanging out. We're really the only ones who know what it's like to miss him. Ellis has so many stories about Rocco, and I can't get enough of them. I spend a lot of time with Ellis. I *need* to talk about Rocco, and no one knew him longer than his best friend.

Thankfully, his girlfriend, Izzy, understands why I come around so often. She welcomes me every time and always listens when I want to talk. Rocco's death made Ellis realise that he had to grab happiness by the balls, and he asked Izzy to move in with him. I'm glad he's got something real.

Rocco and I didn't have long together, but I finally understood what it was like to love a person so completely that it consumed you. Losing him was hell, but I wouldn't give up the way he made me feel for anything.

"I'm going to stay at his tonight," I say, staring at Rocco's name.

Silence hangs in the air, and I risk a look at Ellis. He's staring at the ground, and I have no idea what he's thinking.

"Ellis? Come on, we both know you want to say something."

He clears his throat, kicking his legs out. "Are you sure you want to do that? The last time…"

The last time, I woke up, expecting Rocco to be there, and when I realised why the bed was empty on his side, I freaked out. When I called Ellis in hysterics, he managed to get out of me where I was, and he spoke to me the entire time on the phone as he raced over.

"I'm sure," I reply.

Rocco's smell on the few T-shirts I took to my parents' house is gone. I need this. I want to fall asleep on his pillow and pretend, even if just for a short time, that he isn't gone and that I don't have to face a future without him. I plan on moving back to Rocco's—to home—but it's too soon right now. I need more time.

My parents and Livvy have been so supportive. They were devastated to learn the truth about the day Celia died, but although they were angry that I put myself at risk, they understood why I'd taken the path I did.

None of them hate Rocco anymore either. It took him dying for them to accept how good he was for me. Things are still a bit tense between us, but we're all trying, and I need them so much right now.

Ellis's eyes narrow suspiciously. "How are you really doing, Bella?"

His question makes my stomach roll. I tuck my legs into my chest and rest my chin on my knees.

I'm just trying to make it through, one second at a time.

"I'm okay…" I sigh. "I'll be okay. I wouldn't be if I hadn't promised him I'd live. I owe him everything, Ellis, and as much as it hurts, I won't ever throw my future away. Rocco died saving me, and I would give anything to change that, but I can't, so I will honour him by having an epic life. It's just going to take a lot of time and a lot of strength."

I'm still trying to find that strength, but every time I think about my last conversation with Rocco—after I stop crying—I have the power to carry on.

Giving up is easy, and living is hard.

But, for Rocco, I will fight.

ACKNOWLEDGMENTS

My first thank-you has to go to my Lowdon. I've lost count of how many times you've asked for Rocco over the years, Zoë. Here he is!

Kim, thank you so much for reminding me of all the things I need to get done. Without you, it definitely wouldn't happen. You were the first person to read this, and I really loved your feedback and, well, the shouting! LOL!

Kirsty, thanks for all of the hula minions They were needed!

A massive thank-you to The Indie Girls support group. If you ladies hadn't been around to sprint with me and push me, I would probably still be pulling my hair out.

Jovana, I never quite know how to say thank you for all that you do. I'm never sure of a manuscript before you return it to me.

Sofie, your design talents never fail to leave me in awe. As always, you make my books look beautiful.

And, lastly, thank you to *you* for reading *Reliving Fate*.